STEPHANIE JOHNSON is the author of five novels and two collections of short stories. Two of her novels have been shortlisted for the Montana Book Awards. *The Heart's Wild Surf* and *Belief* were published in Australia and England by Vintage and will be published by St Martin's Press in America. Stephanie is the co-founder of the Auckland Writers' Festival and has been the recipient of several awards and fellowships.

Previous books by the author

Poetry
The Bleeding Ballerina

Short Stories
The Glass Whittler
All the Tenderness Left in the World

Novels
Crimes of Neglect
The Heart's Wild Surf
The Whistler
Belief

THE SHAG INCIDENT

STEPHANIE JOHNSON

V

VINTAGE

With enormous gratitude, I acknowledge my time spent in Menton, France, as the Meridian Energy Katherine Mansfield Fellow 2000, where the first draft of this novel was written. Thank you to Harriet Allan for her genius and patience, to my agent Lois Wallace, to Roxanne Clayton for her hospitality in Aiglan, and to Ursula Woodhouse, Sean Davies, Annabel Lomas, Jan Reeves, Rosie Scott, Moana Avia, Alexandra Johnson and Michael Scott for their advice and kindness.

Thanks are due also to the University of Auckland where, as Literary Fellow for the first half of 2001, I completed the book.

National Library of New Zealand Cataloguing-in-Publication Data

Johnson, Stephanie, 1961-
The Shag incident / Stephanie Johnson.
ISBN: 1-86941-501-9
1. New Zealand fiction—21st century. I. Title.
NZ823.2—dc 21

A VINTAGE BOOK
published by
Random House New Zealand
18 Poland Road, Glenfield, Auckland, New Zealand
www.randomhouse.co.nz

First published in 2002. Reprinted 2003

ISBN 1 86941 501 9

Author photo: Melanie Church
Text design: Elin Termannsen
Cover design: Dexter Fry
Printed in Australia by Griffin Press

In a caveat to his future biographers, Ruskin cautioned that we are made into what we later become only by those external accidents that are in accord with our inner nature.

(*From Dawn to Decadence* by Jacques Barzun)

The wild geese fly across the long sky above
Their image is reflected upon the chilly water below.
The geese do not mean to cast their images on the water,
Nor does the water mean to hold the image of the geese.

(Chinese poem, eighth century A.D.)

One can reflect upon one's life and identify catalysts — certain encounters or ideas — that carried you in certain directions for a very long time. In other cases, one recollects only the journey and not what set you off on it. Or who. In my experience it was a man completely unknown to me who shaped the entirety of my mid-late life.

(Howard Shag, quoted in *An Interrupted Life* by Melody Argyle)

For Tim

1985

The two women running on either side of him are tall, muscular and broad shouldered. He knows that they're women because he can feel the softness of their breasts pressed against his pinioned upper arms. He wonders if they are rugby players, or netballers perhaps — that new breed of giantess created by a powerful alchemy of human genes, steroids and hormone-rich food. Surely they have practised this manoeuvre, one on either side, each with an arm around his waist so that his bare feet hardly touch the ground. Someone pounds directly behind him, hands vicious on his shoulders. There are others, men or women — he can't be sure how many: they blindfolded him almost as soon as they broke into the house — but he can hear their breathing, the thud of their rubber-soled feet, the slick and flick of each departing step on the dark, wet pavement.

He's terrified. His hands buzz and throb, tied too tightly behind his back at the wrists with insulated electrical wire. He could vomit. If they make him keep running he will, he will choke on it, he could die. His bowels are liquid, he clenches his anus, he struggles against that indignity, he struggles again against them and the one behind punches him — yes, that is the origin of the blow — a hard, powerful fist smashing the back of his skull. Painfully open against the cloth of his blinkers, his eyes burn with an effulgence of stars.

He concentrates his senses, the ones they have left him: there's the same smell he first detected when they came upon him, their entry into his house as silent as a falling leaf — he'd heard no smashing glass, no splintering of a forced door. Had he left a window open somewhere? The smell — what is it — fainter in the open air — hashish? Marijuana? Perhaps, on the breath of the woman on his left, gin or scotch. They toked up, had a swig, before they came for him. What other odourless substances are they on — acid? Speed? He doesn't like drugs, he never has: they alarm him. The people who use them alarm him more.

A car door now; he hears it open above the breaking waves. They have run him down his driveway and out his gate, around the corner into Park Avenue, to the little reserve above the beach. It's not his car — the doors sound tinny and cheap. His Beamer is in the garage, or was, last time he looked. They push his head down, propel him into the car and as he struggles again, bent over, a foot, swift, precise, catches him in the testicles. He cries out — for only the second time, he realises. The first was an exclamation of surprise when the first intruder burst through the bathroom door — did he see her face? Blonde, he thinks, acne-scarred — yes, he cursed, a single word — Fuck! — as she came in, a coil of electrical wire held high in one hand, a knife in the other, her voice, ugly with excitement, calling to the other people he could hear pounding up the stairs behind her. First the wire was a weapon, then it was a restraint. They tied his wrists, his knees.

He is weeping, sobbing as the pain spreads from the white-hot agony between his legs into his stomach, higher still until it catches at his heart so that he inhales sharply and screams as loudly as he can. His face collides with vinyl upholstery, his forehead presses against a hard object, sheepskin covered — it's a child's carseat. One of the women curses, he's aware of the door being opened, the carseat being wrenched away. He hears the impact as it strikes the road.

'Don't do that!' A female voice — young-ish, twenty-ish, thirty-ish. 'I need that for —'

'Shut up! We'll come back for it —'

They would know now, how could they not, with his robe flung up over his head, he smells its comforting, everyday smell — they would know he is naked under the robe. He's forced down in the position sleeping babies take sometimes, their bottoms in the air, knees bent under, vulnerable. He's a big man: six foot two, fourteen stone. He hardly fits. A hand pulls at the robe, tugs it down over his arse. An act of kindness? he wonders, until he feels their weight. They sit on him — one on his back, another on his newly covered rump, the third excruciatingly on his legs.

The doors close, the ignition clicks, the engine squeals. He is driven away.

2005: FRANCA

Psichiatra

Driving over the Sydney Harbour Bridge on her way to the prison, Franca was suddenly infused with a sense of warmth and peace, which rushed through her veins like a drug. It was an intense pleasure, deeper than her usual delight in the bridge, and it took her completely by surprise, bringing with it something of the joy and immediacy of childhood. Until she was about twelve years old she and Nònna had regularly crossed the bridge to visit an elderly uncle in Chatswood. Head tipped back on the bus seat, she'd open her eyes to the streaming sky, then close them again to feel the light flicker pink and black through her lids from the latticed girders. She would envy with heart-thudding intensity the pedestrians holding on to their hats on the blowy walkway — then she'd select one to be. 'That's me, Nònna,' she'd tell her grandmother. 'The man in the yellow raincoat.' The bus would pass by, she would lose sight of him and have to choose another. 'No — that's me. That girl with the plait. No — now I'm her, that fat lady —' And if there were no pedestrians she would snuggle into Nònna to imagine herself standing right at the apex of the span, the twin Australian flags streaming on either side of her, the ferries and boats churning the harbour below. 'I'm up there, Nònna,' she would tell her grandmother. 'I'm on the very top.'

This morning a grey dawn fog was rolling up from between the Heads and she wished she could slow down long enough to watch it, to see it slip over the calm winter water, grey on grey, smoke on glass. It was low and dense, a sea-fog that had taken the wrong turn, like whales did sometimes. It would dissipate when it reached the land, it would probably not reach even as far as the bridge piles, it would melt away with the last of the dark as the sun rose.

The bridge never failed her. Even when every lane was clogged with traffic her spirits lifted as she drove haltingly across it; she never took the tunnel and for very good reason. It was in tunnels of any kind, Franca believed, particularly ones that passed under bodies of water, that one could witness — more than in any church — the blind faith men have in the inventions of other men. Should the seabed shift, regain its natural unhollowed shape, there would be no hope of escape. It was quite conceivable that the Earth should want to heal itself, like any living organism. Bridges may collapse of course — succumb to concrete cancer or metal fatigue — and jettison their coursing weight of vehicles from one element into another: air to water. But both elements offered a chance of survival, even for those who leapt voluntarily. Underground, lungs clogged with mud, bones crushed by tonnes of steel and earth, there was none. The psychology of the human desire to choose to survive — or to choose not to — was Franca's singular passion.

Secondly, more esoterically, tunnels were never constructions to be aesthetically admired. Who ever turned to a companion and remarked, at some artificially lit midpoint, as their nostrils stung with monoxide and depleted oxygen, 'What a beautiful tunnel! I'll remember it for ever. Let's stop and take a photograph!'? Human beings only experience a lifting of the spirits as they come back out into the light: a surging, subconscious relief that they survived that unnatural journey. It is bridges that fly, arch and fling; bridges that afford views, inspire poetry and art.

And suicide. The bridge was not a tame, domesticated piece of the city's architecture. It had taken many lives in its time, beginning with the sixteen men who had died during its construction and ending with whatever poor soul had last climbed its wire barriers. Sydneysiders grow up with the idea that bridge-jumpers die more easily over Kirribilli to the north and The Rocks on the city side, when they fall to street and roof. It wasn't true, of course. A body falling at approximately one hundred and thirty-seven kilometres per hour for a distance of fifty-eight metres hits water as if it were concrete. Bones snap and push upward, internal organs burst and implode. It was easy to see in the postmortems she had attended how the physical body had ended its own existence. But what of the brain? What was it doing in its final seconds? Did it freeze over to offer up only blankness — a cold, white, uninhabited expanse — as the organism flew it down? Perhaps it was feverish: a physiological overheating brought about by deficient neuro-transmitters and an imbalance of endocrines. If only it were possible to scan a brain in its descending, uncontrolled flight and describe its activity, its violently adjusting chemical balance . . .

She turned from the outside lane into Cahill Expressway. The mirror blocks above reflected the early dawn, silver and pink. Seagulls wheeled in a flock above Circular Quay, their white wings luminous. On her right the clock of the Customs House read ten past five and a spin of the wheels later a small white-faced figure gazed out of a lit window in the Hotel Inter-Continental. Neither of the early risers was aware of the other, one intent on the fog curling now at Pinchgut's rocky feet, the other turning away from the harbour, all its beauty at her back as she rounded the scooping corner. The mouth of another tunnel loomed. Smoothly, practised, accustomed, Franca swung left into the Macquarie Street exit.

In the cool grey morning light the street was beautiful. Beside her the State Library's columns of stern black basalt rose between tall arched windows, eyes guileless with surprise. The building was greatly altered from the days when she frequented it as a student, but it was grand, serious minded. At the corner of her eye the latticed balconies of the old Sydney Hospital flickered black on stone, the barracks flashed silver and pink after them. The buildings glowed with a kind of stored heat of their own: a heat generated by the weight of history and import, of a beating heart born of being for centuries the darlings of the town.

At traffic lights on Elizabeth Street she slipped Glen Gould's *The Well-Tempered Clavier* into the CD player and a Curiously Strong Peppermint onto her tongue: even psychiatrists are comforted by their little associative rituals. Especially psychiatrists . . . she rolled the powdery disc on her tongue, her gaze fallen on the old tiled front of Mark Foys, which stood on the diagonal corner. It brought with it, as always, a gleaming image of Santa Claus. Nònna had taken her to see him there on her first Christmas in Sydney, intent on giving her prematurely adult grand-daughter at least a glimpse of childhood before that time was lost to her for ever. There was still a chink in the door, Nònna considered. Franca remembered how she had bumped Santa as she'd climbed up onto his knee, knocking her patent leather shoes against his shins. Santa had winced his old blue eyes as he'd pulled her up to sit squarely and she'd worried she'd bruised him.

Green light. Franca, in her shiny red Renault, with her high heels, Italian silk suit and glossy blonde hair, pressed firmly on the accelerator. The surface route to Long Bay was a long one — a journey she could halve if she would go underground. Oxford Street, Flinders Street, Anzac Parade. The university clock was stopped at ten twenty-five. Kingsford gave way to Maroubra, Matraville and Malabar, suburbs of desolate brick houses with ragged, dry gardens and apartments with balconies empty of furniture or flowers, of birds in cages and children's toys. In Bilga Crescent she rummaged in her bag, one hand on the wheel, for the visitor's badge Stambach had arranged for the last patient he'd called her in for: a successful suicide who'd provided useful data.

Long Bay was not a place she enjoyed visiting — but who did? It was necessary for the paper she was preparing, elaborately entitled 'Despair, Revenge and the Desire for Oblivion: Suicidal Impulses Among Australian Prisoners', which she had been invited to give at the Munich Conference at the end of the year. It was almost finished. From Darwin to Hobart she'd interviewed nearly six hundred suicidal men and women; taken down the particulars of their lives: race, gender, age, sexuality, addictions, marital status, relative wealth, memories of childhood; and forced them into pie-charts, bell-curves and Venn diagrams. She'd assembled statistics, crunched numbers, isolated trends. Several of her subjects, most of them Aboriginal, had subsequently been successful in their objective and Franca had been careful to go to their surviving relatives and ask if their contribution could still be utilised. Sometimes this required journeys of several thousand kilometres and relative discomfort. Rising at four-thirty to a phone call from her colleague, Gregor Stambach, the chief psychiatrist at the Special Care Unit in Long Bay jail, was effortless in comparison.

The low-rise buildings of the prison stood beyond the rusted double fence, squat watchtowers topped red brick walls. A guard nearing the end of night shift walked yawning in the grounds with a german shepherd. He looked casual, loose-limbed, as if he were strolling the beach, as if this were a holiday camp. It was a bizarre image, and one that was immediately dismissed from her mind by the icy, slightly accusatory stare from the uniformed man in the gate booth.

Stambach, at this moment thumb combing his nicotine-stained moustache in the small mirror on the back of his consulting room door, thought Franca had a lot to offer. Like most professionals in almost any field Stambach was territorially defensive, but as soon as he'd read the new prisoner's police report he knew Franca would be interested. She was tough, erudite, elegant and still young — mid-thirties, he calculated. He'd be proud to have his name associated with hers. It would prove he'd moved with the times, that he'd kept abreast of the changes, that he wasn't the old dinosaur some of his colleagues thought he was: suicidology was a burgeoning discipline. Not that he really held with it. Not if he were honest with himself. It involved too much talk. He'd read that specious shit written by an American psychiatrist called Danto: 'A psychiatric suicidologist must be part social worker, part psychologist, part cop.' Danto was a dreamer, a cuckoo, he lived in cloud-cuckoo land, a child of the world that emerged after *One Flew Over the Cuckoo's Nest*, Stambach believed: a world where the criminally insane were unleashed upon vulnerable communities, where serial rapists and killers were given wet bus-ticket sentences instead of being incarcerated for life.

Stambach would turn the clock back if he could. Perhaps Danto had never worked in a prison psychiatric ward. Here, there was no time for any of those touchy-talkie niceties and no money for them either. In the majority of cases, drugs and physical restraint were all that worked.

They'd put the new prisoner in the dayroom of Ward D in the prison hospital. Sitting with him was a warden, whom Stambach dismissed with a flick of his yellowed eyebrows. Already Franca had pulled up a chair next to the prisoner, who sat hunched on the bench under the window, his face in his hands. He hadn't acknowledged them — wasn't going to — until Franca touched him on the arm. Stambach imagined her touch: cool, dry, perfumed, and envied him for that and nothing else whatsoever.

'Us thus the bun?' the man asked. He was well built, the muscles of his arms straining against the fabric of the ill-fitting prison greens. Stambach had no idea what he was talking about.

'That's a good Kiwi accent you've got there,' Franca said gently. 'It's Ward D. It's where we put people who are having problems.'

He ripped his hands away from his face then and stared blearily at Franca. His face seemed soft, childlike, vulnerable, and Stambach felt a pang of pity. Part of his distress was grief, perhaps, for his drowned companion. Suddenly, as if he'd felt Stambach's eyes on him, the man looked up at him, startled, as if he hadn't realised he was there. He took a deep breath and his bottom lip trembled. So swiftly he could have struck her, he pivoted his upper body on his hips and grabbed Franca's wrists. Stambach felt himself divide in half: one impulse taking him to Franca's aid and the other to summon the officer who waited outside. He obeyed the former, coming to stand beside the seated prisoner and laying his fleshy white hands on his shoulders.

'Get me out of here,' the man was jabbering, tears streaming on his dark cheeks. 'Not the fucking maddies' hospital — I'm not fucking nuts. Why'd they bring me here? Why did they?'

Franca glanced at Stambach for his permission to engage: this was his patient, after all. He nodded.

'Because you were talking about harming yourself.'

'Was I?' The man let her go. Stambach took his hands away and moved back to the table to take up his notes.

'Apparently.'

'I wasn't.' He turned to look out the window, a view of a horizontal expanse of cracked concrete that intersected a hundred metres away with a vertical concrete expanse, likewise cracked. It was a no view — an anti-view, thought Stambach, revisiting his private non-joke.

'Are you a shrink, then?' the prisoner asked quietly, his eyes on the glass. His focus didn't seem to be any deeper than that: it stopped at the flecks and smears on the dayroom glass.

'We both are,' Franca told him. Stambach envied her tone: a man couldn't use a tone like that, not in a place like this. He'd be taken advantage of, he'd be a favourite with the shirt-lifters. It was a soft, purring, non-threatening voice, maternal but kittenish. 'This is Dr Stambach and I'm Dr Todisco.'

The prisoner was silent again for a moment, then he stood and said in as firm a voice as he could muster, 'It was a figure of speech. That's what they call it, isn't it? When you don't mean it. It's just something I say.'

'What?'

Stambach watched the prisoner look down into Franca's upturned face: fine-featured, dark-eyed, immaculately made up. Maybe she's older than I imagined, he thought: she could be forty.

'What do you say?' persisted Franca.

'That I want to kill myself.'

'How do you say it?'

'Iwantokillmyself. Like that.' The prisoner looked away again, his lower lip flicking from beneath his upper teeth, concealing and revealing itself. It was raw and cracked.

'Why would you say something that isn't true?' Franca asked quietly.

The question bewildered the man. As she watched him his eyes rapidly searched the walls of the room, as though the answer lay in the bright, admonishing posters that advised moderation with alcohol, the safe disposal of hypodermic needles: low-cost decoration that must serve only to remind him of the outside, of choices he no longer had to make. He wiped his eyes and made a desperate attempt to focus himself.

Stambach, sighing, referred to his notes. 'According to the Remand Superintendent you were in a distressed state and repeating that statement enough times for him to be concerned for your safety. Come and sit at the table, Mr Gilmore.'

'I want to go back to Remand.' There was a trace of demand, of petulance in his tone. Franca leaned to her briefcase on the floor, took out her notebook.

'You don't work here,' the prisoner addressed her, suddenly. He folded his arms over his considerable chest.

'How do you know that?' asked Franca, taking the cap off her fountain-pen.

'They wouldn't have a beautiful woman like you in a place like this. It'd be too dangerous.'

'I'm going to ask you a few questions, Mr Gilmore.' Stambach gestured at one of the chairs pulled up to the table and Franca, standing, led the prisoner to it. He came willingly, his gaze on the linoleum tiled floor a few inches ahead of his advancing bare toes.

'If you found a child lost in a park, what action should you take?' Stambach asked the question as he sat down himself, flipping the patient's file open with one impatient movement. Franca's heart sank: his diagnosis would proceed step by slow orthodox step. She felt she had the measure of the man already.

Beside her Gilmore shrugged and Stambach made one mark on the form in the open file. 'What day is it today?'

The man's heavy eyebrows drew together. 'Wednesday?' he asked, uncertainly.

Stambach's only response was to mark the form once more. 'One hundred less seven?'

He had not yet given the patient any eye contact, Franca observed wonderingly. It was if he intended to engender deeper anxiety in this already anxious man.

'Ninety-three,' muttered Gilmore.

'Ninety-three less seven?'

Again the prisoner's eyes raced the peripheries of the room, the lip flicking raw-skinned back and forth. Stambach paused a moment or two before he made a mark in the third column of the form.

'Oh, I see!' The prisoner's chair scraped angrily away from the table. 'I get a tick when I do it wrong, do I?'

'How could you have got it wrong when you didn't answer me?' At last Stambach turned his fierce, don't-give-me-shit gaze on Gilmore, who was standing now, and Franca saw him blink in the onslaught of it.

'Please remain seated, Mr Gilmore,' Stambach said passively and the man did, slumping, his elbows on his knees, his hands against his cheeks so that his fingertips rested against his closed eyelids.

'Repeat this sequence of numbers: 53217.'

'53217.'

'Backwards?'

'71235. I'm not a complete fucking moron!' The fingernails pressed into the man's brow were as black as his hair, the hair uncombed and greasy. Stambach referred to his notes: Gilmore had been arrested at sea, a nautical mile off the coast of northern New South Wales.

'How old are you, Mr Gilmore?'

'Thirty-three.'

'Married?'

The hands fell away, the prisoner glared. 'Waddaya wanna know that for?'

'Because I am examining you. It's standard procedure.'

'No more questions. Take me back to Remand.' His chin jutted. It had several days' heavy growth on it. 'I'm not crazy.' His voice broke on the last word. Blundering, his chair tipping in his wake, the prisoner returned to his window and gazed out.

'No one's saying you are, Mr Gilmore,' Stambach said in as sympathetic voice as he could muster. If Franca weren't here he would've spoken sharply to the patient by now. He was a type, Stambach hazarded a guess — a spoilt boy with all the opportunities, gone bad.

'Why am I here then?'

There was something in the man's body language Stambach didn't like. He was swaggering towards him now, three or four steps, before he stopped. Franca folded her notebook and put it away.

'Excuse us, please,' she said softly, standing and moving towards the door. Stambach had no choice but to follow her.

'Let me have him,' she said, the moment they were in the clinical staffroom.

'I have to do a full assessment first.'

'You know as well as I do he's no danger to himself.' She was following him around the kitchen area as he lifted down cups, spooned in instant coffee.

'Do I? Do you?'

'His impulse is partial. He wants only to dispense with the part of himself that committed the abusive crime. That kind of suicide wants only to clear their head, so to speak, so they can keep going. They usually realise before they're successful that it's not the optimum path.'

Pure sociology, thought Stambach. It irritated him, suddenly, her habit of quick diagnosis.

'If I clear him, he'll be sent back to Remand.'

'That's what he wants and I could see him there. You could arrange that, couldn't you?'

He nodded and Franca flashed him her bright, even smile. Gregor had always been supportive of her work. He'd know how much she wanted this man, this Jasper Gilmore. He filled a gap: educated to a higher level than most of her subjects, well spoken, probably a Maori who had lived in Australia for many years.

'Has he attempted suicide before?'

Stambach shook his head. 'But if he does go back on Remand he'll be on suicide watch.'

'May I —' She gestured at the notes, waved away his specious question and the proffered coffee. 'I never drink that muck.'

Why didn't she tell him that before he went to the trouble of making it? he wondered, sipping gratefully at his own coffee and lighting a cigarette from the crushed soft-pack in the pocket of his white coat. Above his head NO SMOKING was spelt out red on white, but Stambach considered the heinous stress of his daily life made him exempt.

'Perfect . . . yes.' She flipped a page, read hungrily. 'Absolutely perfect. I'll visit him in Remand daily for a week starting on Monday and keep an eye on him. At the end of that time you can have him back if you want.'

'Gee, thanks,' Stambach said dryly. 'How kind.'

'When's his hearing?'

Stambach shrugged. 'A week, maybe. Two. The police are still gathering evidence.'

'There's time, then. For me, I mean.' She had a lovely curvy mouth, thought Stambach, as though she laughed a lot. Unusual in a suicidologist — not that he'd met many. You'd think he would see more of the younger ones, like Franca, who were researching in the prison field. A third of the deaths in this establishment were suicides and he had his own theories based on the data he'd gathered from men who had eventually succeeded after one or two previous attempts. Every blood sample showed the same deficiencies, the same somatic imbalances, the same elevated 17-hydroxy-corticosteroid levels. It wasn't an original theory, of course. But, with luck, he would be the first to present the theory as conclusive, just as soon as he got around to writing it up, which wouldn't be until after he retired. Another two years.

'Hang on a second. It's not up to me, not on my own. There are other authorities that decide whether he goes back to Remand, as you well know —'

'But you can make a recommendation. I haven't got anyone like him. He's Maori, isn't he?'

'Could be, I don't know. He's lived in Australia for eleven years.' He could have laughed then, at her face, which glowed like a child's on Christmas morning. 'Shall I make the recommendation?'

'Yes. Please.'

Stambach drank his coffee, eyed her over the rim of his cup.

'I'd better be getting home. Thanks, Gregor. Can I keep these?' She waved the notes at him.

'Of course. I have another copy.'

'You'll email me about this?'

'Very soon.'

She took his hand, pressed it quickly, and was gone.

It was still early and the traffic flowed easily as far as the bridge, where there was a lengthy queue in every lane, the most stalled and serpentine being the one leading into the tunnel. Franca clicked her carnelian ring — chosen that morning to complement her grey silk suit — on the steering wheel and ate another mint. As she'd predicted, the fog had vanished but so had, oddly, her usual enjoyment of the bridge. It was as if she weren't on it at all, but still at the prison, in the corridor outside Ward D dayroom.

On her way out she'd paused and looked in through the one-way glass. At first she couldn't see him: he'd left the chair he'd been sitting in previously. He didn't stand against the walls or near the table. On the floor on the other side of the table he was doing press-ups. There was something in the angle of his body, the bunching of his muscles around his neck and shoulders, the shape of his calves and thighs in their tight greens, something familiar. It was almost a memory, but so cloudy it was more like the memory of a long-ago dream.

Now, sitting in her car on the bridge, she pulled away from herself, monitored her responses, her old survival trick. She'd done it since before she was a doctor, since she was eighteen. Yes, see — her pulse had quickened, the pupils in the rear-vision mirror were dilated, stomach and thigh muscles stiffened. She was exhibiting all the physical symptoms of fear.

JASPER

Blame

By the time I was eight years old I knew all there was to know about addiction.

That's what I've written on the blank page Franca left me on her second visit today, after she escorted me back to Remand. It's a sentence I've had in my head for years.

It's not strictly true, what I've written, but it's got a ring to it. There's a lot of things I don't know about addiction even now, physiological things. What actually causes veins to collapse after years of needles, for instance. How tumours actually form in a smoker's lungs, how many brain cells an alcoholic is left with after he's drunk hard for, say, fifty years.

But I'd have to start there, when I was about eight, so that she can understand why I did it. Part of me just wants to use the paper to write a note to Bonny and the boys. Two words. 'I'm sorry.' 'Sorry for what?'

the boys will ask and because Bonny knows what the police will find in my flat she'll have to make something up. They'll charge me for it, there's nothing surer. If the boys ask she could tell them about the cocaine, but not the other part. Here's a fact: if anyone tells the boys the full story of why I'm in here I'll get to them when I get out. I won't forget. Richard and Lena, this means you. What you don't know yet, I want my boys not to know either, ever.

Blame. There's a powerful word. I write it above my sentence like a title — BLAME— then I put down the pen and listen. I was always listening as a kid and I heard everything. I saw everything. What kid born in the early seventies with parents like mine didn't? I saw behaviour so loose it could only be defined as raw instinct. On some of the communes Lena and I stayed on, the spectacle of humans mating was more common than dogs fucking, or sheep. I knew a knife with a blackened tip had been used to spot hash, I knew the secondary meaning to the word 'fix' before I knew the primary one; I knew johnny as a condom before I knew him as a man. I was the silent sponge while my mother and her friends discussed with equal vehemence the mysteries of the female orgasm, menstruation, G-spots, divorce, rape, the male psyche, star signs, nuclear proliferation and the abortion laws. On the rare occasions I saw my father I heard him yelling in anger, or laughing inanely, stoned and moronic; I learned to swear at my mother's knee. I heard even when I didn't want to.

Right now I can't hear anything. Can't hear the Aussie screw who's no doubt got his snout pressed to the door outside, watching me with his piggy eye through the spy-hole. Can't hear them going up and down the corridor, or phones ringing, or sirens, or the insane Sydney traffic, nothing. I'm sound-proofed. Maybe they're trying out sensory deprivation on me to get me to talk. There's nothing on the walls, no glossy posters warning about dirty needles or drink driving like in the dayroom in Ward D. There's just me, a table, a chair and a bit of paper. And a plastic cup of coffee Franca brought me before she left.

Bonny was always telling the boys not to blame each other for things, almost like she thought it was a dirty word. Don't know what she tells them now they're older — I haven't been around much for the last two or three years. Not since Vincent was about seven.

I look at my sentence again and I think how I like it. It's well crafted. Maybe I could write the story of my life while I'm inside. The Legal Aid lawyer says I'll have to plead guilty because of the videos, so I'm looking at eight, nine years maybe. Long enough to write it all down; long enough to work out whose fault it is. Maybe Richard could cast his eye over it when it's finished, check it for veracity, being not only a journalist but also my father.

That's another powerful word and I'd rather not use it. Donor's better. If I put my mind to it I could probably remember all the times I've seen him in my life, the life that I remember. Ten meetings perhaps. Fifteen. Scottie was more of a father to me.

Yeah, that's where I'll begin: the time we met Scottie, my mother and me. Not that I blame Scottie for anything — no more than the others.

I was eight years old and skinny as an undernourished ferret. Mostly I wore a pair of denim cut-offs and a brown jersey Lena had knitted. I don't remember any of this on my own; I remember it because until recently I had a photo of myself dressed that way, salty hair curling to my bony shoulders, leaning up against the van, the rolling surf of a New Zealand beach in the background. That van was home for Lena and me for nearly three years — from the time the last of my smack-freak stepfathers cleared out on her once and for all. It was a 1958 Bedford and I loved it. We had a cooker and two mattresses and a little gas-powered fridge. I had a wooden box which Lena had painted bright yellow for my books and crayons and toys. Hanging from the rear-vision mirror was a mobile Lena had made out of Fimo, shells and seagull feathers with a dangling red 'J' for me and a purple 'L' for herself. In the winter we kept ourselves warm with extra blankets and knitted shawls. And because we were true Nomads, Lena said, like the Aborigines in Australia or the Horsemen of Northern Mongolia, we knew to suit our location to the season: winters in the winterless north and in the summer, when it grew too hot and crowded there, we went south, sometimes to the West Coast of the South Island, where we could have whole beaches to ourselves, or sometimes to Auckland or Wellington, where we'd park in one of her friend's gardens and be part of a big city for a while. Lena collected her solo mother's benefit, which was paid into her Post Office savings account, and as I remember it those years were serene.

Maybe Lena was lonely. If she was I never knew. She was the best mother a boy could have: we'd go round the rocks and collect cats-eyes or periwinkles or a feed of mussels; we made outrigger canoes out of pohutukawa twigs and driftwood lashed together with brightly coloured wool and in the evening she'd read me stories or else we'd have the radio on while she knitted and I drew pictures.

In the summer we'd have the door open to let the smoke out: Lena kept her stash in an old tin that had a lady's head on the lid and the words Dorothy Gilmore's Theatrical Cold Cream. She loved that tin — she carried it with her in a beaded bag that swung from her shoulder. The dope made her forgetful and sometimes she forgot where she'd put the bag, or else when we found the bag the tin wasn't in it. When that happened — and it happened quite a lot — we'd both scurry around until it was unearthed from behind a cushion or under the bench seat of the van and Lena would roll up rapido, licking her lips with antici-pation, and I'd watch her, feeling as though I were glowing golden with relief and happiness because Mum would soon feel a whole lot better. When the tin got empty Lena was empty too. She'd become lacklustre, sad, until we got to a town where she knew someone and could score. If she didn't we'd hot-tail it to the nearest pay phone and she'd ring around mates in other towns until she found someone who'd tell her the address of the local tinny house. In winter in the closed van I breathed that smoke, lungfuls of it, but I didn't mind, not when I was a little fella, because I loved my mother more than anything on earth. And even though I was a stick-insect kind of a kid I was robust and hardly ever got sick. Maybe I had a rattly cough now and then, not to mention regular contact-stones, but no asthma or glue ear or any of the complaints that smokers' children are now supposed to suffer.

Now there's an irony in remembering all this — that part of my life and how it ended when we met Scottie. When the cops picked me up years later at Broken Bay it was at the end of a voyage from New Zealand — or, to be precise, that country's territorial waters. We never made landfall, the three of us on *Brian Boru*, we just floated around in

27

the dark — not even a binnacle light — until the Colombians located us by satellite. The seas were calm and easy and the boats were lashed together just like my pohutukawa outriggers while we switched the snow from one hull to another. I didn't realise it at the time but we were right off Taiharuru Heads, on a direct trajectory out into the South Pacific. If the Colombians hadn't showed and we'd gone back to New South Wales empty-handed the cops never would've got us, my flat would never've been searched and they never would've found the videos. If Lena had never driven the van to that beautiful scoop of a bay in 1980, and parked as she did on the metal chipped carpark facing the surf, we would never have met Scottie.

It's as if that little line of coast and ocean is a powerful spot on the globe for me. Big things happen there. From the sea, that last trip with Damian, I saw how the white teeth of Pataua shine beyond the turbulent surf, how the southernmost lip of Ngunguru Bay curls into the corner of a smile at Taiharuru Heads. I remembered how beautiful it was there in the horseshoe-shaped bay, how there's beauty enough to stop your heart. Pohutukawas hang over the striped rocks from high green fields; olive-coloured kelp looms and streams in the clear swell; the sand, examined minutely, has grains of pink and red. A strange conical hill stands a kilometre or so inland, clad in horizontal rows of pine. It's an ancient landform, like a piece of Australia caught there during the dismemberment of Gondwana Land. Each time I've gone near this place some great beak in the sky has let me know nothing will ever be the same, at least as far as freedom and love are concerned.

This last sentence is so cramped at the bottom of the page that Franca is going to have difficulty reading it. I go the door, call through the mesh. This isn't exactly a security cell, I realise: the door is spongy particleboard except for its window of perforated metal and spy-hole above.

'Hulloooo!' I bang my fist. Nothing. Even with my ear against the cool metal there is only silence. It's eerie — have they all buggered off? Where've they gone?

I stand there for a moment, feeling my shoulders droop. It's the story of my life — never being able to finish anything because of the actions of other people, of being obstructed, of what I've really wanted always being out of reach because some other bastard is in the way.

As I go back to the table my eye slides over the freshly painted beige walls of the cell — blank, empty — and the pen bucks in my hand as if it were a live animal or a gun, and before I know it I'm kneeling — an alien posture for a red-blooded heterosexual atheist like myself — and writing. What can they do me for? Graffiti damage to state property? I'm just doing what I was told, officer! Your fault for not giving me enough paper!

As I was saying —

The pen writes easily on the matte surface and I feel as relieved as I did as a kid when Lena located lost Dorothy Gilmore. I can go on — and on and on and on — there's acres of wall —

Taiharuru had only a few houses around the edge of the bay. They were your usual coastal eyesores: brick basement, weatherboard upper storeys and tiled roofs bristling with aerials and saucers, the curtains drawn even in the daytime. It was winter and we didn't see a soul except an old fisherman in a yellow plastic coat who put to sea in his tin dinghy. When I saw him coming back I went down to the beach and his set-line was coiled in the bottom with half a dozen fish — some flapping, some dead so long sea insects had eaten their eyes out. He gave me one with the eyes still in it. Later on Lena and I went round the rocks in the drizzle, found a flattish rock and scaled and filleted it. It was the last meal I ever ate with my mother, just the two of us. It was a schnapper and she made chips to go with it.

I have to stop writing for a moment, for two reasons. One is my knees are hurting — no wonder for centuries kneeling was an attitude of supplication, the posture for prayer, something that must've generally taken longer than a blowjob.

The other is that my eyes are misting up. It so clear, all these years later, the picture of us eating with our plates on our knees, the windows all fogged, the air thick with oil and fish smell and marijuana smoke,

29

and everything so simple and contented. Lena's stripy knitting curled on the end of her mattress like a sleeping animal. Our wet coats dripping on their hooks on the back doors. *The Silver Chair* face down on my pillow, where I'd left it. I was a bright kid — I read a lot. Eight years old and already reading the last of the Narnia books! When I went to university I did chemistry, not that I finished my degree — through no fault of my own. My older boy reads too — each time the boat comes in, so to speak, I buy him books. All the Harry Potters, which have something in them C.S. Lewis didn't understand: humour.

He'll remember me buying him books, my boy, though he won't have a memory like this: the two of us eating a hot fish dinner in a steamy van. Better that he doesn't. If I was to offer anyone any parenting advice it would be this: don't let the kid get too close. It only breaks his heart when he's pushed away, which of course as a parent you have to do, so that you can get close to someone else. In the traditional scheme of things that didn't happen because everyone had a place, you know: mother, father, offspring. But it hasn't been like that for most people for nearly half a century. It's normal now for the parent left holding the baby to want love and sex and security and all the rest, so that when the opportunity arises with another adult it has to be cultivated. Therefore the kid, who up till that point has been kept up late to keep his mother company, who has shared her bed and her every second thought, has to be shoved sideways for expedience. Call me a cynic but it's true — I've seen it happen a hundred times, to rich and poor both.

I didn't think it would happen to me, of course. What kid does? Three years is a long time in a child's life and the smack-freak stepdad was a memory as foggy as the atmosphere in the van that long-ago winter night. I could remember how skinny he was, how he was so weak he had to get Lena to open jars for him. I think he was only around for a year or two anyway, and that intermittently because she didn't like him tasting. And of course before that there was Richard, but he left Lena when I was two and not before he'd broken her rib and collarbone in a stinking drunken rage.

The smoke Lena had after dinner — strong Northland Green — left her too stoned to do the dishes so she just stuck them out in the rain. I wiped some condensation away from the window and watched her as she set them out, moving in and out of the streaky light cast by the single street-lamp in the carpark. Her lips were moving as if she was so out of it she thought I was still beside her, or as if she was pretending there was someone else with her. Maybe she was lonely — so lonely that when she was alone she had imaginary conversations with invisible people. The rain flattened her curls to her head and made her smooth skin shine. Scottie once said she was like a lozenge and that's a perfect description of her — she looked as though she'd been sucked smooth; even when she was dry she looked moist, as though she'd just stepped out of the shower. Maybe it's her Italian blood that gives her that skin. She stayed out there for quite a while, arranging the knives and forks and frying pan for maximum exposure to the elements, and when she came back inside she was shivering and it took us ages to get her dry and warm.

The first thing I saw when I opened my eyes next morning was a surprising wedge of blue sky, with pink clouds scudding, and more surprising still, below the sky, something red and yellow and green, with twiddly carved bits, like a gypsy caravan. The doors of our van were open, the smell of Lena's early morning puff still lingering, and there were voices outside. Whoever it was had arrived in the night and driven over our plates, dented our frying pan and bent the forks. Lena wasn't annoyed at all, though I knew enough at eight years old to suspect she would've been if her tin had been empty. She had the giggles. I slipped out of my sleeping bag, pulled on my brown jersey and went outside.

It was a gypsy caravan! Freshly painted, with yellow and white daisies and polkadots, and instead of a horse to tow it there was a bright red tractor. I thought they looked like toys that had grown magically big. And I remember I thought also — and this isn't supposed to be disrespectful to Scottie, who has been mighty good to me over the years — I thought that if the toys had mushroomed in the rain to grown-up size then so had the boy they belonged to. My first glimpse of Scottie was from behind: blue workman's overalls, heavy boots, denim jacket and spiky red hair. A fat jolly boy with a dirty laugh, who stood holding in either hand the two halves of a broken plate — the one with the pinecones on that I'd eaten my schnapper off. Lena stopped laughing

31

long enough to introduce me and the boy turned around.

'Jasper. This is my son, Jasper.'

'Gidday, Jasper,' said the boy in the same instant my eyes registered her big bazookas and I realised she was a woman. 'I'm Scottie.'

I suppose I nodded and peered one-eyed at her — I was having a lazy eye corrected. Long ago we had lost contact with the doctor who had prescribed the glasses with the flesh-pink blinker over one lens. I wore them now and again for years. I think I had them on that morning. Scottie had pale green eyes and enormous flat freckles — the kind that spread out to touch one another. I liked her immediately. I liked the way she threw her head back and laughed and the way her creamy throat and bazookas jiggled. There was something strong and safe about her. Lena rolled up and they sat together on the grass verge and smoked, and while they were doing that a big round woman came out of the sea in a wetsuit with a diver's bag full of fish. She stripped the wetsuit down to her waist, yanked off her fins and came up to the beach just like that, so even without my glasses there was no making the same mistake I'd made with Scottie. My mother, who for all her life experience so far was still quite moral and Catholic and conservative, blushed — and the two women, Scottie and the other one, exchanged a look. The diver went into the caravan and returned in a T-shirt.

'Lena, Jasper — my sister Foxie.'

It was their father who'd given them their names. Their mother had given them far more sensible ones, not that they'd let on what they were. Scottie and Foxie they wanted to be and it wasn't until we were living in Auckland, months later, that I learned their surname was Terrier, and even weirder, that they had a half-brother called God.

I've reached the narrow skirting-board and my knees are on fire. I stand again, do a turn of the room. Still no sound from outside. Am I being filmed? I snap my head up — one, two, three, four — into all the corners of the room. Nope. Not unless they've invented a camera the size of a bug, which they probably have. I can't spare it a thought now, though I'd envy the pigs if they do have that technology. In my mate Damian's brief career as a film-maker — and maybe I'll get to that around the time I reach the corner if they leave me alone for long enough — he would have made good use of a camera that tiny, that spiderlike, that beneath any normal mortal's notice.

We must've eaten Foxie's fish, not that I remember it. And we must've eaten them off plates out of the gypsy caravan since ours were broken. And Lena and Scottie must've had a courtship of some brief duration before they got together in the way gay women get together, but I didn't notice it particularly. Foxie took me down the beach a lot to let them get on with it, she said, and let me use her snorkel and mask. I didn't stay in for long: the water was freezing and her wetsuit was ten sizes too big for me. She's a good stick, Foxie, not that I've seen her for years, not since I moved to Australia . . .

I'm not bothering to write this down, I'm just squatting here against the cell wall, listening to the silence, and thinking: I don't want Franca to think that it's because my mother went gay that I did the things I did. It's got nothing to do with it. It wouldn't've mattered if she'd fallen in love with an All Black or a brain surgeon or bloody Obi-Wan Kenobi; it was just that she'd fallen in love and I missed her. Terribly. All her little remarks and asides were not directed at me any more, but at Scottie. She didn't wake me in the morning by rolling over, leaning out of her mattress and ruffling my hair. She couldn't, because she was next door and Foxie was in her bed. The food in the van ran out and we were hungry for a couple of days before she and Scottie got it together to drive to Onerahi for groceries. Scottie and Foxie still had food and they shared it with Lena and me, but I wanted her and I to have our own.

I'm starting to get mad with my mother now. I don't want that to happen. None of this is her fault. I pick up the pen and stand to begin a new column. I'm lucky I have such a neat hand: it's printing really, like kids' writing. Franca will have no difficulty reading it.

In the evenings we'd make a bonfire on the beach, which was always deserted except for us. We'd take down rugs and sleeping bags and snuggle up; Lena and Foxie and Scottie would smoke a couple of joints — the little red glow passing back and forth in the night. Every now and then sparks in the bonfire would catch on a dry piece of wood, gorse or pine and send up a flare large enough to show us a glimmer of the tide — a white, bubbling curl out of the dark.

It was on one of these nights that I had my first toke: Foxie was so stoned she passed the smoke to me and Lena didn't notice, being under the rug with Scottie. It was hot and smooth and I must've been born to it because I didn't cough. Not at all, not me, not at nearly nine years old. I blew it out, made the nearest flames jog and jiggle and took another. This one I held down like I'd seen my mother do. Like I'd seen countless adults do and I imagined as I did it how I must look with my lips sealed, my face reddening, my eyeballs bulging just a little.

I must look like The Man, man.

After the second toke I stubbed it out in the sand and put it in my pocket for later.

I've got a roach in my pocket for later, my brain told me and another part of me giggled at how cool that was.

'Where'd that smoke go?' asked Foxie.

'You must've dropped it,' I told her. My voice was too loud. Foxie patted the sand and I could hear the silvery grains rubbing together under her hand, scratchy and small. I wrapped myself up in my sleeping bag and cuddled up with her, my head on her lap, and watched the fire. Castles, dragons, swords, Aslan, waterfalls, wizards, taniwhas and ships in full sail: they were all there in orange and red and gold. The dope roared through my synapses, it zinged and soared, it told me beautiful fragmentary bedtime stories in my mother's voice. It was a good stone.

We were at Taiharuru about two weeks. Lena and Scottie were calling each other Sweetheart and Darling and holding hands even when they were cooking tea in the gypsy caravan, so they did everything one-handed as if they were one person. It was a Friday when we left in convoy along the narrow winding road, Foxie driving our van with me sitting up beside her. I'd saved the roach until just before we left and snuck away to a cave along the beach to suck it up: Lena always liked travelling stoned, so I gave it a try. The cave was really smelly, due to the fact the tide had washed a dead sheep in there. Bits of wool still clung to its bones, and chunks of rotted meat. Its eyes were gone and its lips curled back from its teeth in an evil, decaying grin. It freaked me out — I ran as fast as could back to the carpark where the adults were toked up too. I must've done something to give myself away. Talked in a silly voice for too long, or just acted dumb, imitating the expression on the dead sheep's face. Anyway Lena cottoned on and she went ballistic.

'He's stoned!' she screeched and would've paddled my bum for me but Scottie stopped her. Instead, my mother punished me by riding to Auckland with Scottie. Up till then we were going to be together, alone for three whole hours in our van.

It was the beginning of the end when she did that: the beginning of her pushing me away. It seemed to me that she was less and less interested, that she did the bare minimum, only just keeping me clothed and fed. Anyone who reads this will have figured out by now that I hadn't gone to school since I was six, but I could read and spell better than most kids my age. Lena had taught me.

It was after dark when we finally stopped, and there was a fine misty rain swirling which soaked into everything and blurred in the headlights. The Bedford was as slow as a Galapagos Islands turtle but it was faster than the gypsy van so Foxie and I arrived first. It was an old house in Herne Bay, two-storeyed, white paint peeling off. It won't be like that now, I wouldn't think. It'll have been gentrified: anything in Herne Bay is worth a packet. Foxie took me inside. It was lovely and warm; they had a fire going in a tall, carved wooden fireplace. There were a lot of women in there, fifteen or twenty of them, and they all looked up when I came in.

'Gidday,' said one of them. She gave me a wink.

'Where'd you get that from?' another woman asked. She was one of the younger ones. She had a man's suit on, with a white collar and narrow tie, and a black beret. Between her long white fingers was a long thin cigarette.

'This is Jasper,' said Foxie. She sounded hesitant, almost nervous.

'It's a boy?' The one who asked this had such a deep voice I thought at first she was a man. She was sitting on the floor playing Scrabble with another woman and they had identical hair-dos— red and spiky, the centre bit combed up like a chook's head. Their T-shirts had been ripped and stuck together again with safety-pins. Next to the Scrabble board a glass ashtray overflowed onto the green carpet. It was nice to be in a real house again. I wondered where I would sleep.

'Yup,' said Foxie.

'He's not yours, is he, Fox?' asked the one with the deep voice. There was laughter then — thick, rough laughter — and I remember how I stared at them all, all the laughing mouths, and wondered what was funny and whether there was anything to eat. I reached out for Foxie's hand and held it and though she didn't seem to like me doing that she didn't pull away. Her hand was floppy in mine. Conversation started up again, pockets of it here and there. It was a huge room, almost institutional because of its size. Only one little lamp burned, which made it dim and cave-like, but it was light enough for me to see that one group of women was sharing wine out of a cardboard cask, and one woman was getting up off a sofa to carry a lit joint over to the Scrabble players. An argument was brewing between a beautiful lady with long red hair who'd been playing the guitar when we came in and a young Maori woman who wanted to put a cassette tape in the tapedeck.

I tugged at Foxie's hand. 'I'm hungry.'

She took me out to the kitchen where a long table was covered with plates and bowls and strands of spaghetti and blobs of meat sauce. Foxie didn't mind when I scraped a whole lot of leftovers onto one plate and ate them. It wasn't meat sauce, it turned out — it was something made out of red beans. Foxie leaned up against the crowded bench, swayed gently back and forth, stared glassily at a point somewhere above my gobbling head and looked worried. After a moment or two she picked up a wine glass off the table, rinsed it out and went back into the living room.

My first night in Herne Bay I spent on the ashy carpet in front of the fire. I went back in there after an hour or so. It took me that long to build up my nerve but the women hardly seemed to notice me. I sat down quietly on my own and wondered where my mother was and whether I should go outside and sleep in the van. First I'd have to get the keys off Foxie.

'Do you know where Foxie went?' I asked the Scrabble-playing ladies. They were packing up the game.

'Can you hear something?' one of them asked, and the other one laughed like a kid, like a bully.

It was quite late and most of them were drifting upstairs to bed and the ones who didn't live there went home. The only women left were the ones who'd previously been quarrelling about the music. They were tongue-kissing on the sofa and I watched them with keen interest. I'd heard about French kissing from a girl in the camping ground at Whangamata and I wondered if that was what she meant, or whether it was something only men do to women. They were making little moaning sounds and if it hadn't been so dark I'd've been able to see what they were doing with their hands. After a while they got up and the one who bent down to turn the lamp off noticed me in the corner.

'Getting your thrills?' she asked aggressively, but the beautiful one with the long red hair shushed her.

'He's only a kid, Beck,' she said. 'Leave him alone.'

'Where are you from?' I asked her, 'You talk different.'

'I'm Australian,' she told me. Her friend was pulling on her arm.

'C'mon, Kerry.'

'My dad's in Australia,' I told the red-haired one. Kerry. She was gorgeous. The palest skin and milky-blue eyes.

'I bet he is,' said the other woman, and Kerry and I both looked at her as if to say, 'What do you mean?' but she wasn't looking at us; she was too busy trying to haul her friend upstairs.

When the door swung shut after them I turned the lamp back on, dug around in the ashtrays and found enough roaches to make a little joint. It reminded me of Lena, doing that. She had two tins: Dorothy Gilmore for the new stuff and a little enamelled box for the roaches, which she re-rolled when her stash was gone. I lit it off the embers of the fire, smoked it up, then lay down to watch the pictures but it wasn't as good as the first time. The fire was lower and I didn't have a blanket. The dope made me shivery and cold.

I woke up in the morning with sticky soot on my face and raised voices in my ears. Lena? I flung up and raced out into the high hall. My mother was on the doorstep with Scottie and the Scrabble-playing woman with the chook's head was yelling at them.

'I never heard anything so fucking ridiculous,' my mother said. She caught sight of me at the end of the corridor and I ran for her, pushing Chookhead out of the way and wrapping my arms around her. Mum pulled me close and stroked my hair.

'He's only a kid,' said Scottie.

'He's still male!' said Chookhead. 'That's the policy. We voted on it, remember?' She glared at Scottie.

'Yeah,' said Scottie, 'but —'

'No males, no het women.'

Beck came stumbling down the grand old staircase. It had polished banisters and a curved handrail that went up for miles. I wondered if anyone would notice if I went up and slid down it. Beck put her hand out and stopped me going back inside. Lena's eyes had filled with tears and her body stiffened against me.

'Go out to the van,' she said, her voice trembly.

'It's locked. Foxie's got —'

'Go on, Jas. I'll be there in a minute.' She bent down to look into my eyes so that I knew she meant it. With one thumb she wiped the soot off my cheek. 'Go on,' she said again, giving me a little push down the wide concrete steps. On the way down the cracked, weedy drive I looked back at her. She was slipping her arm around Scottie, who was talking urgently in a low voice to Beck and Chookhead, who were blinking into the winter light and looking grim.

Under my bare feet the grass verge was squidgy, mud seeping up between my toes. I hauled myself onto the bonnet of the Bedford, making muddy streaks on the fender. A boy went past, about my age, on his way to Saturday morning game. He had a short haircut and a pair of footie boots slung around his neck. He looked at me curiously.

'Want a joint?' I asked him languidly. 'I can do you a good deal. Pure sins.'

His face contorted into a sneer. 'Dickhead,' he said, and kept walking.

A while after that a man went by, pushing his little girl in a stroller. I watched them right to the top of the road. The kid was chattering on even though she couldn't talk properly, her little nonsense voice squeaky in the quiet morning street. The father was talking back, answering her as if she made perfect sense. 'Yes,' 'No,' and 'Really?' he said.

Now, there's a dickhead, I thought.

I lie down flat on the floor and do some sit-ups. Fifty, to be precise. I'm built like the old man and I don't want to go to pack like him. Thirty-three years old and still with a washboard stomach. I'm proud of that. It's good to be proud of something.

When I'm finished I take off my green prison shirt and use it to wipe off the sweat, then I hang it on the chair back to dry. Footsteps sound, clip clip clip, shiny screw's shoes down the corridor. I rush to the square of perforated metal, peer through. Whoever it was has passed me by.

They've forgotten I'm here.

The idea drops into my mind pure as the best Huanaco. I could bring it to their attention — I could scream, smash up the furniture, shoulder the door. Why would I want to, though? Food, of course. I'm hungry, but I've gone without food for longer than this. In South America, when I walked up the slopes in Peru with Damian, and on the yachts, when we went to meet the Colombians with nothing much in the galley cupboards and it was too rough to fish. That happened more than once, especially when we had to steal a boat. Foresight has never been one of my strongest traits. I don't see the point of it, really. How can you plan ahead when you don't know the future for sure? Some other bastard is bound to get in the way, stuff things up, make different plans that fuck the ones you've made.

They've forgotten all about me.

Friend of mine went for a job as a screw once, years ago. He had a BA in sociology and they told him he was too intelligent. They like screws to be thick. They make you sit an IQ test and give you the job if you fail it. Actually my friend was no genius, as I remember. He wasn't a patch on Damian, who was my mate for years. But you don't have to be a genius to get a degree in sociology, not like the pure, hard sciences, like the chemistry degree I would've ended up with. He would've been all right as a screw. He wouldn't have lost his prisoners. When I see the lawyer again I'll tell him they did this. Maybe he'll cause some shit.

MELODY

Two Questions and a Whalesong

This morning I have a communication from Howard, asking me not to come. He is unwell, he says, his voice wheezy on the answering service. Howard was unwell last Wednesday and the Wednesday before that. I begin to think Howard is always ill midweek, or maybe it's the winter — the combined effects of the season and his age: Howard is nearly seventy, which even he finds astonishing, given his voracious and continued consumption of Johnnie Walker and Dunhill, both Red. Myself, I put his relative good health down to his sporting youth.

After I erase his message I make myself some coffee and as I do so my old enemy flies in on ragged wings through the window from the grey sky outside, cackling with hatred and doubt. Ha ha, she says, balancing her horny claws on the back of a kitchen chair and with a face curiously like my mother's: you see, he can't stand you, he thinks you're stupid, he thinks you're not up to it.

Even my mother, who is pig ignorant about such things, thinks I

40

am a strange choice for a man like Howard Shag, who could have chosen any biographer. Michael King had approached him, so Howard tells me, as had Patrick White's biographer David Marr, and Nabokov's Brian Boyd, and there were enquiries from as far away as Munich, New York and London, but they were all men. It was a woman Howard wanted, and as I was the only one on offer, he chose me. He felt his life would benefit from a feminine perspective, he felt my youth would be an asset, he had read my only other life and thought I had served my subject well. He was not concerned that *Blood Curdle*, which traced the life of the controversial, grossly underrated Wellington poet/dominatrix Lavinia Mann, sold only three hundred copies, and that the jump from Lavinia Mann to Howard Shag would be . . . well, a considerable one.

Night and day I'm filled with a sharp-edged urge to get on with it. Anyone who has read Howard's novels has been led by the nose on an exciting and often alarming journey through the deepest and darkest of psychoses, and along the way shocked to laughter by the wicked, irreverent humour that runs through even the blacker tales, like mica through a river stone. During his creative life there was no war-torn continent or troubled island Howard would not take his readers to, no perversion he didn't palpitate, no act of violence he left unimagined. He was as elegant as a Graham Greene entertainment, as inventive as Stephen King, as sexually obsessed as the earlier Harold Robbins, had a greater sense of adventure than Wilbur Smith and Henry Rider Haggard and is more famous than the five of them put together. In every airport and mall bookstore all over the western world the Shag books form pyramids and hillsides of glitter-titled tomes, each volume never fewer than seven hundred pages. And in New Zealand we are so proud of him; our chests are so puffed out we can't see the ground, we're falling over our feet. There are streets named after him in all the main centres, and in Levin, where he wasn't born and probably won't die, there's even a Shag Park. Levin is inland, so people know the park is named for him, not the coastal bird. Even the politicians love him — his royalties are so vast they impact on the national economy, the only time in history books ever have. The trusts he funds for disadvantaged children are rich and multitudinous and none bears his name.

Oh yes, he's a national treasure, our Howard Shag: ex-All Black and blockbuster millionaire, a writer whose novels have been adapted for stage and screen, a man who has thrilled, inspired, comforted and terrified millions. And it's me he's chosen to write his life, not because of my PhD, or for any other reason but my gender and my love of rugby. When we first met, Howard and I, we talked rugby for two and a half hours and I don't think he could believe it.

'You've never played though, have you?' he asked me. 'Not in any of those women's teams they have now? You're so delicate and little — you'd be trodden into the mud.'

I've only ever been a spectator. Rugby is one of the reasons my relationship with my boyfriend ended, he being jealous of my affection for a male sport that he neither played nor understood. It was my rebellion, loving rugby: a calculated revolt against my parents and wimpy, clinging ex-partner — at least, it was at the beginning. Now it's just pure pleasure.

The phone is ringing again. Please don't let it be my mother, or Curtis, who even after six solid months of therapy with Mum's friend Lena doesn't comprehend that I don't want to 'service a friendship', let alone 'resume intimacy'. It's possibly the only disadvantage in living alone: there is no one else to answer the phone or the door.

It's Howard.

'Where were you when I rang before?'

'Asleep. I didn't hear the phone. But I got your message.'

'In bed, eh?'

There's a silence after this. I've read most of his books, twenty of the twenty-eight, and the women in them aren't a bit like me. If they're not rare and inconsequential old ladies or little girls then they're tall, dark-haired, full-lipped Latinos or Polynesian princesses, lush with desire, each breast bigger than my head and with no real impact on the plot. If I were to meet one of them I'd stand as high as her solar plexus, eyeball to nipple. Howard wouldn't waste his time imagining me in bed.

'I've changed my mind,' his voice comes. 'I'll see you at eleven.'

'Howard, how do you know I haven't made other —'

BEEEEEEEP. He's rung off already.

So I go, of course. I can't resist — even if I had made other plans I would have cancelled them. I gather up my folders and pens and tapes and arrive at his place, a vast, colonial, two-storeyed wooden villa on the Golden Mile, right on Takapuna Beach, at half-eleven.

'You're late.'

'It's a shit day. The traffic was banked up across the Harbour Bridge.'

Howard looks his age this morning, sitting in his armchair, a tartan rug over his knees, the lamp glowing beside him, his newspaper folded away. A spent cigarette lies in the ashtray, a column of unsmoked grey ash curled like a turd from the filter. The dozen flames of the little gas fire jump rigidly like miniature players in a line-out along their fake logs, putting out a paltry heat to the back of my legs. Beyond the vast picture window the channel is grey and scummy. Rangitoto Island slumps on the far side, triple volcano peaks fuzzed with soft rain. The beach is veiled with seaweed. Nosing in a fallen rubbish bin on the grass reserve beside the house is Howard's old black labrador bitch.

This is only our third session together, but I've noticed already how it takes Howard a few minutes to get used to my being here. He greets me tersely, then we have a short period of silence. Apart from the weekly visits of his cleaning lady, Howard is not accustomed to company. He gestures for me to sit down in my usual spot: the burnt-orange sofa at right angles to his chair. The wall behind me is taken up with a small portion of Howard's vast library — books he has used for research, for pleasure — and books he wrote, translated into nearly every language on the planet.

I flick open the tape recorder on the coffee table between us, slip in a tape, uncomfortably aware as always of how I can see, in the screen of the massive television set on my left, the two of us reflected, or parts of us: my skinny, black-trousered legs and luminous, pasty face; his face with the broken nose flattened at the bridge and distorted even further in the convex plastic; his lopsided smile. He's smiling now, and it's a curiously boyish, teasing smile in his ravaged old battle-scarred face. Purply cauliflower ears on either side, his bald pate shines like a moon-stone. Most of Howard — what I've seen anyway — is pale, milky white, a legacy of having spent the last twenty years inside. Most

Antipodeans his age make regular trips to the melanoma clinic but not Howard. For twenty years he hasn't stepped outside the front door. His groceries are delivered, his whisky and his cigarettes. He doesn't own a car. He doesn't have a current passport. His accountant visits him to prepare his tax returns, his doctor makes house calls, his dentist takes his teeth away to mend them.

Howard's long slender hands twitch now at the fringe of his rug, below the cuffs of an exquisite lemon-coloured shirt, the soft collar open to show a thin gold chain. Who buys his clothes, I wonder? There is no adult daughter to fuss over him; Howard was married only once, disastrously, for the duration of only one year, in his late twenties. I sit in the chair opposite him and go over my notes.

One of Howard's hooded eyes regards me piercingly. The other is focused on the china cabinet behind me, which is stuffed with rugby memorabilia: my famous subject is cockeyed, the result of an injury sustained during a test match against the Wallabies in 1964.

'I've got some things for you. My birth certificate and so on. My Plunket book.'

'Your Plunket book?' I am amazed that he still has it. Howard takes my astonishment for ignorance.

'Oh yes — they had them in 1938.' He hands me a buff envelope, grease-spotted and foxed. 'Take them home with you. Don't bother with them now.'

He lights a cigarette, inhales and coughs dangerously for some time. I take one too — he told me on our first session that he was delighted I smoked and that he would look forward to indulging with me. I had never heard anyone say that before. For the time it takes to finish them we puff companionably in silence because Howard likes to concentrate on his pleasures without distraction.

The rain is suddenly heavier. It flings itself against the window with the sound of hurled sand. Howard pours himself a tot as a dark shape looms on the terrace to sit mournfully at the door: Web Ellis, his dog. Sighing, creaking, Howard gets up to let her in. In the manner of all dogs, Web Ellis waits until she is in the centre of the room before she gives herself a violent shake. Droplets scatter across the glass of the cabinet, the green Turkish rug, the polished arms of the settee, the dark surface of the coffee table and the envelope Howard has just given me.

'Good girl,' says Howard absently, returning to his chair and replacing his rug. Web Ellis settles her bulk in front of the fire and the room smells comfortably old fashioned now: of wet dog and cigarettes. There is no point hurrying Howard. He sips at his whisky, rolls it around his gums, swallows loudly, sighs again and sets down his glass.

'You know, when I was a youngster,' he begins, 'youngster' being a Howard kind of word, 'I used to go to dances. We could all dance then, you know. We were taught and what's more we wanted to know how to do it. All the new dances as well — the jitterbug and so on . . . Anyway, the point is . . .' And he gazes off into space again, his good eye on the swirling rain, his bad eye on a whipping pohutukawa, its upper branches frantic in the wind, the dark leaves flipping and twisting to show their silver undersides. His hand, the forefinger stained yellow, creeps towards his cigarettes — then stalls.

'The point is, I see this process as a little like a dance. You can't do it without me and I can't do it without you. And I want us to dance traditionally, you know what I mean?' The good eye is on me now, a bleary spotlight.

'You want to lead?'

'Bang on,' says Howard. 'And there are parts of the dance floor I will not cover.'

Howard is not big on metaphor, in his books at least. He keeps them down to one a chapter, around about. Mostly they're clichés: sea as mirror, breasts as ripe fruit, men as lions or roaring bulls, blood as wine and wine as blood. He keeps it simple: guns smoke, women pant and men fight iron on steel. One day Howard will discover I am a literary snob, but I'll keep it from him for as long as can. I have already begun the part of the biography that is literary critique — I'll keep that a secret as well, at least until we have finished his life. He's never inquired about my tastes anyway.

'You've been very restrained,' he goes on. 'You haven't asked the two questions. You haven't even hinted at them.'

For some reason I'm blushing. 'I would have, of course, eventually.'

'What I'm saying, my girl, is that I don't want you to ask them. They're journalists' questions. If you want to be taken seriously as a biographer, don't ask them.'

'I want you to take me seriously but you're treating me like a ghost-writer. I have to ask those questions.'

'There's the door,' he says, pointing.

'But Howard, you —' Appeal to his ego, I think, brazen it out. The whisky glass is once again at his lips, which purse to form a proboscis before dipping into the amber fluid. Tenderly his pale tongue licks around to collect the liquor.

'But people will want to know,' I say lamely. 'In a way, they are the two great mysteries of your life: why you became a recluse and why you never wrote again.' There. I've given voice to them.

The veiny lid of the good eye lowers sadly. 'That's a bloody tragedy. After all I've done for this bloody country. Someone called me a Renaissance Man once — a reviewer. I'm not, of course, but there's a fair stretch between rugby and literature. The only blokes who've gone the distance are myself and Greg McGee and I'm a thousand times more famous than him. That tape on?' I nod. 'Don't quote me on that remark about Greg. He wouldn't like it.'

'Mmmm,' I reply calmly, though in truth I'm experiencing a mild panic. The biography will be seriously flawed unless I can persuade him to talk. And in a commercial sense, something my generation understand better than any other since the Depression, these two great mysteries of Howard's life will hook in the general public. His rugby public is huge, but the general public — people who have read his books, or seen the films based on his books, but who have never heard of his legendary prowess on the field — that public is mammoth. A small tremor runs up my spine, a little mercenary current: this book could set me up. Should I so desire I could retire to the South of France at thirty-five.

'That's a scheming expression you're wearing, Melody. Don't think you can talk me round.' He chuckles in a way that I suspect began as a joke, copied from a vampire film, and is now a permanent trait. His yellow teeth glisten as he pours himself another drink and lights a new cigarette.

I have one too and while I smoke it I squat before the china cabinet. When Howard dies I will do my best to make sure it is exhibited exactly as it is in Te Papa Museum. It's perfect. In the centre as altar-piece is a battered rugby ball from his first game as an All Black, which was the first game of the famous Springbok Tour of '56. It's signed by every member of the Springboks, whom they beat that first game in Hamilton 10–6. To the left of the ball is a signed photograph of Sean Fitzpatrick, on the right a cartoon sketch of Colin Meads, also signed. There is a folded jersey once worn by Wilson Whineray and a bent sprig fallen from Jonah Lomu's boot. An entire boot lies on its side, still with a scraping of mud. Once it supported the rarely clad foot of Bob Scott, the much-loved fullback of the 1950s. Many times it would have taken up exactly the position it has now, lying on its side but in the middle of the fields the rugby-playing world over, while Scott wowed the crowd with his famous showtime barefoot kicks. There is a small Samoan carving, a present from Bryan Williams, whom Howard contends was the best wing the All Blacks ever had. Behind the sliding glass front is a rugby landscape: mountains and valleys of souvenirs and talismans frosted with dust, not all of it visible. The space under the dresser is filled by piles of programmes, spines outermost, some of them souvenirs of games Howard played himself. Others are games Howard observed and believed to be so magnificent the programme was worth preserving.

Once I joked with him that under his clothes he must wear a scapular, black with a silver fern, and that hidden in a far corner of the cabinet there was probably a reliquary, containing one of George Nepia's knuckles maybe, or a desiccated strip of Sid Going's foreskin. He was not amused.

I'm home by three, feeling depressed, though I've filled two sides of a ninety-minute tape. Between smokes Howard chattered obligingly on about his childhood on the West Coast of the South Island, his eight brothers and sisters and his coalminer father who fought in the war. Just before his father died he saw Howard play his first game with the All Blacks and when Howard got to this part of the story he took the ball out of the cabinet, very reverently, and allowed me to touch it. The brown leather was crazed like old china. I roused myself to look interested but by then I was hardly listening, a luxury sound technology affords the melancholy biographer. The main worry is this: I have zilch respect for Howard's writing. One thing my loony hippie mother taught me is the foolhardiness of doing anything just for the money. Tell that to a Russian nuclear-power-plant worker or a morgue cleaner, I'd thought cynically at the time. Tell that to most of the fucking world. Unfortunately, in this case — and I'll never let her know it — she might be right. Literary snob that I am, there are only two things that fire my curiosity about Howard. First: why did he become a virtual recluse from the early 1980s? He's a psychiatrist's grab-bag of rare complaints: gamaphobic by his own admission, agoraphobic by professional diagnosis, and haptephobic by mine, after I made the mistake of trying to shake his hand. He hardly even touches Web Ellis. The only thing I have ever seen him touch for pleasure are inanimate objects, in particular a large brass elephant in execrable taste that guards the front door in his hall. Whenever he passes it he gives it a little pat. There's a worn, silvery patch on its head from his caresses.

Second: why did he never write another book after *Black Orbit*? To be sure, *Snow Blind*, *Tombolo*, and *Hard Line* were all re-issued through the 1990s to maintain his profile, but there's been nothing new for twenty years.

I park my car in the miniature driveway outside my dolls-house and let myself in the plastic door. It's one of myriad 'townhouses' they keep building in Grey Lynn and it always seems cruddy to me on my return from Howard's. It's minimalist in every way — size, decor, the sparse furnishings, the contents of the fridge.

The answering machine gives me my mother's voice reminding me about the ceremony on Waiheke Island tomorrow, and then my ex-boyfriend sounding fragile.

'I thought you might be there,' he says, and waits, as if he's thinking I am there and I might pick up the phone. 'I was going to come around.' In the background I can hear voices, American ones. The television. I picture him standing in the chaos of his low-ceiling flat, the one his parents had put in for him in the basement of their St Heliers Bay home, holding the phone with white knuckles. The television cackles and guffaws. It's a chat show, *Oprah* or *Sally Jesse Raphael*. 'Oh well,' Curtis says, 'bye,' and there's a soft click as he hangs up.

I curl up on my bed to read the envelope of Howard's infancy. Perhaps I'll be able to begin his childhood chapter soon. I intend that chapter to be a slim one: it's not a part of his life that fascinates me particularly, and I suspect not many readers will be interested either. The most sensational stuff will come later, once I've tracked down some of his team-mates, and through them some of the women he must have had after his divorce. There could have been hundreds: he was a handsome, discreet and desirable man. I'll have plenty of material. I open the little Plunket book, buff coloured, ruled up in black ink on the inside.

Howard was nine pounds at birth, a giant baby for the times, and gained weight quickly, his first tooth presenting early at five months. He sat up at around the same time and walked precociously at nine months. 'Refuses to take solids' is an earlier entry, at six months, and I know enough about babies to find that strange, especially in the thirties when the fashion for early weaning was having its genesis. 'Taking mashed kumara only' reads another, a month later. An entry on the following page, at ten months, has me sitting up and reaching for a cigarette. 'Intensely dislikes being touched, even by Mother.' I lie with the Plunket book open on my stomach and blow smoke towards the ceiling. If this is the beginning of Howard's haptephobia, I'm thinking — if it is something that dates from childhood and not, as I'd previously suspected, from the onset of his agoraphobia — then how the hell did he play rugby? He was a number eight, the middle row of the scrum, the meat in a heavy, fleshy sandwich. I take up the book again and comb through it. There's no further mention of touching, but considering that Howard was her third child — he had two older sisters — and that by the time he was sixteen months old his mother had had twin daughters and was pregnant with another, she might not have noticed. New Zealanders are not demonstrative parents. More than likely he was potty-trained by then, so she would have had even less cause to touch her first son, except perhaps to lift him in and out of the bath . . .

I'm drifting off. I love to sleep through the afternoon. In the afternoons I don't enjoy consciousness: give me the morning and the evening, with nothing in between. Most nights I don't go to bed till two or three. My sister says I have the sleep pattern of a difficult toddler.

Howard is a tiny boy, running and tackling on a soggy West Coast rugby field. His opponents and team mates are grown men, black shapes heaving suddenly into view through thick mist, with rasping breath and thighs heavy enough to set the ground shaking. Around me, the size of dwarfs, are his seven brothers and sisters, cheering him on. They wear lighted miners' hats, the beams shining on the white fog, and now and then alighting on Howard himself, his little baby legs churning through the mud towards the try line, the outsize ball clutched against his soft, round puku.

The dream haunts me all the following morning and only begins to dissipate as I ride my bicycle down to the Ferry Building to catch the boat to Waiheke Island. As I fly down Franklin Road, through the dappled light of the plane trees, I feel my heart lift: a physical sensation, my blood thrumming, a smile forming on my lips. The harbour spreads below me, still and blue, promising a calm voyage across the Gulf. As long as I don't let my mind rest on the ceremony ahead, my spirits will remain high.

But by the time I'm pushing my bike up the flax-lined gravel incline to my parents' Waiheke home I'm fretting. What compels my mother to do this? It's a shame my twin sister's baby isn't born yet, then instead we might be gathering for a Naming, which would hopefully be less morbid. From the last bend in the right-of-way I can see that the doors onto the deck are open and I can see my father on it with his back to me. Curly grey head bent over his guitar, he croons one of his own compositions, which are all based on recordings of whalesong. It's as if he's singing through the slatted deck floor to Zinnia's new Mitsubishi, which gleams silver and black in the carport like an orca. She must have taken the vehicle ferry from Half Moon Bay; which doesn't surprise me at all. She never liked walking and now she's about a month off giving birth she's probably in a wheelchair.

Either side of the doormat the porch is littered with shoes, mostly sandals even though it's winter. I add my Doc Martens to the collection. It's not for the sake of the carpets we do it — there are none. The floors are chipboard with twenty years worth of stains on them. No, we remove our shoes for reasons of cultural sensitivity, just in case a Maori friend comes to call. As far as I know my parents have no Maori friends.

The narrow lobby I pass into leads straight up a narrow flight of steps with uneven tread. Dad built this house when his career in the bank ended after the crash in 1987. He did it by male instinct, which he and my mother are convinced he possesses in large dollops. Instinct doesn't take you far when you're digging footings, mitring corners and hanging doors. Many of the rooms have doors that stick, fall open or won't close, and one or two have no doors at all, Dad having given up on them. The bathroom and master bedroom are two of these, which visitors of nervous disposition find alarming. Curtis never got used to it.

Up, up I go, into the brilliant winter sunshine of the main room, which has glass walls and roof, the roof blotched with the thick sap dropped by surrounding manuka and macrocarpa, as well as the excreta of various birds: seagulls, starlings, white-eyes and pigeons.

'Hello, Mum!'

My mother smiles from the sofa as I come in, a multi-coloured afghan rug over her knees. She's still pale from the operation, I think as I bend to kiss her. Today she's in a pink leisure suit, one of those outfits of heavy cotton knit so beloved of older American women tourists. Across her chest raised gold lettering reads 'Just Do It!'. Her bare feet rest on a footstool she made herself out of driftwood and I see the afghan rug is still in production: in and out and round about flashes the crochet hook. I think she's pleased to see me: it's difficult to tell. Zinnia's husband comes through from the kitchen carrying a bowl of crisps.

'Hi there, Paulie,' I say and he nods at me with his very tiny head. At least it's tiny in comparison with the rest of his large body, except for his hands and feet, which are in proportion to his head. On tippy-toes he returns to the kitchen. Zinnia and he have been together since they were fifteen and in all those years I might have heard his voice three times, no more.

'More visitors coming up the drive, honeybunch!' Dad's guitar comes through from the deck, followed closely by Dad himself. He gives Mum's shoulder a squeeze as he goes to lean his guitar in a lopsided corner.

'Hi, Dad.'

'Yep,' he says and thumps off downstairs to the basement where the fridge lives, there having been no room allowed for it in the building of the kitchen. I leave Mum to greet her guests and give Zinnia a hand. Or Paulie, as it turns out. Zinnia's buttocks are balanced precariously on another of Mum's glued driftwood collections while she gives Paulie instructions for the garlic bread. When she's sure he's got the right knife, the right action with it and the correct amount of salt she takes time out to say hello in the form of a flash of eye contact. It travels in a nano-second down my leather jacket and jeans to my socks. I could wonder why I bother to come to these family gatherings, given the total absence of welcome — but I've learned not to take it personally. I think it's common in white New Zealand families, but I can't decide if it's origin lies in a paucity of love or an excess of it. For Dad, at least, it's the latter: he was so despairing when Zin and I left home that when we come over to the island a little fiction is spotlit in his brain. It tells him we've always been there, that we've never gone away, so therefore it's pointless extending a greeting. He's never visited me in my dolls-house, or anywhere else for that matter.

'How's Bubs?' I ask Zinnia, giving her tummy a little pat.

'I can't wait for it to come out,' Zinnia says, one foot travelling coquettishly up the inside of Paul's left leg. 'Or she, eh, Paulie?'

'Oh, so you know,' I say. 'Mum told me you were going to ask.'

Zinnia's eyes are turned on me full force, rabid blue, the flesh surrounding them puffy and fluid-retentive. 'Did she tell you the sex? I told her yesterday on the phone. I told her not to tell you. I told her not to. Did she tell you? Did she? Do you already know? That it's a girl? Did you know that?'

'No — I —'

'You're lying!' For someone disinclined to put one foot in front of another, Zinnia can propel herself through space remarkably fast. She's up and out, the driftwood stool toppling in her wake, and her voice echoes back off the glass ceiling, over those of our mother's guests who are arriving in twos and threes from all parts of the island. 'Mu-um! Mum, did you tell Mel my news — you did, didn't you, Mum, didn't you?'

By the time I venture out with the chicken nibbles and sausage rolls Zinnia is having a lie-down while Paulie rubs her feet and Dad is splashing round the bubbly. He's exchanged one stained white T-shirt for another one and put on his best shorts. He and Paulie are the only men in the room, which is often the case at my parents' parties since they moved over to the island. Until recently Curtis made three. He and I were also together since we were fifteen, starting from the exact same weekend as Paul and Zinnia, almost to the hour. Dad loves Paulie and Curtis. He even somehow knew when we lost our cherries — same weekend, same hour, same house, different rooms — and he thought it was marvellous. He and Mum have always been keen on sex. A bit too keen in my opinion — not that they ever did it in front of us, but only because Zinnia and I would wander off if it looked likely.

'Is Zinnia all right?' I ask my mother.

Mum nods. She's distracted by the bowl of home-made fudge she's balancing on her outstretched legs and the three sets of chubby hands that are pillaging it. Our youngest guests are approximately four years old. What are they going to make of the ceremony when it happens? I wonder. For their sake I hope the thing is wrapped up in paper, or solid cloth.

The bubbly has left my father's grasp and in its place is the garden shovel. He looms behind me to whisper wetly in my ear, 'Go and get it, love.'

'It?'

'In our room. Your mother's made a thing for it. You won't miss it.'

'Oh.'

'Off ya go. I'll send everyone out onto the deck so they don't see you carrying it through. Meet you down below.'

In the hall I pause a moment, mentally preparing myself. At varsity I studied arts, avoiding all sciences, unless you call Psych 2 science. I am not interested in pure medicine or anatomy or health or women's problems. Curtis would tell you I'm not interested in sex either, which is not true. It's just that I've not slept with anyone except him and he's not very good at it: a girl can only say 'harder', 'softer', 'to the right', 'lower' or whatever so many times before she gives up.

Through the open portal I go, into the parental bedroom, the glass ceiling of which my father has painted black on my mother's orders. She'd had enough of being woken at dawn. Consequently the room is doused in grey, smoky light, like the aftermath of a bush fire. The bedhead is constructed of driftwood inset with paua shells, which glimmer dully under their coating of dust. Crumpled in a greyish heap beside the unmade bed is my father's discarded T-shirt. Usually my mother burns musk oil in here, but this afternoon there's a mysterious, powerful scent of flowers: early spring jonquils, freesias and paperwhites.

On the dressing table is a sealed glass jar. Around the jar on a heavy pottery platter flowers have been artfully arranged in concentric circles according to colour and type. The jar has a black ribbon at its neck, tied in a floppy elaborate bow. I pick up the platter and the clear fluid inside the jar — formaldehyde, I suppose — sloshes around the tiny pink organ. My mother's uterus is much smaller than I would've thought, considering that nearly thirty years ago it held twins, and more recently, fibroids of rare dimension. Maybe the formaldehyde shrank it.

Outside Dad is ready with his spade and Mum and all her friends are leaning over the deck rail above. As I pass the silver Mitsubishi, through the slatted light under the deck, their excited chatter hushes. Dad must've given a sign. I hold the platter out like an altar boy with the Host and he plucks up the jar, holding it aloft so the women can see. Sparkling and shifting, the glass casts rainbow light on my father's upturned face, the little pink womb spinning in its bath, a translucent membrane trailing behind it like a veil.

'Behold!' he intones, like a prophet.

One of Mum's Waiheke friends, Lena Calonna, stands with her arm firmly around Mum. Lena is one of those people who shine with health and vitality and happiness, as if she's never ingested a food additive or suffered a regret. She's a mystery to me, but Mum is very fond of her and right now it looks as though Mum could faint and Lena is all that's holding her up. Lena's girlfriend Scottie is there too, wearing her usual delighted grin, and Scottie's sister Foxie with her enormous male german shepherd dog Hausfrau. There are a few other faces I recognise, but not many — Val, Mum's old best friend from school, who's looking a bit disapproving and pursy-lipped; Sheree, the next-door neighbour; Sooze, who runs surprisingly lucrative Becoming Orgasmic workshops in the Onepoto church hall; and of course Auntie Lil, Dad's sister, who wasn't invited but came anyway seeing as she only lives down the road and she'd seen Dad at the wholesaler buying the case of Seaview. Right now Auntie Lil's not at the deck rail — I can see her through the glass wall chomping on sausage rolls, glass in hand.

'You want to say a few words, love?' Dad asks tenderly.

Mum opens her mouth but nothing comes out, so Lena pats her arm and speaks for her.

'Thank you, Supreme Mother, for the gift of Helen's womb, a womb that gave the world the priceless gift of two lovely daughters, Melody and Zinnia. This afternoon we give the womb back to the earth from whence it came. From henceforth Helen's womb will lie in the Womb of All the World, the Womb of Woman returned to you, oh Mother of All the World.'

Someone, I think it's Sheree, says Amen and a bird begins hooting from one of the macrocarpas above the house. It's a kind of natural funeral music, dirge-like and repetitive. Dad unscrews the lid from the jar and tips the fluid away into a bush, then puts it back on my tray while he digs the hole. The hooting bird grows louder and, in the same instant I register how damp my socks are from the wet grass, I realise it's not a bird at all but Zinnia, who is leaning bulkily on our mother, who in turn is being propped up by Lena. Very gently Dad takes the jar back and empties Mum's womb into the little grave. Into the dark soil it plops like a pink fish. Zinnia's hoots give way to wails.

'It's so sad, Mum, it's so sad!' she sobs. 'It's all over for you and it's just beginning for me!'

I could strangle Zinnia. Instead, in keeping with the solemnity of the occasion I pluck one white flower from the tray and drop it into the hole. Dad is crying too, but he brushes his tears away and takes the tray from me. All the flowers cascade in now, a thick layer of them, scented and colourful, and my heart gives a tiny pang. As funerals for body parts go, this is probably a good one.

'I'll fill it in later,' Dad mutters, putting his arm around me, and we go upstairs for another glass of Seaview and what's left of the food, though I haven't got much of an appetite. Lena brings me a plate of salad and pats me on the head.

'That was a lovely touch,' she says, 'dropping the white flower in.'

'Yes, it was, dear,' says Mum. She's got some colour in her cheeks now: maybe she's relieved it's all over. She's back on the sofa with the rug, Zinnia beside her with her head on her shoulder, eyes closed. Auntie Lil hauls herself into the chair beside us.

'I just let them munch mine up,' she says wheezily. Soy sauce from the chicken nibbles stains the whiskery corners of her mouth.

'Pardon?' says Lena sharply.

'When I had my hysterectomy. They've got a thing at National Women's that munches them up. Wombs and afterbirth and so forth.' She lights up a Pall Mall Menthol while Lena glares at her and I think to myself how I wouldn't want to cross Lena. That glare is just the pilot light of what could easily fan up to be a furnace.

A wisp of cigarette smoke trails across Zinnia's blind and tear-swollen face and evaporates before her nostrils. Her nose waffles, rapid, tremulous, like a rabbit, and she heaves herself up, wounded and betrayed by her aunt's utter selfishness and cruelty to her unborn child, and goes to look for Paulie. On the other side of the room Dad is waiting for her.

'This was your mother's day,' he says in a hoarse whisper, 'and you had to do your best to ruin it for her.' Zinnia claps her hand to her mouth and stares wild-eyed at him. 'Why do you have to carry on like that?'

'Sorry,' she squeaks through her fingers, and though I have a sense of sneaky delight at seeing her upbraided I'm also thinking that it's not really her fault. It's the way we were brought up. I don't recollect ever hearing the word no. We truly thought we were the centre of the universe.

'Oh, Jesus — Foxie!' Scottie's thumping in from the deck makes the whole house vibrate. She's jabbing her finger backwards, over her shoulder. 'Foxie, quick!'

From the deck, where Dad and Zinnia and I arrive at the same time, we see the devastation: clods of soil and bruised flowers, a brown vacuum, an absence. Disappearing around the bend in the right-of-way is the grave-robber Hausfrau, his small pink prize clamped between his teeth. Zinnia bursts into fresh tears.

'Don't tell your mother,' says Dad, but it's too late: she's on her way in.

I go downstairs, pick up the shovel and fill in the hole. While I'm tamping down the earth Mum and Lena come out onto the deck to watch me. I glance up at them once and it seems to me my mother might have the ghost of a smile.

'In the end,' Lena tells her firmly, soothingly, 'it doesn't make much difference. We still had the ceremony. It'll still go back to the Supreme Mother.'

'Yes, I s'pose it will,' Mum says dreamily. '. . . After it's been through Hausfrau. It's him I'm worried about. Won't it make him sick?'

RICHARD

Metaphor as Calculus

We were in Paris, Michaela and I, when we received the news. It flashed across my laptop screen one evening in our hotel and as I stared into the light and read the words I was engulfed by darkness. Now, 'engulfed by darkness' is a literary phrase and not one I use lightly. I'm not a literary man: I am a journalist and true to my profession I get lost after about two thousand words. But I had a sense at that moment of being engulfed and of the room growing dark, as though some evil nameless horror had settled its rank buttocks around me, as if I would be suffocated. I was only just aware of Michaela flopped on the bed, her shoes kicked off. We'd walked for miles that day I remember, from the Isle de la Cité and Notre Dame and all through the Latin Quarter, and she'd shopped, shopped, shopped. It was hot, far hotter than I'd imagined Europe could be in my predictions about the place: I'd never been to Europe before. The chill and endless rain we'd left behind in Auckland. In Sydney we'd spent the evening of our stopover with my daughter-in-law Bonny and my grandchildren, and Bonny was quiet and distracted, or so Michaela told me later — I didn't notice. I was much too taken with the boys, who at eight and ten are delightful and not at all like their father was at that age. And it was strange, because as I sat reading the message on the laptop and Michaela stirred behind me and asked 'What is it?' I wasn't thinking of Jasper as he is now, but Jasper at eight or nine, which, given the circumstances and in hindsight, is not so strange at all.

'What is it?' Michaela asked again and she got up and came to read over my shoulder. She gave a little gasp and her damp hand came to rest on the back of my neck.

'We'll have to go back,' she said.

'Yes.' I switched the laptop off and a cold, rational part of my brain cursed modern technology. I had bought the machine with me in order to keep in touch with the office and it was only as an afterthought that I handed the address out to friends and family. It was someone I didn't know who'd sent the email: a woman called Franca. If Franca — whoever she was — hadn't been able to feed the misery out into cyber-space, if she'd been compelled to telephone, she may well have missed us. And a letter would take eight days — I would have lived eight days more of my life feeling entirely alive, instead of, as I do now, as if part of me has died. I remember my mind shot along these runnels, like Bonny's boys' Tamio cars in their slots, until I realised I was trying to delete the message from my mind, minimise its gross importance in all our existences.

'Who is Franca?' asked Michaela.

'Buggered if I know,' I said, but she'd gone, not waiting to hear my answer. From our ensuite seconds later I could hear the sound of gushing water and energetic scrubbing. She was brushing her teeth, as if the words on the glowing screen of a few minutes before had left her, literally, with a dirty taste in her mouth.

A man finds it less and less easy to truly love a new woman the older he gets. Many would disagree with me on this: they would point to their old Uncle Ted or Jimmy down the road, who met his heart's desire just as life's tide was on the turn. I put these kinds of marriages down to exhaustion and need, not affection, and certainly not concupiscence — with or without Viagra. I have not married Michaela, nor do I intend to. As I listened to her in the bathroom, my sixty-year-old body rigid on the edge of the chair, it became abundantly clear to me that considering what lay ahead, the monolithic unravelling of it all, a continued relationship with Michaela would be problematic. God knows she's a beautiful woman: late forties, tweaked and tucked, private-school educated, the ex-wife of one of the wealthiest business-men in Australasia. She's vivacious, funny, sexy — and bloody emotion-ally demanding. Also, given her sheltered life spent in the various compounds of Double Bay, Remuera and Toorak, there is a definite childlike naïveté to her. I found that attractive, of course, when I first met her: her lisping soft voice with its ersatz English accent, the plump, breathy vowels of the postmodern, post-colonial upper class.

She came out of the bathroom lipstick pearly, her breath smelling of toothpaste and a fresh blast of Dioressence emanating from her throat.

'Darling,' she said, 'we have to talk about this. You mustn't close me off. I know you'll want to close me off. You mustn't.'

When I was a young man I'd shut women up by kissing them. As I watched Michaela's pinky-white mouth move above me I remembered doing that to my second wife, and before that to my delicious Liquorice Lena. At that moment I never felt less like kissing anyone in my life. I never wanted to be touched again.

My poor jumbled-up boy.

'Richard?' Michaela reached out to stroke my hair and I dipped my head to avoid her.

'Ah — so we're going to play the prickly old journo again, are we? I think we need a drink.' She went to the telephone and dialled the bar downstairs, ordering in her excellent French a bottle of Bordeaux, the best. Money is no object to Michaela. When we left Bonny's sad little dive in Tempe she pushed a cheque for a couple of k's into my daughter-in-law's hand. Ex-daughter-in-law. There should be a better name for the relationship I have with Bonny — that countless men have with the woman their son was once married to, the woman who bore their grand-children, a woman who is closer to them than their own flesh and blood. Bonny's brown fingers had closed wonderingly around the cheque; her huge dark eyes had stared asking, silently, 'Should I accept it?' And I had nodded, of course. Of course.

Sitting on the bed, Michaela arranged her long, toned legs along it and by the thoughtful expression on her face I could see she was settling in for a long, deep discussion.

'One thing, Michaela,' I beat her to it. 'You have met my son only once and as I recall you didn't like him —'

'That was because of Bonny, what he did —'

'And!' I was almost shouting. Audibly Michaela's mouth snapped shut and she let her head fall back on the pillows. 'And this whole episode is none of your business. I don't wish to discuss it.'

'With me, you mean.'

'With anyone. I think you should continue on to Spain, as planned. I would rather go back alone. Could you ring the airport for me?'

For a moment I thought she would refuse. I gave her time to consider by getting up and lifting my suitcase to the bed. Bending is almost a pleasure now. Greatly diminished is my beer belly, less whiskyish is my whisky nose, my hands no longer shake and my tachycardia is a tacky problem of the past: I imbibe in moderation, as they say. I am reformed; I am a social drinker. I look ten years younger, more Michaela's contemporary than ten years her senior.

'You're ashen, Richard.'

'I'm having a shower.' I left the door open while she dialled. First she cancelled the bottle of wine. Then she rang Charles de Gaulle and began the torturous exercise of trying to get us on the earliest and least nightmarish trip back to Sydney: twenty-seven hours of continuous flight.

In the end I was relieved Michaela was coming with me. Over the next couple of days, the more the news sank in, the more monosyllabic I became. By the time we reached the ferro-concrete octopus that is Charles de Gaulle, it was all I could do not to scream out loud. Michaela was repaying me for my earlier 'rejection' by not speaking to me — though she spoke for me very graciously. There is something to be said for private-school education in a woman, particularly when it has been allowed to mature and gather grace in the sitting rooms and salons of uppermiddle-class Europe. Michaela's first husband took her to live in Berlin for a number of years, another to Paris, and the same one — the third, I think, an ambassador — also to Milan. She is multi-lingual and macro-mannered. I have implicit faith in her ability to conduct herself in any situation.

Politically, of course, we are diametrically opposed. As yet, as a couple, we have not faced an election: it could be the breaking of us. There's one later this year and I suspect, given the endlessly downward spiralling of our economy, her lot will get in. Not that they will arrest the decline. As a nation we own nothing — not our telephones, nor our railways, our bus services, our electronic communications, most of our forests, our newspapers, our television stations: none of the utilities New Zealanders daily spend hundreds of thousands of dollars on. Mostly they were sold in the 1980s and no bastard had the brains to ask the obvious question: how do you harvest a garden when you've sold the bloody soil? Like many of my generation, once my mind latches onto this economic obscenity — which it does with monotonous regularity — it won't let go. Round and round and round it goes in my head, a hopeless rat-wheel.

On our third night in Paris we ate with some French friends of Michaela's and I regaled them with a Brief History of How We Destroyed Aotearoa, while my interpreter Michaela rolled her eyes a lot. These people, with their national pride, their self-respect, in a room where not a garment, stick of furniture nor mouthful of food originated anywhere but France — the fourth largest economic entity in the world — could ask only one question: 'Pourquoi?'

I click in my seatbelt and recline my seat the moment the plane levels off and I'm thinking as I do so, Fucking pourquoi indeed. And then I think that if Jasper were a country he'd be New Zealand. Is it my absence of religion that's making me have these ideas? I have no God so therefore I must have metaphor? I'm having these thoughts more and more and they frighten me. They're unfamiliar and the rational part of my mind, which I've worn for most of my life like a baggy old cardigan with the elbows out — Christ, there I go again — scorns them at the same time as my heart pursues them. Metaphor as calculus, metaphor as a way of seeing, of comfort, of solving problems.

If Jasper were a country he would be the bifurcated country of his birth, not the broad, effervescent land of plenty he's made his home for the past eleven years. He has no sense of himself, except maybe in the grey no-man's land between his warring factions; he has no aptitude for bliss or generosity — the same atmosphere of mean-spirited gloom surrounds him as it does countless small New Zealand towns. These are harsh opinions for any man to have of his son, let alone his country, and I wouldn't share them with anyone. I've scarcely had to confront them, having had so little to do with him. I saw him perhaps four times as a teenager and then not at all until we staged a reconciliation when he became a father — he must have felt the need of one himself on that occasion — and I said to him then, with great honesty, that I hoped he would make a better go of it than I had. That was ten years ago now. Ten whole years. A drop in the bucket, an eternity in a bubble. A decade that passed more quickly than this hellish flight.

When we leave Bangkok I drink too much too quickly and drown the words I might otherwise share with Michaela, who sits beside me cool, impeccable, eerily unruffled: it's that breeding again. It's hard to conceive of her as belonging to the same species as Lena, let alone the same gender. Maudlin on Bloody Marys I consider again how Lena ruined me for life before I fall into a stupor, earplugged and blind-folded, willingly deprived of all external stimulus.

At Kingsford Smith Airport I arrive looking and feeling like the Ancient Mariner, complete with albatross. Why does no one see it rotting and stinking around my neck? Then, while we're outside queuing for a taxi, a question occurs to me suddenly: why the hell have I come back? What in God's name am I expected to do? It was Michaela who said, 'We'll have to go back, of course,' and I must have had a moment of weakness, of directionless conscience, the same compulsion that makes a human being travel thousands of miles to the funeral of a relative they never liked.

Michaela directs the taxi to the Novotel, a luxurious monstrosity at Darling Harbour, and insists I shower and shave before taking another taxi to Long Bay, where Jasper is being held. Although she is aware, she tells me through the fug of my jet-lag and hangover, that I am entirely uninterested in her state of being, she actually feels like a rubber band about to snap and to that end she is booking herself in for a massage and aromatherapy. I manage a smile and a kiss to her brow: I've always admired a woman who knows what she wants.

Sydney does not have winters any more. That much is obvious as the taxi skids its way past gridlocks and through streaming rain: it's sticky enough for my clean shirt to adhere to my back. At the prison gate I lean forward with a tearing sound to pay the cabby.

'Visiting?' he asks, turning with my Visa slip.

I nod and the words 'my son' well to the back of my throat like beery vomit but I swallow them down.

It is 4 p.m. when I approach the visitors' desk and ask for my son under his various aliases: Jasper Brunel, the name I gave him; Jasper Colonna, which is Lena's name; and Jasper Shag, an ambiguous and ridiculous name he copied from the famous writer and ex-All Black. The desk clerk, a pock-faced brunette of sullen disposition, can't find him on her terminal.

'Jasper Pomare?' I try. It's Bonny's name, though to my knowledge he's never used it. On the other side of the Plexiglas the dark head gives a negative.

'Next,' she says, bored and nasal, pointing at the man behind me. She also points at a bench seat on my right. Obedient as a well-trained dog I sit down to wait, assuming that between 'clients' — as these mostly sad and bewildered relatives would be called in my homeland — she will continue her search.

Three-quarters of an hour later I try again.

'Do you have a database of first names?'

'Nup.' She's looking at me as though she's never seen me before in her life. I take a deep breath and begin again.

'I'm here to see my son Jasper Brunel, who might also go by the names —'

'Yeah, I know.' She gives her head a backward toss. 'They're looking him up.'

'You mean you've lost him?'

'When was he brought in?'

I try to figure it out. He would have been arrested a week and a half ago — I received the message on a Monday, about ten days after his arrest. They must've caught up with him on a Wednesday, or Thursday perhaps . . . The woman is narrowing her eyes at me as if she thinks I'm making it up, as if I'm some kind of old nut who likes to pretend his son is in Long Bay. We both start to speak at the same time but she's louder and wins.

"Cause if it was the Thursday before last all our systems were down. They crashed. His data mightn't've gone in yet.'

'A hacker?' I ask, conversationally. Her lips tighten.

'Come back tomorrow,' she says, 'you might have more luck.'

'Your security too? Is it all part of the same system?' I'll check the papers of the last few days to see if it's been covered yet. It'd make a good story; I could stump up to the *Herald* with it. Someone there'll remember me. And I could do with earning a few Aussie dollars. 'Can I at least get a message to him?'

But the lady is not interested in chewing the fat with me any further. A strip of white plastic appears across the lower half of the window with CLOSED, large and black, and she presents me with her profile.

'Tomorrow, then,' I say jovially, to no response. As I take my leave I hope for the ten or fifteen prospective visitors still in the waiting room that Frau Commandant reopens for business soon.

Our box at the Novotel is empty of Michaela. Her masseur must be taking his time. I take off my shoes and trousers and lie prone on the bed in my Y-fronts. The last time I lay flat was about forty hours ago. It's blissful. More than anything else I would like to sleep, but sleep, like so many other functions these days, is no longer summoned on demand. Instead my exhausted subconscious gives me my son, two years old, dragging his bright plastic trike to the top of our steep driveway while I watched him. I didn't think, did I, that he would lack the control or dexterity to avoid a collision at the bottom? When Jasper was born he was the first baby I'd ever held in my life. More incompetent I could not have been. We spent the night at Casualty, he with a greenstick fracture, a split lip and a black eye, me weathering suspicious looks from the staff. They thought I'd done it to him, which I had, but not with my fists.

'Have you been drinking, sir?' asked a young intern with a keen sense of smell. I had been, of course, at the same time as hoovering up a quarter ounce of dope. It was a Saturday and Saturdays for my twenties and most of my thirties were devoted to getting out of it. This was okay, but then it became Sundays too, then Wednesdays and Fridays, and sometimes Tuesdays and Thursdays, and it's a miracle I kept my job at the rag I wrote for.

Lena now, Lena appearing on the same occasion at the hospital, in full Latino fury. She was stoned, having spent the afternoon with some friends, but it wasn't because she was off her tree that she attacked me. It was her hatred of booze, her own father having been a boozer and a basher, and she came at me with her nails out. Even while she screeched and scratched I admired her beauty, my Liquorice Lena, her smooth olive skin, her flashing eyes, her flailing, coal-black hair. She had tits like gelati, a mons of angel-hair surrounding the finest calamari; she was Raquel Welch to my James Bond. I loved her like I've loved no one else since. Even now if I think about her for long enough — and I think about her every day, no matter how fleetingly, and only ever as she was then, when we were young — if I let my mind dwell — oh yes — even now on this lonely hotel bed, I get a hard-on.

Where are you, Michaela? She'll be disappointed: this is almost an historic event. I sit bolt upright. Where's Lena? Not Lena as she was then, but Lena as she is now: self-satisfied, homoeopathic, techno-phobic, holier-than-thou Waiheke dyke? Has anyone told her? I stumble up, my eyes scarcely able to focus, a sick whirring in my guts, my ears still thumping with spectral Boeing 707 engines. It's comic, I suppose, or would be to an observer, the way I stagger around the room holding out the plug for my laptop as I search for the jackpoint, my dick so shrunken it may as well have been dipped in embalming fluid.

Success at last and I'm before the screen, scrolling through my address book and relieved that Michaela isn't here. She would want to know what's wrong with me: why are you weeping, Richard?

In involuntary spasm my shoulders lift to my ears, my stinging eyes are awash. But it's not my pain. No, it's Lena's, it's her grief, I've had a preview of it: even after all these years it's as if we share a piece of our hard-drives, a common microchip. She will be inconsolable.

This is pointless, searching my address book. Lena's hatred of new technology is only minimally surpassed by her hatred of alcohol. I knew that. The jet-lag is making me forget things I know. Just as I pick up the telephone and ask for international directory, Michaela comes in laden with boutique bags.

'I've bought something to wear to court,' she says, as if she's being presented to the Queen.

LENA

Why I Did Not Answer the Telephone

I am a woman who has learned the passageways, bridges and avenues of her own mind.

I am a woman who does not rush her responses.

'Should' is a word I have banished from my vocabulary. It implies duty, guilt, remorse.

When the telephone rang in the other room I did not hurry off to answer it. I was with a client, the only male I have on my books. Curtis requires careful handling. His first serious primary relationship has ended. The girl is the daughter of a friend of mine, here on Waiheke Island.

In my Work Room Curtis was talking. He was weeping. He was using the box of tissues.

In my Work Room Curtis was working.

The telephone was ringing. I did not answer it. The telephone answered itself.

When the telephone began to ring I had an idea I should answer it.

I had a moment of clairvoyance, a strong aura: that is an important call.

Answer the telephone.

But I did not. I stayed in my chair by the window, the island's winter sea glinting grey behind me, Curtis's tufty head bowed, his body humped into the cushions of the lilac sofa.

The telephone was ringing.

Curtis looked up. He paused for a moment, but went on. He knew my commitment to him was strong. He trusted me not to desert him. I did not.

The telephone answered itself. Perhaps it should not have.

1985

He could smell duckweed, rank water. And something else: manure and lots of it, as if they were near a concentration of animals. A barn maybe. Had they driven to a farm, were they near a dam? They had travelled on the motorway; he was sure they headed south. There was the rise of the Harbour Bridge, then the fall of it. The driver took an exit soon after. It was not a long enough journey to have reached the country. Which exit was it? Ponsonby? Fanshawe Street? The car had travelled fast, swerving around corners, gears screaming. Monoxide still scented the air — they were in the city.

Before they hauled him out of the car, a pair of ungentle hands on each leg, they took the wire off his knees. He fell heavily onto the ground, his back cramping, folding him over; he couldn't stand up. The same hands again now, on either side, hauling him upright. One of the women cracked his spine and he cried out at the sudden, sharp pain, tributaries of it fierce in his legs and neck.

'Shut up,' hissed a voice.

'Why isn't he gagged? You forgot to gag him. You were supposed to do that.'

Could he recognise the voices yet, tell them apart? The one that just spoke — was that the voice who'd griped about the carseat?

'Do it now.' There were four of them then: the three who sat on him in the car and the one who drove. Or had there been two in the front seat, making five all together? That voice was older, smoke-roughened.

'What with?'

Someone giggled — not one of the women holding him. It came from behind him. 'Pair of knickers?' She said kneeckers, with a double e. Was she Australian?

'Gross.' That voice — she didn't say much. She'd offered directions to the driver in the car.

'I've got a scarf.' A cloth with a faint tang of sweat and perfume arrived in his mouth. His tongue crushed against his teeth — he shook his head to show his discomfort — but they were forcing him back onto his knees to tie the gag so tightly his ears went numb.

'Up. Walk.'

As he stood he tried — even though he was certain now they were all women — he tried to kick out. If he'd heard a male voice he would have kicked out before, when they came upon him in the house. He would have fought back immediately. But not against women. He'd never hit a woman; he didn't think he ever could. But now, he realised, because they'd untied his legs, he could lay about with his feet, kick them away, outrun them, scrape his blindfold off on a tree. He made one attempt. Instantly a body pressed up against his back; he could feel her breasts against his constrained arms and the fists of a second woman punched him in the temples, both sides at once.

Strange, how pain had colours. He'd never allowed himself the observation before: pain was a sensation best ignored. The bruises and broken bones of his youth he had turned his mind away from, as he had been brought up to do: his mother wasn't a woman for kisses-better and gentian violet. If one of her children suffered a surface wound then they were culpable and made to feel guilty for the trouble they'd caused her. Fractures and breaks were dealt with at the doctor's, the child left at the door. This new pain in his head blossomed febrile blue, his back a mess of reds and oranges, the pinpoints of gravel in his knees were purple, the remaining ache in his balls and stomach pale green. He stumbled along, aware his robe was flapping open, two women on either side and one behind in the same configuration they'd taken on the street outside his house.

Suddenly from nearby came a sound — a sort of strangled, monolithic trumpeting scream. He froze, and as the women dragged him on he realised what it was, where they had taken him. It was an elephant: they were near the zoo, at Western Springs, by the lakes. His feet left the asphalt path — he knew this park: once or twice he'd walked his dog here. He tried to picture where they were exactly. They must've already passed through the children's play area, yes — there, above the panting exertions of his abductors, the faint squeaking of the swings moving emptily in the damp breeze. They turned right, still on the path, and their feet sounded hollow over the little bridge. They were on grass now, and it was cooler here, the night air not so humid, they were among trees, away from the lakes.

Away from the water. His mind let go of the black terror it had been holding away from itself, doing its best to deny: they were not going to drown him then. What did they want from him? What was going on? Was his house at this moment being ransacked, his valuables taken? Surely women would not value the things he did; they wouldn't take the things he deemed priceless. There was his car — would they have taken that? Why hadn't he questioned them before they put the gag on, when he had a chance?

He landed on his face in leaf litter, scratching his forehead on the fine branches of a tree as he fell.

'Tie him to the trunk.' The older voice again. 'Taihoa a sec.'

Then, oh God, what did they plan for him? They were removing his dressing gown.

'Use the cord.' That was the carseat voice. He'd isolated only three: the older smoker, the carseat woman, the one who gave directions. He must concentrate, he must think harder, learn everything he could about them. His own long-dead father — had it been like this for him when they caught him and almost starved him to death in a Japanese

POW camp in Sumatra? Had he felt this terrible potent mixture of humiliation and pain? Of course not. He was a hero: he knew he had been doing the right thing; he knew what they wanted him for. His father was caught in action, blowing up Allied airfields the length of the Malaysian archipelago so the Japs couldn't make use of them. Imagine if his father were alive now to hear about this: the shame, the ignominy, his pathetic son abducted by women. They were busy, two of them tying him to the tree with his own dressing-gown cord, the other two re-tying his legs.

'Take the blindfold off. It's dark enough.' The fourth voice and for some reason he came to the conclusion it was the one who had hit him, twice now since they'd left the house. Was it the blonde acne-scarred one, the only one he'd actually seen? The blindfold was yanked away from behind him, from behind the tree trunk, and he made out they were in a little grove where the manuka met on all sides and closed overhead — the sort of place children would play house in. It was almost completely dark except for a faint fuzz of light from one side, from a distance away, one of the park lights.

'Do you know why we've brought you here?' The Australian voice. It was sweet-toned, he thought, surprising himself, the voice of a singer perhaps. She sounded tremulous, apprehensive.

'Nod your head,' said the rougher voice.

'If you do know,' added Carseat, and giggled.

'Shut the fuck up, you dumb bitch.' The Hitter's voice. 'You're off your head. This is serious.'

There was a silence then and he realised they were waiting for him to respond. He shook his head violently, his hair catching on the rough bark of the tree.

'Fuckin' liar.' A heavy boot caught him in the shins and he moaned through his gag.

'Say the other thing we worked out. Where is it?' The voice was close, belonging to the woman who'd kicked him, the rougher, older voice. There was a rustle of paper. Dear God, had they prepared a speech? A lighter flared beside him, illuminating a cloud of red hair and a pale, intent face.

'Crimes such as the one you committed are not adequately

punished by the courts.' She was the Australian, thick with tears. 'You ruined a life. You took cruel advantage of a defenceless human being. You are a monster.'

The lighter was extinguished and a face loomed in out of the dark, a new face. He took in as much of it as he could, which wasn't much. Just the eyes and a strip of sweaty brow beneath the balaclava. She clicked her fingers and behind her he saw another flash of a lighter, the glow of a cigarette. It was passed to the woman in front of him.

'See this?'

He nodded, fearing the boot.

'Every time you lie you'll get another letter till we spell the whole word.'

Nothing made sense. What word? What was she talking about? They'd got the wrong man — they thought he was somebody else.

'Ask again.'

The tremulous voice repeated the question. It was the woman who had volunteered the scarf. She was sitting behind him, on the other side of the tree. 'Do you know why we've brought you here?'

He had never lied about important things. Certainly he had concealed the truth sometimes, but he was basically an honest man. It was easy for people in his profession to be thought of as liars and he never wanted to fall victim to that. He'd made a point of it. He shook his head. He didn't know.

The balaclava leapt out of sight, the cigarette poised like a pen. He felt her stretch the flesh of his upper arm between thumb and forefinger to form a flat surface and the cigarette plunged then, a fiery, torturous nib, beginning the downward stroke of a letter.

He filled his lungs, bellowed through the muffling cloth and the Hitter came in then, came in hard, a blooding punch to his nose. When he was a little boy he and his sister used to make letters with their pointer fingers on each other's backs and guess what the other had written. There was no guessing this time. He knew intimately by the smell of his scorched flesh, by the blood and tears mingling on his face: he knew she'd made the letter R.

RICHARD

Lollies for Grown-ups

As I cross the narrow strip of concrete between Bonny's place and the screaming four-lane road, there's a stink of cat piss and stale fat from the deep-fryers of the next door Mixed Business. That's not unusual. What is unusual are the packing cases and cartons piled up on it and the solitary red balloon tied to the fence railings. Have I missed one of the boys' birthdays again? I turn it around to read the white writing — 'Bon Voyage' it says. The front door is wide open so I wander in, drumming my knuckles on the crumbling door frame.

'Bonny?' She has her back to me, her hair tied up in a green bandanna, the table covered in kitchen gear. She turns with a handful of forks, her free hand over her heart.

'Shit! Oh, it's you —' The forks hit the table with a clatter and we stand for a moment, staring at each other, neither knowing what to say. In the end she comes to me, puts her arms around me and gives me a quick squeeze. She smells of cleaning fluid; I sniff loudly.

'Want the landlord to give me the bond back, eh,' she says, smiling.

'Where're you going?'

'Home. Back to New Zealand. The, um . . .' She looks at me uncertainly. 'The money your girlfriend gave me? Yeah, well, I used that. Best use for it, really. Considering.'

'Will you come to live in Auckland?'

Bonny shakes her head. 'My sister is meeting us in Wellington and then we're driving to the Wairarapa. That's where most of us are, round there.'

We're staring at each other again. I'm thinking how brave she is. At her young stage of life eleven years is a long time in one place, even though this is a place that hasn't treated her well. I'm pleased — she's made the right decision.

'How'd you get here?' she asks suddenly. 'Where's Michaela?'

'At the hotel. I had precisely ten days in Europe before I had to come back again.'

'Shame,' says Bonny casually, getting on with sorting the motley collection of cutlery. She's heard the note of complaint in my voice and is offended by it.

'Yeah, it is,' I persist, regardless. 'I'd never been there before. Cost me a fortune.'

It didn't, of course. I'm lying. It cost Michaela a drop in her capacious bucket. It cost me a bucketload of male pride — but only when I think about it. Clunk, clunk. She drops the utensils back in their compartments.

'Next tenant can have these,' she says. 'Buggered if I'm going to lug them all the way back.'

'Have you been to see him?' I ask.

'Why would I? You got a rental car?' Both questions are asked with identical intonation: flat, disinterested.

'Yeah.'

'Could you take a load of stuff to St Vincent de Paul on your way home?'

'Sure.' She's passing me on her way to the cupboards at my back. I catch at her arm. 'Bonny, I want to ask you —'

'I don't want to talk about him.' She's pulling away.

'Look. I know you're not together any more. But you and he were into drugs together for years.'

'I don't do them any more.'

'No, I know. Good on you. But at least you can understand, more than I can probably, what compelled him to —'

'Shut up, Richard. You don't know half the story.' She tries again to get past me but I step sideways, block her way.

'What story?'

'The police don't know what I know. When they find out, believe me, the shit is going to hit the fan. That's why I'm leaving, taking the boys away from it all. It'll be in the papers, on the telly, it'll . . .'

'What?'

'He made these videos. They're . . . with kids. They —'

'With Vincent and Jack?'

'No. I don't want to talk about it.'

'You can't start telling me something like that and then just stop.'

'Oh, yes I can.' She pushes me to one side.

'You have to tell me! I'm his father. I can't just have half the story!' I'm shouting now. I don't mean to, but I am. Bonny glares at me and only breaks off when the front door bangs shut and footsteps sound in the hall.

'Hi there, Grandpop.' It's Vincent, with Jack pushing in behind him.

'Why not? Half the story's all you ever wanted before,' hisses Bonny, and I see to my horror I've made her cry. She stomps off to a room off the hall, the door slamming behind her, while the boys sit at the table, their fists releasing handfuls of lollies onto the chipped surface. Vincent, the eldest, has deep shadows under his eyes. They weren't there when I saw him two weeks ago.

'Have you come to get Dad out of jail?' asks Jack as he chooses a large red soft lolly shaped like a teardrop and bungs it in his mouth.

'I don't think I'll be able to do that.' It's as careful an answer as I can think of.

'Why is he in jail?' Jack asks then, a trail of chemical red escaping from the corner of his chomping mouth.

'You know that already.' Vincent punches his brother on the shoulder. 'Mum's already told you.'

'What, um . . .' I lower my voice. The walls of this shit-hole are probably tissue paper. 'What did your mum tell you?'

'Drugs,' answers Vincent, attempting a complacent tone. 'Have you heard of cocaine?'

I nod and Jack passes me a green snake. 'I don't like them much,' he says. 'You can have it.'

'Thanks.' I put the end of the lurid green sweet on my tongue and bite a piece off. It threatens to remove a filling. For a moment everything is quiet save for the nearby roar of traffic and the boys' and my energetic jaws. Bonny stays in her room.

'Maybe I should go and see if Bonny is —' I begin.

'We're going back to Aotearoa,' Vincent tells me as he tenderly unwraps a cube of bubblegum.

'I know.'

'Mum says we're going to learn tangata Maori.' Vincent again, through his bubblegum.

'Oh. Good.' And it will be good. Bonny's father is a fine, upstanding man, an elder in their tribe.

'Do you like drugs?' Jack asks conversationally. 'Dad says they're lollies for grown-ups.'

'Does he?' I feel sick. And guilty, of course. I never moderated my behaviour in front of Jasper — he quite obviously has done the same with his own sons. With one major difference, I think self-righteously. With me it was only dope and booze; these kids have seen hard drugs and adults doing them. If only I could open up their little skulls and see what they're thinking. They sit quite still at the table, side by side, heads bent intently over their sweets, each a larger or smaller version of the other. They have Bonny's smooth, manuka honey-coloured skin but their faces are more like Jasper's: close-set eyes, strong noses, square chins.

'Lollies are bad for you,' I try, 'and drugs are much worse. Not all adults take drugs.'

'Mum doesn't,' offers Jack, grinning proudly. 'She's even given up smoking.'

'Drugs fuck your head,' intones Vincent solemnly. 'That's what happened to Dad.'

I nod again, not sure if this is information imparted to him by his mother or something he has worked out for himself by observing his other parent. If Bonny were with us she'd chide him for his language and I wonder for a moment, dully, if I should do so in her stead.

'Mum said we weren't allowed to stay with Dad any more anyway,' Vincent goes on, casually, as though his father being in prison is not such a change for him. 'Not since *he* played dealers.'

'Me,' says Jack. 'Me and my mate from school, 'Anyway —' he turns on his brother vehemently, 'it was only chopped-up bits of grass.'

'You still got in trouble,' says Vincent, 'You still got caught by Mr Leith.' He turns his tired, serious eyes on me. 'They wrapped it up in tinfoil and everything.' The eyes roll exasperatedly to the ceiling. He's world weary, I realise. Ten years old and world weary.

The phone rings then, interrupting any further stories from Jack, who is just drawing breath around a huge yellow sphere of sugar to begin another one. Neither of the boys shifts to answer it and Bonny remains on the other side of her closed door. Perhaps she'll answer it in her room, I think, but it rings on and on.

'You boys —'

'We're not allowed,' says Vincent.

'Why not?'

He shrugs. Is it journalists Bonny's worried about? Or Jasper's druggie mates? The phone reaches its allowable number of rings, then cuts out, pauses, then rings again. The druggie mates wouldn't call here, surely — Jasper left Bonny three years ago. Maybe it's Michaela . . . I locate the phone under a pile of folded tea-towels.

'Hello?'

'Richard? Good God — is that you?' The voice, a woman's, is deep and sweet, an older version of a voice I once knew very well.

'Lena?'

'I got your message. What's going on?'

'Just what I said. Jasper is in prison.'

'What for?'

I put my back to the boys and lower my voice. 'Coke. But I think the police will lay charges for something else, which I don't know much about. The, um . . . boys are here, so I can't really —'

'I understand.' There's another voice, a woman's, close by, talking to Lena.

'Who's that?'

'Scottie. Have you seen him?'

'Jasper?'

'Yes, of course. Who else would I mean?' Testy.

'No — I . . . I, um, I went to Long Bay but they, um . . . they couldn't find him.'

'What?' An earth tremor. A shifting of tectonic plates.

'They'd temporarily lost him in the system.' A moment's pause. It occurs to me that Lena thinks I'm lying.

'Is Bonny there?' she says, snappy.

'Wait a moment.'

Vincent obliges by going down the hall for his mother. I hold the phone away from my ear but I can still hear Scottie and Lena. They're talking about air tickets, and who will feed their cat while they're away. I imagine the room they're standing in — an essential oils burner, a dreamcatcher in the window, a poster of Katherine Mansfield, a white stone fertility goddess, pot-plants, a hammock, a dildo . . .

Bonny appears with a face like soggy bread. She snatches the phone from me and points with a sweeping gesture towards the front door. Obediently the boys and I file out.

'Your new girlfriend's rich, eh?' Jack announces, plonking himself beside me on the narrow sooty veranda.

'Hmmm,' I answer, wishing I still smoked, because this is exactly the kind of situation that requires a cigarette: I'm waiting, I'm anxious, I'm full of conflicting emotions, I'm thinking about Lena — how she is now, how she was then, how weighty she's become. Not just physically, but in every other way. She makes me quail.

'How come?' Jack asks. His older brother leans against the thin veranda post, squinting into the blue haze of the traffic. It's something about women in their fifties, I think — or rather, contented women in their fifties. New Zealand has a whole raft of them in power, most of them terrifying and appalling, beginning with Cath Tizard in the

1980s, Jenny Shipley in the nineties and now Helen Clark. Left wing, right wing, doesn't matter — they accrue themselves with a sense of wisdom and self-righteousness and Jesus Christ it sticks in my craw. I swallow it down and strain my ears to hear what Bonny's telling Lena but she's shut the connecting door.

'How come she's rich?' Jack persists. Careful, I think, be very careful. Do not tell Jack she's rich because —

'She's had some wealthy husbands,' Vincent tells him. 'She must've had good settlements.'

'How do you know that?' I ask.

'Sometimes I watch daytime telly with Mum. Happens all the time on there.' I put my arm around Jack, though it's Vincent I really want to hug. Was Jasper like him? Did he know so many facts about adult behaviour at ten — base details of drug use and divorce? I can't remember. There's no comfort in any of this, though perhaps Jack is taking some from me. He's snuffling into my chest.

'You smell nice,' he says. 'What's that smell?'

'French aftershave,' I tell him, just as a rustling sounds behind us. It's Bonny coming down the hall, stuffing something into a super-market bag.

'Here,' she says, handing it to me. 'The boys bought it back from his place by mistake, mixed up with their *Star Wars* and that. He doesn't know I've got it. Not even sure it's all still there — I might've put something over the top of it. Take it anyway.' Through the opaque blue plastic of the bag looms the darker, rectangular shape of a video cassette. It looks ominous, like a submarine rising out of the depths.

'Thank you.'

Infinitesimally Bonny shakes her head. 'Oh no. You won't be thanking me. But at least you won't be asking me any more questions. Come on, boys, we'll start packing up your room now.'

'Bye, Grandpop,' says Jack, and Vincent gives me a manly nod, mature beyond his years, before their mother shunts them inside and closes the door after them. It's a moment or two before I realise that she didn't say goodbye, nor did she tell me when Lena is arriving. Before I walk the three blocks to my parked rental, I scrawl a note.

Bonny

Didn't want to disturb you again — forgot the load for
St Vinnie's. I'll ring tomorrow.

Kia kaha

Richard

All the way down Parramatta Road and into Bridge Road the morning slants unnaturally hot through the windscreen. With my left hand I shunt the video in its incubating plastic bag onto the floor out of the heat and as I do so it comes to me what Lena must have said to Bonny.

'Give Richard the video.' I can hear her as clearly as if she were sitting beside me. 'You don't have to tell me about them. He can.'

Good old Richard, who never minds sticking his nose in the muck. Other people's muck, especially. If only Lena knew the truth of how clever I've been at avoiding my own, at staying out of trouble and covering my tracks: obviously not a trait I've passed on to my only child. I resolve not to indulge in any conjecture about the tape and look out the window instead at the passing terraces and shops, but the draught from the air conditioning catches the bag, has it crack and whistle and draw attention to itself like an irritating child. Finally, when I stop at the lights by the Fish Market, I find the little dial that redirects the blast to the stick-figure's face only.

From the Novotel carpark I carry the plastic bag up to our room on the fifth floor, hoping that Michaela has gone out on another shopping expedition. One stiff scotch, I plan, and another to sip once the thing's in the player. But she's here, on the telephone, laughing, one long brown leg crossed over the other, a glass of Perrier glinting on the bedside table. She waves at me, newly varnished red fingernails catching the light.

'He's just come in,' she says. 'I'll ask him. Darling?' That's me. I open a drawer, drop in the bag and close it. 'Dodo wants to know if we can come to dinner tonight, since we're here.' I shake my head. 'Why not?' She's cupping the phone, her gay voice transmuted to a hiss. I look past her to the window, see the traffic stream off the Western Distributor onto the bridge. 'Richard?'

'Previous engagement.'

'Where?'

'Long Bay.'

'Excuse me, Dodo,' she says into the phone, 'he's being difficult again. I'll call you back.' In one fluid moment the phone is replaced in its stand and she's on her feet, which are bare, I notice, with toenails painted pearly pink, contrasting nicely with the beige hotel carpet.

'You can't possibly be going to the prison tonight. It's not visiting hours.'

'How would you know?' I open my duty-free bag, fish out the Johnnie Walker.

'Put that back.'

I don't even bother to shake my head. Two fingers, three — and thick ones, bricklayer's fingers.

'Don't you like Dodo?' She's wheedling now, the little-girl voice. It's on the tip of my tongue to tell her a woman with her bank balance need never talk like that — the silly high pitch, the upward inflection, the slight lisp — it makes me want to puke.

'Never met her,' I say instead.

'You have! Remember? We went to Prego's together in Auckland last November — Dodo and her new friend Bernard, and Gerard Linck and Nicolette Myers and we all had such a lovely happy time —'

'Oh yes. No, I don't.'

'Don't what?'

'Like her.'

'Richard — she's my friend! And I need to see her. I've been having such a rough time lately with you and Jasper and I think, frankly, that you owe it to me —'

I close the curtains, squat before the VCR, pick up the remote.

'What are you doing?'

'Movie time.' I retrieve the tape, put it in, pull up the little grey two-seater closer to the screen and pat the seat beside me.

'Come and join me, darling.'

Michaela makes a snorting noise, similar to the ones she makes in her sleep — though I would never tell her that — and shoves her feet into sandals as if she's going out. She's staring at me, tears trembling in those huge hazel eyes.

'You seem to think that you have a monopoly on despair,' she begins. 'I have never told you about my brother . . . and —'

'Your bag's over there,' I point, helpfully, at the pink Lacroix bought on our first day in Paris, and that seemingly is the last straw. She flings it over her shoulder and out she goes with a sort of agonised gasp while my thumb rests lightly on the Play button, suppressing it only at the slam of the door.

MELODY

Possibles and Probables

I have been in Howard's kitchen — a first — and put a quiche in the oven to warm slowly for our lunch. We have the day planned: work this morning, then our quiche and fruit, then the game — the fourth of the Tri-nation test matches, the Wallabies and the All Blacks.

I like the kitchen: the old cupboards with white paint yellowed to cream and black Bakelite handles, the cracked grey lino tiles, the chipped porcelain sink. There's a little mullioned window above the taps that looks out onto his garden — a grapefruit tree with green lichen and black saltburn; a huge, leafless liquidambar; an old green park bench set beneath it; rose canes cut back for the winter; a row of daphne bushes just coming into bud; and a pair of snowball trees, the flowers still small and pale lime, backdropped by a cartwheel painted white. It's like stepping back in time to the 1950s. Nothing's been changed since then, in the garden or the kitchen. Against the wall opposite the cupboards stands a chrome-legged table, with a top made of swirly orange and white Formica. One bandy-legged, plastic-upholstered stool keeps it company. It's where Howard has his breakfast, the paper spread out, Web Ellis solid and wheezy at his feet.

I touched the table top, ran my finger along an orange swirl and felt a kind of solidarity with Howard and his solo morning repasts. It's one of the few things Howard and I have in common, living alone, and I decided then to think of him tomorrow while I eat my muesli — him and all the millions of others like us who begin the day purely, our mood and intent unsullied by the company of others. The biographer Ian Richards wrote in *To Bed At Noon*, of Dan Davin, an obscure writer of the twentieth century who, despite being married, always breakfasted alone while he did the *Times* crossword. He and his wife never spoke until lunchtime — it was a rule of their co-habitation. If I ever marry — which is unlikely — I'll duplicate that rule. Couples always argue in the morning. Curtis and I always did, but then we argued in the afternoon, at dusk and all night. Arguing was our modus operandi; by the time I was twenty-four I had deep frown lines, the first lines to form on my face, and a perpetually heavy heart. It makes me bleak to think of it. What a waste of all my twenties, that most vital decade. Sometimes I feel so old, now that I'm nearly thirty. Or is it? The most vital decade? Howard was married at twenty-seven and divorced at twenty-eight.

When I came back into the living room to join him he was smoking, so I had time to jot this down as a question for later: Do you see any period of your life as being more pivotal than the other? Did I or do I? he'll respond, more than likely, before sucking on his yellow teeth and saying no more. It's a leading question, in more ways than one: it could be a doorway into the reason for his agoraphobia, if agoraphobia is indeed the cause of his seclusion. Besides, leading is something I am not allowed to do.

Now, as the smell of warm pastry fills the house, Howard is talking about 1956, his first year with the All Blacks.

'You wouldn't be able to conceive of it,' he says, leaning back in his chair, hauling his Shetland rug up to cover his crossed arms. 'The excitement. All Black Fever, the papers called it, for months, leading up to the arrival of the Springboks.'

'I know. I've read about it. It always amazes me that there were no protests.'

'Against what?' Howard looks annoyed.

'Well, you know. Racism in South Af —'

'Listen, lassie. You've had your head screwed by all that 1981 nonsense —'

'I was six years old in 1981,' I say, 'and anyway there were protests before the 1960 South Africa Tour —' but he's talking over the top of me.

'None of us cared about that rot then. Fact was, the last time we'd met the Boks we'd been taken to the cleaners well and truly. That was in '49, before my time. The country had seven years to prepare for the re-match. So the selectors went from club to club — came to Ponsonby, of course. Over the years there have been more selections from Ponsonby than any other club except Otago. You wouldn't know that, necessarily.'

'Actually, I do,' I say, with a hint of indignation, and Howard looks pleased, as if I've passed some kind of test.

'The season before the trials were announced I'd already played five games — for Ponsonby, of course — and was about to get on the train for Palmerston North for the Junior All Black trials.' Howard pauses for a moment, extends his right arm from the rug and takes up his cigarette packet. He lights one, but as soon as it rests between his fingers he starts to cough, in a sudden violent spasm that folds his upper body towards his knees. After a moment or two I go to him, helpless — I should sit him up so that his passages are upright, more easily cleared, but I can't; I can't touch him. My conscience conducts a speedy debate with my instinct — save his life and endure his embarrassment and anger, or stand by while he chokes to death? Web Ellis lumbers up from her possy in a square of sunlight cast by the French doors and gazes at him with rheumy sympathetic eyes. Even she knows not to rest an enquiring paw on his foot, or push her wet nose into his ear.

Carefully I reach out, hoping Howard will see me coming, and in that instant the hacking stops. He pushes himself back away from me, against the cushions of his chair, a trail of yellow sputum hanging from his chin, and hauls in a jagged, desperate breath.

'Tissue,' he whispers, flapping his hand at me for the box from the windowsill. His left hand holds the cigarette still, and the moment he is clean he picks up his lighter and holds the flame to it.

'Jesus, Howard,' I say, weakly.

'You're here to write my life, not preserve it,' he mutters, taciturn, and holds the packet out. I shake my head, not that he's looking at me directly — I'm still too close for that — and he puts it down.

He smokes, gazing out his window at the winter sun hot and hazy on the bushy slopes of Rangitoto, the channel between the beach and volcano blue and milky with wind-churned chop. My father, who on behalf of the continued existence of whales follows weather patterns world wide, told me last night that they've had this weather in Sydney — temperatures in the eerie mid-twenties and gusty, hot winds. While I rewind the tape I tell Howard this and his shoulders stiffen with irritation.

'I don't expect you to reply — I'm just passing my time talking about global warming while you smoke,' I say, and press the Play button. Howard's recorded cough blasts out of the machine, louder than it was in reality, bubbling and poisonous. Now he's glaring at me, eyes slitty, thin lips in a rigid line, while I bumble for the volume.

'Little bitch,' he says, as the recorded coughing fades away. I rewind again, my face burning with embarrassment. 'You did that on purpose.'

'Of course I didn't.'

'How dare you?' he says, louder.

'It was a mistake, Howard. I'm trying to wipe it. And don't speak to me like that.'

'You're blushing,' he says then, and he sounds pleased.

'Let's just get on with it, shall we?' My finger rests on the Record button and Howard stubs out his cigarette, grinning at me. No wonder he has no wife, I think maliciously. The only human interactions that please him are antagonistic ones.

'So,' I resume, 'did you go to Palmerston North?'

'Oh yes.'

'By train?'

'Sleeper. I shared with another chap, Warren Clayton. Snored and farted the whole way. He did, I mean. I couldn't sleep. He got in, of course.'

'To the All Blacks?'

'Don't be silly. The Juniors. Then he was killed in a motorbike accident a year later. Had a bloody enormous Triumph.' It's almost impossible to keep Howard on the right track. It's as if he makes a point of taking every tangent that appears. He's downcast now; maybe he's remembering his travelling companion, that young life ended abruptly.

'Was he a good friend?' I hope I sound sympathetic.

'Not at all,' says Howard. 'Hardly knew the chap.'

'So,' I take a deep breath, 'if you were playing in the Junior trials, then how come you were selected for the All —'

'Obvious, isn't it? Selectors were there. They were bloody everywhere that season. Picked me up after the first trial and put me on another train, this time for New Plymouth.'

I wonder if I should keep him talking about Palmerston North, if it's important, but Howard moves on rapidly, his tone wry, as if he's not sure even now whether he was badly treated. 'It was pissing with rain when I arrived. Six o'clock in the morning. I walked to my billet carrying my suitcase and I got lost. Didn't find the place till half past seven. Only had time to bolt down some breakfast and get to the clubrooms to change, get my boots on and get onto the field. We played two games that day, one after the other, Possibles against the Probables.'

The smell of burning pastry dismisses the last of the aroma of Howard's cigarette. He's oblivious to it, his mind on those long-ago games, and I don't want to stop him.

'Some chaps,' he's saying, his good eye on the display cabinet and his bad one on me, 'remember every step and turn of the game that got them in. I was so darn tired I can hardly remember a thing — except that for the second game they pushed me into the second row.'

'So you were a Probable already, before you played those two games?'

'The second one I was.' Howard nods, both eyes achieving that particular blind, icy shade of blue that they do when he thinks I'm obtuse or stupid. 'And they packed me in as a lock.'

How have you had a rugby career at all given your dislike of physical contact? I want to ask. But I can't, of course. I'm certain he thinks I haven't observed that in him. If I do mention it, suddenly, without softening or preamble, he will think I am assuming an intimacy we have not had time to develop. I swallow the question down, reluctantly, and ask instead, 'How much did you weigh then?'

'In '56? Fifteen stone, bit over.'

'And you were six foot two,' I add.

'Not sure I like the "was" there,' says Howard, grimly.

'Perfect for a number eight,' I say, to cheer him up, and he smiles proudly.

'I was perfect all over in those days.'

Looking at Howard now, at his thin shoulders and scrawny neck, I'd say he wouldn't be much more than half his original weight.

'You burning my lunch?' he asks suddenly, and, obedient as the perfect wife or daughter, I jump to my feet and race out to the kitchen.

Parts of the pastry are dark brown, a shade of black, but once the slices are arranged on a platter, with tomato quarters, lettuce, oil and vinegar tossed together in a bowl to accompany it, lunch looks presentable enough. While I'm doing this girl thing I hear the clink of glasses and scotch bottle in the other room, and a moment or two later the rustle and crack of paper. Howard is searching for something — an old programme maybe, or photograph.

He has his lunch off a tray in his chair: the least charred slice of quiche and two shots of scotch. In keeping with the house rules we don't talk, but he gives me something to think about.

'When you've finished — and make sure your hands are clean,' he says, tapping a large envelope with one long finger.

Howard eats slowly. Each swallow seems to cost him greatly, almost as if it hurts him. Is there something wrong with his throat, I wonder, something he hasn't told me about? It's not a line I want to pursue and I stop watching him, finish my lunch, and wipe my fingers on my jeans.

Inside the envelope is a pen-and-ink drawing on heavy white card, slightly foxed, the corners and edges yellow with age. A beautiful young man stands with one leg slightly bent, his arms at his sides. It's not the sort of body usually favoured by artists: there are the thick flanks and heavy shoulders of the forward, the bullish neck of the heavy-weight boxer. The figure's hands are immense, as out of proportion with the rest of him as those of Michelangelo's David. The young man's hair is dark and straight, cut close in a brutal short back and sides. His expression is curious; he looks almost embarrassed, as if he feels shy, standing there with no clothes on. His eyes and mouth are soft, innocent, country-boyish. There is nothing in the background — no rolling fields or mountains — to hint at who or what he might be; the body is suspended in space. One of the giant hands is spread against his upper thigh, as though he longs to lift it higher and cover himself, that part of his body rendered in delicate strokes of the fine nib and just as generously proportioned as his hands. I think. I've only got Curtis and my father as comparisons and I never looked that closely at my father.

In the corner of the picture are the initials 'J.A.B.' and on the reverse, in pretty copperplate, 'Howard, 1961'.

It's me who's embarrassed now, for having examined Howard's twenty-one-year-old body with such concentrated fascination. I don't dare to turn the picture around but leave it face down on my lap. Swilling his last mouthful of scotch, Howard is watching me. Without looking up at him I know this and I know also that after he swallows, his mouth forms a wicked grin.

'Who . . . um . . .' For some reason my throat requires clearing. Howard is holding out the cigarettes and I take one, compose myself. 'Who was J.A.B.?'

'A friend.'

'A girlfriend?' I attempt a light, teasing tone. Howard looks thoughtful, exhales smoke. He's not going to tell me. 'An artist?'

'Amateur.' He chuckles, that vampire wheeze. 'We were all amateurs in those days.' Leaning forward he picks up the envelope and holds his hand out for the drawing. Before he puts it away he gazes at it, tilting it to get it in focus for his good eye. His face is impassive: I have no idea what he is thinking.

'Ears are still good there,' he says suddenly, 'and no broken nose.'

'When did that happen?' The cigarette tastes vile. I stub it out. 'The broken nose?'

'During the first test with England in 1963. No Blood Bin then — you played on, even if you were streaming with it. That was a famous game — Don Clarke put one through the posts from sixty yards out and we won 21–11. Hasn't been a kicker like Clarke before or since.'

'Grant Fox,' I say automatically. 'Andrew Mehrtens.'

'Nothing on the Boot,' he says frostily, picking up the remote control and pointing at the vast television. 'Wheel it out a little from the corner, lassie. I like it closer.'

Sound roars out of it as I bend to the trolley handles. It's an ad, underscored with the Elgar cello concerto, the All Blacks tastefully filmed in black and white, semi-nude in the dressing rooms. Howard, who watches television in profile to give his good eye the full benefit, has a sneer on his face.

'What is this?' he asks. 'Beer or bootlaces? Where's their pride?'

'Sponsorship, Howard,' I tell him.

'Tragic. Pathetic,' he growls. He's holding out his glass for another scotch.

'Professional teams are expensive to maintain.' The glass is smeary, with flakes of pastry at the rim.

'They should just concentrate on the game. Look at that! Unbelievable! It's almost pornographic.' The ad is finishing with a colour close-up of Te Atu Lal, the new right wing, in a gloriously pouchy g-string. He's as beautiful a human being as anyone could imagine: huge clear eyes with whites so pure they're almost blue, a strong nose and chin, his Indian heritage visible in his straight, thick, glossy hair, his Maori blood making his shoulders and chest broad and powerful. The camera pans from his wide, sexy grin, across his shoulder and rounded biceps to his elbow and upraised fist which contains, limpid and sparkling, a bottle of Pounamu Mineral Water.

'I'm dying of thirst,' Howard says. 'Shake it up, will you?'

'Needs a rinse,' I say, and take his glass through to the kitchen, the excited, barking tones of the rugby commentators following me: the teams are jogging onto the field.

It's while I'm drying the glass on a suspect tea-towel Howard keeps on a hook by the window that my eye is caught by a flash of bright yellow passing slowly at the mouth of Howard's driveway. The driver pauses long enough to peer through the bars of the security gate. My own ancient Toyota, which was once pale blue but is now a patchwork of rust and bung, is parked just on the other side. The yellow VW, lovingly polished and buffed, horribly familiar, parks with its gilled rear end just visible in the gap between the gatepost and gate.

In the living room the volume swells: 'Australians all, let us rejoice for we are young and free —'

'Melody, what the devil are you doing?' It is a soprano singing for the Australians and Howard's voice almost achieves the same querulous tremolo. I give him the clean glass and the bottle and accept one for myself. Our anthem begins then, sung in Maori by a world-famous Samoan tenor, and Howard leans forward as the camera moves slowly along the line of All Blacks.

'Look at that,' he says disgustedly. 'Hardly any of them know the words.'

'Hamish Wong does,' I observe.

'Huh,' says Howard, then a moment later: 'There's Jonah. I just saw his bald head in the stands.' The anthem ends, the haka begins.

'They all know that one, Howard. Better than your lot did. Fifties hakas were a disgrace.'

'As was the game itself, in many ways. It was pretty bloody dour. A lot of crash-bang stuff up and down the touchline, not much finesse.' He's rummaging for his lighter, which has slipped behind the cushion of his chair. Before the sanctity of the smoke and the game, I seize my moment. 'I think we have a visitor.'

'What?' He takes the unlit fag out of his mouth.

'From the kitchen window I saw —'

'Who? Go and tell them to piss off. I don't want anybody here.'

'The gate's shut anyway. He might just —'

'Who is it? Friend of yours? Did he follow you? Get rid of him.'

'Howard, I —'

But he fixes me with such a ferocious glare, one hand roving over his heart as if he has a sudden pain, that I rise once more to my feet, Web Ellis following me, and go out the French doors and around the house.

I'm missing the kick-off. Bloody Curtis.

There he is, standing outside the gate, one hand on the bar like a prisoner, the other hand cupping the roach end of a joint at his lips. He blows a pungent stream of smoke in my direction. The closer I get to him, my feet scrunching on the red gravel, the more despairing I feel.

My mind goes instantly blank, an internal void with shiny grey walls where no thoughts can gain purchase; my shoulders are weighted with invisible sand-bags; my stomach feels bloated and achy. Her nose coasting through the stubby grass at the edge of the drive, Web Ellis snorts like a walrus.

I let Curtis speak first.

'Your mother sent me to find you. Directory didn't have Loverboy's phone number.' This close his eyeballs have their particular, characteristic red tinge; the pupils are asinine pinpricks.

'It's unlisted,' I say mildly.

'Why? He's not that famous, not any more. People've got short memories.'

Some more than others. 'What do you want, Curtis?'

'Let me in and I'll tell you.'

'Howard doesn't want me to —'

'It's important. Family news. Zinnia.'

'Zinnia what?' Keep calm, I tell myself. Your sister is young, well nourished — overly nourished, actually, a candidate for fluid retention, for haemorrhage, for embolism, for sudden death.

'Let me in.'

I know Curtis in this mood. It's easy — he has only two: stoned and arrogant, or straight and melancholic. I check over my shoulder: Web Ellis is waddling back towards her master in the back room of the house, who need never know. If I let Curtis in so that he'll tell me about Zin, he's stoned enough for me to take him by surprise and shunt him out again. Curtis is only five centimetres or so taller than me and doesn't weigh much more either. People used to mistake us for brother and sister — we're more alike than Zinnia and I are, with our fine bones, straight, brown hair, eyes the colour of dead grass. When I was fifteen I revelled in our similarity but as the years went by and I struggled time and time again to extricate myself from our stifling relationship, I grew to hate it. I knew it was finally over the day I dyed my hair cerise.

I depress the square orange button on the stone post, the gate swings open and Curtis, the third twin, steps inside. Today his hair sticks out in mousy tufts on either side of his head, stiff and rough, as if he hasn't washed it for weeks.

'I'd like to meet the object of your gerontophiliac passion.'

'He's busy.'

'Got his pants off, have you?'

'Fuck you, Curtis.'

'Big game on this afternoon, isn't there?' He inclines his head towards the roar of the game, which is carried to us by the onshore wind.

'Only if you have pay TV,' I tell him, not that he'd care. The neighbourhood is quiet: most houses have satellite dishes on their roofs. No lawns are being mowed, no cars are being tinkered with on the street. The vast block of apartments next door shows no signs of habitation — its multitude of windows are shut and curtained.

'What's happened to Zinnia?'

'Um . . .' He screws his eyes up, as if he's trying to remember. 'Um . . . oh yes. She dropped her sprog. Couple of hours ago now. Girl.'

'Thank you.' I hold the gate open, hot with relief. 'You can go now.'

'Not before I've had a look around.'

'No — Curtis —'

But he strides off up the path. The gate clanging behind me, I hurry after him and grab his arm, which is clad today in a World sweatshirt, probably a cast-off of his wealthy older brother's.

'Please,' I whisper, panicked, 'you'll upset him. He's not well. You mustn't — please go now —'

He pulls away and with his other hand shoves me up against the wall, where I knock my head against a rusted bracket that once held a lamp. 'Don't tell what to do. You know I don't like it.'

'But the doctor's with him,' I say, with sudden, desperate inspiration.

'During the game?' he asks, suspiciously.

'Yes. And Howard's niece and nephew are here too. They're all inside.' But fifteen years of crawling around under my skin give him the upper hand: he knows me too well.

'You're full of shit.'

We've come to the northern wall of the house, where further on the French doors stand open. I can see the shape of Web Ellis slumped on the carpet, just inside, her black nose on the step. The sound of the game is louder here and there's Howard's voice, suddenly, 'Yes! Yes!' The All Blacks must've scored.

'Whatever is that doctor doing to him?' says Curtis, with devastating wit, and I wheel away into the garden, hoping he will follow me, but it's a last-minute ploy that doesn't work. Softly, his bare feet take the two low steps up to the terrace. It's only by breaking into a run that I pass him and get through the doors first.

'Howard I'm sorry — I —'

Howard stares at Curtis for a moment — his grubby toes, his Hawaiian board-shorts, his stubbly chin — then he waves him away, his gaze returning immediately to the screen. The game seems to have put him into a kind of trance — how extraordinary that he doesn't lose his temper! But then, as Curtis flops into the sofa as comfortably as if he were an invited guest, I notice Howard's cheek is pulsing, the hinges of his jaw working in and out, and his fingers have gone back to plucking the rug. I go to him, bend over him to whisper.

'He's an old friend. I didn't mean to let him in — he tricked me —'

'Wait till half-time. Kindly sit down,' Howard spits.

I sit on the sofa beside Curtis, who indulges his stoned, simian sense of humour by waggling an admonishing finger at me. From a seemingly impossible angle the Australian fullback Jacques Skelton, a Matt Burke protégé, is taking a penalty kick. The score in the right-hand corner reads 13–7 to the Wallabies. Maybe Howard's symptoms of anxiety relate directly to the fact that our boys are losing. Even though he doesn't venture out, I reason, he is used to people coming to his house. Other people, apart from myself, must know the security code for the gate: the man who delivers his groceries, the cleaning lady, the gardener, friends . . .

The ball sails between the posts, Skelton runs into the centre of the field with his arms upraised. Two of his team-mates rush towards him and wrap him briefly in their burly arms. Half-time.

'Bloody soccer players,' mutters Howard.

'Yeah, bloody homos,' rejoins Curtis. 'Bloody repressed turd burglars.'

Howard mutes the sound and turns his attention to our visitor.

'Who are you?'

'Mel hasn't told you about me?' Curtis asks, in mock surprise.

'Don't fuck me around, young man.' Howard's voice is level, his eyes laser blue fury. 'I did not invite you in.'

Curtis blushes suddenly. That first, powerful rush of his stone must have ebbed. 'Curtis Lodge,' he mumbles.

'Speak up.'

'Curtis Lodge,' he repeats, louder.

'Your father is Christopher Lodge? The construction engineer? The firm with the contract for the new harbour tunnel?'

'Grandfather.'

'Really? You're not short of a bob, then. It's still a family firm.'

Curtis meets the criticism of his lousy appearance in Howard's eyes and looks away again. Maybe he's thinking this visit wasn't such a good idea.

'How did you find out where I live? Did Melody give you the address?'

'No. Drove along looking for her car. I mean — I knew you lived on the beach-front. Her mother told me that.'

'Why did you want to see her here? Couldn't you have waited?'

'Helen — that's Mel's mum — wanted me to give her the news that she's an auntie. She would've rung, but we couldn't find —'

'Is the baby unwell? The mother?'

Curtis shakes his head.

'Then why have you barged your way in here, disturbing us?' Curtis looks blank, his lower lip quivers slightly. 'What do you do with yourself during the day?' Howard asks. 'Have you got a job?'

Instantly, Curtis's face takes on the perturbed, traumatised cast I know so well. 'No — well — after Mel and I — after we — since we split up I've been having a very bad time. I'm in therapy — it's hard for me to talk about —'

'How old are you, Lodge?'

'Twenty-nine.' He's thirty-two.

'Bit old to be behaving like this, aren't you?' Howard is completely baffled. It's as if he and Curtis are of different species, let alone generations.

'People go through different shit at different times of their lives.'

'You went out with this sorry creature?' Howard says to me, shaking his head and reaching for a cigarette.

'Can I have one of those?' Curtis asks. Without looking at him Howard holds out the packet, his own cigarette between his lips, unlit.

'Go now, Curtis,' I say quietly, but Curtis is leaning forward, waiting for the lighter.

'I've read all your books,' he says in an urgent whisper. Howard holds the flame to his own cigarette and puts the lighter on the table between them. Curtis grabs it up. 'How come you haven't written any more? Before Mel got this job I thought you were dead.' Howard is smoking with all systems shut off, but Curtis doesn't seem to notice. He stands, pulling in smoke, and goes to the window on Howard's left.

'I thought you'd have a better place than this. I mean, you must be loaded. Great location, but your house is kind of run down.' Smoke billows from his mouth and curls against the glass. Howard has closed his eyes.

'You give a lot of your money away, though, eh?'

'Come on, Curtis.' I stand and take his arm once more. Sluttishly, softly, my middle finger caresses the crook of his elbow. I have to get him out of here.

'You be good to Mel. I love her.'

Oh no.

Tears well in his eyes. 'I understand that she no longer loves me. I don't feel guilty about the fact that I still love her. I've worked hard on not giving myself a bad time about it. It's just how it is.' He moves suddenly, his right arm encompasses me. The tears are falling copiously now. His nose drips.

'For God's sake, Curtis.'

Howard opens his eyes. The good one steadily regards the mute picture on the television.

'Come on.' Very gently I draw him away down the side of the house, the television booming now with the half-time analysis at our backs. Web Ellis stays put this time.

'Sorry,' blubbers Curtis. 'Shouldn't've had that smoke. Keep thinking I need it, you know, to give me confidence —'

'Shut up.' I open the gate, he stumbles through and I close it after him without a backward glance. Instead of going back to Howard, the idea of which fills me with trepidation — he's bound to hold me at least partially responsible for the intrusion — I go into the garden and sit on the slimy bench under the liquidambar.

I must be a monster. The phrase pops into my head out of habit. It's one of my mantras. At the end of every argument with Curtis I would think it, or something like it. At the end, after whatever shouting and tears there were, Curtis would accept in some way that he was a fool, that it was the dope that made him more so, that he was weak. Our relationship was so juvenile that there had always to be an absolute polarity, a child on either end of the see-saw: if he was weak, then I was strong; if he was gentle, then I was a monster. And I must be. What kind of woman spends half her life with a man and then loathes him entirely afterwards, without even a speck of residual affection?

My heart thumps and I feel sick with myself, glutted with wishes: I want to make love with a man I respect; I want a close girlfriend; I want not to dislike my sister so much; I want my mother to pay more attention to me; I want to feel excited about being an auntie; I want a bigger bum so that I can be comfortable on hard seats.

'Melody —' Howard's voice, thin and plangent, sounds from the other side of the house. I go inside to watch the second half.

Some of my garden bench crisis must still show in my face because Howard gives me as sympathetic smile as I've ever seen.

'It's all right, lassie,' he says. On the coffee table in front of my place on the sofa is a fresh scotch and a new cigarette reclining in a clean ashtray: Howard's pacifiers. I push Curtis out of my mind — I'm good at that now, I've had months of practice — and absorb myself in the game. By the end of it I can offer myself cold comfort — at least I'm not an All Black. They bumble and drop the ball. Te Atu Lal is sinbinned for a high tackle, Hamish Wong is lucky not to walk after giving Skelton a face massage. The boys get rattled. They lose 29–10.

LENA

List

Ring travel agent — two tickets to Sydney.
Check Scottie's passport is current.
Bank. Buy Australian currency.
Contact all clients. Will resume sessions in a fortnight? Or longer?
Tell Curtis to work on his own for a while/Arrange for Curtis to see White Hawk from now on.
Email White Hawk to check.
Ask neighbour to feed cat.
Ring Foxie to come and get Hausfrau.
Ring Helen — sorry will miss Naming Ceremony.
Get lock on back door fixed.
Pack clothes, yoga mat, Rescue Remedy.

FRANCA

Piece of Luck

She took Jasper to an interview room at the end of a corridor where they would be undisturbed. It had taken Stambach longer than he had anticipated to get back to her. As far as he could make out, he said, the authorities were happy for Gilmore to go back to Remand and happy for Franca to visit him.

The intervening week Franca had spent treating her private patients, working on her paper and vacillating between the desire to dismiss her apprehension about Jasper and the desire to analyse it. First she would have to accept that he had frightened her and she was reluctant to do that. Fear had never got anyone anywhere, she believed. One simply used one's intellect, made sure that frightening situations never arose, such as — in her own case — finding herself in a tunnel. It was a useful emotion to engender in children, to teach them the dangers of the world — busy roads, fire, hard drugs — but for adults it was pointless, a waste of energy, a physiological archaism as obsolete as the coccyx

101

or the wasted directional muscles behind the human ears.

There had been one occasion in her life when she had been terrified out of her mind and she had handled the situation badly, freezing herself into paralysis like a frightened opossum. Her attacker had been fed and strengthened by the smell of her fear. Besides, in this instance, she was less interested in why Jasper had frightened her — than why he was frightened of his own life, or weary of it. And as time went on she may well discover, she knew, that he was not suitable material for her Munich paper: in the session with Stambach he might have been telling the truth. Perhaps his threats were just a figure of speech; perhaps he had only been grandstanding. He may not make a serious attempt. The police report she had given only a cursory read: cocaine possession, theft of a yacht, possession of pornography. It was enough for now to know why he'd been arrested — she wanted to draw her own conclusions from the man himself.

Jasper sat across the table from her now in the silent windowless room and the word 'begrutten' sprang to her mind: his eyes were red and streaming, his nose disgorging. It was a word you never saw any more. It belonged to the novels of Durkheim's time. From her briefcase she took a small packet of paper tissues and made Jasper a present of it. He had been talking about his father, calmly at first — so calmly in fact that she'd had no hint or warning of the ferocity of his grief. He wiped himself up, took a second tissue and dabbed at his brow, attended to his hands. He was sweating — a dark butterfly of moisture formed across the front of his prison shirt, though the atmospherically controlled room was cool.

As quiet and still as the officer at the door she bided her time, her hands clasped peaceably on the table, and waited for him to offer eye contact. After a moment or two he did, though it was not sustained for longer than a few seconds.

'All right?' she asked. He nodded.

'Are you worried about your father?'

'No. Of course not. Stupid fat fuck.'

'Then why were you crying?'

'Not about him. Someone else. Someone who's dead.'

'Does your father know you're in jail?'

'No. I want him to know, though.'

'Yes?'

'I want you to let him know.'

'Why me?'

'Then he can tell Bonny, my wife.'

'Your wife?'

'Ex. We have two sons.'

'In New Zealand?'

'Sydney.'

The silence again, enduring for whole minutes. It was unnatural, thought Franca, how absolute it was. It was almost apocryphal, final. No insects or traffic, not even the hum and click of the air-conditioning unit. Jasper was doing his best to gulp down tears, his throat bucking as though he'd swallowed something live. The silence opened and rejoined around his hiccoughs until he gave up the fight. His arms collapsed onto the table, his head cradled and shoulders heaving.

'Do you want to talk about the coke?'

He reared up, looked at her now. 'I don't regret that. People use coke, they like it. I'm not responsible for that. I didn't hurt anybody. I just got caught.'

'Have you given the police the name of the other man? The fair-haired man who was with you?' The table caught her in the midriff and knocked the breath from her, but she thought he hadn't meant it. It was because he'd stood so quickly, three strides to cross to the far wall and lean against it, glowering at her.

'Are you working for them now or what?'

'Them?'

'The cops. Who the fuck else do you think I meant?'

She shook her head, stood up herself and placed her briefcase on the chair.

'Why do you carry that thing around with you?' he demanded. 'You never write anything down.' Instead of answering him she laid a piece of yellow paper on the table, a pen beside it. 'Must have a good memory,' he said then, answering himself.

His tone was wheedling, noted Franca, almost apologetic, the New

Zealand accent noticeably thicker. He ran a hand over the stubble on his chin. It made a scratchy sound, amplified in the dull air.

'Are you going?' He really was whining now, like a child, or a spoilt husband.

'Perhaps I'm asking you the wrong questions — or at least, questions you dislike.' She spoke so quietly he had to incline his head to hear her. Experimentally he clicked his fingers: was there an acoustic anomaly in the room, he wondered, one that made sounds louder from where he stood? He was sure she'd heard him rub his chin. Now she was looking at him queryingly and he realised that every action of his was being monitored, its motivation weighed for normality. She and the doctor, that weird old guy with the Dr Seuss name — they may have decided he wasn't going to top himself straight away, but the jury was still out on whether he was loopy or not. He shrugged his shoulders at her, clicked his fingers again in the rhythm of an old TV ad from his childhood — M-I-L-O, M-I-L-O, Milo! Let her think he had a screw loose. At this moment he couldn't care less.

I'm not going to tell her your name, Damian. Never. I'll never tell anybody.

She laid a lilac-polished fingertip on the paper. 'Write what you like. The things you want to talk about. Your childhood, for example, or your recent experiences. I don't mind. I'll visit again tomorrow.'

'On a Saturday?' he mocked. 'Married to the job, are you?'

'Oh — no, of course not. I'm sorry. On Monday.'

'No shame when the shrink doesn't know what day it is,' he said nastily in an undertone, and for a moment or two Franca wondered what on earth he was talking about. Then it came back to her — Stambach's initial examination.

'Will you get in touch with my father?' He sprang towards her, ripped a narrow strip off the bottom of the paper.

'It would not be ethical for me to do that. Ask your lawyer to do it.' She was at the door, lifting her hand to knock for the guard outside.

'You do it or I won't talk to you again. What are you doing with it all anyway, the stuff I'm telling you? You doing a survey?'

'Yes, of sorts.'

'Making your name in the shrink world?'

She shrugged at him now and he saw as her shoulders lifted how the fabric of her linen jacket gaped at the buttons to show a lacy chemise, flesh-toned. She was a classy chick, he decided, a career woman.

'You with anyone?'

It was curious, thought Franca, how his accent changed when he was asking intimate questions. It was a self-deprecating voice, the stronger New Zealand accent, almost cartoon Maori. When he was relaxed his accent was more cultivated, which was why she'd assumed a level of education that he quite possibly didn't have. Perhaps the cultivated voice was the false, secondary one.

'You know, are you in a relationship with anyone?'

'It's not necessary for you to know anything about my private life.' While she watched him he very deliberately took up the pen, wrote down an email address and handed it to her with a flourish. Without looking at it she dropped it into her pocket and motioned to the guard to open the door.

He stood looking at the closed door for two or three minutes, the silence welling around him. Then he sat down at the table, sipped at the coffee she'd given him, which was cold now, weak and bitter. He sighed. Picked up the pen. Examined his nails, which were black-rimmed. He remembered her lovely lilac ones. He remembered his old sentence and wrote it at the top of the page:

By the time I was eight years old I knew everything there was to know about addiction.

She should have gone home — there was an abundance of work waiting for her there. Not of a domestic kind because Franca, as she liked to think, was scarcely domestic. She lived alone in an expensive eyrie high above Lavender Bay and what little detritus she created was taken care of by a daily cleaner. In order of urgency the waiting work was: an article on suicide among senior citizens for the British medical journal *The Lancet*, due in a fortnight and currently still in note form; a letter of referral for one of her patients to a dermatologist, the woman being afflicted with what was once called a nervous rash; a letter of thanks to her recent hosts in Darwin; and lastly the rewriting of her introduction to the Munich paper, which she had decided was necessary only that morning, Jason having introduced a whole new element, one that she had previously been missing: the threatened suicide of the egoist.

Unfashionable though he now was, Franca remained a devotee of Emile Durkheim, whose 1897 classic on suicide partially informed all her diagnoses — along with a grab-bag of twentieth-century psychiatrists such as Beck, Maltsberger and Farber. She would subject her cases to Beck's Hopelessness Scale, to the psychodynamic formulae of Maltsberger, to Farber's Equation for Likeliness of Suicide. She would take into account Marie Asberg's discovery of a shared low level of 5 HIAA among suicides and her accompanying Deprivation Theory. But it was the French sociologist who offered the best and most sensible tool of assessment. According to Durkheim there are three different classifications of suicide: egoistic, altruistic and anomic. Prisoners, in Franca's opinion, fell heavily into the latter category, being, as Durkheim outlined, morally, culturally, spiritually, politically and geographically isolated. One of her case studies, a kleptomaniac Asian woman in her sixties, formed her only demonstration of the altruistic, being certain that her death would relieve her family of the burden of shame.

Light rain hissed on her windscreen all the way along Parramatta Road, until she turned off at Johnston Street towards the Leichhardt house where she had been raised, and where her grandmother lived still, alone. A time would come, soon, when Nònna would need to be taken care of, and Franca hoped she had made it clear to her by indirect comments and descriptive statements about her apartment that they would not be cohabiting. Nònna would not like the clear, cold surfaces of Franca's minimalist decor, nor would she enjoy the predominance of white and pearly grey, the abundance of natural light, the absence of clutter. This last translated to no sanctity — no Sacred Heart, no Virgin, no Saints, not even a tiny unobtrusive crucifix. And there were only two bedrooms, one of which Franca used as a study. It was imperative she kept it for that; as she eased herself out of practice and into research she worked more and more at home. Home, to Franca, all her adult life, meant somewhere cool and quiet, peaceful and, aside from herself, utterly empty.

Stopped at the traffic lights at Annandale Road she made a note in her diary: Investigate Italian home. There were lots of them now. The first Australian-born generation of Italians looked after their elderly parents; successive generations did not and would not. There were retirement homes in Haberfield, Leichhardt, Strathfield, suburbs familiar to the Nònnas and Nònnos.

The old lady was on the side path of the house, almost obscured by the extravagant oleander which for over a year Franca had been nagging at her to get pruned. To find her, she followed the sound of running water and the scraping of bristles on wet asphalt. Everything was already drenched from the rain: the little rectangle of grass at the front was now almost underwater, a tiny waterfall rushed down the low step below the gate. This was a new eccentricity, noted the grand-daughter: cleaning the paths while it was raining.

'Nònna!' she called out, loudly, because her grandmother was deaf and Franca did not want to startle her. 'Buon giorno, Nònna!'

The little face turned towards her, almost entirely obscured by her huge spectacles, the lenses a centimetre and a half thick. Magnified, Nònna's eyes widened still further and the hose was flung aside, sending up a plume of silver that arced against the wall and caught Franca on the sleeve. Neither of the women noticed the dampening, the elderly one so delighted with the sudden appearance of her grand-daughter and Franca, her arms around her grandmother, thinking with a wrenching jolt to her heart how old Nònna was now and how, when she died, there would be nobody left to her. For years, until Franca was in her mid-thirties, Nònna would question her about her singularity — why was there no boyfriend, no close women friends even? Why did she not want to get married? And Franca, knowing full well the reason, could only tell the old lady that this was the way she liked it. She was happy with her life, she'd say, and Nònna would scowl, dissatisfied. It was as if she took Franca's decision as an insult to her own chosen, crowded way of life — her beloved husband now dead for twenty years, though outliving his doctor's predictions by at least five due to her own leviathan will and complete devotion; her two sons who lived in Melbourne; her youngest daughter in Milan; and her eldest daughter, Franca's mother, whose portrait photograph rested on the polished side-board between the marble Madonna and St Michael made of sea-shells.

In the kitchen Franca made coffee and opened the tin of butter biscuits that had lain undisturbed since her last visit, a fortnight ago. Nònna sat at the little table and chattered on in Italian, while Franca replied loudly, in the manner of so many migrants' children, in English. Nònna had had a letter from another grand-daughter, Kerry in Melbourne; the neighbours had had another baby; the dog at the top of the street had been killed by a car.

'God is good,' she sighed, not mourning the dog, which had frightened her on her daily walk to the Norton Street shops. 'Where have you been this morning?' she asked when Franca put the coffee down in front of her.

'At the prison,' said Franca with a tiny smile. Nònna would not like that.

'The prison! Again? Which one? Why?'

'I'm studying one of the prisoners.' She nibbled a biscuit; powdered sugar coated her lips and tongue.

'A prisoner? Again? What for?' Nònna was bewildered. 'Why don't you study nice people? There is too much attention given to bad people now — you should study what it is that makes a person happy and kind.'

Happy and kind people don't tend to commit suicide, Franca thought, but said nothing. Nònna knew only that she was 'psichiatra' — her specialist area would distress her.

The coffee drunk, the two women went into the tiny sitting room. There was only just enough room to wedge themselves in between the rolled back of a vast sofa to stand before the overburdened sideboard. Nònna lit the votive candle that sat before a photograph. It was dark in the room. Heavy patterned curtains, yellow and blue, were drawn against the wintry daylight. The single flame doubled in the glass, giving movement to the image, a temporary, eerie quickening. It was a black and white studio portrait taken in 1970, three years before she died. Franca gazed on her mother's face, her small sharp nose and heavy-lidded eyes, her dark hair swept away from her face. Her lips were curled in a reluctant half-smile, one bidden by the photographer.

She did not remember her mother like that at all. Away from her grandmother's house the woman in the photograph and her own image of her mother were memories of two separate beings. Her own image, rarely summoned, was of a skeletal body in a bed in a room as shadowy as this one, and a bony hand too weak to clasp her own six-year-old one, or to take up a spoon or fork to eat whatever her childish self had prepared in the grimy Broken Hill kitchen. She remembered her mother's protuberant, luminous eyes, made enormous not by spectacles like Nònna's, but by voluntary starvation. She remembered how purely she had understood her mother's desire to die, how she had accepted it in the way children can accept the most tragic of adult realities. It was only after her mother had achieved her end that she had gone through bags and drawers and found the estranged grandmother's telephone number in faraway Sydney.

'God forgive you, Paola,' muttered Nònna, and Franca felt washed by relief: there would be no tears today. There was enough grit in the old lady's voice to tell her that they would remain standing; she would not kneel and weep. Those times, the times of weeping grief, were impossible to bear and though Franca would weep with her, part of her, her Australian half, would afterwards take weeks or months to recover. Perhaps Nònna understood now that it was the weeping that made her stay away, that made her require a period of convalescence.

Nònna leaned forward and wiped away a non-existent smudge from the glass, her customary caress. 'Poor foolish girl.'

During her teens Franca had resented these criticisms of her mother. She would draw close to her mother, put her young arm around her ghostly waist and confront her grandmother.

'It wasn't her fault she died,' she'd say. 'She was alone. Why don't you blame my father?'

But Nònna would never reply to these accusatory questions. Her thin lips would narrow further, closing against any vitriol she held against her absent son-in-law, the tall, fair Australian who had disappeared during Franca's infancy.

The heavy drawer slid open, a rosary clattered in Nònna's fingers and while she prayed for her daughter's soul Franca stood behind her, her hands resting lightly on the old lady's bowed shoulders. The candle was low and sputtering now and Franca wondered idly, while her grandmother prayed, how many candles they had burned for Paola — five hundred? Five thousand? What panoramas of guilt and remorse had they lit in Nònna's mind, the suffering of her daughter not ended by her death at all, but transmuted and intensified by her long sojourn in limbo?

Later, Nònna led her to the front door, picking her way down the narrow hall made narrower still by the shelving that rose high on either side, each shelf a universe of figurines and baubles: china, porcelain, glass and plastic. There were shepherdesses with lambs on tiny gold chains; blue and gold plates on uncertain stands; a fragile menagerie of blown glass; an aerial photograph of Milan laminated onto a plastic ashtray; a propped-up photograph of Franca in her graduation robes; an apple in bubbly green glass with a gilt leaf; a tiny pair of Limoge shoes; an enamelled trinket box stuck all over with red coral; a painted wooden Russian egg; and in a coffee mug printed with the Virgin, a bristling sheaf of memorial cards for Nònna's many departed friends. Gazing into the shelves as she passed through, the way lit by a small, cheap chandelier, Franca did not so much appreciate all the things that had delighted her since childhood as use them as a gauge. An examination of Nònna's collections was a good way to see how she was coping — according to how dusty they were. Dust coiled among the coral of the trinket box, lay in spheres among the Venetian glass, furred the gold chains and the china netting of the shepherdesses petticoats. When Franca had arrived in Sydney as an almost pathologically serious six-year-old, the shelves and their populations were wiped with a moistened cloth every other day. Nònna appeared to have given this up, Franca noted, though she was keener than ever on scrubbing the concrete. Did it signify anything, she worried — was it the beginnings of dementia?

On the porch Nònna slipped her dry hand into hers; it felt cool and consoling. There was nothing wrong with her, Franca thought — she could go on for ever, and she bent her head to kiss her grandmother's brow. Immediately the old lady's arms closed around her in a firm clasp and Franca was further reassured. How strong Nònna was still!

She drove home to Lavender Bay in the dusk, across her grand and shadowy bridge, with her heart at rest. Foolish, she knew, to love above all other humanity a lady in her eighties, but as she daily prepared herself for Nònna's death she was convinced she would contain her grief.

She closed the door on Nònna now, a skill her mother had unintentionally left her; a technique in survival: the ability to make absolute, rapid changes in focus, and turned her thoughts to Jasper.

What a piece of luck he was.

JASPER

Mr Shag

In late 1980 Scottie, Lena and I set up together in a little house in Grey Lynn. There was a shed out the back for Scottie to do her cabinet making — she had a genius for it. Orders came from all over the country for her furniture, made from recycled kauri, rewa and matai. She made bed-ends, chests of drawers, sideboards and bookcases, some of them as intricately carved as her gypsy caravan, some of them inlaid with paua shell and pieces of agate. She fashioned table tops from heavy slabs of swamp kauri, clock cases from hollow puriri trunks. When I came home from school I loved to sit out there with her: I had tools of my own, mostly her cast-offs, and pieces of wood to whittle or carve while I listened to the radio. It was even better when Scottie showed me how to pull nail heads from old floorboards and joists, or how to plane away charred or discoloured wood to reveal the sweet-smelling pale timber underneath, or how to dovetail, glue and brace. Looking back I can see how I could have become a carver, or a cabinet maker. It's something I like to do even now, sit with a piece of wood warm in my hand and shape it with a sharp blade.

The house sat high on the south-facing ridge above Williamson Avenue. In winter it was freezing: the wind roared through the gaps in the floorboards and made the scrim on the walls billow and sag. Our breath frosted in the kitchen and we slept in our jerseys. Scottie fixed it up a bit, but we were only renting so she didn't want to do much. For the first time that I could remember, I had a room of my own, which I hung with psychedelic posters and a batik bedspread with elephants on. There was less than a metre between my long, skinny double-hung window and the house next door, which was painted a luminous turquoise and flung a ghostly green light across my floor and bed. These days, if ever I hear on retro-radio my favourite bands of the early eighties — Police, Split Enz, Australian Crawl, Midnight Oil — I'm back there, burning camouflage incense, stoned off my face on dope filched from Dorothy Gilmore, head on my pillow, floating and dreaming in the marine light.

Lena took a while to settle down. She'd been on the road for so long she'd forgotten how to live in a house, or how to keep to any kind of routine. It was Scottie who got up early to make sure I left for school on time, to pedal my old bike along Ponsonby Road. Scottie did all the cooking as well, as I remember, and what little housework they bothered with. Mates of mine who came from 'nice' homes sometimes remarked on the mess and smell: I never noticed it. Until I was eighteen I lived happily with Mum and Scottie. That was the year Mum took herself off to MAA, Marijuana Addicts Anonymous, and got herself sorted out. She would've been thirty-seven years old then and she had a complete personality change. She cleaned the house, made curtains, had elaborate dinner parties, joined an organic vegetable co-op, trained for and then got a job as a drug and alcohol counsellor. At first she and Scottie fought furiously and I worried for a time that they'd split up — 'You're not the same wommin, darling,' Scottie would say — but they weathered it. They're still together. And I reckon they wouldn't be if they hadn't shoved me — and my lucrative dealing business — out. But I'm getting ahead of myself.

The year I remember best, the year I'm filling this particular piece of wall with, is 1981, when I turned nine, the year of the Springbok Tour. Until then I hardly saw any men, except for the lone male teacher at school. I wasn't a sporty type then, but even if I had been Lena and Scottie would never have let me join a rugby club. Or even a cricket club, which would be not only sexist but classist. They were bringing me up to spearhead the sexual revolution for my gender, they said — to break with masculist tradition. I was to be raised by wimmin, shaped by wimmin; I was to live and breathe feminism. I would never oppress a wommin.

Taihoa a mo. 'Spearhead' was never in the dialect — it's phallic. Phallicist? They would never have said it.

In the centre of the floor I take up a yoga position, one of my favourites, the Full Lotus. Not many western men can achieve it but I find it very restful. Soles uppermost, palms together, I resolve to keep to the truth. For most New Zealanders the '81 Springbok Tour is remembered as a time when barriers and distances formed between members of the same families and between friends; a time of near civil war, when communities were temporarily ruptured. Heaps has been written about it — not only books, but films and plays as well. Franca, being an Australian, won't know anything about it and I want her to understand that for me it was a time when barriers fell down, one after another. It was also when I met a really famous man — a superman, a Renaissance man — the man who's been my life-long hero.

After I've meditated for a while I go to the door and try to peer through the fish-eye, which is of course inverted so that they can see in. It's not for prisoners to look out of. Maybe it's night time — the light out there is gloomy, artificial. I wish I'd paid more attention to my surroundings when Franca and I came down the corridor yesterday — or was it the day before? Was there a window in the far end wall? How far down the corridor did we come? What are the rooms on either side of me? Maybe there's been a stir, a breakout, or a sudden epidemic. It's freaky, like the fairytale about the castle where everyone goes to sleep for a hundred years. Another scenario flares through my mind: a prisoner, a chemistry genius, such as I wanted to be, has concocted a potion that he's fed through the air-conditioning ducts. It's a lethal gas and it's only a matter of minutes before it starts hissing through the grid above the door. Suddenly I'm bathed in sweat, prickling all over, strangled by the collar of my shirt. I rip it off, fling it away.

Breathe, breathe — the air is thick, dull, metallic. The lino tiles are cool against my side. I lie with my nose pressed into the almost non-existent crack between the floor and door. Breathe. It's out there too, the lethal gas, in thirty seconds I'll be dead . . .

Fuckwit. Drug-fucked paranoid. Cocaine brain. I roll away, onto my stomach, cushion my forehead on my hands and before I realise what I'm doing I've numbered twenty push-ups, forty, fifty, sixty. I'm really breathing now, great heaving, rasping breaths and with each rise and fall my vision dances and blurs over the writing on the wall, the columns of it. I could have called out, could have brought them running, but it would have been the end of all this.

The end of all this remembering. The pen still has ink in it.

The Herne Bay house, the same one I'd spent my first night in Auckland in, was where Wimmin Against the Tour held their campaign meetings. We were regular attendees, or rather Lena and Scottie were. I had to stay outside in the garden, me and any other boys that were around. There were other boys — a surprising number of them. One family was of four brothers, two for each of the mothers. They were turkey-baster/hot-spoon boys, do-it-yourself artificial insem-inations. I've read since that when sperm is exposed to air the XX sperms die off and the XY ones survive. Maybe that's why there were so many boys in that garden. We outnumbered the girls eight to two. The four brothers were allowed inside because their sperm donor was Maori. They used to get food for the rest of us and sometimes their father came to the parties too. That's what I mean about barriers coming down — they used to let Maori men into that house, for parties and meetings. The boys' mothers were blondes and even though I was darker than the four brothers, because of Lena being Italian and Richard being what he called Black Irish, I wasn't allowed in.

I joined in on the marches up Queen Street and the rally outside Eden Park. Scottie got me fitted up with a crash helmet and shield and I stood up the front with her, 30,000 protesters behind us. I was a soldier for human rights, a freedom fighter. We watched the Topp Twins bravely front up to the stony-faced pigs and sing to them; we cheered the little plane when it dropped flour bombs right onto the field where they were playing; we sang 'Ngai Iwi E', 'We Shall Not Be Moved', and chanted 'Remember Soweto', and we stood up to the riot police when they came at us with their PR24 batons — the special extra-long ones with the handles fixed to the sides.

'Move! Move! Move! . . . Move, move, move . . . Move! Move! Move!' the cops sang, phallic symbols thrusting under their elbows — it was rap before rap, they were musicians ahead of their time, but it wasn't entertaining, or even slightly amusing. It was terrifying. They attacked us — Scottie pushed me behind her and I ran, ran as fast as I could down Onslow Road towards the safehouse she'd shown me on the way. I waited there for her, and when she came she had a sprained knee, a black eye and a bloody nose.

It came out later, about the cops, how they'd teamed their black helmets and perspex visors with epaulets empty of their numbers. Some of the protesters were hospitalised by police brutality; the police themselves sustained broken arms and legs, wounds to their heads. The perpetrators of the police violence could never be identified, but that wasn't the worst of it. The worst of it, of course, was that a whole generation grew up afterwards with no respect for them. Out of our impressionable child eyes we saw them for what they really were: a gang of thugs, verified, purified, sanctified and protected by the law.

We stopped the game, though. It seemed like a miracle — we were few and they were many. They were the macho men, the rugger-buggers, the gun-toters and stick-wielders, the Establishment. We were the women, the disenfranchised, the children, the left wing — and we won. After Lena patched Scottie up we went to a huge party in an old city warehouse. Most people had gone home and changed into their party clothes. The women wore huge earrings, bush singlets, bone carving pendants and short-cropped hair. The men wore longer hair, smaller earrings, bush singlets and bone carvings. It was a night of high feeling. There was a fantastic atmosphere of victory and success, of occupying the moral high ground, but some of the adult faces I looked up into looked stunned — and it wasn't just from the dope and red wine that was passing round — it was the aftermath, a residual horror from the day, a chilling awareness of how nasty it had been and how much worse it could have got.

I met up with a boy from school and his brother, who got us a half-smoked spliff someone had left on a window ledge and a full bottle of Müller Thurgau. The older brother was called Damian. He was three or four years older than us, about thirteen. He had dreads in his thick blond hair under his rasta hat, and his voice had already broken. He smelt of sweat and some kind of musky cologne. Hiding in the stairwell we got really smashed and I never took my eyes off him. I felt so envious of my friend, having a brother as cool and wild as Damian.

Years later, when I met up with Dam again in Sydney I reminded him of that night and he said he remembered it. He said he remembered me because I stared at him all night, like a possum in the headlights. That was the expression he used. I never told him how much I thought about him in the years we never saw each other, because I worried he'd think I was weird. And I wasn't sure whether I should believe him or not, that he remembered that long-ago party in New Zealand. Why would he? I was just a poxy little kid. For Damian it would've been one night among hundreds, just the same: getting out of it with people who gazed at him, at his beautiful luminous face, while he talked shit and showed off. I remember him balancing on the handrail, with a twenty-foot drop on one side, until some girls came out of the party, girls about his age, and he pretended to fall. When they screamed he jumped down, laughing maniacally. He grabbed one of them and kissed her and as far as I could tell, watching intently, she didn't seem to mind.

When we got back into the big room it was really crowded and smoky and almost as soon as we pushed our way in the door I lost sight of Damian. I reeled around for a bit, looking for him, banging into people. Finally I lay down on an old sofa, which had been turned to face the wall, and tried to go to sleep. Voices and music buzzed and whirled around me, I could feel a fizzing and popping inside my skull, and when I opened my eyes I felt as though I were tipping forwards. When I closed them I fell backwards through whirling white space into infinity: I wanted to die. I wanted to be violently ill. And pretty soon

I was. I spewed into a conveniently located velvet shoulder-bag that someone had left hooked over the sofa back.

Feeling much better — hungry, in fact — I went in search of Lena. I found her in the kitchen, which is always a good place to find your mother. There was a delicious fishy, creamy smell. Water boiled in a tall pot on the stove and there was a long table with men and women — Maori and Pakeha — seated around it. They were eating crayfish. Mum and Scottie were there and I pushed in between them, reaching out for a red and white gleaming cray tail on a plate in the middle of the table. Everything fell silent. It was as if I'd sworn, or farted. Lena slapped my hand and scowled at me and I realised she and Scottie were chewing on a spiny leg each. So were all the other Pakehas — the legs and the antennae. The tails and heads were for the tangata whenua.

It seems stupid now. Weird. But at the time I was excited by it, by being in a room with these people. There were some famous activists there; one of them went on to live a life as an MP dogged by scandal in the late eighties. There were writers, and a couple of actors I'd seen on television. The whities were happy to chew on the hard orange bits and they were fairly quiet — the Maori people did all the talking.

Franca will think all this is irrelevant, unless I get on to what happened the next day. It all seems so real to me now — I can smell the crayfish, the cigarette smoke, the frangipani essential oil Lena wore as perfume. I can see all the shining faces around the table, but I can only recall snatches of what they talked about. There was a sense of discomfort among the Pakehas — of flagellation, of the minute cuts inflicted by the cray legs to the lips and gums being small recompense for a century of colonisation. There was talk of white greed, guilt and general soullessness. Lena and Scottie and the other Pakeha grown-ups all sighed and nodded with self-loathing, as if they were responsible for what was happening in South Africa now and what had happened in New Zealand in the past. I hung on my mother, propping my chin on her head, and didn't understand. I was only nine years old, I was stoned, drunk and very tired.

The next day Richard picked me up in his two-seater car, with the roof off. Lena had agreed to this only because he was relocating to Sydney the following week and he had got 'emotional' about wanting to spend his last Sunday with me. Mum and Scottie had put up a lot of resistance — it was bad enough that I shared genetic material with Richard, let alone be influenced by him. Nobody had explained to me that Richard was pro-Tour, which was the main reason they hadn't let him see me for ten and a half months. As I barrelled out the door my sweatshirt clicked with badges: Stop the Tour, Dykes Against the Tour, Physicians Against the Tour, Gay Men Against the Tour, Teachers Against the Tour, Scientists Against the Tour, MPs Against the Tour, Librarians Against the Tour. My father was leaning against the steering wheel smiling at me, but as I flung the car door open his smile became lopsided. When I put my arms around him for a hug he pushed me away.

'You'll have to take those off, where we're going,' he said.

Happily I unclicked them all and tossed them into the glovebox — the political convictions of a ten-year-old boy are secondary to the desire to be one with Dad. We headed down Curran Street towards the Harbour Bridge and as we went I told him all about the riot and the party the night before, and how Damian had got us the wine and dope. I wanted Richard to see how grown up I was now, how in the ten months since we'd seen each other I had become a man — I left out the bit about being sick in someone's handbag.

We turned off the motorway at Takapuna and while we waited at the first set of lights he took out his notebook and jotted down a few lines. I didn't think it had anything to do with what I'd been telling him. He was in his work suit, I noticed then, the same one he'd worn for years: baggy, grey, with a faint wide check through it.

'Where are we going, Dad?' I asked him, my heart sinking suddenly: he was dragging me along to some work thing.

'You, young man, are about to meet the most famous New Zealander in the world, more famous even than Kiri Te Kanawa.'

'Who's he?'

'She. Kiri is a she.'

'The most famous New Zealander is a wommin?' I asked. I should have known that.

'No — he's a man, of course. Howard Shag.' Dad slipped a sideways glance at me and must've gathered from my blank incomprehension that I had no idea who he was. 'Rugby player extraordinaire, world-famous blockbuster novelist. Here —' He reached behind me, rummaged around on the narrow back seat and shoved a thick paperback at me. 'You should be able to read that.'

FLASHPOINT, the title read in raised gold and glittery letters, and there was a picture of a soldier with a tin hat holding a machine gun. Behind him was a tropical jungle with grass-roofed shacks and under the trees stood a wommin with big bazookas and not many clothes. 'What's it about?'

'What all his books are about — good triumphing over evil, honour among men, loyalty, courage — all that stuff. Sells like a bomb.'

'Who's she?' I ran my nail-bitten finger over the lovely lady. Her nipples were little red nubbles under my pad. Maybe they do them like that for blind men, I thought. Dad shrugged.

'She'll be the love interest,' he said. 'You know, for the sexy bits. A horny oriental incidental.'

'Doesn't he have wimmin main characters?' I knew about this problem in male literature — I'd overheard enough conversations.

Richard laughed. 'No,' he said.

'Can I read it?'

'Sure,' he said, 'You can have it. I've got a proper present for you, for later.' He was undoing his tight seatbelt, exhaling gratefully. He was only young then, Richard — a bit older than I am now, mid-thirties — and he had a beer gut. Too many long lunches.

We were stopped before a rich person's house, the sort of place where the oppressors of the proletariat lived. It had huge spreading trees, rose beds, three chimneys, a high gabled roof and a wide veranda that went right around the house. A tall, broad-shouldered man in a white panama hat came around the corner carrying a gardening fork and a spade. He wiped his right palm on his muddy shorts and shook Dad's hand.

'Brunel. Nice to meet you.'

Richard nodded. 'And you.' He put one hand on the back of my head and pushed me forward. 'My son, Jasper.'

At the back of the house we sat on the veranda that overlooked Takapuna Beach. A young man waited on us, bringing Richard and Mr Shag coffee, and me a lemonade. It was the first time I'd been in a place that had a servant. He was Asian and not very friendly, as if we were the source of extra work for him.

'This is Raymond,' said Mr. Shag, introducing him. 'I brought him back with me from Taiwan after I finished writing *Fire Dragon*. He's what we used to call, in less enlightened times, a house-boy.' Raymond gave an almost imperceptible bow of his head. At least Mr Shag doesn't make a wommin wait on us, I remember thinking. I wondered if that meant he was a feminist. First, he and Dad talked about the house, which Mr Shag had lived in since the early sixties. Then Dad got out his notebook and wrote in shorthand squiggles while they talked about the tour.

'Haven't got much to contribute, really,' said Mr Shag. 'I think the behaviour of the protesters is execrable.'

'Were you at Eden Park yesterday?' Dad asked. Mr Shag nodded.

'Of course. I have a seat in the Members' Stand. The whole thing was appalling — the fool who dropped the flour bombs, the noise from outside. Moronic.'

'Should they have cancelled the tour, do you think? After the Waikato game?'

'Absolutely not.' The servant was loitering by the French doors. Mr Shag held up a finger to him for some more coffee and another lemonade and he turned back into the house.

'They should of!' I wished I'd left my badges on. 'The Springboks should never of come here.'

'"Have",' said Mr Shag, '"Have come here." Why not?'

'Because . . . because of how the black people are treated in South Africa.'

'Are you a black person from South Africa?' Mr Shag leaned in to me so that I could see where his nose had been flattened at the bridge. He had odd ears, too — warty and rumpled and swollen. I'd never seen anything like them. His eyes were a deep, clear blue and he was looking at me sternly.

'Are you?' he prompted.

'No.'

'The first lesson in life, young man, is to fight your own battles. Keep your nose out of other people's business. I'm sure your father tells you the same.'

I shrugged. 'He doesn't tell me hardly anything. My mother hardly lets me talk to him.'

Mr Shag was embarrassed. He sat upright again, made a deferential gesture towards my father. 'I'm sorry,' he said, 'I didn't mean to pry.'

'Quite all right,' said my father. 'Would you like to go down to the beach, Jasper?'

He wanted to get rid of me, I could tell. Mr Shag pointed to a gate that led down to the sand between two huge pohutukawa trees and I set off along the terrace in that direction. On my way I peered in all the windows. There was the living room, with its carpet and old-fashioned furniture, and there, in a part of the veranda that had been closed in to make a sunporch, was the servant. He was lying on his back on a narrow bench lifting weights. He must have forgotten about the coffee and lemonade. The room — not that I recognised it then for what it was — was a fully equipped gym with rowing machine, exercycle and tread-mill. It was all gleamy and shining new.

After a few minutes the servant sensed me there, sat up and gave me the fingers. I tore off, through the gate and up the rough, scrapy bark of a pohutukawa, where I waited for Richard to come and fetch me. It was ages since I'd been to the beach. Mum wouldn't take me any more because of the new discoveries about UV rays, and there's no reason to go in the winter. I breathed in the lovely sharp, salty smell of tree sap, and from the high-water mark on the beach the woolly brown stink of drying seaweed, thrown up in a recent storm. I lay along a bough, my cheek on the silvery bark, the grey sand below blurring with tears. Why didn't my father tell me to only fight my own battles? Why didn't he give me advice on what to do? My stomach felt raw and uncomfortable from the night before and I thought I might spew again. A few experimental dribbles of spit fell in long sinewy strands to the orange and red leaves and fag-ends on the sand below.

'Jasper?' It wasn't my father, although when I looked down into the upturned face it could have been. Mr Shag and my father were about the same height and they had similar eyes with heavy lids and dark eyebrows. Mr Shag's hair had more grey in it though, because he was older. Dad's hair was silvery at the temples and he wore it longer, curling around his ears. 'Your father's making a telephone call. Do you want to come back now?'

'No.'

'Why not?'

'Did you know he's going to live in Sydney?'

'Who? Your father?'

I nodded and the bark grazed my cheek, making my eyes water again.

'Come down and we'll go for a walk along the beach.'

Even now, when I remember him saying that, I get a warm, seeping feeling in all my veins. This handsome, rich, famous and kindly man took an interest in me. It was the beginning of a friendship that sustained and nurtured me for three and a half years.

We walked along the hard sand towards the St Leonard's end of the beach, and when the wind blew Mr Shag's hat off I ran after it, and when I shivered from the cold he gave me his jersey to wear. It hung down past my knees. As we walked I told him all about Lena and Scottie, and how I hated school, and how I did wood carving. I had enough nous not to tell him about my dope smoking. He didn't bat an eyelid about Mum and Scottie, though — he even told me I was lucky to have what amounted to two mothers.

'But don't let them push you around, son,' he said. 'Men are different to women — always have been, always will be. There's a fashion at the moment to try and make us all the same. Stupid and dangerous in my opinion. What sport do you play?'

'Nothing,' I said.

'What would you like to play?'

'They'd never let me play rugby,' I told him.

'No. I don't imagine they would. Athletics. How about joining an athletics club?'

I remember nodding eagerly, the salt spray tangy on my lips and the wind blowing at us from the other side now as we walked back towards his house. Dad was still on the phone, arguing with someone, so Mr Shag took me into his study and sat at his desk. While he was busy I looked at all the books — lots of them were about wars in different countries, and different kinds of weapons and guns. There was a book called *The People of Kau*, with photographs of tribal people nearly in the nuddy. There were big heavy dictionaries and books of maps. One whole wall of shelves was full of Mr Shag's own books, translated into English, French, Spanish, German and other languages I'd never heard of. I started counting the different versions of the same book and had got up to sixteen when he interrupted me by putting a letter into my hand.

'You should read this before I seal it up.' It was written in his round, rolling script.

'I can't read running writing — only printing.'

He stared at me for a moment, shook his head. 'All right,' he said eventually. 'I'll read it to you,' and he began:

> Dear Lena,
> This morning I made the acquaintance of your son,
> which I very much enjoyed. I would like to make him
> a gift of membership to the Central Suburbs Athletics
> Club. Enclosed is a cheque for his joining fee and first-
> year sub. I should think they will be taking
> enrolments in the spring.
>   I do hope my offer does not cause you any unin-
> tended embarrassment. It has been a pleasure talking
> to Jasper.
> Yours faithfully
> H.G. Shag

'It sounds kind of English,' I said when he'd finished.

'Formal, you mean,' said Mr Shag, severely. He put the envelope in my hand. 'Don't lose it.'

For the rest of the day I only wanted to talk about my benefactor and new friend. I hammered at Richard, who could tell me very little except about Mr Shag's moments of rugby prowess and the titles of his books.

'He's a very private man,' he said. 'He likes it that way.'

'I wish he was my father,' I said while we ate fish and chips for lunch on North Head. 'He would be a neat dad. I wish he was my dad. Has he got kids?'

'I don't know,' said Richard. 'I told you, he doesn't answer questions like that.'

'He'd answer me if I asked him. He's my friend. I wish he was my dad. Do you think I could go and visit him?'

Under its usual five o'clock shadow Dad's face, blue from the cold, hardened. He lit a cigarette and inhaled deeply, into his capacious stomach. 'No,' he said, 'that's not a good idea.' The wind whipped around us in the open car; a few keen yachts lurched and flew in the gulf below. 'You don't want to make a nuisance of yourself.'

'Will you take me?'

'One day, maybe,' my father lied. After a moment he chucked away his butt. 'I needed that. Tell you one thing about your hero — he's a health fanatic. Decaf coffee and he won't let you smoke around him.'

After the fish and chips we went to the movies — can't remember what we saw — and in the car outside my house he gave me my present. It was a Swiss Army knife — a real one with a pig-stabber and little scissors, a magnifying glass and three blades. I wanted to tell Damian about it and I could have. I could have rung his place, pretending I wanted to talk to his little brother. But I had a feeling he wouldn't approve — a present from an All Black and a knife from my father — they would have no currency with a right-on boy like Dam. I didn't want to spoil my pleasure. That night I slept with both presents under my pillow, without showing Lena or Scottie. They were all the more precious for being secret and I felt clean and pure in my resolve: no more filching from Dorothy Gilmore and no more fighting other people's battles. As I drifted off to sleep I even planned to change my name to Jasper Shag — and I have of course, subsequently, on a number of occasions.

My hand aches and I'm starving. It's all the food that's come into it — the crayfish, the greasies on North Head with the old man. I've always had a weakness for the old kai moana — even on the long hauls in

125

yachts out to make the pick-ups I'd cast a line over and fry up the catch for Damian and whoever else was with us. Even the fucking plain-clothes D who was with us on the last run, he got a taste for my genius for fish, the catching and the cooking of. I curl my right hand into a fist and push it into my growling stomach. It's all because of Howard Shag that I have this body that people cream their jeans over. Lena let me join the athletics club and I kept it up for a few years until I discovered gyms, which I liked better. She and Scottie were pissed off with me for telling Richard about the party — he wrote something in *Truth*, about it, the same day's edition that had the interview with Mr Shag. It was on the second page, all about how anti-tour people let kids drink and take drugs, and how they were so rotten with white guilt they indulged in kind of apartheid themselves when it came to sharing out a crayfish.

'How does he know this?' Lena yelled at me. 'He makes us look like fools!'

'I fight my own battles,' I told her, but I wrote to Richard in Sydney and told him how mad she was with him. He sent me a card with Darth Vader on it. Inside he'd written 'May the Force be with you.'

I'm drifting off to sleep, my back against the wall, when voices and footsteps wake me and the door opens. It's two screws — a fat ugly one and a fatter, uglier one — and Franca, who looks like an angel beside them — she looks like Uma Thurman. The three of them stand there, horrified, whether by the corner I've been forced to use as a urinal or by my life story — my neat, ordered printing on the walls — I can't tell.

They take me away immediately, Franca and the screws, march me towards my cell, and as much as I yell and plead for Franca to go back and read it all, that it's all for her, she pretends to be deaf to me. On the way we are passed by a prisoner with a bucket.

1985

It was dawn and he was alive. He knew these two conditions of his existence as if they were one, homogeneous and interchangeable. A chink of grey pearly light penetrated the membrane of fine leaves above him, illuminating the fair hairs on his arm, just beyond his open eye. It was the arm that cushioned his aching, pummelled head; the other was crooked, held in close to his naked chest, the soft white inner skin of it raw with pain and sending to his nostrils in waves, with each pulse of his blood, the stink of cooked meat, of his own singed flesh.

He was cold; he curled onto his side. They must have untied him before they left. Would he die, still? Why had the women taken away the dressing-gown cord and the insulating wire? They must've thought they had finished him off.

A flash of white slipped through the bushes in the gloom, at the edge of his vision, and he thought for a moment they'd come back. Adrenalin surged through his body — potent, too rich a chemical brew

— and he felt his sight blacken, his heart seize and grab, but it was only a cat, intent on an early morning hunt for baby coots and ducklings. Or were they grown now? It was February, nearly March. Later he would think how much worse it could have been if had been winter — how they could have succeeded, those women, in what he had to believe was their objective. He could have died from exposure and shock, breathing his last in the dark cold hours before sunrise.

Wriggling, he extended his lower leg until the knee was straight, then thought better of that and tried instead to rock over, the tender rim of his hip pinching and grazing on the hard twiggy ground, until at last he achieved a position on all fours, his legs splayed away from his balls which were swollen and blue, like alien life forms ballooning out from the fork in his body. They didn't belong to him, surely; he dropped a hand to investigate, but the idea of contact was abhorrent, horrifying — even though the centre of the pain was much higher, in his abdomen, a steady, polar roar as if he'd been frozen to the core and had melted only now at his extremities.

Gingerly he drew that enquiring hand back and examined on his other arm, in the half light, the brutal calligraphy of the woman in the balaclava. There was the 'R', the formation of which he had witnessed, then an 'A'. He remembered then how the first diagonal of that letter had knifed across the blue veins in the crook of his arm and how he had bellowed through his gag, struggled with every last remnant of his strength. To quieten him, one of them — he supposed it was the blonde one — kicked him three times with her heavy boots: twice in the balls and once in the head and mercifully, at long last — it might have come earlier to a weaker man — he slid into unconsciousness.

How many hours ago that was he didn't know, or how long they had gone on torturing his limp and unresponsive body. On all fours he looked, through the one eye that would still open and then only to a slit, at all the parts of himself that he could see. They'd continued with the cigarette, completed the 'A,' and executed a 'P'.

'RAP,' he repeated to himself and wondered if they were a vigilante gang, if this was their collective name. Rap. The Rap Girls. Midway on his forearm there was a single vertical line, an 'I'. RAPI . . .

RAPIST. That's what they were writing on his arm, that was their accusation. The final two letters were missing, something must have interrupted them, or maybe one of the women themselves — the one with the sweet voice that he heard only once, maybe she'd pleaded clemency on his behalf. Or the one who'd provided the scarf, which even now left a floral taste amid the blood in his mouth. It was a perfume that reminded him of the islands: hibiscus, or frangipani.

His head was falling, it was on its way to the ground; his forehead smacked into the fine, powdery dirt and a tree root opened the skin above his eyebrow. The gathering black was sweeping in towards him again — not that he welcomed it, not this time. His last thoughts, just before he fainted, were about how his arse was in the air and how he was naked, and how the women would come back and find him this way.

Madagascar, or Maddie, as her keeper had got into the habit of calling her, very much enjoyed her dawn walks around the park. Picking up each of her four round feet in the delicate and ponderous manner of elephants, she would convey herself out of the lower zoo gate and around the lake on the asphalt path. The little wooden bridges Murray avoided. Although they were sturdily built, he considered they may not support an adolescent Indian elephant of just over one tonne. Maddie seemed to understand this, somewhere in the globe of her vast pachy-derm skull, so her human devotee was surprised when, on this particular morning, she refused to advance any further on her usual route. Paused at the mouth of one of the bridges she swung her head and flapped her ears, an agitated expression in her pretty, long-lashed eye. Murray touched her once on the flank with his rod, which was usually enough to persuade her.

'Walk on,' he said, but Maddie responded by moving instead onto the grass at the side of the bridge and parting the ti-tree with her gentle grey trunk. The first world Maddie had known was the concrete environs of a zoo in Madagascar, so it wasn't a long-ago memory of shifting tree trunks in Burma or Thailand that motivated her. The keeper hesitated — did she want to forage? She might have smelt a banana skin or a peach stone, he thought, or some other discarded article that would not be good for her health. He came level with the waffling end of her trunk and together they pushed the flimsy trees apart.

On the ground at their feet was a dressing gown. A very nice one, too: purple silk. Its cord lay beside it, not far off. The keeper picked them up and turned to take them out into the brighter light to examine them for tears and stains, but the elephant blew lightly through her trunk — a warm whooshing with the scent of hay — and pushed her shoulder against him.

'Maddie,' he said warningly, 'back!'

Heavily the elephant leaned, and heavier still, until the keeper knew she wanted him to turn around. She took another step, weighty and inexorable, and the keeper was obedient to it, turning back and taking three steps through the low trees, pushing into a tiny clearing — where he gave out a yelp of shock at the condition of the body on the ground. It was in the most peculiar of positions, mooning the grove, the head twisted unnaturally to one side. Kneeling behind the head, Murray held two fingers to the man's throat and felt his pulse, steady and strong. He wasn't dead then, only unconscious.

FRANCA

Ink

She went with the guards to Jasper's cell to make sure he would not require sedation — or rather, that if he did she would be there, with her leather doctor's bag clasped in one hand. Once he'd given up on trying to explain his graffiti's pertinence to her understanding of him, Jasper went quietly into his tiny room, his shoulders slumped with defeat. Immediately the door was closed Franca, escorted by only one of the officers, hurried as fast as her yellow high heels would allow her to the administration block and the superintendent's office. There was a reek of stale cigarette smoke and the dry, soapy smell of instant coffee.

'Superintendent's in a meeting,' interrupted the clerk when she was halfway through her story. 'We've got nothing here about a Gilmore coming back from Ward D.' He wheeled his chair closer to the screen. 'Nothing about a Gilmore at all.'

'But he did,' said Franca, 'He came down with Dr Stambach.'

'According to our records he didn't. Anything else?'

'Yes. Interview Room 12 needs cleaning. He had no access to a toilet.'

'Believe me, sweetheart, even when they have got one they don't use it half the time.' He wasn't smiling. 'I'll get it seen to.'

'Could you ask them to leave the walls?' asked Franca.

'The walls?'

'He wrote on them. He wants me to read it —'

'If you'd kept him in the hospital then you could do that if you wanted. But not here. Graffiti's got to be cleaned off.'

'At least let me read it and take notes.'

'Take *notes*? How much did he write?'

'Enough for it to be useful to me.'

The officer shrugged, a gesture of someone whom nothing could amaze — and who wasn't going to go out of his way.

'I'll make the phone call for the cleaner — if you're quick you'll get there before him. But you'll need to speak to the superintendent about this and he's in a meeting.' He picked up a phone, punched in a short internal number.

'I'll come back later, then.'

Rage was a primal motivational emotion, Franca believed, like fear, and it had no place in her psyche. From the time she was seventeen until her mid-twenties rage had governed and fuelled her every waking moment and often her dreaming ones. There was no one moment that she remembered it going away: it was a slow path to tranquillity brought about not by a lover, or a friend, or even Nònna. It was revenge. She would take it, finally, effectively, by being happy, by not giving the perpetrator the unknown satisfaction of ruining the rest of her life. Life was too short, she had realised at about twenty-five, to ruin it by staying caught in one disastrous moment. She had bid goodbye to rage and fear, she hoped for ever.

So when she stepped outside into the corridor she was surprised, horrified even, at how quickly anger blew up in her. It was a tumour, a shining wen, pushing hard at its poisonous, encircling membrane. It threatened to tear, to spill, explode. The officer who had escorted her down from the cells had vanished. She could not go back to Jasper on her own. Behind her the door to the superintendent's office opened and closed — there was the clerk, locking it, and regarding Franca warily.

'You still here?' he asked. 'Office is closed now — twenty minutes,' and without waiting for a response he hurried off along the polished floor towards the main entrance. The interview room walls would be cleaned off if she didn't hurry, she thought, and steeled herself: she'd go back, prison officer or no prison officer. She set off, retraced her footsteps — or had she? She found herself after several turns at a locked door with no guard attending it. She felt desperately disorientated now — the remand cell that contained Jasper was directly overhead, surely. Or was it? She hadn't watched her escort when he'd operated the buttons on the descending lift. She turned back again, passed the superintendent's office, still closed, and headed outside, across the carpark and into the concrete alleyway that led to the back entrance of the hospital.

Her colleague was in his office writing up case notes and answered Franca's tentative knock with a snappy 'What?' that almost made her turn back yet again. What in God's name is the matter with me today? she wondered. I'm an exposed nerve. She heard footsteps on the other side, the door was flung open and there was Stambach, welcoming her with an expansive, yellow-toothed grin.

'Franca! Good to see you!' He waved her in, held out a chair for her and opened his window an institutional few centimetres for the egress of his cigarette smoke. As Franca told him of what had greeted her that morning in the interview room, only an hour or so ago, Stambach moved things around on his desk, saved the document he'd been working on on his computer and raked his stained and agitated fingers through his hair.

'Deplorable! Unbelievable!' he said when she'd finished.

'Yes. I need to see him now.'

'We should have kept him here. I'll ring the superintendent and do my best to —'

'No, don't bring Jasper back here, please. He hates it here, even more than he hates Remand. His whole childhood was on the walls, he told me he'd —'

'But there has been no opportunity to read it?'

Franca shook her head.

'Come on, then.' Stambach stood, shrugged on his jacket. Behind him the window was glossed with fine rain, the rectilinear featureless remand block, clumped together with other parts of the jail, varying intensities of grey against grey against grey. 'We'll go together.'

They went first to the interview room, which reeked of disinfectant. The smell met them as they came up the corridor, as well as the sound of two voices. There were three men in the room, one of them a prisoner, who knelt with a bucket and scrubbing brush, the water turned blue with ink. All Jasper's words, gone for ever, Franca mourned. The other two men were standing close to the wall near the last column of writing that remained. One of them, a guard, carried a camera.

'My colleague, Dr Todisco,' Stambach announced to their backs. 'Franca, this is Deputy Superintendent Cooper and — sorry, mate, I don't know you.'

The deputy flicked his fingers in the photographer's direction as if his name didn't matter and turned on Stambach. He was a little man, balding uncomfortably in the lampshade style, one side-lock grown long enough to flick over the top of his skull and approximate a full head of hair. Knife-edge creases ridged his trousers, his regulation boots had a mirror shine. Below his luxuriant russet moustache the thin-lipped mouth was spitting.

'This is appalling! The superintendent will want an enquiry and if Justice Action hear of it we're all in the shit. How was he forgotten about? It's your fault, meddling where you're not wanted.'

Stambach crossed his arms and smiled tolerantly.

'Before we get on to apportioning blame,' he said, 'May we ascertain that you have preserved the prisoner's writing on film?' This question was addressed to the guard with the camera, who nodded.

'It's our evidence of damage to prison property,' hissed Cooper. 'Nothing to do with you.'

'I'll sort it out with your superior,' said Stambach, implacable.

'Excuse me,' said Franca, moving closer to what remained of

Jasper's work: *'Where'd you get that from?' one of them asked. She was one of the younger ones —,*

Cooper pushed in between her and the wall.

'I've got special visiting rights to Gilmore,' she said tersely, side-stepping him.

'Gilmore?' Cooper's high voice squawked into its piercing upper range. 'Gil-more?' He drew the word out, looking at this so-called doctor pityingly, this ageing dolly-bird, who'd gone back to studying the wall: *She had a man's suit on, with a black beret and was smoking a long, thin cigar —*

Cooper went on, 'Jeez, you shrinks know nothing. His name isn't Gilmore. That's just an alias he gave when he was arrested. His name's Shag. Maybe that's why he fancies himself as a writer. Thinks he's the real one.'

Franca took a step away from the wall. The tiny, neat print on it blurred and leapt and she brought her hand up to her mouth. It wasn't possible. His son? Shag's son? She took another step, her ankle twisting on its elegant heel, her body urging flight.

'Thank you for that,' said Stambach coolly. 'Please don't allow us to waste any more of your time.'

Franca felt suddenly dizzy, aware that she was swallowing frantically, struggling for breath. You're being stupid, she told herself severely. Control yourself. It's not as if you haven't heard the name again, or seen it — in every bloody bookshop, every airport, website, newspapers, magazines . . . She found herself at the door, facing out into the corridor, and Stambach was beside her, offering her his arm. Gratefully she took it, her ankle burning — though so far away, over a distant horizon. She felt immensely tall, thin, stretched, as fragile as a charred twig.

Once they were out in the open air she chanced a look up into Stambach's face and he was looking at her kindly, quizzically.

'I don't suppose you'd like to tell me what's up?' he asked when they reached her car. 'Was it something you read on the wall?' She shook her head in answer to both questions and lifted her face to the sky. It had stopped raining. The air smelt of wet concrete, car fumes and a hint of the sea from the other side of the correction complex.

Oh, how pathetic she was! She was hot with embarrassment. She found the keys. 'Do you think his name really is Shag? Or is that another alias?'

'Who knows?' said Stambach, lighting a cigarette and dragging hard on it. 'It's not a name you'd choose, is it? Given its secondary meaning, I mean.' He almost sniggered.

'Maybe it's a common name in New Zealand.' Franca concentrated on keeping her voice level, calm, but Stambach was not to be fooled.

'I don't think so. Look, what is this, Franca? Do you want to forget about this chap? D'you really need him for your paper or not?'

Sinking into the driver's seat she slipped her shoes off. The twisted ankle had begun to swell already.

'Part of your initial enthusiasm, you might remember,' Stambach went on, 'was due to the fact that you thought he was Maori. He's not —'

'He might be,' interrupted Franca. 'He lies about his name. He could easily be Maori, pretending to be an Italian. He might have found a Latin ancestry more advantageous in Sydney than a Polynesian one. More fashionable.'

'And furthermore,' Stambach continued as if she had not spoken, 'he's not suicidal. We know that. I suggest you drop him — it's all got very problematic. After this graffiti episode the super's not going to be keen on you having ongoing contact with him anyway.'

'Why not?' Franca asked, rolling her keys in her hand.

'Oh, come on. They'll be looking for a scapegoat, someone to hang it all on, and it'll be you — the pointy-headed outsider.' He dropped his cigarette and stood on it. 'The fact that the computers crashed on the day of his arrest, that the super gave permission for him to return to Remand — all that won't matter. You know what goes on in a prison this size.'

'Okay.' Franca clicked her long fingernails on the steering wheel. They were mauve-coloured today, noted Stambach, the colour of bad circulation. 'Okay. I'll drop him. Easier all round, considering.' She felt abandoned by Stambach and resented him for it. She turned the key in the ignition and reached for the door but he closed it for her. Usually she found his old-European manners charming but today they seemed insulting, infantilising.

'Goodbye, Gregor,' she said through the glass of the closed window and accelerated, her back wheels splattering greasy water over the shins of the doctor's trousers.

Driving was agony, as was the walk from her basement carpark to the lift. Inside her apartment she gritted her teeth for long enough to assemble on the coffee table beside the sofa ice, scotch, a glass and a plastic bag. She spent the afternoon there, gazing out at the seeping sky over the towers of the CBD and Darling Harbour, her ankle packed and her mind numbed by the medicinal doses of whisky. She wished she believed in fate, or God, or Jung, or any superstition at all that supported the idea of signs, or weighty coincidence. Then she could accept that Jasper had been sent to her, that he had entered her life like a pawn on some celestial chessboard. She could try to unravel him; she would obey a cosmic order to search for clues, to finish off unfinished business.

Shag. The glass lifted to her lips and the scotch slipped between them to stop her repeating it to herself, the small word. A consonantal digraph, a long 'a', a glottal stop. A crested cormorant, strong tobacco, thick carpet and two men. The latest man new, strange, mysterious; the other from twenty years ago, the one everyone knows, the pulp writer — the Common Shag. She giggled, a little drunkenly, and rearranged her bag of ice.

At four o'clock it was dark enough to reach for the lamp beside her.

This is a fucking consulting room, she muttered thickly, seeing her apartment through new eyes. You live in a fucking hospital. All this white and grey and black. New eyes? Whose eyes? Jasper's eyes? She flicked on the lamp and gazed around, excited, the way she'd felt as a child in Broken Hill when new games would occur to her — different identities to try out as she played at being a grown woman in her mother's kitchen. How would he see this room?

She pictured him coming in the door, walking in his heavy-shouldered way to the sliding glass wall that led out onto the balcony. Bracing his firm, shapely legs, the muscles of his buttocks tight, he'd put his hands on his narrow hips and look out over the harbour. He'd like the view. 'You can see the bridge!' he might say. The value of her furniture, the Sidney Nolan painting, the Brett Whitely heads, the designer lamps — that would all be lost on him. She would have to educate him, teach him the finer points of living, how to dress. She took another mouthful of whisky and removed him from his prison greens, re-clad him in a navy blue Versace suit, leather shoes, a Rolex wristwatch . . . no. That wasn't right. It wouldn't be him; it wouldn't be Jasper. The game started to fade even though he was somehow dressed again, now in a black T-shirt, Levis and leather jacket, even though he was walking towards her as she lay on the sofa. No, she told herself again, don't imagine that, that he is kissing you, taking you in his arms — and the fading, the moment of paling indecision acted as a patch of oil and her imagination slipped, collided with memory — those clothes were what the first Shag wore when she met him in 1985. Franca hugged her drink, fought down the panic.

Think about it. You will think about it, just enough to remember him as clearly as you can. Does Jasper resemble him?

She closed her eyes, swam against the effects of the scotch and tried to conjure up that face.

It was no good. It was a hopeless exercise even then, all those years ago. The memory of his eyes and mouth would only come unbidden. If she consciously tried to summon him, recall only provided her with words: 'tall', 'dark', 'grey at the temples', 'youthful'. Or maybe that latter perception had been formed by a snippet of an ABC radio interview she'd heard soon after it happened. Affecting a cultured, old-fashioned voice Shag had told the interviewer he'd just celebrated his forty-seventh birthday. To Franca, only two weeks earlier, he'd seemed to be in his late thirties — at the most. As soon as the interviewer mentioned the writer's name she'd turned the radio off and sat shaking over her textbooks. She was studying for her first-year med school exams at the time, in her little room at Nònna's house. After that, for all the years since then, it hadn't been difficult to avoid hearing of him, really. Authors were rarely on television, especially ones like Shag who didn't win literary prizes. On her holidays Franca read Elias Cannetti, or Saul Bellow, or Rick Moody, Russell Banks, David Malouf: she wouldn't be seen dead reading crap like Shag.

There! She had his hands: square, attenuated fingers, small palms

— not what you'd expect in a man of his build and strength. And she was shivering again. After draining her glass she reached for the remote and turned on the television. The two soporifics had their desired effect and though she fought sleep — out of habit, as she always did — it overwhelmed her quickly and deeply, until the morning.

Tuesday. A consulting day. She'd woken blank, dry, her skull as empty as a scraped-out gourd and not knowing what day it was, which was frightening. She remembered just before she reached the wall calendar in the kitchen and as she stood gazing at it — a tasteful reproduction of twelve of Matisse's cut-outs — she also remembered her foot, which hurt possibly as much as her head did. It was only wrenched, though, not truly sprained, and as she self-diagnosed she had a vision of herself standing just like this, peering at a wall, in the prison yesterday. And last night, hadn't she pretended, at least, hadn't she fantasised — or at least imagined — that Jasper was here and that he was about to make love to her? The memory jolted her out of her hangover, bringing a sting of shame to her eyes. She was a tragic lonely heart if ever there were one, she thought, stepping hard on her sore foot as reached into a cupboard for muesli. At the chrome and glass breakfast bar she ate it as she always did with non-fat milk, and mineral water and a calcium tablet to follow. She showered, dressed and drove to her consulting rooms in North Sydney.

All morning she felt engulfed by a sense of loss. Between patients she sat motionless at her desk, foot throbbing, mind sluggish. There was a solution, of course. She could visit him during prison visiting hours as a friend, or acquaintance. Otherwise he would wonder why she had deserted him so suddenly: she had to consider his feelings in this. It was imperative that he did not guess at hers, which were delusional, of course. The man was a criminal, a drug-runner, quite possibly a depressive with violent tendencies. She was consumed with curiosity about him — yes, that's what it was. Curiosity. She had been in danger of mistaking it for attraction. It was only that she wanted to know his origins, the narrative of his life.

At lunchtime she discovered she was starving so she took herself to her favourite restaurant, a small vegetarian shop-front nearby. Its internal walls were painted a lurid green, bright enough to beckon her hangover's return. Soft, pearly light refracted off the low grey clouds and intensified the colour, made it more luminous. She put on her sunglasses and addressed herself to the dairy-free carrot soup, bread and salad. The plethora of restaurants in North Sydney meant that often she had the place to herself but today there was another woman there, one who had a nest of boutique bags gathered around her smooth, tanned legs. Winter clothes, possibly, thought Franca, as the woman was dressed for summer, except for a fine, hot pink woollen pashmina draped around her slender shoulders. She had smiled at her when Franca came in, a forkful of frothy green leaves halfway to her mouth. She was carefully made up, her blow-waved hair bright brown with new dye, and Franca envied her for a moment, seeing how pampered she was — a man's woman — but envy turned quickly to disparagement. When the woman had finished her spartan lunch she lifted a jangly gold wrist to her ear, a tiny cellphone cupped in her jewelled hand, and engaged in conversation with someone called Richard, evidently her keeper. Franca pictured him: a harassed executive high in one of the surrounding towers, a creature compelled by his gender and social conditioning to fritter his life away in the accretion of money, money that his wife made it her business to spend. Throughout the conversation the woman's voice grew lower, descending from purr to hiss and both registers in a cultured New Zealand accent. I'm surrounded by them, thought Franca. By comparison the man's voice grew louder, a tinny squeak emitting from the tiny phone. The call reached a possible denouement.

'Richard!' whispered the woman, sibilant, slightly threatening. 'That's enough! You've told me enough. I don't want to know any more.' But she listened again attentively, an olive-skinned furrow forming in her gleaming brow.

It's a good facelift, thought Franca. In a few years etiquette will have changed enough for women to ask one another the question: 'Could I have his name, darling? Wonderful job.' Franca had seen some shockers.

'Don't watch any more of it, then . . . Have you been drinking? Turn it off . . . Whatever you like. I'll be back by —' but it seemed the man had rung off. Turning the phone to face her, Dior glasses perched on the end of her nose, the woman searched for the off button. A new purchase perhaps, guessed Franca. The woman glanced across at her, acknowledging that she had overheard her part of the conversation. She gave her a wry smile and just a hint of a roll of the eyes: maybe her lids were pulled too tight to allow a full rotation. Sometimes that happened. One of Franca's private patients, after her seventh lift, had been driven to the limits of her sanity by not being able to close her eyes to sleep.

Franca pretended she had not seen and stood sharply to pay her bill at the counter. She would not collude with females who sacrificed independence for the triumph of the malls. Determinedly, she limped back to her rooms in time to make a phone call of her own before the next appointment. As she returned the phone to her desk it seemed, just for a moment or so, that there was a whirring thud in the dull air-conditioned atmosphere that surrounded her, and then another — the sound of pieces of machinery falling back into place. It was a ghostly sound, far off: a low, subterranean vibration.

Roadworks, thought Franca. Either that or I'm writing my own score.

The African savannah of her screen-saver gave way to notes for the next patient — a young woman who had so fervently embraced the new fashion of neck-rings she had required surgery to mend a snapped vertebra. Depression had ensued — she was the classic fashion victim: vain and stupid. Franca wouldn't hold it against her, not in the confines of her professional life. The world seemed swollen with kindness and possibilities, suddenly, healed by the therapeutic dose of a single phone call. She was even whistling quietly, though her teeth, a pure and tuneless melody of contentment and hope.

MELODY

Enter Godfrey

Maybe, because of the unseasonable warmth, Paulie and Zinnia have forgotten it's winter. It's not the right time of year to conduct a ceremony in the Parnell Rose Gardens. The canes are bare but for tiny budding leaves, all lined up in regimental rows. At least it's not raining: the sky is pale and clear, the same shade of blue as —

I nearly think it, but I stop myself in time. Howard's eyes. Do I think about him too much? I wonder. Are my feelings for him erroneous, misplaced? I begin to feel like a character in a French film, falling in love with a man old enough to be my grandfather.

At the bottom of the hill at Judges Bay I find a park. The pocket of sea corseted by the railway bridge and Tamaki Drive reflects the silver of the sky, with tiny footbound waves hobbling at the shelly shore. If Howard would leave his house I could have brought him with me today. We could be walking together up this path, under the huge old pohutukawas towards the crest of the hill and the Nancy Steen

142

Memorial Garden, where the family will gather for the baby's Naming Ceremony and a picnic afterwards. My heart pangs slightly at his absence. He is my constant companion. Even when I am not with him I'm still surrounded by his life, absorbed in all its detail. A biographer knows more of her subject, the whole complex map of his life, than any lover could.

This morning in bed I finished *Black Orbit*, Howard's last book, and surprised myself by liking it very much. I can see why it was so successful — it's a tough, twisting yarn, simply and baldly told with a no-bullshit tone. The story is of a father and son returning to the north of Italy, where the father fought in the Italian Campaign in the Second World War. After a chance encounter with a Russian mafioso on a train they become his guest in his luxurious villa in Menton, across the border in the south of France. The Russian has, of course, a beautiful daughter, who becomes the lover of both the father and the son. With maturity and skill Howard weaves the love story — and it is a love story, not only sexual but paternal and filial as well — with a tale of corruption, of drug money, lawlessness and deception. It's his best book, I think. I also think, against my will, that Howard must have been a consummate lover in his time. The erotic passages surge with sensuality and longing: he knows what women like. More than that — he knows what women need. When I had finished it I turned back to the recto leaf and puzzled over the dedication: For Jasper. Who was he, I wonder again, as the path branches off towards the Memorial Garden. Howard has never mentioned him.

Wafting in a long lilac and turquoise dress Zinnia is standing under the archway of the walled garden. A small white bundle curves over her shoulder. She lets me stand behind her to gaze into my niece's face, which is cross looking and screwed up against the light. The baby has a tiny head. Anyone who didn't know Paulie could suspect micro-cephalia, but I suppose a small head has its upside: it made for an easier birth. Paulie himself, bestower of the titchy skull, is talking to a group of other pinheads who have arrayed themselves along a wooden bench — his mother and sisters.

'Are you letting the secret out yet?' I ask my twin.

'What secret?'

'What you're calling her.' I go to tickle the baby under the chin and Zin moves sideways.

'Don't!' she says. 'You'll have germs on your fingers.'

'For God's sake, Zinnia. Don't be too precious.'

'I can't be too precious. Not about Zanipula.'

'Who?'

'It's a . . . what do you call it? An anagram of our names. Zanipula. We made it up.'

'Shit,' I say inadvertently.

'Don't you like it?' Zinnia swivels to face me, the baby's head lolling alarmingly.

'Yes, it's lovely,' I tell her. 'What is it again?'

'Zanipula. One "n".'

'Zanipula. Very original.' We look at each other, me smiling desperately, she searching for signs of disapproval.

'What about middle names?' I ask her. 'Melody's a nice name.'

'They're Maori, of course,' says Zinnia airily. 'Names that belong to the land.'

'Oh, there are some lovely Maori names,' I gush. 'Which ones did you pick?'

'I didn't pick them!' Zinnia is severe, as if I should already know this. 'They were chosen for her.'

'Oh. Right. What are they?'

Zinnia opens her mouth and closes it again. An expression of extreme panic crosses her face. 'Zanipula Roi . . .' she tries. 'Roi. Ho. He . . . Ih . . . Paulie! Paulie!'

Paulie abandons his mother mid-sentence, who looks after him with a scowl as he rushes to Zin's side. 'What's wrong? Is she crying? I'm sorry, I didn't hear, I was —'

I have never heard Paulie make such a long speech.

'Shut up,' says Zinnia. She whispers in his ear, then pulls back to stare into his face. 'Can you remember?' Paulie shakes his head. 'Oh no!' wails Zinnia. 'What are we going to do?'

'Shshsh.' Paulie takes the baby. 'It'll be all right. Don't worry, Zin . . .' But Zin's face is in his neck and she's sobbing loudly.

In a pair of faded orange beach shorts and his best Save the Whales

T-shirt, Dad is bending over to examine the label on a yellow rose.

'Look at this, Helen,' he's saying to my mother, who stands staring in an unfocused kind of way at the harbour below us. 'It's a Gold Bunny. Didn't we have a Gold Bunny in Ranfurly Road, before the Crash?'

'Hi, Dad,' I say, kissing him on his lowered cheek.

'Didn't we, Helen?' Dad persists, acknowledging me with a wave of his nearest hand. Mum remains transfixed. 'Look at her,' Dad says to me in an undertone. 'She doesn't take an interest in anything.'

'Yes she does. Don't you, Mum? She's looking at the harbour.'

'Do you know something?' Mum says slowly, looking at me now. 'I've decided to have all the amalgam taken out of my teeth. Just then, I decided that. That's what's causing it, Ray.'

'Do you think so, love?' Dad asks softly. He comes between us and touches her on the cheek.

'Causing what?' I ask. Neither of them replies.

'Who else is coming?' I ask Dad's back.

'Just family and a few friends,' says Dad. 'Zinnia wanted it small. She asked Poor Curtis but he said he wasn't up to it.'

'Who's that?' A tall Maori man all in white with a single long bone earring is walking down the wide path towards us from Gladstone Road. He has a beatific smile and silver hair frosting his temples.

'The celebrant, I think,' says Dad.

'No,' says Mum firmly, 'the celebrant is in the Memorial Garden — she's a little grey-haired Pakeha all in pink.' We watch Zinnia greet the Maori man with enormous relief. Impatiently she beckons to us and we go in to begin the ceremony.

By the time all the guests have arrived it's shoulder to shoulder in the tiny garden. Short as I am, I'm compelled to stand on one of the benches to get a view of the proceedings. The celebrant, Paulie, Zinnia and the tall Maori stand with their backs to the end wall, facing us. To their left, on the other side of the fountain after a ceremonial gap, stand Mum and Dad and Paulie's mother and sisters. All the flowers are white, there is a white shell path between the beds and a fountain tinkles.

Maybe a late incarnation as a celebrant is a popular career choice for retired primary school teachers, ones who previously had aspirations to be poets or priests. It is as if we are a group of mildly handicapped five-year-olds and she is explaining to us patiently, kindly, the most profound spiritual realities of human existence. Her tone rises and falls with rhythmic symmetry as she recites a poem of her own composition.

'For Zinlupa,' she begins, looking coyly at us over the frames of her pink lenses,

'Little one, you are blessed

oh yes,

blessed by having loving parents

who welcome you

who will care for you

all the days of their lives.

Zipilu — Zanipa — Zupilup —'

'Zanipula,' whispers Zinnia urgently.

'Yes, sorry dear,' the celebrant tilts her chin and goes on, triumphantly,

'Zanipaulie, you are luckier than most,

little parcel sent by cosmic post

to Paul and Zinnia now Paul and Zinnia didn't want any mention of God today,' she goes on seamlessly, leaving us groping for the final lines of the poem.

'But Matiu is going to say the Lord's Prayer in Maori.' Is the logic here that most of us won't understand it, so that makes it all right? Dad, dedicated atheist, looks as surprised as he would be if someone goosed his shorts from behind. Conflicting emotions race across his face, fighting for dominance, until in the end peaceful, worshipful acceptance wins.

The celebrant holds a hand out towards Matiu and steps backwards as he steps forward, head bowed. Most people likewise incline their heads. Paul and Zinnia gaze at Zanipula, who is rubbing hungry fists on her cheeks and making whimpering sounds.

'E to matou Matua i te rangi,' Matiu begins, 'Kia tapu tou ingoa. Kia tae mai tou rangatiratanga —'

He is joined by one other lone voice from the back, near the archway. It belongs to a big man in a suit, his black hair slicked back off his forehead and a gold tie-pin glittering at his throat. He must be six foot four at least, this man, praying in a soft, deep voice with his eyes closed.

'. . . engari whakaorangia matou i te kino. Amine.' The two men finish.

'What name do you give this child?' asks the celebrant then, though I'm not looking at her but at the stranger at the back. As he raises his head he sees me looking at him and winks one startling green eye in his dark face. By dint of standing on the bench, I'm the only one on his level. I smile at him and he looks suddenly reproving, nodding his head towards the continuing ceremony at the front, to which I return my attention. Matiu is passing Zinnia a piece of paper and she reads aloud, stumbling only slightly.

'Zanipula Ngaone Hohi Irihapeti Argyle.' She smiles with relief when she reaches the end. Argyle is our name and Dad looks delighted.

'Thank you all for coming to share this special time with Paul and Zinnia,' says the celebrant. 'They would like to invite you now to share picnic lunch with them.'

'Kia ora,' says Zinnia, and blushes.

Paulie's mother and Mum and Dad are busy spreading blankets on the grass and opening chilly-bins. Paulie pours me out a white styrofoam cup of Seaview, left over from Mum's Womb Burial. Guests mill around, drinking and talking. Under the archway Zinnia and Matiu stand in earnest conversation. In her customary position, draped over Zinnia's shoulder, Zanipula is like an oversize toga brooch. Zinnia is rummaging in her handbag, which hangs from her other shoulder. Maybe Matiu is helping her with the pronunciation of her daughter's names I think, lighting a cigarette down wind of her. But Zinnia is handing him a thin roll of red hundred-dollar bills. Matiu smiles, pocketing the money, and as Zinnia gestures towards the evolving picnic, he shakes his head. They bid farewell and part, Zinnia smiling broadly after him as he makes his way back to Gladstone Road.

'What was that for?' I ask, joining her.

'Consultancy fees. Mind your own business.' She rearranges Zanipula, who has slumped sideways.

'What for? Her name?'

'Yes.' Zinnia is prim, maternal. She rubs Zanipula's back.

'I thought he was a friend of yours!' I'm angry; a knot of rage forms in my empty stomach.

'It's got nothing to do with you,' snaps Zin.

'How did you find him? In the *Yellow Pages*?'

'Paulie knows him from the museum. Why're you so worked up about it?'

'Because it's stupid!'

'Oh! Stupid, is it? To give your child a beautiful Maori name?' She rears back, pink self-righteousness suffusing her cheeks. A breeze lifts the lowest corner of Zanipula's shawl and waves it like a white flag. 'You're a racialist, Melody.' Spinning in the red gravel on her high heels she stalks off, her swollen feet puffing around the buckles of her shoes.

I finish my fag, one last draw, under a Morton Bay fig. Zinnia has a point. Why am I so angry? I should be proud of her, I suppose, but instead I'm overwhelmed by the senseless, hollow trendiness of it. Or is it just that I don't understand her motives? It reeks of political correctness of the worst kind; it seems insincere. Maybe I'm giving the issue too much weight. Later I'll question Paulie, find out who this Matiu is, whether choosing names for Pakeha is his main trade, or just a sideline to a job at the museum.

'Hello,' says a man's voice behind me. 'You must've been standing on something before — thought you were taller.' It's the man who joined in the prayer. Good clean living shines from every pore: he looks disapprovingly at my cigarette, which I'm dropping to grind beneath my shoe.

'You'll have to give that up,' he says.

'Oh, I do everything bad,' I tell him. 'I smoke and have "racialist" thoughts. According to my sister.'

His thick black eyebrows rear towards his hair-line.

'Really? You're Melody, then? Zinnia's twin?' I nod while he looks from me to Zinnia and back to me again. He's thinking what everybody thinks when they find that out — you're not identical — but he doesn't say it. I'd like him for that alone, even if he weren't so gorgeous.

'Which one is your mother? That one?' He points at Helen and I nod again. Paulie is making his way over to them with the Seaview and a towering column of white cups.

'Who are you?' I ask. He doesn't fit with Zinnia and Paulie — he's not their type. The tie-pin, which I can make out this close, half a metre above my head, is a tiny golden football.

'Oh — sorry.' He smiles and there's a tooth, his left incisor, gold to match his tie-pin. 'I'm Scottie's brother, Godfrey Terrier.' He holds his hand out for me to shake. It's big, fleshy and warm; a musky after-shave zings in my nostrils. 'I've come to offer Scottie and Lena's apologies,' he continues. 'They couldn't get through to your parents last night.'

'No, Mum and Dad stayed with Zin in Howick,' I tell him. 'Why couldn't Lena and Scottie come?'

'Had to go to Sydney. In a hurry,' says Godfrey, accepting a foaming cup from Paulie. He tastes it and grimaces.

'What for?'

Godfrey shrugs his magnificent shoulders. 'Asked the same question. Scottie wouldn't say.'

'You must be a lot younger than her,' I observe.

'Yep — eighteen years. I'm her half-brother.'

'I never knew Scottie's name was Terrier. They all call her Scottie Dog.'

Godfrey laughs. 'Years ago she was going to change it by deed poll. But I don't think she ever got round to it.'

'Have you got the same mother?'

'Father. Dad married again late in life. He's a goer, Dad is.' He grins at me. 'Runs in the family.' I wonder if he's referring to himself or Scottie.

'Come and meet Mum, then,' I say, before my thoughts run too far in that direction, and lead him across the grass. Clustered around Zinnia and the baby on the rug, Paulie's sisters lean their heads together to whisper as we pass.

'Is that her boyfriend?' one of them says, loud enough for me to hear. Godfrey doesn't appear to — he doesn't even look in their direction, which, given that he seems to be a man with high standards of hygiene, is a good thing: among the chicken, bread and cheeses Zinnia is changing a nappy.

I introduce Godfrey to Mum and light another cigarette while they talk. Paulie appears just as I drain the cup to the bottom: he gives me a refill.

'Nice ceremony, Paulie,' I try. He nods his ferrety head and offers Godfrey another drink but he puts his left hand over the top of his cup and I see, with a sinking feeling, that not only does he have a golden tie-pin and tooth, but also a wedding ring, fat and broad, set with a tiny, flat-cut, trembling diamond.

'Do you live in Auckland?' asks Mum, made sociable by Seaview. 'You have very nice teeth.'

'Thank you,' says Godfrey. 'No, I live in Wellington. I'm up here on business. I was supposed to have dinner with Scottie last night but she'd forgotten. Lena was worried you'd be upset when she didn't show up today so they asked —'

'Wellington?' interrupts Mum. 'That's a shame. I was going to ask you who your dentist is.'

'Mum —' Zinnia is at Godfrey's elbow, a white plastic bag cupped in her hands. 'Is this normal? It's kind of green.'

Just as I perceive that it's not a plastic bag, but Zanipula's nappy, Godfrey steps backwards. No longer is his elbow at the nappy, but in it. He lifts his arm, horrified, and a mucoid, khaki web drips from his sleeve.

'Now look what you've done!' yelps Zinnia. 'You can't see the lumps in it any more! I wanted Mum to look at the lumps. You've squashed them!'

Godfrey looks as though he's going to be sick. His eyes protrude slightly, he swallows rapidly, holding his arm out with his face turned in the opposite direction — towards me.

'Come on — we'll find a tap.' I hand Mum my cup and take Godfrey by his nearest hand — which is forward of me, I know, but the man needs help. Past the archway and under the Morton Bay fig trees we go.

'There's one down at the bay,' I tell him.

'All the way down there?'

'It's not too far.' I point to the concrete loo block above the beach. As soon as Godfrey sights it he takes off down the steep slope, running, and I know without the slightest of doubts, watching him — the subtle hunching of his shoulders, the rolling, powerful gait of his pumping thighs — that he is, or was, a rugby player.

I reach the bottom of the hill long after he vanishes into the Men's and sit on the stone wall, dangling my feet above the winter's detritus collected above the tide-line — a red child's bucket, almost split in half; cigarette ends; McDonald's boxes; supermarket bags; a broken wine bottle. From behind me, in the Men's, comes the splash of running water and frantic scrubbing. But I don't feel frantic at all: it's not contagious. I feel deliciously calm — or is it just that I feel delicious? Or as if I'm on the brink of doing something delicious?

Out of the now cloud-flecked sky a helicopter comes in to land at Mechanics Bay, shining silver, a miracle. Behind it, across the channel at Devonport, an ancient frigate thrusts backwards from the naval dock. I can smell spring — even above the rubbish on the beach, the pungent mud of the receding tide. There is the smell of growth, of renewal. My mind fills with images from Northern Hemisphere Easter cards: fecund bunnies, amorous birds, nest-building, eggs and daffodils. The cheap champagne has gone to my head.

The tap shuts off and I hear the squeak and step of Godfrey's stylish shoes. Carrying his jacket he plonks beside me, the offending sleeve dripping. He spreads it out to dry.

'I've ruined it,' he says dolefully. 'I rubbed too hard.'

'Maybe you could get it dry-cleaned,' I suggest, then add, 'or get your wife to fix it.'

Godfrey laughs, one single peak of bitter hilarity. 'My wife!' He leaves it hanging. Does that mean the ring is ornamental, or that she's an idiot in the laundry?

'Quite nice down here,' he offers after a pause. 'Never been here before — don't know Auckland that well.'

'No?' Do people call you God for short? I want to ask. Instead I say, 'What do you do, for a living?'

'Manage a football team. You heard of the Wellington Wolves?'

'League?' I try to keep the disapproval out of my voice. I succeed.

'Yeah,' Godfrey says proudly. 'New last year and bloody good. This is their second season. You don't follow the league?'

'Not really. I'm a Union girl.'

'Ah.' A black-backed gull lands at the water's edge and picks with its yellow beak at a small brown mound. A dead fecund bunny, perhaps.

'And, um . . . you? Do you work at all?'

'Of course. I'm a writer,' I tell him. 'A biographer.'

'I thought you'd be something like that,' Godfrey says, surprisingly. 'You look brainy.'

'Do I?' I never buy glossy women's magazines, so my reading of them is limited to the back issues in my doctor's waiting room. His remark resonates in the tiny part of my mind that might hold a memory of an article on this problem. 'How to Strip for Your Man — Professionally!' is one I remember. That's not much use. 'How to Make Him Believe He's More Clever Than You Are'. 'What to Do if Your Brain is Too Big'. I can't recall any titles like that. Am I more clever than Godfrey? I decide not to worry about it.

From far away, somewhere over the Waitakeres, comes a roll of thunder. I tip my head back, aware as I do so that Godfrey is doing the very same thing. We have the same responses to natural phenomena, then. Above the hill the sky streams from the west with ragged black clouds: the sun is covered in an instant.

'It's going to rain,' Godfrey observes.

'My car is just here. Would you like a lift?' We're standing, brushing ourselves down. He picks up his jacket, gives it a good shake.

'Shouldn't you go back and help pack up the picnic?' he asks, with the same censorious expression he wore when I gazed at him for too long during the ceremony. Maybe he's a Mormon, or a Baptist or something. I don't know anything about Scottie and Foxie's family.

'What's that word mean? "Should"?' I ask him, with all the potent, amoral reasoning of our times. 'It's not part of my vocabulary.'

'You are a bad girl, then,' says Godfrey, 'You were telling the truth.' He's cast me now as someone I'm not. Actually, I could tell him, I'm bookish, judgemental, untravelled and lonely, and, aside from one devastating, damaging and finished relationship, practically a virgin. But I say nothing: my limited life experience and prodigious reading have taught me that men don't find that sort of woman attractive — particularly men like Godfrey.

'I'm hungry,' he says as he straps himself in beside me. 'We missed out on the picnic.' We zip up the steep road, circumnavigating the Rose Gardens. In the distance, through the now swirling rain, Zinnia's lilac and turquoise dress flaps under the shelter of a tree; Dad's orange shorts are a blur as he rushes about flinging food back into chilly-bins; in slow motion Mum folds a rug while the guests hurriedly depart around her for their cars.

'Looks as though they've got everything under control,' says Godfrey, relaxing into his seat. He was genuinely concerned, I realise. How sweet and old-fashioned.

On Godfrey's suggestion we go for yum-cha in a vast, steamy Chinese restaurant at the bottom of Victoria Street West. It's crowded, mainly with Asians in large family groups. They sit at vast circular tables: adults of two and three generations and immaculate, indulged children. Our table is by the window, overlooking the park, which is deserted. Some of the old oaks that rim the oval are speckled with new, pale green leaves. Yes, it really is spring; that primeval seasonal force is coursing and thrusting its way through the systems of all living creatures . . .

Jasmine tea and dumplings arrive. The tea is fine, of course, but how can I tell what the dumplings contain?

'Eat up,' says Godfrey, his lips glistening. I can't bring myself to tell him I'm a vegetarian. A man like Godfrey would think that vegetarian women lack passion, that their blood is thin. I peel a shiny white steamed creation and sniff its pink insides. Swine flesh. I take a deep-fried one between my chopsticks and lever apart its crispy envelope: shark.

'Don't tell me you don't eat meat!' says Godfrey. 'Why didn't you say so?'

'No — well — yes. I don't. But it's okay. I can have rice and —'

Godfrey beckons the waitress with the trolley and picks out, knowledgeably, a tiny plate of three brown lacy-cased ovoids.

'Taro,' he says, as they're placed before me. To oblige him I eat one, though it tastes of dead animal: everything does, even the rice. Godfrey eats everything, including chicken feet, nibbling around the tiny bones. It's a fascinating spectacle — his lips, teeth and tongue work nimbly, adeptly; he wields the chopsticks as though he were born to it. Maybe he was. We don't talk much. His eyes are heavy-lidded, his face dreamy, all his being devoted to the pleasure of eating. It reminds me of Howard, though Howard's rule of silent consumption seems grim and dour by comparison. Godfrey eats joyously, sensually, in a private, happy ritual. Quite suddenly I decide he doesn't have a wife. This man is used to eating alone.

'Come back to my place for coffee,' I say, as he swallows his last mouthful and wipes his lips. 'It won't be any good here.'

I appease my hunger with a plate of rennet-free cheese and biscuits, most of which Godfrey eats with his coffee. In the tiny rooms of my house he seems even bigger, as though my furniture were built for a different species. He seems to be aware of it himself, moving carefully in the narrow spaces.

'Howard Shag!' he says suddenly while I'm in the kitchen pouring myself a second cup. He comes to the door, holding my copy of *Tombolo*. 'I read this when I was a teenager. It's fantastic.'

'Yeah, I know.' I'm dying for a cigarette, but I won't have one.

'He was famous All Black in his time. Did you know that?'

'Yes I did.' I follow him out to the living room.

'Did somebody leave it here?' he asks suddenly.

'Pardon?'

'Well, look —' He's running his finger along the spines of the books on my shelf — Jane Smiley, Elizabeth Knox, Pat Barker, Germaine Greer, Katherine Mansfield, Barbara Kingsolver, Mary Doria Russell, Antonia Fraser. 'Chick-lit. Every single one.'

'No, I think —' I squeeze in beside him, search for a bloke. There must be one. Do I only ever get men out of the library?

'See?' he says triumphantly. 'It doesn't make sense, a girl like you reading Shag. He's a man's man.'

'In my bedroom,' I tell him, 'I have a whole stack of Shags.'

'Do you? Why?'

I shrug. 'Good bedtime reading.'

'Show me.' I lead the way. What would Howard think if he knew he was part of my seduction technique, such as it is?

Godfrey really isn't interested in the books. When I lean over to retrieve *Black Orbit* from the top of the pile on the other side he cups my buttocks with one hand, runs his other one down my inner thigh. I turn to him and his yum-cha lips are soft and tender on mine; the solid, yielding mass of his body bears me down onto the duvet.

One Shag leads to another, I think, blissfully, and we spend the rest of the day in bed.

RICHARD

The Fall

In Castlecrag Michaela parks the car at the bottom of the steep right-of-way and insists we walk up to the house. She thinks it will do me good, sober me up, though she knows better than to say so. Actually, considering my inebriated state, I've been relatively acquiescent. I dressed for dinner in the very nice clothes she'd bought me in North Sydney; I agreed to squire her to Dodo's.

Above us, through the trees, Dodo's expansive deck is lit up and peopled with guests, their voices rising above a recording of busy electronic jazz. The damp air smells of eucalyptus and wet earth, and something more appetising: garlic.

'This Dodo's a good cook, then?' I ask, panting a little at the incline. Penetrating and tasteful external lighting shines up the legs of palms and ferns and illuminates Michaela's pained expression.

'I have no idea,' she says, 'but I can guarantee her chef is.'

She's still cross with me, then. Usually she finds my naïveté at how the rich conduct their lives endearing; sometimes it earns me a kiss. Passing ahead of me she nods at the young man at the door who offers us a glass of champagne from a tray. A second later, at the bottom of the stairs inside the terracotta tile and limestone wall lobby, she grasps my arm, which makes the champagne slop over my fingers.

'You will behave yourself, Richard. Or I will never forgive you.' She lifts the hem of her long loose-weave skirt — though which I can see the shape of her pretty legs — and begins her ascent. Handbag that I am, I go behind her, forewarned and obedient until we emerge — our little convoy — into a large low-ceilinged and too brightly lit room. Female voices erupt like startled cockatoos.

'Mikie! How lovely to see you! We had no idea you were in Sydney! Dodo — you should have told us! What a superb surprise!'

Michaela is surrounded by them. They pluck at her dress, admire her earrings, her sandals — all bought in Paris a season ahead. The men in the room stand in circles, each clutching a glass filled from a long table that is attended by another young man in a white shirt and black trousers, clone of the one downstairs. The men look up at our entrance but go back to their conversations, shutting me out. They do not do as well in the neon light as their female companions, I observe. Gone are the days when middle-class women aged faster — though lived longer — than their husbands. The women get stretched and lifted while the men pop off with cancer and heart disease. I finish my champagne and request a glass of red from the young man.

'You do this for a living,' I ask him, 'or as a fill-in?' Very professionally he avoids my eye while he pours it and gestures for me to pick it up. 'Are you a student?' I try. Engineering, I think. Or zoology.

'We're from an agency, sir. For casual wait staff.' Wait staff. Australian American. It's loathsome. I repair to the deck, where Dodo — whichever one she is — has set up gas heaters on poles like enormous fiery mushrooms. Underneath one I sip my wine and after a moment a hot chemical smell rises from the warming shoulders of my new jacket. What is my son doing now? I wonder. Sitting on his narrow bed? Having a last cigarette before lights out? Any desire I had to visit him has ebbed away. It's farcical, I silently tell the half-moon, that you can shine on up there, fuzzy among the rainclouds, as if nothing has happened. This afternoon on the phone I'd started to tell Michaela how disturbing I'd found the video but she'd interrupted me.

'Turn it off,' she'd said.

'He's my son!' I'd yelled at her. That's the secret to her unrelenting optimism, of course: anything nasty and unpleasant must be turned off, ignored — and quickly — or you'll ruin your day and give yourself a wrinkle. I can see her through the glass, sparkling, laughing with her head back, showing her amalgam-free, newly capped teeth.

'Giles Muir,' says a voice at my shoulder. One of the grey-heads from inside has joined me, his hand out. He wears white trousers and blazer, with brass buttons and gold-striped epaulets.

'Richard Brunel,' I tell him, shaking his hand.

'You're —?' asks Giles.

'Richard —' I begin, before I realise he's not deaf. He wants my credentials.

'Journalist. Ex-*Truth*, ex-*Dominion*.'

'New Zealand papers, obviously, by your accent,' says ex-navy Giles, dismissing them. 'You must be here with Mikie.'

'You're a Pom, aren't you?' I ask him, broadening my accent further. Giles finds the idea absurd.

'Not at all, not at all! Australian born and bred — South Australian, actually. Adelaide.'

'Come on. You must have spent time in the UK to have a plum in your mouth like that.' I watch him over the rim of my glass. Childish, but I can't help it. Giles narrows his eyes at me.

'Do excuse me,' he says, and returns inside. Michaela, coming to meet him on his return, flashes me a shaft of pure antagonism and offers her cheek for a kiss. The old lech puts his hands on her shoulders and leaves them there. They're talking about me, of course: Mikie's bit of rough trade.

Dodo, who is a large, yellow-haired woman in an electric blue dress seemingly made of two vast rectangles of cloth sewn together with gaps for her arms and head, takes up a central position in the room. 'Welcome, everyone!' she says, hooting, genteel. 'Do come through to the dining room.' On cue two wait staff persons open a long concertina door that previously formed the wall behind the drinks table. Beyond, below an execrable modernist chandelier of frosted glass cubes, is a long white table already set with a cold entrée. The fifteen or so of us file through. Michaela, that good breeding showing again, waits at the brink for me to take her arm.

'You mustn't be rude to dear old Giles,' she whispers. 'He's just lost his wife.'

'Overboard?' I ask, before going on, sotto voce: 'He's a pompous old Tory shit.'

An expression of extreme distaste crosses Michael's face, though she leaves her arm in mine until Dodo directs her away. Dodo is placing us all at the table. I am to sit at a corner, Dodo at the head of the table on my left and Michaela opposite me. The Admiral is seated to her left and on my right I am joined by a new arrival, Elise. Tall, fair, forty-ish, elegant, a compulsive and unapologetic smoker, Elise is French. She speaks loudly in heavily accented English, handing her silk jacket to one of the black-trousered ones who stands for a moment with it in his hand, non-plussed, until Dodo points him through to an adjoining room. Elise lights up, calls for an ashtray.

'We have just got back from France, Richard and I,' Michaela leans forward to tell her.

'Ah — from Paris?' Elise exhales a luxuriant plume.

The Admiral's immediate neighbour, a baby-cheeked seventy-year-old, gym thin and sinewy in a backless black dress, narrows her cat's eyes in disgust. 'You won't smoke while we're eating, will you?' she asks sternly, but Elise doesn't hear her.

'Oui,' Michaela answers Elise. 'Nous avons passé dix jours à Paris.' She goes on for another sentence or two and I don't understand a word. Show-off, I think, and tune out. One of the young men comes to fill my glass and I indicate an uncouth level with my thumb. He pays no attention to me and moves on down the table. In the same instant he departs Dodo arrives. All wobbly white arms and shiny brow, she flops into her chair with a sweaty squeak from her colliding inner thighs. The guests are all seated and it seems she feels she can relax now, beginning with a great gulp of chardonnay. Dodo, I suspect, was once a good-time girl and still likes a drink and a bone to chomp on.

'How are you, Richard?' she asks. 'We have met before, you know. In Auckland.'

I nod, though I have only the vaguest alcohol-hazed recollection, and apply myself to the round pink fishy mound on the plate before me. It's the size of three French entrées put together.

'Mikie tells me you cut your European trip short because of family troubles?' An upward inflexion makes it a question, not a statement. I nod again, take a sip of wine.

'I wasn't aware that you had family in Australia.' Dodo scoops up a dainty portion of mousse and inserts it seamlessly into her mobile mouth between words. 'A son? A daughter?'

'A son.' Michaela could rescue me here, cleverly guide the conversation away in another direction, but she has her head prettily inclined to dear old Giles.

'What does he do? Your son?' asks Dodo.

'He's in jail,' I tell her, too loudly. I drain my glass of wine, help myself to another, while beside me Elise lays down her fork.

'Who? Who is this? Someone we know is in jail?' she asks. From across the table Michaela meets my eye and microscopically, infinitesimally, shakes her head.

'My son,' I tell Elise, who immediately lays a comforting hand over mine on the table.

'Mon Dieu. How awful for you,' she murmurs. She looks across at Michaela. 'Do you have other children?'

'Yes — I —' begins Michaela.

'No.' I feel trembly suddenly, like a menopausal woman, a vertiginous hysteria welling at the back of my throat. 'He's my only child.'

'Where are you staying in Sydney?' Michaela asks Elise in a quiet, level tone. The Admiral is considering me, while he masticates his parsley garnish. A fleck of it remains on his lip.

'At a very nice hotel in Kirribilli, quite small but very pri —' begins Elise.

'What's he in for?' barks Giles, as if I'm a rating standing to attention beside a poorly scrubbed deck. He would never speak like that to a man he perceived as his social equal — he's taking his revenge for my rudeness outside. I let him have it.

'Drug-running. You might have read about it in the papers. He and two others on a yacht called the *Brian Boru*. Colombian cocaine.'

'How long's he looking at? I suppose you've got him a good criminal lawyer?'

The wait staff are clearing the entrées. One white-sleeved arm eclipses my view of the Admiral's sun-battered face and shows me Michaela's. I smile at her comfortingly — that's all I'm saying, the smile says: I won't embarrass you by describing his other, worse crime. She understands and immediately engages the old fella in a conversation about dogs.

'Giles breeds pugs!' she tells me brightly, as the main course flies in on white wings and settles before us. It smells of cinnamon and cumin. There's rice and a dark meat. I sample a little, discreetly: it's lamb, Middle Eastern style, with prunes.

Jasper hates lamb. On one of my rare trips back to New Zealand during his teenage years, before I returned to live there permanently, he and I went away on a holiday. One night I cooked a roast dinner for us in our motel. He refused to eat it. He'd seen a dead sheep in a cave once, he said, when he was kid, and now the smell of lamb made him feel sick. Don't be such a fucking prima donna, I'd screamed at him, I went to a lot of trouble — and Jasper had slammed off into the night, not returning until after midnight.

I can't eat it either. Not tonight. I drink instead, another glass, and another, while Michaela laughs her high, ringing laugh at some hilarious pug antic and Dodo talks across me to the geriatric gym bunny beside the Admiral, and Elise discusses art with the tall, black-garbed man on her other side. He looks an arty type, his hair dyed the same saturated black as the rectangular frames of his designer spectacles. I listen in for a few seconds.

It's not art they're dissecting, but film.

'Oh, I love his films!' says Elise, clapping her hands together winningly. 'Have you seen his latest?'

'The erotic one?' asks the man.

'Yes! Yes! The one about the young violinist falling in love with the famous old conductor —'

'Aren't all French films about that?' interrupts the muscle-toned old girl. 'Old men and young girls? Why can't they make a film about an older woman and a young man? And I mean genuinely older — a woman in her fifties or sixties.'

'But they do,' says Elise.

'Name one,' challenges the other woman. There's a pause while Elise ponders.

'See! You can't!' The gym bunny is triumphant. She smiles and an alien, diagonal ditch forms across one cheek. 'It seems to me,' she goes on, 'that everyone is a sexual being except women over thirty-five. Young women are erotic, and men of all ages. Even boys.'

'Oh, especially boys.' Who said that? Was it me?

'Well . . .' says Elise, doubtfully.

'Greek men universally have sexual experiences with boys,' I go on, warming to my subject. 'You read this everywhere. It's well known. They've done it for centuries and they continue to do it with no shame.'

'We're talking about French films here,' says the man in black, 'not Greek perversion.'

'Patrick is a film director!' Dodo tells my left ear, as if I care what the silly prat does.

'We should emulate them. There's nothing wrong with it,' I say.

'You'd be the first out on the streets to protest if the government lowered the age of consent,' Patrick says, jabbing a finger at me. 'I know your type.' Lighting a cigarette, Elise leans back in her chair so that her friend can address me more easily.

'Really? What type's that? You've only just met me.' I drain my glass, pour another.

'Narrow-minded, middle-aged, middle-class, middle-fucking-New Zealander pissheads!'

Dodo leans towards me again. 'Patrick's a New Zealander too,' she whispers, fish-breathed.

'Patrick — shhh.' Elise offers him a cigarette, which he takes. Both pairs of eyes alight on me.

'Richard, I'm curious,' she says. 'Why should you take this position?'

'Well, ah . . .' I adopt a proud, paternal tone, 'During my son's film-making career —'

'Name?' Patrick sneers. 'Do we know him?'

'— which is now at an untimely end due to his incarceration, he concentrated on breaking down social barriers.'

'Richard —' Michaela's voice from a long way off. I ignore it, picturing instead Jasper dressed in the same stylish noir as Patrick at a press conference, expounding on his creative impulses and elucidating his themes to the paparazzi.

'Children are sexual beings who like to give and receive pleasure.' The whole table is giving me their attention. I pause for a moment, roll some more of Dodo's excellent Hunter Valley red around my mouth.

'Richard —' Michaela again, from the other side of the moon.

'This is a taboo, but also an absolute truth. In my films — I should say, my son's films — the children you see are not acting. Oh no. It's all for real. They suck and fuck, take it and give it. If they cry it's with pleasure, not pain. They moan, they pant. Are they children, though? This is a contentious point. Is a thirteen-year-old a child? Given the phenomenon of precocious puberty in the twenty-first century, I would argue that very often they are not.'

'I think you should leave now, Mr Brunel.' The Admiral has sprung to his feet. He's surprisingly agile for such an old chap. Patrick, too, stands and disappears from his place. A moment or two later I feel my chair tugged away from the table and hands settle on my shoulders. Several pairs of hands in fact, including the white-cuffed ones of Dodo's little helpers. My feet scarcely touch the ground until we reach the room in which we took our pre-prandial drinks.

'Let me go!' I thrash around furiously, my right fist almost clocking the waiter on that side, but he ducks and it continues on to catch the Admiral, who flies backwards into Michaela who, white-faced, was coming after me. They land in a sprawl of bare legs, Parisian loose-weave skirt and white trousers on the carpet and the last I see, when I pause for a nano-second at the top of the stairs, is Dodo's vast blue bulk hanging over them and Elise and several others hurrying from the table.

All the way down the drive I can hear footsteps behind me, but they keep their distance. I don't turn around to see who it is. I sit on the bonnet of the rental car and wait, checking my watch every two minutes: the keys are in Michaela's Lacroix evening bag. After half an hour I have to accept that she's not coming to drive me home. I don't want to be with myself. I want to be with her. Fuck you, Jasper, I think, you perverted, twisted little turd. I never want to see you again. And I blubber a bit, as quietly as I can, because through the trees is the gleam of a white shirt. One of the young men has been sent to watch me.

Why doesn't Michaela come? She has no psychology. She has no understanding of me. Another twenty minutes pass, during which time I dispose of a lot of red wine and my entrée into the gutter on the other side of the road. A few minutes later, returned to my roost on the car bonnet, I hear the light trip of a woman's feet down the driveway, accompanied by the heavier tread of a man. It's not Michaela, but two guests who were seated at the far end of the table. The party must be over then, prematurely. Male pride nudges to the surface of my bewildered brain. Do I want Michaela to find me here?

'Are you going into town?' I ask them. 'Can I cadge a lift?'

The man takes his wife's arm and hurries her on.

'Arseholes,' I say, loud enough for them to hear. 'Sanctimonious shits.'

'Perhaps we should ring the police,' says the wife in an undertone as they cross the road to their car.

Suddenly I don't want to wait for Michaela. Sobriety wings in at me with all the finesse and landing accuracy of a one-wheeled plane: Michaela would take pot-shots at me, she'd fill my fuselage with lead. I head off, up the steep street. On the way here I didn't take notice of the route; I sat beside Michaela silently as she drove, brooding, remembering. There had been only five minutes or so of Jasper's film on tape — Bonny was right, she'd taped over it. Satin sheets and boyish bodies gave way to gunfire, sirens and New York streets. But from Darling Harbour to Castlecrag that five minutes had played over and over in my head, without my permission, in an endless loop.

The main road — an arterial road at least — is up ahead. I can hear the traffic, the muted roar of it, along the ridge. Damp and vaguely feverish I struggle on: at the top there will be a taxi. At the top there will be a taxi, a taxi, a taxi, my pulse thumps relentlessly, my head throbs . . .

All the houses are set well back from the road with long, winding right-of-ways. Now and then, through the trees, is the smooth, silky gleam of a swimming pool landscaped into the hillside, set around with retaining walls and ornamental shrubs. They're aberrations, open sores that send up a stink of chlorine to mix with the antiseptic smell of the gums. Maybe I should do a story on swimming pools, I think — on what they cost in real terms: the water, the wildlife lost in them, the toddlers . . .

A bird — or is it a possum? — moves heavily in a branch over-hanging the narrow footpath just ahead of me. It sounds as though it's falling; there's a snapping of twigs and I almost hold out my arms to catch it. Peering up into the sparse leaves, the hazy, rainy sky above glowing with reflected city lights, I make out the shape of a cat. I think it's a cat, a white-tipped tail lashing furiously with wounded dignity — unless it's another species of weird Australian fauna that's previously eluded me. It swivels its demon head with its two chewed ears, hisses and clambers up to a wider branch. My arms relax.

I would have saved the little creature if it had fallen. Fate had placed me under the tree to do so, strong and willing, and then had made me surplus to requirements. The cat's own muscles and claws had halted its earth-bound descent. All sound is muffled by the rain but I'm sure I can hear it now on the other side of the gum, its paws thudding to the ground. It didn't see me as a saviour but an enemy, a black shape reeking of vomit and despair, a bottomless pit it could have fallen into with no hope of escape. And who's to say, I think, plodding on up the wet hill, that I would not have taken pity on it and broken its neck? It might have been diseased, covered in sores, wormy and blind. I might have afforded it that final act of kindness.

A full hour and a half later I find a taxi. Street signs swarm and flicker in the rain-flecked light. When the cab with its light on pulls up ten metres in front of me and a woman gets out, I run against the leaden muscles in my exhausted legs, my heart heaving its arteries into my throat like bungy ropes, and sink into the back seat before the cabby has a chance to turn off his light.

JASPER

My Lovely Mate

I am back on Remand in a single cell and although I've asked for pen and paper they won't give me any. Retribution seeps from every brick and stone, every impermeable surface is pocked with it. Every half an hour around the clock a screw comes to look at me and sees — in the thirty seconds he holds his eye to the door — a model prisoner. I don't acknowledge him, I don't go to the door or call out: I remain motionless on my bed. A strange, paralysing calm fills me. I don't want anything: not food, or water, or human company. It was immediately after my first request for the pen and paper was refused that this new peace came. The same screw who told me he'd bring paper, but not a pen — as if it was a joke I'd share — described how my early life had been wiped from the wall by a sweeper. Franca will never read what I had written. It was an exercise in futility, a microcosmic demonstration of the greater futility of my continuing life.

At first, when I was brought here, Franca following with her bag of tricks, I was so hungry I ate what they gave me. It was revolting, of course. My horizons temporarily shrank to the prison perimeters. While I ate I didn't think about Bonny or my sons, or even Damian, but whether or not the sweeper would take the time to read what he had been set to erase. In the primitive psychology applied by the Corrective Services, it seems prisoners are rewarded for good behaviour with cleaning duties. I reckoned out his course of action: having cleaned the piss and shit from the corner he'd be after payback later in the showers, or the exercise yard, or the slop-hall. If I were a character in an American film that is what would happen to me. My generation is the first to be cursed with self-consciousness so schismatic and absolute that we can see ourselves from an outside vantage as physical beings in the blink of an eyelid. That's why at nightclubs you see us dancing alone, eyes averted; why single-person dwellings are mushrooming in tower blocks all over the world; why we love the cocooning membranes of 'social' drugs.

Shine the light on me, we say, *so that I might watch myself.*

I see the sweeper corner me against a concrete wall and tip the saved bucket of ink-stained shit over my head. I see my reaction, my whole face in close-up, I hear the score in a minor key, and the emotion of the moment is this: the prisoner doesn't care. The sweeper balls his fist, Jasper Shag offers his slimy chin. He says nothing, but his expressive and soulful eyes call out to his myriad audience of one, out there in the soft, sympathetic darkness — those heart-wrenching eyes beg and plead: knock me down, mate, they say, put me out.

I've never been in prison before, except for the one night I spent in the holding cells of Auckland Central for being drunk and disorderly, shortly before Bonny and I left for Sydney in 1994, when we were twenty-two. The cops let me off with a warning. A saggy-faced old cop gave me a lecture, then Scottie arrived to take me home to Lena, who was waiting with a cooked breakfast, her sympathetic counsellor's face and a ready ear.

It's better in here than in the interview room — better not to have the pen and waiting wall, better not to go on dragging it all up. If I lie still enough for long enough surely my mind will slow down too, it will empty, it won't give me what it is now: Lena's new saintly persona falling away as her eyes fill with tears. She gives out a plaintive bleat: 'I wasn't such a bad mother to you, was I? I never stopped loving you, you were always fed, you had a roof over your head.' I remember it exactly for its unconscious rhyme, for her longing for me to verify her truth. It wasn't my truth.

The day Bonny and I left for Australia I gave Lena and Scottie the wrong departure time so that they missed seeing us off. I did things like that then, to punish her for all her crimes, for all the times she'd failed me. As the plane took off I thought of them hunting the airport for us, scouring the bar, and it gave me a sense of achievement and sweet utu. A door closed on them then: for a whole year I scarcely spared them a thought. It was Bonny, after Vincent was born, who insisted I ring Lena to tell her she was a grandmother. Lena wept and I had the horrible sensation of time not having moved on at all, that once again I was sitting in the Murdock Road kitchen looking at my mother's over-wrought face and getting caught up in a sticky web of mutual blame and recrimination. She was probably weeping for joy, though I didn't realise it at the time. It was probably her hot Italiano blood pumping in her veins: when Bonny took the boys home for a holiday in 2000 she asked the boys to call her Nònna — Grandmother.

The walls of the interview room would never have held the whole truth, even if I'd filled them all and started on the floor and ceiling. If I was famous — as famous, say, as Howard Shag — and a biographer wanted to write my life, I would withhold pages worth of secrets. I've got lots of secrets. But then so has Shag.

Damian was always going on about discretion and caution. One of the first parties Bonny and I went to in Sydney was at Damian's place in Randwick and it took a moment or two for him and me to figure out where we knew each other from. At first I thought he was one of the turkey-baster boys who'd hung around in the garden of the Herne Bay house, but he wasn't. He was the older kid who'd got us the wine and joint at the party Richard later wrote about. I'd been miserable in Sydney until then; meeting up with Damian gave me a charge, helped me to remember who I was. After that party, for the next eleven years, we were closer than brothers, Dam and me. I loved him more than I've loved anybody else in my whole life — more than my mother, more than Howard Shag, more than Bonny even. Together we were invincible: we were tough, fit and smart; we had a gift for the sea, for pleasure and for business. Our clandestine voyages on stolen yachts were bliss and even better if there was only the two of us on board, if Dam thought we could handle the boat and cargo on our own. We'd read and talk; we stayed away from drugs and stayed sharp. We had two enemies out there, both of them unpredictable, Damian would say: the sea and the fucking coastguard. The Colombians weren't our enemies, but they were unpredictable and Dam handled them perfectly. He was fluent in Spanish and a crack-shot with the gun he kept in a shoulder holster — they seemed to know not to fuck him round. On fine days on our voyages out, bored with reading or eating the fish I'd cook for him, he'd shoot seagulls out of the air — knock them off the mast point. He had one of those laughs that stick in your head for ever — sudden, big, wild. He'd throw his head back, his fair hair hot-white in the sun and whipping wind, and his laughter filled the world around him, even a world as vast as the Tasman Sea. Once a dolphin put its head up, right by the stern where Dam was lounging with the tiller in his hand, and it looked at him as if it wanted to share the joke. The sound of his laughter must've reached a thousand leagues to the seabed.

How'd you get taken in, Dam? That's what I want to ask you. Why'd you decide to trust Monty or Ponty or whatever the fuck his real stupid name was? There was something about him that excited you — his crass Western Australian way of talking, maybe; his conceited, tight-arsed strut; his outsized muscles — even bigger than mine — the result of hour after senseless hour in the gym. Mine are at least natural. God or whoever made me this way. He was just a snake, a lying cunt, an undercover D. I would've written all this on the wall; I would have let those bastards have it.

It was just on dawn when they got us. We heard the pump of their 800-horsepower diesel engines — they came out of the dark without their lights on like a ghost ship — and that was when you twigged. You went for Monty, you reached for your gun, but the cop was too quick for you. He got behind you and twisted your arms behind your back and when I came up from below, woken by your shouts and the thud of the engines closing in, you were already bent over by his weight while he bashed your head against the rail. He sensed me behind him and turned, kicking your legs out from under you. He held your gun on me and you slipped — or did he push you? — whatever, you slipped, fell, vanished, probably unconscious, into the sea, into the narrowing gap between the coastguard's powerful boat and the yacht. The bastards probably went over the top of you.

I'm not crying. I did all that when they didn't look for you, when they only talked about sending divers out. They shone their searchlight around a bit and I looked with them, scanning the chop for a glimpse of your white head, but it was too dark and the sunrise played tricks with shadows in the waves. I thought I saw you; I kept screaming and pointing until two of the coastguards wrestled me downstairs and locked me in the secure cabin. There were twelve men on board, Dam. Twelve — four crew and eight officers. We wouldn't have stood a chance.

I didn't stop crying until I met Franca. She reminds me of a lot of different people. My mother, because she's Italian. Damian, because her hair is the same colour. Even Bonny. She's tough and tender in the same way Bonny is. Like Scottie too. Franca will save me. I don't know how I know this, I just do. I know it as surely as I know Damian's dead.

'You've got a visitor.' The screw has unlocked the door and come in before I'm aware of him. I sit up, feeling dizzy and light-headed. The slop they gave me for lunch is congealed solid.

'You not eating, mate?' asks the screw, as if he cares.

On the ground floor he has me sit on a bench in the short corridor where you wait for contact visits. From a room at the end of it, on my left, is the buzz of voices — women's as well, and even the squawky tones of a kid. I listen harder: not my kid, I hope. Bonny hates me even more now than she did before; she wouldn't bring the boys to see me.

A door opens directly in front of me and for a split-second I have no idea who this woman is, gazing at me with welling eyes. Her black hair is streaked with grey and cut close to her head. She wears tight, screen-printed pants that accentuate her wide hips and rolling stomach. Her baggy T-shirt is embroidered with a lurid picture of a gynaecological orchid and a long piece of pounamu swings on a thong in front of it, like a stamen that's come loose. In the eleven years since I last saw my mother she's doubled in size. For a moment or two neither of us says anything.

'Is Scottie here?' I manage, at last.

'She'll come next time.' Lena is almost breaking down. She digs in her bag for a tissue.

'Take her through, Shag.' An officer appears from the visitors' waiting room. He points towards the room at the end of the corridor where all the noise is coming from. Lena follows me and we see that there are two areas to choose from: an outside one and an inside. Except for the absence of a roof on the outside one they're pretty much the same: bare, desolate, with benches and tables bolted to the floor. It's been raining so the inside area is crammed. Taking the initiative, my mother leads me outside to where water pools on the concrete bench seats. Silently, from her handbag, she removes her sunglasses, then lies the bag on the seat. It's flat, square, made of a woven taupe-coloured string, with a long handle. She sits on it and I stand beside her.

'Sorry,' she says, dabbing at face again. 'It's not like me to lose it like this.' My mother the solipsist, I think, looking at her. Slumped like an abandoned puppet she's crying for herself, not for me.

'It's all right,' I tell her. She sits upright, as sharply as if I've pulled a string in the top of her head.

'Oh no, Jasper. That's where you're wrong. It's not all right at all.'

A seagull cries out suddenly, above us, and we both tip our heads to watch it wheel over the high walls and away. The mournful, desolate tones from its yawping beak fill me with impatience — and dread. Whatever my mother intends to put me through I don't need it. I feel dizzy still. My stomach growls.

'You'd think they could put some plants out here or something, wouldn't you?' Lena looks around. 'A bit of greenery would be nice.'

'It's not a fucking hotel. It's not supposed to be nice.'

'No, of course not. I'm sorry.' She apologises again. They're not real apologies. They don't appear to cost her anything. 'Have you seen your father?' she asks quietly.

'Richard? No.' She never calls him 'your father'.

'He's in Sydney. He came back early from Europe because of . . .'

'Me.'

'Yes.'

I hunker down beside her. Perhaps if my head is closer to the ground I'll be able to think more clearly. Lena pats me on the shoulder and caresses my cheek, then she pulls her hand away as if I burned her.

'Oh, Jasper.' She's putting her sunglasses on so I can't see her eyes. 'What about Bonny? Have you seen her?'

'Bonny chucked me out two years ago, as you know. Why would she come?' Lena shrugs and opens her mouth to reply but I don't give her a chance. 'If she hadn't chucked me out I wouldn't be in this shit.'

'She wanted you to go because of Damian. She wanted you to choose.'

'Between her and Dam? That's bullshit. She's filled you up with crap.'

'She thinks you and Damian were lovers. Bonny didn't understand and she couldn't cope with it.'

I come to stand in front of her and bend over, hold my face inches away from hers and lift her sunglasses onto the top of her head. 'Get this, Mum. Damian was my mate. We never fucked each other. Not even out at sea, when we could have, when we were alone. We were only —' my voice chokes off. She's seeing me, she's got into my head, she's holding one of my hands.

'But you wanted him, didn't you?' she says softly.

'I'm not gay.'

She pulls me down onto the seat beside her, hooking her arm through mine, holding me firmly against her side. Water penetrates the thin prison greens, through to my skin.

'I didn't know I was either, until I met Scottie.'

'Don't you fucking give me a lecture about fluid sexuality or any shit like that.' I give my arm a wrench, but not hard enough to pull it away.

'It wasn't only Damian,' Lena goes on, as if I haven't said anything.

172

'It was all the other stuff you got yourself mixed up in.'

'What's she told you?' I need to know suddenly. What've they been doing, having long trans-Tasman phone calls, or sitting opposite each other in the kitchen of Bonny's shit-hole in Tempe with Lena doing the mother-in-law act, making endless cups of tea? Did they talk in front of Vinnie and Jack?

'Enough.' Lena pulls her arm away now and uses the crumpled tissue in her other hand to blow her nose.

'She doesn't know everything.'

'She's got a fair idea.'

'No, she hasn't.' A tall, dark-skinned boy, fourteen or so, comes out of the inside room with an older inmate who could be his grandfather. They light cigarettes, the old man drawing hard, the sinews in his raggy neck straining, and look around for a dry seat. There isn't one, so the boy takes off his neon-coloured nylon jacket and spreads it out on a bench. They sit side by side, on the other side of the yard, not talking and staring at us. Our voices will carry to them. I don't want Lena to say anything more.

'She gave Richard one of your tapes.'

'She . . .' I begin, but the old man opposite smiles at me suddenly, showing his broken yellow teeth, then he turns and says something to the boy in Arabic, or Lebanese. The boy ignores him, his eyes downcast. Maybe the old man is his father.

'What tapes?' I'm not giving anything away. Lena doesn't reply. She's looking at her knees.

'Richard's got one. Bonny gave it to him. He has a video-player in his hotel and he's watched it.'

There's a loud thudding in my ears suddenly, and a fluttering at the edges of my vision like black curtains lifting and falling in a draught from an open window. The thudding swells, thickens — it's a plane approaching, or an outboard engine with its throttle open in the bay on the other side of the wall.

'Jasper?' Lena's voice is coming from above me. 'Are you okay?'

Slowly, inexorably, the concrete floor is coming up to meet me; my head is slipping between my legs. I am a snake, a clod of earth, a ground-dweller. I'm going where I belong. But arms pull me up: the soft, fleshy ones of my mother and the thin, bony ones of a boy. My face crushed to his narrow chest, I can smell his sweat, his last meal of spices and meat and hot grease. I set my lips against the skin of his throat and taste him, drink him in, and the boy doesn't notice, he thinks only that he's helping me away from this bass, mechanical pulse of blood and shame, away from the flapping black curtains — or are they wings? — that want to wrap me like a shroud. I coat my mouth with him: his freedom, his youth, the air of the streets and rooms he inhabits, a faint, babyish trace of soap. Around us, around our brief embrace — my mother and this boy and I — there's the sound of the old man shouting and the hard shoes of the screws running on polished floors. Strong dark-sleeved arms clamp in on me from either side and walk me away. I feel my mother fall back and lose the scent of the boy who would save me, who would take away my pain like so many tender boys have.

The screws have got a wheelchair from somewhere and they're bending me into it, strapping me in. It's unbearably hot: the sun rises over the sea, the boat rocks under my feet and I'm searching for Damian, screaming out his name because I love him and he's gone, lost: these cunts have killed him. I've got one of them now, his fat ugly neck between my hands, and I'm choking the air out of him. It's Monty. What was he doing, holding you like that, like he wanted to fuck you up the arse and you couldn't get away?

You'll answer me now. You'll hear me now, Damian, my beautiful mate.

My voice is louder, as if it's bouncing off walls — and I'm knocked sideways, punched in the head and my skull lolls, heavy, as if it would snap off. Their voices are harsh, they stink of evil, their arses are near my nose, stale and old. I'm wheeling down a corridor lined with closed doors, my tongue circling for the last of the boy, the final strands of his taste caught in the runnels of my lips. But there's only the stench of the screws — they're ruining the boy for me, taking all I've got left of him.

The heavy doors open and I know where I am. I know because when I lift my head I can see the shrink coming down the corridor, his white coat flapping.

LENA

Talk

I am losing my mind with grief and despair. My skull is a plasma-ball whirling with wordless trauma and horror. I tell Scottie this and she says nothing in reply, because there is nothing to say. It is the truth. She fetches me from the prison in a taxi. I cannot speak. When we get back to the hotel I sit on the edge of the bed.

'Tell me what happened,' says Scottie.

I say, 'I am losing my mind.'

All my life I have talked. I have talked my way into tomorrow, I have talked myself out of the past. I have talked hundreds of women out of their depressions, out of their phobias, out of their oppressive relationships with their husbands, their mothers, their children. When Jasper was in my womb I talked to him. When he was born I talked to him. He spoke in complete sentences at thirteen months because I talked to him. I surrounded him with talk, garlanded him with it, put him to bed on it. I crooned, I read aloud, I whispered.

Talking is how I have shown my love for Significant Others in my life. It is how I have shown my love for the world.

It is time to be silent.

I draw Scottie down beside me on the bed to explain it to her. Despite the grieving of my spirit, Scottie smiles. I extinguish my anger by visualising a thumb and finger pinching out a flame. I explain again.

'It is time for me to be silent. You must speak for me.'

1985

During his lifetime Howard had woken from deep sleep to tender smiles from the most exotic and beautiful of the human race; he'd come round from surgery, once or twice, to the same severe visage of a tartar nurse; he'd been revived by cold water on football fields with a real and virtual audience of millions. Never before had he opened his eyes to the pink insides of an elephant's probing nostrils, which at first, to his groggy and pulped brain, seemed like an outlandish face consisting entirely of two hollow eyes with fine hairs prickling their edges. As it nudged against him, terror and cognisance fought from opposing hemispheres of his brain to possess him. It's an elephant, his conscious mind informed him, though it failed to gain control of his struggling, scrabbling limbs.

There was a flutter of something large and purple falling softly on him from above. His silk dressing-gown. A man in cotton khaki — was he a soldier? — bent over him. Young, with a weather-beaten face.

'It's okay, mate. She won't hurt you.' Murray patted his breast pocket but his cellphone wasn't there. He'd left it up in the staffroom on purpose: early morning walks with Maddie were sacrosanct, never to be disturbed by electronic jingles. The man on the ground was writhing, as if he were trying to get away, or to stand. The silk dressing-gown, which must belong to him, had fallen away with his movement. Blisters were forming on one of his arms, bruises and abrasions welted his legs, his face was swollen and bloodied.

'Just stay where you are. You'll be all right. Give us a second.' The keeper picked up his stick and tapped the elephant on the shoulder. 'Back, girl. Back.'

One of Maddie's black eyes regarded him; a pale-soled foot lifted and fell. On his side now Howard watched. He knew nothing about elephants. Jungle instinct could compel her to crush him, to put the miserable creature on the ground out of its agony. But she was moving backwards; he could feel the warm, hay-scented huff of her breath as she retreated with a rolling, careful tread. The keeper followed her.

'Don't leave me here —' There was blood in his mouth, the words were jumbled, made indistinct by his engorged lips and tongue. Through the trees he could see them, the keeper tapping her again. An insect scuttled in the dirt near his ear; there was a crushed, empty ciga-rette packet above his bent knee. Pall Mall Mild. Is that what they'd used on him? It was another thing he could tell the police — another tiny, almost useless detail.

'Down!' came the keeper's voice. The tapping rod moved above the elephant's back, the keeper's shoes sounded on the path. The elephant snorted, a reluctant, resigned sigh and there — she was kneeling — Howard watched as she curled one knee under her massive chest, then another.

'Down,' said the keeper again, tapping her on the rump this time and the elephant snorted again, her resignation perhaps tinged a little with irritation as she drew her vast bulk down, level with the ground.

The man was back again, among the trees in his green shirt, bending over him, helping him to sit up. Howard howled with pain: his inner thighs had brushed against his ballooning balls. He brought his hands down to hide himself, his body shuddering, but it was too late. The keeper had seen them, drew his hands back, his face set with horror.

'Jesus Christ,' he said, then a moment later, 'You poor bastard.'

The pain subsided in waves. Howard found that he was panting — like a whelping bitch, he thought, like a lambing ewe. He sucked in air, filling his lungs against his complaining ribs, and forced himself over onto his side, as he had been before the keeper tried to help, and then onto his hands and knees. The keeper draped the dressing-gown over his back and went ahead, scuffling twigs and stones out of Howard's slow, crawling progress with his boot, holding aside manuka branches.

'She's called Madagascar, Maddie for short,' said Murray. 'She's twelve years old. We've had her since she was seven. She had people on her back when she was younger.' The man was advancing with short, jagged movements, favouring the arm that wasn't blistered. Under the silk his legs were splayed, the soles of his upturned feet were lacerated.

'It'll be fine,' Murray went on. 'After all, elephants never forget, do they? It's true, you know. Amazing animals.' More than likely the man wasn't listening, but it seemed to Murray that he should carry on talking, that the sound of his voice would soothe him, whoever he was. Sometimes, on their dawn parades, he and Maddie would come across tramps sleeping under the trees, or street-kids, and he'd pretend he hadn't seen them. People were wary of elephants — it was like walking with an unmuzzled rottweiler. Nobody approached you; they just stood aside and gazed, their faces translucent with awe.

'She's a good, sweet girl,' he said as they came nearer the elephant, as much to soothe the beast as the man. The vast banana-leaf ears were twitching.

It seemed to Howard suddenly that he was on a long, difficult and vastly ridiculous journey along a pre-determined path that had an elephant lying across its terminus. Then, pain drained him of thought, left him only with a savage instinct to continue: hand, hand, knee, knee. Hand, hand. Knee, knee. There was no alternative.

The keeper bent to Howard and carefully inserted his arms in the robe, knotting it closed with the cord. He made no sudden movements: years of working alongside captive animals had made him rhythmic, empathetic, as gentle as a nurse for the terminally ill. As he drew the

179

cord around Howard's waist like the saddle-strap of a horse he caught a flash of blue from the man's least injured eye and had a sudden sense of the face under the swollen tissue and grazes. It was a face he knew, he thought, from years ago. Did he used to be on the television maybe? Or he'd seen him in the newspapers. This was a famous man.

'What's your name, mate?'

The lid closed over the eye and the face swung minutely to one side. Later, in his hospital bed, Howard would be supremely grateful for his failure to answer.

On the other side of the grey leathery mound the keeper extended his arms to take hold of Howard's wrists and was pulling him, dragging him, up over the elephant until he lay across it. Whoever the stranger was, famous or not, he was a man who had endured other injuries in his time — he had a high pain threshold, Murray observed. He did not cry out, he only bit his lips hard enough to draw fresh blood.

The sun was rising above the shops at the crest of Chinaman's Hill and dew glossed the littered grass as Maddie made her slow, quiet way back to the lower gate of the zoo by the elephant enclosure. The roads that bordered the park were empty of traffic. It was too early even for dog-walkers or joggers. The only other creatures to observe them were swans and geese, ducks and pukeko, and they saw nothing remarkable in the spectacle of a tall, badly beaten middle-aged man slung across the back of a plodding elephant, her keeper walking alongside with a steadying hand on her silent, silk-wrapped burden.

LENA

After only a few days I see what a precious gift speech is. I am renewed by my silence. Silence is the Primeval Mother. Silence holds me in her quiet, warm arms.

I meditate. I am still.

In our hotel room the telephone rings. Scottie answers it. It is Richard. I prepare myself for necessary speech.

MELODY

Mystery Shag

While I'm driving out to the airport I remember Ms Harris at school who used to talk to us girls about the fallacy of Romantic Love.

'You gels are the victims of the popular song, the Dream Machine, women's magazines and your own hormones,' she'd tell us, nodding her shorn grey head and waggling one ferocious nail-bitten finger. 'Only the most determined and intelligent of you will resist it.'

It was an idea that persisted through my university days, in discussions and even some Women's Studies papers which dismissed its existence — or, at the very least, its relevance to the emotional lives of post-feminist women. At the end of the twentieth century Romantic Love was at a low ebb among intellectuals and academics, which, as everybody knows, are not the same thing. Romantic love was an archaism, a leg-iron; it was a lemon we'd been sold for centuries, and everything I experienced with Curtis backed that up.

Maybe that's why I've fallen so hard for Godfrey — why I'm

incapable of thinking about anything else. When he holds me in his arms — those big, soft arms, which can metamorphose in an instant into solid, sculpted, sun-warmed stone — I feel tiny, delicate and precious. I understand why for decades men have called women 'Babe', which previously I held as derogatory, diminishing and infantilising. In Godfrey's arms I am his babe, absolutely. My heart ceases to ache for him — he's all around me, the wide expanse of his brown, hairless chest, the smooth, scented rise of his creamy throat, the curl of his dark hair at the nape of his neck . . .

Careful! Subject to a swoon that has me swerve I'm nearly off the road, my left hand pulling harder on the wheel than my right, my left foot pumping the pedal, the tyres throwing up gravel. The car behind me slams on its brakes then zooms out and past me, its driver a blurred white face looking my way. The white face of a cow looks at me also over the fence of the only paddocks left on this stretch of road. I ease the car around and continue on.

I'm in love, I'm in love, I'm in love — the spin of the wheels has a rhythm that beats the mantra out, the swish of cars zipping by in the fast lane say it too, one after the other: I'm . . . in . . . love I'm . . . in love I'm . . . in . . . love . . . I'm in . . . love . . . I'm in love . . .

I'm late. Godfrey is standing outside the airport waiting for me, a sports bag over his shoulder and a large suitcase on wheels beside him. Five days since I saw him: a whole five days since last Sunday night when he flew home to Wellington. How am I going to control myself until we get back to Grey Lynn?

Why has he got a suitcase I could ask, but it's difficult to talk when your mouth is hosting another tongue, when there's a warm dry hand the size of a land crab spanning your trembling back under your shirt, when you're so wet between the legs you wonder if it's showing. Very vaguely I'm aware that people are watching us — quite a lot of people, in fact — but I don't care: his prick is hardening against me and my head is full of an image of him lifting me up and lowering me deliciously onto it, up against the Pick Up Drop Off Only sign.

'Jesus, Mel — stop it — you're killing me,' says Godfrey. 'Get in the car.' I peel myself away and he puts his suitcase — which really is substantial, now I look at it — in the back seat. He leans in the passenger window.

'One minute, Babe,' he says. 'Just got to say seeya later to the boys.'

The boys? Little boys? Sons? I watch him walk back towards the automatic doors, heart pounding. I can see them already, what they must look like — green-eyed and toffee-skinned like their daddy, two tiny chaps hand in hand — but no. Godfrey passes the automatic doors and approaches instead a big group of twenty or so twenty-something blokes, who are ambling out of another set of doors pushing trolleys laden with luggage. There's a woman with them — a tall, sporty-looking Maori woman in a dark suit — and it's she whom Godfrey talks to, pointing to where the shuttle buses leave for town and the international airport. He hands her a narrow blue and red folder with white lettering on it, smiles at her, then turns to jog back towards me. I watch him in the rear-vision mirror: poetry in motion.

In the car we kiss again, for ages, until the parking warden tells us move along out of the five-minute bay. All those blokes, I presume, are Godfrey's league team, the name of which escapes me just now. This is one of the things I love about Godfrey: he doesn't waste his breath — or mine, since our breathing apparatus is quite often joined — explaining obvious things. He and I can assume a level of cognisance in one another.

It's hard to concentrate on the motorway with his hand between my legs but I manage it. I even manage to park with only a few inches of tyre in my neighbour's driveway — and although he's nuzzling my neck and nibbling my ears I manage to get the key in the door and kick it shut after us. Making it as far as the bedroom is an impossibility, however, at least not until we begin for the third time and I decide my derriere requires cushions, as do my knees. The hot, slightly stinging sensation in those parts of my anatomy is quite possibly due to carpet-burn.

The phone is ringing.

'Leave it,' says Godfrey, lifting his mouth from my nipple.

'Oh, don't you worry,' I say. 'I have no intention of —'

'Melody. Are you there?' Howard's voice comes loud and tinny from the fingernail-sized speaker in my antique answering machine. 'Melody.

This is important. Pick up the phone.'

Godfrey freezes. 'Who's that?'

'No one.' I reach for him.

'Ring me immediately you get this message. This quite simply isn't good enough. I chose you over a number of contenders and you should be available to me . . .' There's a pause while Howard thinks. '. . . should I want you.' He finishes.

Godfrey stares at me. Does Howard's voice sound old, I wonder? I mean, I think it sounds old because I know Howard is old. I hope it sounds completely ancient. Godfrey has no idea. 'Who the hell was that, Mel?'

'Work person. Don't worry about it. Come here.'

And he does. Intensely. And so do I.

Funny how good sex can leave you aching, and how the aching is pleasurable. Heavy-limbed and warm, Godfrey and I sleep tumbled around each other in my bed for an hour or so after we finish — until the phone rings again.

Godfrey — who, let's face it, I don't know all that well and could be a suspicious kind of person — beats me to it. 'Melody's phone,' he says in a falsetto, while I gurgle foolishly into my pillow. 'One moment. I'll just enquire . . . No. I'm afraid Miss Argyle is rather sticky and indisposed —' He breaks off, listens intently. 'Pardon?' he says in his normal voice. 'No, I'm not. Who's Curtis?'

'Give it here —' I rear up. Godfrey scowls at me before his eyes drift to my breasts. I hold out my hand. 'Who is this?' He keeps a grip on the phone. 'Howard Shag?' Incredulous, he hands the phone over.

'Why didn't you tell me?' Godfrey wants to know as we drive down Curran Street towards the bridge.

'We haven't told each other anything much,' I reply carefully, lightly. 'Have we?' Godfrey shrugs his delicious shoulders, now reclad in his dark suit jacket. He looks more like a Mormon than ever. 'For instance,' I continue, 'who were "the boys" at the airport?' Perhaps it would have been nice if he had explained, I think.

'My team of course. The Wolves. On their way to Sydney.'

'Why "of course"?' Shit — are we going to have an argument?

'I told you about the Wolves. At your sister's stupid Claytons christening.' I haven't heard that word for a long time. Claytons. It's a word that belongs to my parents' generation. And why would he think the ceremony was false, anyway?

'Are you religious?' I ask him.

'What do you mean by that?'

'Do you go to church? You knew the Lord's Prayer in Maori.'

'Learned it as a kid.'

'I thought, when you said "the boys" that you might be talking about your sons.'

'Christ. You think I've got God and sons.'

'You could do. It's possible.'

'No to both.' He squeezes my upper thigh, rests his hand in my crotch. 'But you still haven't answered my question.'

'I like to keep things separate. Like you do.'

'Me?'

'For instance, when you're with your wife do you think about me? And vice versa?' His hand leaves my lap like a startled cat. 'Godfrey?' He doesn't answer. 'I'm sorry. Jesus. Sorry. I shouldn't have said —'

'Don't worry about it. It's okay. I should have told you. I, um . . . well. The truth is, I hardly think about her now. Since I met you.'

'You've left her?'

'No. Claire, my wife . . . she died three years ago. She was killed in a car accident.' Curtis is right. I am a bitch. A bitch with a red face and a pounding heart. 'Don't be embarrassed,' Godfrey is saying now, 'It's all right. Really. I mean, I'm still wearing the ring. How could you have known?' I want to stop the car right here at the apex of the bridge and fling my arms around him. 'It's not your fault.'

'Curtis is my ex,' I offer. 'You know, when Howard rang and he thought you were him?' Godfrey nods. 'He's still . . . He's finding it hard to let go. He's doing therapy with Lena. He rings me a lot. And on the day my niece was born he showed up at Howard's place.'

'What did Howard make of him? Do you think he'll like me better?'

It's all too much too fast, I think worriedly. I can't take him to

Howard's. I launch into an explanation of Howard's various phobias and suggest he might like a solitary walk along the beach — even though, as we turn off the motorway, a fine, straight-falling rain is speckling the windscreen.

'That's fine,' says Godfrey. 'I need to get some things to take to Sydney, anyway. I'll take the car up to the shops and come back to pick you up.'

'You're going to Sydney too?' I ask, as I pull up outside Howard's. You should have told me before, I want to wail. 'When are you off?' I ask instead, casually, as if I don't care.

'Tomorrow,' says Godfrey, taking the keys. 'See you in an hour?'

Howard had told me on the phone our meeting wouldn't take long and it's only now, as Godfrey zooms away at my back and the security gates swing open to admit me, that I begin to have a slightly ominous feeling. The house is completely closed, more so than usual, every window latched and curtains drawn. The French doors, when I get to them, are covered by their thick green drapes.

'Howard?' I knock on the glass. At thigh height the olive cloth is pushed aside and Web Ellis looks mournfully out at me. A moment or so later Howard shoves the curtain aside and points with one long, nicotine-stained finger towards the front door. As I make my way up the steps on the other side of the house I can hear Howard sliding open a plethora of bolts, locks and chains.

'Come in,' he says tersely. 'Quick.' He glances down the drive. 'Where's your car?'

'A friend dropped me off.' I edge in the tiny gap he's allowed me and the door closes again. Keys turn, deadlocks are secured. When Howard has finished this process, which involves a lot of quiet grunting and running his tongue over his thin, dry lips, he leads me down the hall towards our usual room. On the way he passes his hand over the smooth dome of the brass elephant's head, his gold ring clicking above the elephant's enamelled eye. Instead of veering left to the sitting room above the beach he leads me further down the hall to a part of the house I've never seen.

We are in a long, narrow room that lies along the full length of the beach side of the house. There is an air of neglect. A vast mahogany dining table is finely veiled with dust, all its leaves extended although it hosts only two chairs. There is a low window seat on the far wall below a wide expanse of dun-coloured curtains. At the far end of the room looms a dark-lacquered, over-bearing antique chiffonier with cupids carved into the wood at its corners and bunches of burnished grapes dangling from its one heavy shelf, which is empty, save for a framed photograph of a boy. From this distance, at the other end of the table, I can't make out the child's features. He is perhaps ten or twelve, black-haired.

'Sit down,' says Howard. 'Wait here a moment.' Taciturn as ever, he vanishes back up the hall and I can hear him muttering as he goes: 'stupid', and a moment later 'old fool', then 'I had it in my hand'.

From a corner shadowed by the dresser comes a glint of chrome. It's some kind of machine. On investigation I decide it's an exercise machine, quite old. Some of its parts have been disconnected from the main body — chains that once held weights, some supportive pads for knees or elbows with perished leather covers and a narrow bench that must once have fitted beneath it.

'Come away from there.' Howard has padded in behind me and is spreading today's *Sunday Star-Times* on the table. 'D'you get the paper, Melody?'

'No.'

'Why not? How ignorant do you like to be?'

'I get my news off the Net,' I tell him.

'Over here.' He is circling a small article with a blue ballpoint pen, about halfway down the page: 'New Zealander Faces Drug Charges'.

'Read it,' says Howard. 'Aloud. So that I know you haven't missed anything.' If I weren't so blissed out on sex I could get really annoyed with him. He's in one of those moods where he's convinced that everyone on earth except himself is an incognate, blithering idiot. He stands aside to let me at the paper and I read him the article.

'"The name of the New Zealander apprehended earlier this month off the coast of New South Wales has been released. He is Jasper Brunel, who also goes by the names Shag and Gilmore. Brunel, aged 33, faces charges of smuggling Class A narcotics and possession of child pornography . . ."' That's who you dedicated your last book to!'

'Well done,' Howard lowers himself stiffly into a chair.

'"Brunel, who has lived for the past eleven years in Australia, is believed to be suffering drug-withdrawal in the Long Bay Prison hospital and is expected to go to trial later this week —"'

'That's enough,' says Howard. 'You've made the connection.' For a moment the only sound is rain drumming on the roof. Howard looks mournful, his fingers interlaced on the table, fuzzily reflected through the dust. 'It's bloody odd,' he continues. 'I get the paper every day and this is the first I read of this. The boy has been in detention for a fortnight. Usually when Kiwis are implicated in drug busts all the news is covered with it.'

'Maybe he has powerful friends,' I say quietly, finishing the article. This new, mystery Shag has been caught with 500 kilograms of cocaine — $290 million worth. 'Someone who wants to keep it quiet.'

'His father knows people who could do that for him,' Howard mutters. 'Richard Brunel. Wrote for *Truth* in the seventies, moved over to the *Herald* and then television in the eighties. He was a good journalist in his prime, very influential. Until the booze caught up with him. He's still around, I think, in a small way. He came to interview me once and brought Jasper with him. Brunel was a what-do-you-call-it — a Sunday Father, or as they say in the States, a Zoo Father. One day I was the zoo. I tried to help out — we became friends, the boy and I. He was . . .' Howard trails off.

'He was what?'

'Devoted to me.' Howard's voice sounds muffled and when I lift my eyes from the newspaper I see that he has covered his face with his hands. Is he weeping? Yet again, as so often happens with Howard, I don't know how to behave. I don't know what is expected of me. I can't put my arm around him, I can't comfort him in any way except . . .

'I'll get your cigarettes for you,' I suggest, and as he doesn't reply I slip away to our usual room and retrieve his smokes and ashtray from the little table beside his armchair. When I return Howard is blowing his nose. I light a cigarette for him and go to open the window for fresh air.

'No,' says Howard. 'If they're not there now, they'll be there soon.'

'Who?'

'The paparazzi. How long will it take, do you think? Until one of them remembers the dedication and puts it together: the "Jasper" and the "Shag"?'

'It's highly unlikely. You know for yourself the standard of journalism in this country. Besides, nobody reads dedications.' To illustrate my point I whip the curtains open and the room fills with a pure, trembling grey light. The beach and foreshore are deserted, the sea still, dark, receiving the steady rain on its dimpling surface like a vast puddle. Howard smokes quietly behind me.

'How long was your friendship with Jasper?' I ask when I hear the ashtray clatter on the table and know that he's stubbing out.

'About three and a half years. I met him in the winter of 1981, just after the Springbok Tour, and we . . . parted in the summer of '85. After that we had a few phone calls, and I kept sending money. I set up an account for him, with regular deposits, a kind of allowance. It turned out it wasn't his fault, you see. In fact, if I had responded differently, if I had believed him when he warned me, well then . . .'

'Warned you? Against what?' My bag rests against one of the swollen-ankled legs of the old table. I pull it out, retrieve my notebook.

'Put that away,' snaps Howard.

'Why?'

'Because all this is off the record.'

'For God's sake, Howard. Do you think it's your fault he's locked up in prison?'

Howard fixes me with a bloodshot, emotive eye. 'Yes. Partially. It is my fault. And everybody else's who failed him — his mother, his father.'

I pick up the newspaper, find the article. 'See here. It says he's thirty-three years old. He's an adult now.'

'Oh yes. He's a father himself. Two sons. He wrote to me when they were born.'

Slowly, openly, calmly, I put the notebook on the table and click out the nib of my pen. 'So in a sense he was like an adopted son?'

'Pretty poor father who adopts a child and only makes him a part of his life for three years. Stop it, Melody. Put the book away. We will leave the past behind in our discussion today. It's the present I should like to concentrate on.'

I'm enraged, of course. Has Howard forgotten what I'm here for? Maybe he thinks he's hired me as a friend, a dogsbody, a daughter. I doodle with my pen on the cover of my notebook: an ornate 'G', an ornate 'o', a 'd', 'f', 'r', 'e', 'y', — Christ. Howard is wasting my time. I could be with my darling: we could be walking in the rain hand in hand.

'Very unfashionable drug now, cocaine,' I tell him. 'Hardly anyone takes it any more, except as crack. And those people are morons.'

'Do you think so? Where do you get that information from?'

'Round about. Friends.'

'This friend who dropped you off?'

'God, no. He's as straight as they come.'

'Pure cocaine is a marvellous drug. Don't let anybody tell you otherwise. Taken it myself a few times in the States — years ago now. It's just that it's too expensive — the champagne of narcotics. You should try it.'

'Howard, I hardly even drink,' I tell him, 'and it wouldn't agree with me.' I have the strangest feeling that Howard is lying to me about taking cocaine. It doesn't fit. He's told me before he hates the drug culture.

'Jasper is a very bright young man. He wouldn't be wasting his time importing a product with no market.' There is an edge of defensiveness in his voice, the dull blade of it.

'Is that him, up on the shelf?'

Howard nods. 'I got him out for you. To give you some idea of what he looks like.' I lift down the photograph in its flimsy cardboard frame. Its edge leaves a clean, dark line in the layer of dust on the shelf. It's a school portrait. As I thought, the boy is about eleven or twelve and the photograph must have been taken in the summer. He wears a lime-green T-shirt, slightly frayed at the collar, and his thick black hair sticks out from his head as if it's laden with sea-salt. He has high cheek-bones, a straight-edged nose and smooth olive skin. There's something tough about him, something resilient. It's the expression in his eyes, I think, which are an unusual greeny-brown colour and cautious, defensive, alert to the betrayal of secrets, ready for seismic changes in the world around him. It's as if the kid is on permanent night-watch.

'He was a good-looking boy,' I say.

'Absolutely.'

A seagull caws past the window, wheeling towards a pile of seaweed and rubbish on the beach. We both start — the air seems electrical, charged.

'Close the curtains, Melody. Please.' A vein is jumping in Howard's throat, the skin around his mouth is drawn tight. I do as I'm told. As soon as the room is dimmed Howard speaks quickly.

'I want you to go to Sydney.'

'Me? Why?'

'I want you to go and see Jasper for me. There's no one else I can ask. You're perfect for the job — you have no connection with anyone in my life, you can just go, as my emissary. I'll give you a letter to take to him. I want you to make sure he's got enough money for a good lawyer. And I want you to keep this quiet. Not a word to anyone. Not even your family.'

'What about his real father? Can't he do something?'

'I shouldn't think so. As you point out, the boy is in his thirties now. He quite clearly isn't a boy. Brunel as good as rejected him, in any case.'

'What about his mother? His wife?'

'My dear Melody, you are horribly naïve. You see these words — "child pornography" — there in black and white? His mother, whom I may well once have met, will disown her son if that is true. His wife — or at least the mother of his sons — I know nothing about. But even the most broad-minded of women will not forgive a man for that crime. I'm convinced he will be quite alone.'

There is a small pause, during which, I realise later, I am dangerously close to suggesting to Howard that he go to Sydney himself, that he stop all this stupid agoraphobia–heptaphobia nonsense and get on a plane like the avenging uncle he obviously sees himself as. But Howard is rapping his knuckles smartly on the table.

'You do have a passport, a current one?'

'No. Never been out of New Zealand.'

Howard looks surprised at this. 'Never?'

'Once — Curtis and I made plans to go to Fiji to try to sort out our rela —'

'I'll make some phone calls to get you one.' Howard interrupts. Too much information, the tone of his voice tells me, too much intimacy. He doesn't want to know. Sighing heavily he continues, 'We'll get you on a plane tomorrow.'

'How can you organise it that qui —'

. 'I'll have everything covered for you.' He speaks over the top of me again. The most charitable diagnosis of Howard's churlishness would be surdity — but he's interrupting me on purpose. I know he has radar ears. Sometimes he hears Web Ellis scratching at the door before I do. His dismissiveness is more a symptom of fame, a learned response to banalities from rugby fans and journalists.

'I'll pay you well, of course.' He stands up. 'Will you be home tomorrow morning?' I nod. 'I'll courier over my final instructions. It'll be quite a package: air ticket, letter for Jasper, bank draft, a few other bits and pieces.'

We begin our way down the hall and I'm thinking how strange it is that I seem to be going to Sydney when I have no recollection of saying yes. At the front door Howard applies himself to unlocking the ten padlocks, chains and barrel locks that keep him safe.

'Good luck,' he says once the door is open and although I can scarcely believe it he puckers his lips, applies them to his own finger-tips and blows me a kiss.

Despite his seclusion, Howard obviously still has friends in high places. The courier wakes Godfrey and me at the crack of dawn the following morning, banging on the door with a red plastic-wrapped parcel. My flight leaves an hour after Godfrey's.

'Why didn't you organise it so we could be on the same flight?' asks my loved one while we're in the shower. It's a tight squeeze and he's getting all the flow.

'I didn't want to bother Howard with that,' I say. My stomach is a hard knot of anxiety. What am I going to say to this man when I see him? That is, if the prison authorities let me see him. Which they may not. The packet, opened and spread out on the bed, contains a sealed envelope with 'Jasper' written on it in Howard's perfect copperplate. There's my ticket, a bank cheque for $5000 Australian, a faxed confirmation of two nights' accommodation in a city hotel and a small knobbly gift-wrapped object, also labelled 'Jasper'.

In the cab out to the airport Godfrey is as quiet as I am. Nerves, he explains. 'I've got a lot riding on this. A lot of other people's money.'

'Other people's?'

'Yeah. I've got three major sponsors — Telecom, Adidas and Malachy O'Dea, my best mate. Heard of him?'

'Can't say I have.' The taxi is stalled in a long column of traffic on Manukau Road. The meter ticks over faster than a petrol pump.

'One of the richest men in New Zealand. Inherited it all. Overseas interests and real estate. Offered him naming rights and he didn't want them. "O'Dea's Wolves" — got a ring to it, don't you reckon? Malachy keeps a low profile. Sunk all my own money into it as well — sold my house and car,' Godfrey continues. Why does he choose this moment to impart this information, I wonder? He's not looking at me, but out the window. I remember the gift of French perfume he had hidden away in his suitcase; the delectable dinner last night at a beautiful restaurant overlooking the sea; the taxi that took us there and the one that drove us home; and before that, in the late afternoon, the oysters we ate in bed; the bottle of Moët we drank to wash them down. Godfrey wouldn't let me pay for any of it. Maybe he's profligate, a spendthrift. 'Not husband material' a voice says in my head, a voice curiously like Ms Harris's from school. But that's okay. I don't want a husband anyway. After all these years walled up with Curtis I want to play the field. I think.

'This is all very cloak and dagger this mission of yours,' he says now, turning to me. 'Why can't you tell me what you're up to?'

'Howard wanted me to keep it quiet.'

'Is it for the book? Or are you doing him some kind of favour?' He sounds jealous.

'Don't, Godfrey.' I squeeze his hand. 'I wish I could tell you. I'm pretty fucking tense about it, actually.'

'You're not going to be in any kind of danger, are you? Now he's worried.

'Of course not.'

'You could tell me where you're staying, at least.'

'All right. Okay. The Inter-Continental.'

'Very flash.' He nuzzles my hair. 'I've got an idea. How about,' he breathes, hot in my ear, 'I stay there with you? We can have the nights together.'

Howard wouldn't mind, I think. I feel a sudden sense of relief at the thought of having my darling staying with me. 'You have such good ideas,' I tell him, snuggling up. As he bends his head to kiss me, his gold tooth gives off a tawny glare.

We go through the gates together and after Godfrey is safely on his plane I find my own crowded departure lounge and settle in for some reading. I've brought with me the manila folder Howard gave me weeks ago now, and also a recent bestselling history of the All Blacks in which Howard's name features largely: it'll take my mind off visiting this drug-dealing pornographer, I tell myself. I might even be able to convince myself that my biography is continuing, that it isn't completely stalled — which it is. Idly, I leaf through the papers, ignoring the little old Plunket book, casting my eye over Howard's leaving certificate from Auckland Grammar. He left school at fifteen and went out to work as a builder's labourer, finally getting his Trade Certificate at eighteen. It's here too, mottled and cracking at the edges, dated 1956. There's a crisp black and white photograph, white-rimmed, of Howard and a young woman in a tiny sixties bikini, one arm resting on the boom of a broad white sail. Howard is in profile, looking at her. The young woman's head is thrown back in laughter, her deep-set eyes are lively, her long, dark hair whips behind her in the sea-wind. Her teeth are as luminous as the low white buildings on the craggy hills behind her — is it Greece, perhaps? — and her body could be the one Howard describes over and over again in his books — sometimes, in my opinion, fairly cursorily and repetitively: 'tanned breasts, firm to the touch'; 'legs strong and slender, scented as sandalwood'; 'waist so small a man could cup it between both palms'; 'a woman made for love'. The epithet 'sex goddess' occurs in his first book, *Snow Blind* no fewer than five times. Curiously, I turn the photograph over. In faded ink it reads 'Mrs Shag 1965'. The date appears to have been added later: it's in a different-coloured ink, and not as faded.

So this is Howard's ill-fated wife, who died in a diving accident in the Maldives a year after their separation in 1966. She seems so very young, though I suppose, on consideration, Howard was young himself then.

The next papers are clipped together, with an Auckland Hospital letterhead. I lift them away and read avidly. Howard has never told me about rugby injuries so extensive he spent several weeks in hospital. There are the notes from the doctor who admitted him. 'Fractured L.H. metacarpal, R.H. carpal . . .' Hand bones? '. . . broken radius', which, if my limited anatomical knowledge serves me right, is one of the bones in the forearm. I compare the dates on his admission form — 16 February, and the discharge document, which is from a private hospital, Brightside, and dated 20 March. A full month. And not even during the season. 'Lacerated soft tissue surrounding R. eye . . . Ruptured spleen and associated abdominal swelling,' the notes go on. 'Extensive bruising to the scrotum and anal area . . . second-degree cigarette burns to the upper arm . . .' There is an addenda at the bottom of the page: 'Patient wishes case to be treated with utmost confidentiality which, given the circumstances, I heartily recommend.'

Howard's rugby career finished in 1964, well before the lunacy of the Privacy Act. Maybe people were more decent in those days — maybe he was already such a hero the media accorded him some respect and left him alone. Perhaps these injuries resulted from a well-liquored summertime game that got out of control . . . but the burns, the genital bruising? Baffled, I return to the front page of the notes and there, staring me in the face, is the year: 1985. In 1985 Howard was forty-seven and his rugby career had been finished for twenty-one years.

The departure lounge is emptying. As I join the queue and go through the mindless herding process onto the plane I have a deep sense of unease. Somehow, I realise, Howard's appalling injuries are connected with Jasper. Wasn't it the summer of 1985 that his contact with the boy ceased?

'If I had believed him,' Howard said yesterday, 'If I had accepted his warning . . .' Warning of what?

I keep the manila folder on my knee all through the flight. Perhaps Jasper, this mysterious, rather distasteful-sounding crim, will be able to cast some light. He might tell me what Howard never has and never will: what exactly it was that happened during the night of 15 February, twenty years ago, that stopped him ever writing another book or taking pleasure in the world outside his front door.

There is no doubt that Howard, or at least the Howard I have come to know, is irascible, surly, sometimes downright unpleasant — but what did he do to incur an attack of such viciousness? Did he pick a fight with some younger men and come off the worst? The burns puzzle me more than anything — they could be part of a ritualistic torture, as if Howard had done someone so grievous an ill that this attack was a revenge.

A flight attendant with sticky pink lipstick offers me a drink and despite the early hour I accept a gin and tonic. The mixer fizzes into the glass, the ice cubes clink, and in slow replay in my head a fist smashes into Howard's face . . . But it isn't, of course, his old face, the way he looks now. It's a face halfway between that and the young one in his team photographs. It's his middle-aged face, the dark hair only slightly silvered, his features fleshier, his neck and shoulders as strong and sculpted as they are in the pen-and-ink portrait by J.A.B.

I finish my gin, decline the airline meal, recline my seat and sleep almost the whole way to Sydney. At least, my body does. My mind retains an eerie, all-seeing consciousness. I see how my head, twisted into the blue headrest, has squashed my mouth hard up against the coarse fabric and a small stream of dribble forms there. I see the flight attendant moving up and down the aisles and I hear somebody saying my name.

It's the woman beside me, my travelling companion. She is holding my hand, tracing with her forefinger the veins on my inner wrist. She's a big woman, big bosomed and broad shouldered. Revealed by the lift of her full and smiling lip is a glinting gold tooth.

'Now that you know about Claire I'll wear the ring on the other finger,' she's saying, and I watch as she transfers the wedding band to the other hand. How silly I was to worry, I tell myself, and how pleased Lena will be to know I finally have a close relationship with a woman. It was a delusion to think my life was dictated by men. Look at this: my dearest one in the whole world, a raven-haired Amazon with execrable taste in clothes, in her chinos and Bob Charles golfing shirt, holding my hand and beaming at me. She may bear a close resemblance to Godfrey but she isn't Godfrey at all. In the logic of my dream she is Jennifer. Jennifer Adrienne Blucher. J.A.B. Or is she Jillian Alison Brown? My own J.A.B. Joanna Annabelle Brinks? Jocelyn Arabella Bodkin?

J.A.B. The artist who sketched that long-ago portrait. Howard's ex-lover.

Jasper Andrew Brunel. Jasper Aaron Brunel. Jasper Anthony Brunel.

We are beginning our descent as I startle myself awake. Eyes bleary I scramble through my backpack for pen and paper, scrawl out dates, years, subtractions. But I know it couldn't possibly have been Jasper who sketched the portrait, it's a ridiculous notion. The picture was dated 1961 and Jasper wasn't born then — he wouldn't even have been thought of. The newspaper article said he was thirty-three, which makes his year of birth 1972, a decade later.

The drawing isn't important anyway, I tell myself. The business-man sitting beside me is looking at me curiously. I suppose it is a strange thing to do, to jolt yourself awake and indulge in rapid math-ematics. I glance away from him, and see that beyond the oval window, racing up to meet us, is Sydney — my first view of it. Red roofs, wide roads, brick and tile houses, the dusty tops of gum trees, an ever so slightly different light.

'Those are the northern suburbs,' the businessman tells me. 'We'll pass over the Harbour Bridge soon.'

Almost as soon as has finished speaking the bridge appears, a grander, busier version than ours, with a railway line on one side. The city is a mass of tower blocks at either end of the bridge, and the harbour between streams with dozens of boats of all sizes. It's a sunny day here, the sky an immaculate blue: for the first time excitement and curiosity outweigh my apprehension.

RICHARD

Nothing Stays the Same

Staggering along Oxford Street with my third blinding hangover of the week I see Lena and Scottie before they do me: they're sitting at an outside table at the café where we've arranged to rendezvous.

'It must be neutral ground,' Lena had said when I'd suggested my hotel, 'my' being the operative pronoun since Dodo's dinner party — I haven't seen or heard from Michaela since. I've stayed on, though: she'd paid up front for a week so there's no point in leaving.

'And not a pub,' Lena had added. So I'd named a place near the Academy Cinema, one of the few cafés I know in Sydney without resorting to the *Yellow Pages.*

Hearing the phrase 'neutral ground' in Lena's voice was like listening to a song from our courting. It was like a seek-and-destroy heat-sensitive warhead cruising the chambers of my heart. It was a phrase from the time she was still part of my life.

As a counsellor it's probably one of the stock sayings of her trade.

Maybe it came loose from her lexicon because the trauma of seeing Jasper in the Bay had peeled the years back to the battleground in the first months of our separation, when I couldn't believe I wasn't allowed to touch her any more. Once or twice my hands had done so of their own accord and Lena got a young lesie lawyer who'd slapped a non-molestation order on me.

There's no physical contact this time, not between my ex-wife and me anyway. Scottie and I shake hands.

'You all right, Tricky-dicky?' she asks me. 'You look a fright.'

I resent with every cell in my body her infantilising of me, but I force on a smile and sit down. Lena scarcely raises her eyes from her coffee cup. It's twenty-four years since I saw her last. And that was from a distance, from my car, on that long-ago day in 1981 when I collected Jasper to take him to meet Mr Shag. The ensuing article, which arose from interesting information my son imparted on the drive over the bridge, was the final obstacle to all communication between my ex-wife and me: she never forgave me for it. Mr Shag the Alpha Male stepped into the breech. Mr Shag, the man who stole my son away for the next four years. It was Shag who took him to Eden Park, Shag who gave him his first bicycle, Shag who heard all the small triumphs and losses in Jasper's life between '81 and '85 — and after that let me have him back, damaged and silent.

Whenever I came to Auckland, during all my years in Sydney, I booked into an old B & B on Ponsonby Road and made direct contact with Jasper, independently of his mother. He could walk up to see me from home — it wasn't far. Fatherly affection would metastasise in my breast and I would sit out on the villa's sagging veranda, watching out for that loping, evasive boy, all bony shoulders and elastic limbs. After the first year I gave up feeling guilty about how I could summon paternal amour and then dismiss it for months at a time. It was how it had to be.

'Hello, Lena,' I say, and my voice has a certain nasal thinness to it that screams of nerves. A crack in my shell. Are there subcategories of Alpha Male, I wonder? As a younger man I was not that far off Shag's turf; I was snapping at his heels. Maybe I'm Alpha B1 or B2, like a vitamin or one of Jack's Bananas in Pyjamas.

Minutely, Lena raises her eyebrows and drops them again, in the pseudo-Polynesian way that many white New Zealanders have adopted, usually younger ones.

'Hello, Lena,' I repeat evenly. But Lena is not man enough to look me in the eye. Scottie does. 'Flat white,' I tell the waiter, before she orders for me as well. How old would Scottie be now? I wonder. Mid-fifties? All that post-menopausal hormonal soup pouring through her system, giving her balls, while the real ones God gave me shrivel up. Her face shines and as I look away from her, back to Lena, I think it must be religion. You couldn't live so pure a life of organic veges and island air without something to get you through the boring bits, which on Waiheke Island must be multiple and manifest.

Even lowered, Lena's eyes are still splendid. Submerged in her satin-skinned, unlined face, which in mid-life is composed of a pattern of cushiony ovals, they have a dark animal glow. They are as unchanged as the rest of her is unrecognisable. Pulvinate in her soft cotton clothes her body has undergone a metamorphosis, which would be alarming if I hadn't seen Jasper's photograph of the proud grandmother holding Vinnie. She looks up at me now and there — I have it suddenly — the face of the younger woman passing briefly over, as if it were etched on glass, all that high-cheeked beauty gone for ever.

'What are you doing about Jasper?' she asks me quietly, moving her coffee to lean her elbows on the table. 'When are you going to see him?' She thinks I have a plan, which I don't. I must look gormless — Theta Male, Omega Male — because she goes immediately on. 'Did you bring the tape?'

I have no plan *because* of the tape, I want to tell her. Because of the tape I can't sleep. I drink.

'The tape, Richard,' says Scottie, firmly.

'It's in my bag,' I tell her and she looks curiously to my shoulder, then to the chair leg under the table where I might have leaned it. 'In the hotel,' I add.

'You forgot it?' Lena's voice rises suddenly, an upward swing, that old beloved rage.

'You don't want to see it.' My coffee arrives and I remember the packet of fags I bought in a bar last night. I light one and inhale like a drowning man.

'That's not up to you; it's not your decision whether I watch it or not. You said you'd bring it.'

'Next time.'

'I don't want there to be a next time. We'll make all the arrangements now. Have you found a lawyer for him? A good one?'

'He gets Legal Aid.' The back of my throat feels sore. This is the third-to-last one in the box.

'Pardon?' says Lena, fairly belligerently. 'We have to get him a good lawyer. Don't be ridiculous.'

'Can't afford it.' I lean back in my chair away from them. 'Nothing in the world will get him off, Lena. We don't even know what the police must know now. It could be worse than we imagine.'

'You seem to be imagining a fair bit these days, Rickie,' says Scottie. 'That's not like you.'

'There's no "we" in this equation,' Lena says, speaking at the same time as Scottie, and I am filled with dread. Am I to be subjected to another dual conversation of the type I remember from early in their relationship, when I would cower under fire from twin guns? They've got me perfectly lined up, sitting at the table opposite them.

'Have you been to see him yet?' asks Scottie.

'You know more than we do,' says Lena. 'You've seen the tape.'

Scottie puts her hand on top of Lena's and regards me sternly. 'You haven't? Bit of an oversight, isn't it?'

'I want to see the tape,' says Lena.

'It's not here.' At the next table a couple of bald young women sporting brass neck-rings on necks that are approaching breaking point turn their heads stiffly to order coffee from the waiter. It's something the West has borrowed for a minute from a Burmese hill tribe and I have to say it can look wonderful on the hip thirty/forty somethings, especially the girls gone jowly. For the not fully formed it's dangerous and stupid and they can't dance properly. I much preferred the piercings of the last fin-de-siècle.

'Richard. Pay attention!' Lena sounds cross.

'Look — ' I say, my eyes unable to tear themselves away from the pair of aliens. One of them has colour-washed her bald scalp to look like pink marble. It's quite beautiful. 'Don't you see enough shit in your life? You know what it must be. Boys and body glitter. Hotel rooms and satin sheets. Joints back and forth. Scotch. At least the drugs in it are pretty tame. That's one thing.'

Lena's coffee is untouched. It's formed a brown skin.

'What do you mean, I know? How could I know anything more than what you told me on the phone?'

Warning lights flash in my brain. There's a subtext here — something female, maternal and deeply neurotic. 'Better you stay optimistic,' I suggest. 'Better you float above it.' Bad choice of word: float. It means chiffon, lightweight. It means balloon-shaped. It could be a word Lena is sensitive to.

'I'm not optimistic now, Richard. Fuck you.'

Scottie picks Lena's hand up off the table altogether and holds it somewhere beneath it. 'How good are the Legal Aid lawyers?' she asks. 'I'm sure they'll be good,' she answers herself. 'But if they're not, we'll get one and split the bill. Okay, Dickie?' I nod.

'Where'd he get the boys from?' Lena says quietly, deadly.

'I don't know. Ask him.'

'We can't ask him anything. He's back on the psych ward, didn't you know? He's had some kind of breakdown. It happened while I was there.'

'What do you mean breakdown?'

'He collapsed.'

Scottie puts her arm around Lena and gives her a squeeze. 'That's all that's worrying us now,' says Scottie. 'That's all that should be worrying us. We don't want to obsess about anything else.'

Lena is talking over the top of her. 'Will the police try to find the boys?'

'I s'pose. Of course. I don't know.' God, I wish I'd stayed in France. I wish I'd kept my distance. At least the sun is out today, with racing clouds streaming in from the west. The wind is high up, in some outer atmospheric zone: there's not so much as a ruffle of a serviette or cappuccino froth down here. It's cool and still and the air stinks of monoxide and burnt rubber. We should have met in a park somewhere — the Botanic Gardens or Centennial Park. At least then we could have looked at trees and ponds and ibis and kids playing.

The women are looking at me as though they expect me to contribute something to the discussion. I wonder if the pink marble head would be cool to the touch.

'Where are you staying?' I ask.

'With friends,' says Scottie, 'in Rozelle.'

'Nice, is it?'

'Richard,' says Lena, 'Jasper is back in the hospital. He's had a breakdown. I don't think you took it in.'

'Some counsellor you must be. It wouldn't occur to you, I don't suppose, that I don't want to take it in. Not just as this moment. It's my choice. You can't impose on me like that.' Give her a taste of her own jargon, all those merry bells ringing out behind those depleted words.

'What?' she says. 'Pardon?'

'Leave me alone. Of course I heard you. I'm going out to the prison this afternoon. I'll find out what's going on and let you know.'

'I don't believe you,' says Lena. Scottie is gazing off into inner space. When she relaxes her focus an optic muscle must also soften to allow her right eye to swing away from its axis, at a forty-five-degree remove from whatever the gaze of her left eye rests on. Is it a distortion come about from an accident, like Shag's rugby-injured eye, or is it an effect of ageing? I wonder. I don't remember Scottie's eyes being like that before.

'Does he need anything? Should I take him something?'

'It's not like he's walled up in some fucking nursing-home, Richard.' I'm stabbing out my cigarette, I'm standing and pulling five bucks out of my pocket and putting it on the table.

Lena keeps talking. 'I'll make some phone calls and try to get on to one of the psychiatrists out there.'

'Don't bother telling him,' says Scottie. 'He's not interested.'

'Don't you dare bugger off, Richard,' says Lena, but I'm picking up my cigarette packet with two smokes left in it and I'm going, I'm gone, as fast as I can, back down Oxford Street to Taylor Square, dodging the traffic on the diagonal into Burke. I'm walking into Surry Hills. Narrow leafy streets open up on my right. Down Foveaux Street and across Crown I go, as if I know where I'm going. Which I don't.

I had a night on the ink here once, in a pub further down the hill towards the railway station, sometime in the early nineties. It was full of blokes and I thought at first I'd walked into a gay bar. But there was none of the effervescent hilarity, tragedy and charity I'd witnessed in a boys' bar before. Most of these guys seemed sullen and glum, bewildered even, mostly alone or sitting in small groups. I sat with a trio of them and heard their sorry tales of ex-wives and family courts and kids and loss of access. They pointed out men who'd had an even worse time of it than they had. They talked of bedsits and broken-down cars, debt and dead-end jobs. They were the lost boys of Sydney. All that was missing was a crocodile with a clock in its stomach. It was hideous. One of the most dreary nights of my life, even though — I remember — I tried to liven it up with a joke.

'Why is a woman like a hurricane?' I asked the morose trio, who shook their heads and waited mirthlessly for the answer. 'Because she arrives wild and wet and leaves with your house and car.' Not a glimmer of a smile. I wasn't going there again. I was descending the hill, emptying my mind, trying to keep it cool and still.

When Jasper was about four he had a pair of green gumboots that were magic. He'd sit on the floor to pull them on and the boots would walk him around the rooms of whichever dreary flat he was visiting me in. Flatmates would be alarmed by his sudden appearance in the bathroom, or at the foot of their bed. He couldn't be dissuaded; he believed utterly that he didn't arrive in those places of his own free will: the boots made him do it.

So I'm walking through Strawberry Hills in the way he got about at four, in his seven-league green gumboots. Left into Elizabeth Street I go, and left again into Chalmers Street.

The Journalists' Club is gone. Demolished. In its place stands an ugly apartment block. 'Clarion 2000' reads the sign on the wall and I remember suddenly that *The Clarion* was the newspaper some Sydney journalists put together during strike of the seventies. When I first crossed the ditch I wrote one or two things for it. I stand on the street, looking up at its blind windows, wondering if a journalist had some part in the naming, or if it's yet another mindless coincidence of the sort my world bursts with the older I get. Collective memory is a phenomenon of the past, I remind myself; this is not a cultural reference. How many of us are left who will see the connection? I wonder. When I lived here, during Jasper's boyhood, I came here often, to the now-vanished club. There were countless nights of staggering out the door legless and falling into a taxi or a mate's car. There were plenty of ladies I won around the pool table — beautiful girls delighted by my debonair ways, drop-dead gorgeous babes who would spend a night, a weekend, maybe as long as a month. I was still pulling them in my late forties.

I sigh, light my second-to-last smoke. I'm a lonely heart, that's all. What did my subconscious think: that I'd get here and find it all unchanged, that night would miraculously fall from the noon sky and I could climb the steps to a loud and crowded room, that the journos I knew from Kippax Street would be there unchanged, drinking up large?

Nothing stays the same. All those girls, where are they now? The ones who were twenty will be forty, the ones who were forty — and there were a few of those, I remind myself — could be dead, or as good as. They'll be like me, trailing long and complicated lives behind them like wake behind a boat, and not wanting to turn to watch the disappearing land. I can't afford to let my mind drift for fear of entering some no-go zones, some rough and unforgiving seas. Compartmentalising they used to call it in the eighties. It was a kind of buzz-word. It enabled you to inflict wrong on other people, to take the upper hand when you had no right to, to eschew guilt. Conversely, then as now, if you were the victim, you had all of society's permission to dwell and mope, to let the wind go out of your sails and wallow for ever in stagnant waters.

I'm dropping my smoke to grind it underfoot when I hear a female voice call my name from behind me, from the other side of the street. At first a heavy truck puts a wall of sound between me and the voice and I hear only the first syllable — 'Rich —' As I turn a flash of blue catches my eye: it's Dodo in the same dress she wore to the party. Without my glasses she's an obelisk of royal blue, regal and ecclesiastical, with legs. No, it's not the same dress. Today it's a pant suit in an identical shade.

If I were Dodo and some pissed and deranged bloke had ruined my dinner party as effectively as I ruined hers I would have passed on quietly by; I would not have hailed him from the other side of the road.

'Richard!' she calls again, fully revealed, the truck passed. She steps out onto the street, her face retaining her warm, welcoming smile as she negotiates the traffic.

Why does she want to speak to me? Perhaps she's forgotten what I did; perhaps she has amnesia brought on by too many dinner parties over too many years and they've all blurred into one long evening of good manners and dull wits.

'How are you?' She takes my hand between hers, which despite the heat are warm and dry. It's the end of August and about thirty degrees. The morning news showed pictures of crowds at Bondi. 'I've been worrying about you.'

'You shouldn't have.' I tug my hand away.

'But you're in a terrible situation. Michaela's told me all about it.'

'She's staying with you, then?'

'Oh yes. Of course. Is there somewhere around here we could sit down? Have a drink? This isn't my usual stamping ground — had to see a specialist just up there, in Buckingham Street — don't ask — a woman's thing — took a cab in — much easier than driving, don't you agree?' And Dodo, legs and tongue pumping, leads me off down Elizabeth Street. Biddable as a lobotomised lamb I go along with her for block after block until we reach a pub on the corner of George and Hay streets.

We sit at a table outside the Club Paradise with the light rail clicking and hissing past at regular intervals and Dodo tells me over her gin and tonic that Michaela is fine and that they have been talking about my son and what I should do. And no, she says, before I ask — not that I was about to — she doesn't want to see me. It's quite wonderful that we met, she says, because they had decided that she, Dodo, would ring me to give me their advice and pass on Michaela's regards.

'And I would have told you that you're welcome to stay on at the hotel until the end of the week. I suppose you know she's paid the bill till then. After that you're on your own.' Above Dodo's head a sign flashes in an oblong of red strip lights: 'Open for Fun and Gambling'. The lettering in the centre of the red board is white, Chinese. Does it say the same thing, I wonder, or something completely different? 'Stay away from here or you'll lose all your money'?

'However, Richard,' and Dodo pauses to take a long, giraffe-lipped sip at her gin, 'there have been some developments. Mikie and I have a lawyer for your son. Top class. The very best. A man called Lamb.'

'We?'

'We're doing this together, Mikie and I. We'll meet all the costs.'

'Why?' I ask. I'm having water.

'We have our reasons.'

'What reasons?'

'There's a connection. For Mikie. Something that compels her to help out as much as she possibly can.'

'Me, you mean?'

Dodo erupts, her breast a vast blue shimmering oblong that jolts with each with deep, percussive hoot. 'You? I don't think so.'

'She doesn't even like Jasper.' Dodo raises her eyebrows and makes a small moue before applying herself once more to the rim of the glass.

'Why, then?' I'm completely at sea with this one. Dodo meets my eyes once and looks away.

'I don't think . . .' she says steadily, 'that she likes either of you much. It's another connection completely.'

'Bonny? Has she been talking to her? Lena?'

'No, no, no. You mustn't try and work it out. You won't be able to anyway. It all goes back to yonks ago. To her darling brother. We all loved him.' Dodo drains her drink and stands up. 'I really mustn't say a word more. Goodbye, Richard.'

And she's sailing off, a full blue spinnaker, a ship of mystery, down Hay Street towards a taxi rank, leaving me to puzzle over my Adam's Ale alone. I thought I had listened attentively enough to Michaela's late-night life-stories, but try as I might I cannot remember any mention of a brother. 'We all loved him,' Dodo said. Past tense. Was he dead? It's that breeding again, I realise. In Michaela's world it is unseemly to dwell on unpleasant aspects of one's life. Admirable really, I think, and old fashioned. She never told me why her marriages had broken down, or of any hard times she may have experienced. I just assumed her whole life had been a doddle: a smooth clicking together of private schools, travel, husbands, children and friends, with all the parts well oiled by lashings of money. I imagined her gears had never graunched.

Silly me. I light up my very last smoke and order a beer with a whisky chaser.

FRANCA

Snake Handler

Diffused light melted cool and pale through the long white curtains of Franca's bedroom and a frantic figure formed a trajectory between the wardrobe and full-length mirror. In turn she discarded the grey silk suit, her black trousers and jacket and a red linen dress and stood eventually in a pair of designer jeans and an apricot cotton jumper. She added a gold necklace and drew her hair up in a loose knot at the nape of her neck.

How much younger she looked like this, she thought, calculating the difference in their ages. Four years. They were almost contemporaries. The bathroom mirror, lit by a blazing frill of naked bulbs, was not so kind. She took a step back from it and smoothed makeup over her skin, applied lipstick and mascara, and was debating which of her cluttered perfume bottles contained the right scent when the phone rang. Standing at her bedroom window, parting the curtains to look out at the concrete wall of the neighbouring apartment building, she answered it. On the parallel floor a man in an orange bathrobe sipped from a mug at his kitchen table, the newspaper spread before him. On his tiny balcony a pot-plant trembled in a sharp breeze off the harbour, a large fluffy ginger cat curled up in a patch of weak sunlight.

'Ciao, Bella.'

'Kerry?' Her cousin never introduced herself. One year would pass into another without Franca ever hearing her voice, but she was supposed to recognise it. It always rankled. 'Are you in Sydney?'

'No, no. Melbourne. At home.'

'Is something wrong?' It was Nònna, Franca knew suddenly. She'd been taken ill, collapsed, the phone had rung before, while she was in the shower, she hadn't heard it, the emergency services had got through to Melbourne, her aunt had asked Kerry to ring Franca with the bad news —

'No,' Kerry was saying, 'I was just lying here in bed reading the paper and I saw something I thought might interest you.'

'I'm about to go out,' said Franca. Despite the intermittent sun it looked cold outside. That busy wind. She'd need a jacket.

'It'll really interest you,' said Kerry, and then to a questioning voice in the background she said, 'Yeah. Why not?'

'Who's that?' asked Franca.

'Only the most beautiful woman in the world offering me more coffee. She's tall, she's funny, she's gorgeous, she's too sexy for her hat!' Kerry laughed.

'You amaze me,' said Franca, envious.

'We're wildly in love,' said Kerry. 'I can't believe how intense it is. She's —'

'Kerry, I have to go —' She wondered about her cousin's capacity for love, the decisions she made. Did she really fall in love every single time? She was slightly older than Franca, in her mid-forties now. Since she'd come back from New Zealand, where she'd spent most of her twenties, there had been a series of dearly beloveds, most of whom Franca had never met.

'You and Kerry,' Nònna used to say, shaking her head at their mutual unmarried states. Franca never attempted to explain the vastly differing reasons for it. Even without their individual sexuality they couldn't have been more un-alike: Kerry, with her exuberant red hair, now helped along by regular applications of henna, her wide, wicked smile, her big tumultuous heart; and Franca herself, cold, bottle-blonde, solemn, careful as a cat on a high wall strewn with broken glass.

'What was it? In the paper?'

'Oh yeah. Hang on.' There was a rustling as Kerry shifted in the bed. 'Page eight, the *Age*. "The name has been released of the New Zealand man apprehended last week ten kilometres off the coast of northern New South Wales. He is Jasper Brunel, who also goes by the aliases Gilmore and Shag. Brunel is being held on remand at Long Bay Prison, Sydney, facing charges of smuggling and possession of a Class A drug. A police search of Brunel's flat revealed a number of pornographic video tapes of amateur quality. Police intend to interview Brunel, who . . ." blah blah blah.' Kerry broke off. 'Shag, Frankie. One of his names is Shag!'

Franca said nothing. Her neighbour in the orange bathrobe had risen from the table and come out onto his balcony to place a bowl of food near the indifferent nose of his cat.

'Franca? You there? Did you already know about this?'

'Yeah, I'm here.'

Knowing that Kerry and her friends had taken revenge on him when Shag had returned to Auckland had made her recovery quicker. She had always believed this. There were gaps in what she remembered, in what she had been told. She'd never known the names of the other women who'd acted for her, or the details of what they'd done to him. They'd made him suffer, Kerry had written in a letter signed only 'K'; they'd given him an experience he was unlikely to forget. 'Please destroy this note as soon as you have finished reading it,' it finished, in the best of *Mission Impossible* style, and Franca had obliged, setting it alight in Nònna's kitchen sink.

'Maybe he's his son,' said Kerry. 'He's too young to be the same guy. Howard Shag must be nearly seventy now, at least.'

'Maybe he just liked the name. Or the books.'

'The books are all shit,' said Kerry, then, 'Thanks, honey.' The new love was talking to her.

'Look, thanks, Kerry, I'll buy a paper later and read the whole article,' Franca said.

'It's pretty short,' said Kerry. 'Won't take you long.'

She drove quickly, automatically, forming a list of questions she would put to him in order. Her mind returned to the day she'd met Jasper, when she'd looked in the door at him doing push-ups and there was that resemblance, that flash of something familiar that had frightened her. Back then she'd known nothing about his Shag alias; there was nothing to prompt that moment of recognition. There was no point in surmising any possible relationship, she'd decided by the time she'd parked her car at the prison. Neither was there any sense in indulging in meditations — sober, this time — on serendipity, coincidence or karma, or any foolish attributions of intelligence to fate.

He was still sedated, Stambach told her as he led her down the corridor. She could see him if she really wanted.

'Absolutely. No question,' Franca replied too quickly, and Stambach paused to look at her curiously.

'I know you're no longer seeing him in a professional capacity,' he said gently, 'but I'm sure I hardly need remind you to keep your distance.'

She flushed and kept walking, drawing level with the doctor and then passing him. She must be an open book, she considered, if you took into account some of the damaged minds and motivations of the men he'd treated here for most of his working life. For a second she hated him for his perception.

'Through there.' Stambach caught hold of her arm before she overshot the door. 'The far bed.'

There were four beds in the room, two of them empty. Franca passed the only other occupant, a painfully thin, pallid skinhead who looked up at her once with dull eyes and away. She stood at the foot of Jasper's bed and watched him for a moment. He was asleep, his breathing shallow, his face young and peaceful. There was a chair against the wall and Franca sat in it, wishing suddenly she'd bought something with her: a gift of fruit, or a book. Perhaps it would be against regulations. She pulled the chair closer to the bed and its rubber-stoppered legs squealed loudly on the polished linoleum. Startled by the noise, the skin-head swore with fright and turned carefully in his bed, presenting her with his bony back. Jasper's eyes flickered, opened, regarded her and as she looked into them she saw him come back into himself. They were lit by a sharp edge of panic that was immediately blunted by whatever Stambach had administered. Librium or Xanax.

'Hi, Jasper,' she said.

He gazed at her still and she wondered if he had forgotten her, if his mind was so fogged he couldn't work out who she was. Then his lips parted and he said her name, dry-mouthed. She poured him some water from a plastic jug and held it to his mouth, pulling the sheet away from under his chin. His head lifted, his lips pursed and she saw he couldn't raise himself up to drink comfortably because he was tied down, strapped to the bed. Water dribbled from the rim of the glass and pooled in the hollows of his collarbone.

After she'd replaced the glass she took a tissue from her bag, went to wipe it away and met his eyes, the pupils dilated.

'Can I ask you something?' she asked, holding his gaze.

'If you like.' His speech was slow and slurred.

'Why do you call yourself Shag?'

''Cause . . .' he paused, considered, and she hoped he wasn't working against the sedative to spin her a line. 'I knew him when I was a kid. I met him and he was kind.'

'Howard Shag, do you mean?' The name came unnaturally to her lips. She hadn't pronounced it for decades, she realised. Jasper was nodding.

'Blackorba,' she thought he said.

'What?'

'S'mine. *Black Orbit*.'

'Oh.' It dawned on her. One of Shag's books. He'd dedicated one of his books to Jasper.

'You're not related to him? I thought you might be his son.'

One side of Jasper's mouth twisted up in a doped smile. 'If only,' he said quietly. 'If only.'

'So your father really is Richard Brunel, the man I emailed for you?'

She thought he nodded. 'Why don't you use his name?'

Jasper had closed his eyes but he murmured, 'Fuckin' frog name.'

'Don't go to sleep again, Jasper,' she pleaded, leaning forward to pat his cheek. His eyes opened blearily.

'Go 'way now,' he said, turning his face from her, towards the skinhead, dismissing her.

The road ahead seemed clearer suddenly; the relief she felt at Jasper's explanation was intense. Children are often poor judges of adult character — the young Jasper was not to know what Shag really was.

'Jasper?' she tried again, putting one hand on his unresponsive shoulder. 'I want to ask you about these tapes the police found in your flat.' The nameless man on the yacht, the one who'd drowned, perhaps they belonged to him, she thought. Or to one of his other criminal mates. In his sleep Jasper's head turned to face her again and she longed to lift her hand from his shoulder to trace the line of his soft lips, the high, tanned arches of his cheekbones. He looked innocent, boyish.

Stambach's voice came back to her, the words he'd used in the corridor. 'Maintain your distance.' She could teach him a thing or two about that: she was an expert. The neurotic wealthy women who made up the bulk of her clientele were no doubt easier to treat than his patients were and sometimes she felt a keen sorrow for them, for their empty, lonely lives. It wasn't difficult for her to empathise: on the surface their existences were not dissimilar. They resided in clean, comfortable, empty homes, eschewed domestic tasks, rarely cooked, dressed carefully and well. It was just that instead of a husband who philandered or worked too hard or made unreasonable demands, Franca had her career. Aside from Kerry she had no real friends, no brothers or sisters. Yes — it was too significant to be ignored: this beautiful troubled man had come into her life with two powerful coincidental factors — their shared Italian blood and his connection with that other Shag, the man who could have been her nemesis.

For so many years she had held herself apart from the world, loving scarcely anyone and making sure the succour she offered the depressed, the overweight, the anorexic, the alcoholic, the addicted — whatever specific disease of privilege her patients suffered — was first class, beyond reproach and administered at no real cost to herself. The faces of the attempted suicides she interviewed for her paper were usually forgotten by the following day: an intentional and necessary amnesia.

But this man . . . She was prepared to give as much as he required from her. She would deny him nothing except the truth of her feelings. Why had he been asking for her? she wondered. Had there been something he had wanted to tell her, something the drugs had suppressed? Had there been a period of lucidity before Stambach got to him?

There was Stambach himself, at the door, beckoning, and it occurred to her as she stood that he could have been there for some time, watching. Surreptitiously she slipped her hand away from Jasper's shoulder, along the sheet.

'Remand sent these up,' Stambach said in the corridor, handing her a sheaf of papers. It seemed to Franca, as she took them, that he was avoiding her eye.

'But I'm not —' she began.

'I've kept a copy for myself,' he interrupted, 'and I'd be interested in anything you have to say about them. Keep in touch.' He was holding the ward door open for her. A number of responses rose in her mind — 'Of course', or 'I'll ring tomorrow', even 'Let me know if he asks for me again' — but she went out with the papers rolled in her hand and only a muttered goodbye.

Puzzled, Gregor returned to his office. The image of Franca's face as she'd sat at the prisoner's bedside glowed mysteriously in his mind. He knew nothing about her private life except that she lived alone. When she first came to the attention of the psychiatric world with her work on suicide there had been some gossip that her mother had gone out by her own hand — but he had never achieved any degree of intimacy with Franca that would have allowed a discussion of her past, or even the circumstances of her present. She struck him now as isolated, a singular woman. It was common for women with successful careers in the early twenty-first century to have no family and few friends. And if they did have these things, they sometimes regretted them: his own wife, also a doctor, had often bemoaned her marriage and the hindrance of children.

From his window he watched Franca crossing the carpark, the sheaf of papers held close to her breast like something precious, like an infant. She walked quickly, the wind ruffling her hair.

She didn't want to go home. Neither did the idea of visiting Nònna appeal. The two options struck her as arid, empty and confronting in a way she didn't welcome, not in the strange, tender and vulnerable mood she found herself in. At the exit of the carpark she turned left and remembered as she did so coming this way with Nònna one summer when she was a teenager. They'd gone to La Perouse on the bus, which had stopped outside the prison to let off a group of women who could well have been on their way to see their men inside, she thought now. She had hardly been aware of the prison. At La Perouse she and Nònna had stood with other families and tourists around a rectangular canvas pit, like an outsized paddling pool, and watched an Aboriginal man and his son handle snakes. Nònna had seemed on the verge of fainting, fanning herself for the heat and wincing as though the mere sight of reptiles caused her pain, but Franca remembered herself as wide-eyed, fascinated. She had seen snakes before, of course, in Broken Hill, but never so close or so large. When the handler bought one over to her to touch she had stretched out her hand, expecting a moist sensation that corresponded to the glinting, shining scales — like a fish, or a worm — but the snake was dry and warm. Draped passively in the strong, dark hands the animal regarded her. There was a primitive intelligence there, the shape of an equation passing through its black lidless eye as if it were measuring the meat on her bones.

As Anzac Parade swung around to enclose the green ellipses of lawn that held the museum and monument, Franca passed the spot where the snake man had stood in a bay at the side of the road. The bay was no longer there; the shape of the road had changed. She parked and got out of the car, shrugging on her jacket. The Frenchman's monument sprang up before her, like the grave of a stake and crossroad suicide, the pointed column rising from the midriff. The fine wrought-iron fence encircling it was a septum, fraily guarding all that was left of Monsieur La Perouse. But it wasn't his grave, she remembered. It was just his name, that being all that remained of him.

The wind off the sea was stiff and much colder than she had

expected it to be, but she forced herself out of her car and bought a takeaway coffee from the Boatshed Café. For a moment, as she waited for it, she considered staying inside, drinking it on the veranda above the grey expanse of Frenchmans Bay. Beyond the white sand of the beach below, the sea was whipped into a scummy chop and further out was inky black, reflecting the sky above, like the reverse side of an old mirror. Franca felt dreamy, excited, like she had as a child at Christmas or birthdays, even before she came to live with Nònna, who celebrated them with far more vigour and joy than her poor mother ever had.

Balancing her coffee, the papers Stambach had given her tucked under her arm, she stepped over the low barrier fence and picked her way over the low flat rocks of the point. There was a fisherman below her, in trackpants and a woolly hat. A red puffer jacket was folded on top of his tackle box behind him. She sat down on the rocks, cross-legged, and opened the papers, turning the pages to the shifting, tumultuous light. It would be difficult to decipher, the letters blurred black on a grey fuzzy background. The photographs must've been scanned and enlarged, then printed out: the quality was very poor and Jasper's script tiny, a childlike, unsophisticated printing. Someone, she supposed it was Stambach, had hand-numbered the pages. She bent her head and read avidly, tracing the smudgiest words with a fine-nib pen, the coffee growing cold on the limestone beside her.

A flicker of raindrops spotted the last page. On the far side of the bay an aeroplane was coming in to land, its wings glinting blue-white in the thundery glare. The man in the Boatshed Café was moving around his few hardy patrons on the veranda and rolling down plastic storm-blinds. For a moment Franca considered returning to her car, getting out of this icy wind and beginning rain, thawing out her stiff, chilled limbs —

I must have done something to give myself away.

How would it have been if she'd met him earlier, even only three or four months ago, before he went on that last run? She could have offered him salvation — enough financial security for him to find his own place in the world. How clearly she saw him on the day he described when he was eight, a lean-limbed, hungry-eyed boy, stoned out of his mind in the cave of a remote New Zealand beach. Then that very night on the floor of that vast living room in Auckland. The comfort of dope. The beautiful girl with the red hair, whose written name blew up in a raindrop landed on the page. She wiped the water away and the name smeared and obscured. Kirsty?

Come down and we'll go for a walk along the beach.

The boy fetched from the tree, on the last day of his boyhood he'd spent with his father. His mistaken lionising of Howard Shag. How clearly she saw it. The older face tipped up to the younger, that winning, wicked but somehow safe smile. That I've-seen-it-all-and-you're-safe-with-me-kid glint in the eye. It was raining in earnest now, but Franca was miles away, oblivious.

She was remembering how she'd gone with Karleen to the Journalists' Club in Surry Hills. Karleen with cropped blonde hair and thick black eye-liner, who lived two houses away from Nònna and was older than Franca, nearly twenty. She was a cadet reporter for the *Sydney Morning Herald* and Franca was captivated by her reckless behaviour, her peerless consumption of vodka and orange juice, her blood-red finger-nails set with glittering moons and her tight, sexy clothes — the sort of gear Franca could never wear around Nònna. That night she matched her drink for drink, changing when Karleen did to tequila slammers. Around the pool table she borrowed the more raucous elements of Karleen's personality. She might not have had the black leather jeans or legs as skinny as her friend's, but her skirt was shorter than Nònna liked it to be and her long hair — still dark in those days — shone down her back, as lambent as her cheeks and lips, which were smeared with Vaseline. It was a Friday night and the club, in a long upstairs room with a wooden floor and long, streaky multi-paned windows, was packed. Five or six deep at the bar stood not only journalists but cab drivers, advertising executives, secretaries, rock musicians, business and television people . . . and oh! There was the pop star Grace Knight! She felt quite breathless.

The fisherman propped his rod between his legs and put on his jacket, squinting at the sky. The rain wasn't going to put him off.

Two men had challenged them to a game of pool. One of them was a New Zealander, a square-shouldered, barrel-chested man with curly hair greying at his temples. Even though he was old, he kind of glowed with health. There was something curious and proud about him and she was fascinated. Was he really ancient? she wondered. Was he forty? She loved the way he looked at her with those sharp, warm eyes under their heavy lids: he was slightly predacious, there was a hint of danger. She couldn't remember the other man at all. Younger. Fair-haired. He had paled beside the older man into insignificance. She remembered he'd had to resort to ribbing him about how dozy and dull his homeland was.

'Name one New Zealander who's changed the world,' the younger man had said as he went off to chalk their names on the board at the far end of the room, 'apart from Rutherford.'

'Changing the world isn't such a good thing unless you change it for the better,' she'd called after him, slurring slightly, and the men had laughed at her. Perhaps they weren't friends, she thought now, perhaps they'd only just met. The New Zealander hadn't liked her coming to his defence.

Around midnight she and Karleen had gone for a smoke in the ladies and giggled a lot. The chrome taps flared, the sound of a woman pissing in the next cubicle set them off hysterically for what seemed like hours. Then they'd reeled out again, Franca swallowing frantically against her dry throat. The younger man accidentally/on purpose leaned against Karleen who lunged forward on her shot, missing the white ball completely and driving the end of the cue into the baize. It left a hole. Was it the older man who'd bought them the first tequila slammers? They could hardly focus on the end of the cue enough to bring the blue chalk against it. The men could have beaten them in five minutes but they kept giving them extra turns.

It was three o'clock in the morning when they left. Franca remembered looking at her watch as they went down the stairs and turning to tell Karleen this astonishing fact, and also that they should hurry because Nònna would be waiting up, worried. But Karleen wasn't there. She'd disappeared. It was the kind New Zealander who stood on the step above her.

'Your mate? Girls' loos,' he said, smiling.

'What for?' she'd asked, innocently, thinking Karleen might be unwell.

'Must've felt like a bit,' the man told her, making her blush. The stairs rolled nauseatingly one after the other down the well. Outside on the street they'd sheltered from the rain under a shop awning. The cool air began to revive her.

'So you're Karleen.' He was behind her, lighting a cigarette and using her body as a wind-break.

'No, I'm —' but he didn't give her time. He wheeled around her now almost as if they were dancing, with his right hand extended.

'Howard Shag,' he said.

'The writer?' She was amazed. 'But why were you —'

'Had an interview today for my new book,' he said airily. 'Wound up here after a long lunch.' She'd leaned against the wall while he hailed a taxi. It was strange — she was sure she'd heard his mate upstairs call him something else. Robert, was it?

'I should wait for my friend,' she'd protested as a cab swung around the corner. 'I came with her in her car.'

'She's in no fit state to drive,' Howard Shag had said. 'I'll give you a lift. Where do you live?'

'Leichhardt.' She climbed gratefully into the car, let the warmth of it and the soft upholstery scoop her in — and banged her head on the back of the seat. The world wobbled.

'Alone?' Howard Shag dragged on his cigarette and ignored the cabby, who swore at him and told him to put it out.

'With my grandmother.' She wound down the window, prayed that she wouldn't be sick.

'How cute. You're very sweet, Karleen, you know that?' and he'd put his arm around her. She'd pretended he hadn't and asked him a question.

What was it now? She shifted on the cold stone; her hair felt slicked, glued to her head with rainwater. Yes, she'd asked him where he got his ideas from and he'd laughed again, in the same hard, superior and infinitely alluring way he had in the club when she'd defended him.

'Which ideas?' he'd asked. 'I'm full of them. Here's a good one.'

And he'd taken her hand, laid it in his groin. She'd left it there, moved it a little, excited and curious. A famous man, Howard Shag, turned on by her!

'Good girl,' he'd whispered into her hair, and he'd leaned forward and given the cabby the name of his hotel.

There was the vague ghost of the memory of the rest of the journey, of the two of them standing side by side at the brightly lit front desk to pick up his key. In his room they'd had another drink — a scotch each from the mini-bar, with ice. As he moved around adjusting the lighting the skin of his face was the same shining beige as the curtains. The first time he kissed her he'd come from behind, tipping her face up from where she lay slumped against the sofa. Her neck and jaw had begun to ache; she burped at the end of it and hoped he didn't notice.

How swiftly he'd removed her clothes and his own, and how pleased she was with everything until he had her lying on his bed. There was something in the smell of him, in the way that he was with her, that made her think this was not what she wanted. Not for her first time. He had been with a hundred women. She could tell. There was an over-caressed quality to his skin. A pallid tongue lapped at her nipple and she gave him an experimental push away.

He looked up, one eyebrow raised, and she thought perhaps, on the other hand, that she did like him. He had a neat sense of fun. They'd had such a great night together. He was sophisticated, he knew a lot. He was a famous writer whose books she had not read. But she knew his name. It was everywhere. They made films of his books. He gave her breast a parting kiss and rose above her, pushing something — his cock, of course — between her legs. It felt huge. Why hadn't she looked at it when she had the chance? She'd never seen one with its trousers off completely, outside of heavy petting with a boy during Year Ten.

It took ages and it was embarrassing, but he finally got it in. The pain made tears prickle at the corner of her eyes and she thought it might stop once he achieved his goal, but then he began to move — once, twice — and she made her mind up. Finally and absolutely. If this was sex, she did not want to have it with this man. She had made a mistake.

'No,' she said, in what she hoped was a firm voice. He put his arms around her shoulders, tightly; his face pressed into her neck and she struggled against him. 'Please — stop!'

'It's all right.' He was moving, whispering gently, 'It's all right, Karleen.' Did he know she was a virgin? Could he tell? She tried to do it right, to do it better. She kissed him on the underside of the jaw and felt it hot and prickly on her lips; his skin tasted sour. Groaning slightly, he lifted himself to his elbows and she imagined what they must look like, his pulsatile bum.

'I want to stop now,' she said again and stopped crying. The pain had lessened and she could see her knees rising on either side of his body like the boards of a boat. Anger flared suddenly; it replaced her fear — it was more powerful than what she imagined desire to be. One hand lifted from the crumpled sheet and struck him hard on the ear. Shag paused momentarily and shifted something from behind her head: a pillow, which he placed over her face, pinning it down with both his arms.

'You little bitch.' His voice was muffled, half amused. 'Don't try that one.' And he went on fucking her for what seemed like hours but perhaps it was only a few minutes more. She stopped calling out, tried only to breathe with her head twisted to one side. Finally, somewhere above her, on the other side of the suffocating foam, he gave a great shuddering sigh and all the tension in his body released.

He was still and heavy and Franca waited a moment or two before she flung the pillow away and wriggled out from under him, carefully pushing him to one side. Why was she strong enough to push him away now, when she hadn't been before? she wondered. He'd rolled over onto his back and in the bright light that he'd flicked on as they lay down — 'Let me look at you,' he'd said — she saw he was asleep. He looked older, louche, debauched, his mouth fallen open and his teeth nicotine stained, his eyelids flickering already. As she got out of bed the room tilted, the carpet swam up to meet her, the walls shifted forward and receded. She was still drunk: her stomach burned and roiled.

The first door she opened, hand clamped over her mouth, proved to be a wardrobe, but it was too late: she was sick all over Howard Shag's jacket sleeve and the shoes paired below it. Reflecting on this twenty years later Franca supposed Shag would've thought she'd done it on purpose. At the time it had been another unendurable shame, but now the recollection of it pleased her. It was a tiny revenge exacted before the greater one.

Afterwards, through the only other door, she'd found the bathroom and rinsed her mouth. In the mirror she looked exactly the same. There was nothing to show in her pale, exhausted face that she had just been with a world-famous writer in a grotty hotel room. His toilet bag was open on the vanity and she'd peered in at its contents — the bottle of Tabac aftershave, the splay-bristled toothbrush. He must be mean with his money, she'd thought. Surely someone as famous as him could afford to stay in five-star hotels and wear expensive cologne? She'd wondered what the real Karleen would do in this situation. Go through his pockets and steal all his money? The thought of touching anything that belonged to him filled her with revulsion. In the bedroom she'd dressed quickly and then hurried downstairs to take one of the taxis home from the rank outside.

'I fell asleep at Karleen's,' she'd lied to poor Nònna, who came to open the 5 a.m. door.

Stiffly, Franca stood and made her way down to her car, where she took off her jacket and wrung water out of it. Inside, she gave the ignition a quarter turn and flicked on the heater.

What had become of Karleen? she wondered, noticing idly that her finger had left a black smudge on the heating switch. They'd lost touch years ago.

The rain was easing. High above Botany Bay the clouds shifted enough to let through a shaft of light. It burnt pale and white on the dark water for only a moment, then extinguished. How black her hands were. She opened them flat — the palms, the undersides of her fingers sooty. It was ink, she realised, feeling mildly panicked. Reaching into the back she retrieved Jasper's papers and saw, horrified, that they were ruined, illegible, streaked and sodden. The rain had glued them together, obliterated even Stambach's careful numbering. Crumpling them up into a ball she wound down her window and chucked them out, watched them blow around the carpark. A seagull flew down from the top of the sign that explained the origin of the fort, but the chemical smell of the paper must've been enough to convince it there was nothing worth eating. It tucked in its wings and drew down its head, disgruntled.

It's no great loss, thought Franca, as she reversed the car. I can still remember what he wrote, the parts that matter. And he will tell me anyway, slowly, as we get to know each other better: he will tell me about his life, the things I've already read and the events he'd missed out, or hadn't got to yet. If Shag had really taken an interest in you, Jasper, he would've looked out for you more. He wouldn't have just written a cheque and then forgotten about you. He could've made himself a real presence in your life.

Then, as she drove past the prison, a wave of pity rose in her, from the toes of her sodden boots to prickle at the flattened roots of her hair. Poor, lonely Jasper, sedated and bewildered on the other side of that rusted double-wire fence, that red brick wall. No matter what you've done I'll stand by you, she thought.

That's a promise, a vow. I won't ever abandon you, or let you down, not like Shag did.

JASPER

The Nature of Other Men

There's a nurse who will give me whatever I like. He seems to have taken a liking to me and his liking translates into Sinequan, Serepax, Melleril and Rohypnol. The medication cards are written up every six weeks by the doctors, but the nurses are allowed to add things in. I've been here for three weeks now, my trial delayed. Nurse McCutcheon wangled paper and pen for me too, which I keep in the locker beside my bed. The pad is blank, unsoiled, virginal — except for the top page, which has a list of names on it and in one corner some numbers.

It's the drugs Nurse McCutcheon gives me, you see. I thought I'd keep writing down my life, my childhood and everything that came after — Bonny and Damian and the boys — but I can't be bothered. There's no desire to remember it any more, no sense of life being a continuum. The drugs fuck my memory. That's why I keep the list, so at least I can remember who's come to visit me. So far it says Lena, Franca, Lena, Franca, Scottie, Lena, Lena, Scottie, Franca, Lena, Lena.

Scottie comes some days, to give Mum a break, but Mum comes more than anyone. She always gives me a cuddle and tells me she loves me. And she does, too. I can tell. She doesn't cry any more, not in front of me anyway. She's gone back to calling me Jazzy, which was her baby name for me. We sit side by side and hold hands. After she leaves I feel like a kid left at a day-care centre.

Richard stays away. Last time Lena came I asked her if she'd seen him and she said not for weeks. There's another name there, written only once, with the date. Mr Lamb, my lawyer, who wears a grey suit, a grey face and grey hair, a snotty voice and a sarky laugh. He laughed when I asked him if he was Legal Aid.

'Most definitely not.'

'Did my mother hire you, then?' I asked him. All I got for a reply was: 'Let's just say I'm a friend of a friend of a friend.' And he said something about six degrees of separation, which I didn't understand. He's as cagey as a spy in a James Bond film or one of Howard's books. He's manicured, groomed and smells of money. He let me in on what I could expect once the police have finished gathering evidence on me. He'd been looking over some similar cases, he said, before he explained some of the finer points of the law.

A 'trafficable' amount of cocaine is only two grams, which is a joke. Two grams'd scarcely get me through a heavy night. 'Commercial' is two kilograms and over. Considering Dam and me had 400 kilos pure aboard the *Brian Boru*, the judge'll have to have me deep frozen so's I can serve out my two hundred years. That's why I've written two 2s in the upper right-hand corner of my page, to remind me: 2 grams and 2 kilos. Underneath I've written '25' which is life of course, and Lamb says life is what I could get for that amount of coke, let alone the other charges. In 1996, he tells me, some poor bastard got caught with over seventy-seven kilos, worth more than $44 million on the street. He got eighteen years, with a non-parole period of thirteen years — and he was like me: no previous record. I could tell Lamb was surprised by that, that this was my first time. People like Lamb don't appreciate that the world is full of people like me, who like their drugs, their boys, their girls and their good times and who quietly go about it week after week, month after month, and never get caught. People like Lamb don't appreciate that quite famous people can be into one or other of these things happily for years. Damian used to say we'd have to want to be caught to be caught, he and I, because we knew exactly what we were doing.

Lamb asks me questions as much as he tells me things. He asks me about Damian and whether or not he was the boss. I could only smile when he asked me that. It's the kind of question that could only be asked by someone who never knew Damian.

'Well, did you always do as Mr Frost instructed you, or not?' Mr Lamb demanded and I couldn't see his face clearly because we were in a room that had a window — barred, of course — but the bright light was coming in striped around him, shadowing his face.

'Don't grin like an idiot,' said Mr Lamb, who was having no trouble seeing my face, though he had no idea what I was thinking. I was feeling sorry for him because it had occurred to me just then that Mr Lamb would never know Damian. He'd missed his chance.

'It's important you tell me this,' said Mr Lamb, 'because it will make a difference to your sentence, at least as far as the smuggling is concerned. The Crown's case will hinge on whether you were acting as an active liaison, or as a significant link, or whether in fact you were a victim of coercion.'

Even in the hospital you can't have a private conversation. There's always an officer hanging about. If I had told the lawyer even a little bit about my friendship with Damian old Officer Flap-ears by the door would have had it all over the prison. They'd have me off to Berrima as soon as I'm off Remand because Berrima's where they put the queers.

Right now I'm lying on my bed going over and over Mr Lamb's visit, which was only yesterday, or maybe the day before. I wanted to tell him about the tapes, and I would have done if we were alone. I would have told him about how we cruised the city streets in Dam's car, which before our first run across the Pacific was a rust-bucket Datsun and afterwards a brand-new Porsche. We didn't go for high-class boys, though after the car got more up-market so did they. I would have told Mr Lamb how we found sunny days were better than rainy ones, because in bad weather those bad boys stayed inside with their buckets of soapy water and rags and rubber blades. When the sun shone every major intersection bloomed. Boys appeared as if by magic, shirtless shoulders in every shade of brown gleaming in the blue smoky air.

As they approached our car Damian would show them his money — twenty dollar bills, fifties sometimes — far more than the two dollar coin they expected for cleaning the windscreen. Some boys didn't understand and would clean the window anyway, foaming the glass with soapy sponges, dragging the squeaking rubber blade back and forth across our faces. Once we became better known at certain cross-roads, so I would have explained to Mr Lamb, there were boys who would come to us the moment we arrived, calling out to their mates to mind their buckets and gear, and they would get in the back seat.

Because Dam and I knew what we were doing we never took the same boy to the same place twice — there are enough motels and cheap hotels in Sydney to go around for years. Sometimes we took them back to the flat in Redfern.

'How old are the boys in the tapes?' asked Mr Lamb. 'Do you know?'

'When does a boy stop being a boy?' I asked him. 'I was never one.'

'Don't waste my time, Brunel.' Mr Lamb was snippy.

'We never forced any of them. They were always willing,' I said. 'There was never any pain or distress.'

'We?' asked Mr Lamb and I knew I'd said too much. 'You and Damian Frost?' he asked, and Damian, if you were looking down on me at that moment, you might have seen me nod. You would have under-stood, just as I did, what Mr Lamb was trying to do: he was going to make out that everything was your fault, that I just tagged along after you like some retard kid brother. He won't see the equation: that I was always smarter than you, but that I loved you more than you loved me and so, because of that, I allowed you to take the lead even in tiny ways. You had words you fixed on and then pronounced incorrectly, like lascivous for lascivious, and lujubrious for lugubrious; and words you used in the wrong context, like portentious for pretentious, slither for sliver. You said 'woe to go' instead of the other way around; you said nucular for nuclear. I never corrected you — I never wanted to knock you down in any way. I did everything for you out of love, even though I suspected that sooner or later we would get caught. I tried desperately

229

hard to believe what you said, Dam, that we never would be, but every brain cell I had left told me we would.

I share this shit-hole room with four other men, which I don't like. Right now Blondie's bald head is snoozing on one of the beds. He looks a fright without his wig and makeup. He's definitely headed for Berrima. If they send me there too I might get a hut of my own. I can ask and see. I'd need my own hut so I can get away from the faggots.

Franca has come to see me three times since they shifted me here and she's always dolled up to the nines. She likes me as much as Nurse McCutcheon does: she looks at me all moony-eyed. Does she think I don't notice? She tries to act all professional, though, asking me shrinky questions, but I can see through that. I know she isn't doing anything to try to get me out. Last time I told her I had a dosette in my locker.

'Who gave you that?' she asked, her mascara'd eyelashes sticking out like twigs, and I considered for a moment playing her off against McCutcheon, but the drama ran itself out in my head in a lightning flash: she would confront him about it being an unsuitable means of medication for a prisoner on suicide watch; he would ignore her and it would have no entertainment value because it would happen somewhere else, not in front of me. Franca is an outsider and McCutcheon only has to listen to Stambach and the other shrinks employed by the prison service.

The officer comes to get me at five to three to go down to the dayroom. My visitor is there already, he tells me. While we walk down the corridor I concentrate on walking normally, lifting my feet, imagining my tendons and muscles to be as taut and elastic as they used to be. Sometimes I worry I'm developing a kind of lunatic shuffle, every bit of me drugged slack.

I don't recognise the woman waiting for me. She isn't one of the usual trio. Angular, thin, bones too close to the surface, she smiles at me when I come in. She's got thin, dyed red hair that falls straight as wooden boards on either side of her face. I don't know her.

'Melody Argyle,' she says, holding out her hand.

'Gidday,' I say and sit down opposite her. My fingertips coast over the cigarette-burn lunar pits in the vinyl armrest, which are crunchy at their singed edges and soft in their yellow sponge interiors.

'I've come on behalf of Howard Shag,' the woman says, which is not what I expect at all. I don't expect anything.

'What did you say your name was again?' I ask.

'Melody. I'm, um . . .' She trails off.

'A friend of Howard's?' I suggest, sympathetically.

'No. Well, yes. In a way. I'm his biographer.' What I know about biography would cover one side of a matchbox but it seems to me she's an odd choice for a man's man like Shag — a skinny, nervous female.

'What do you want?' I ask her. She's fumbling in a red velvet bag with glittery braid and pulling out a packet of cigarettes. It's got a health warning written on it; the words blur as she holds the pack out: 'Ka mate koe i te kai hikareti' — a little piece of New Zealand. I've lived in Sydney for so long now I never feel homesick, but the Maori words give me a little start of nostalgia, a pang of longing. If we'd stayed there, Bonny and I, we might have stayed together, gone straight, set up house in the 'burbs, never let Damian back in our lives, just been Mr and Mrs Normal. But the idea of never knowing Dam, never having that thrill and tumult in my life . . . It'd be as if I'd never lived at all.

We light up.

'I've brought you a gift from Howard.' It's a letter and a parcel which has been unwrapped and checked out by security and then clumsily refolded in its wrappings. It's an elephant, one of those ones from Thailand or India, black plastic and covered all over with hundreds of tiny mirrors and coloured beads. It's small enough to stand in the palm of my hand, the size of a grenade, pin out and ready to throw.

'So he believes me now,' I say. 'Bit bloody late. Is that what he sent you to tell me?'

The woman opens her mouth to reply but I'm too quick for her, my heavy, fuzzy brain like a truck hurtling down a steep hill in fourth gear.

'He didn't believe me when I rang him. I'd overheard the women talking, you see. They sent me out of the room, but I hung about outside and listened in. They said they were going to get him — watch his house until they knew he was alone, then break in and get him. They were going to show him what it was like to be raped; they were going to pay him back.'

The woman is staring at me, one hand up to her face. It's a small hand, a boy's hand, with nervous, bitten fingernails.

'Pay him back for —' she begins.

'I don't know. It was supposed to have happened here, in Sydney, to one of the women's cousins. He was here promoting one of his books at the time she was raped.'

'But Howard isn't a violent man —'

'Look, lady. You don't have to defend him to me. I don't know if he did it or not. He's a bloody strange fish, don't you reckon? Playing Big Daddy one moment and cold as the fucking grave the next.'

'When did this happen?' The woman is leaning forward, her bag open on the floor, to lift a hardback notebook onto her knee.

'Hasn't Howard told you anything about this?'

'No — he —' she pauses, begins again. 'Well, yes, of course he has. It was a major event in his life and he thought perhaps you could remember more of the details. He's blacked a lot of it out because it was so traumatic.' She might be lying, I think, watching her steadily. I can smell her excitement: little pink spots have flared on her skinny cheeks.

'Why did Howard send you an elephant?' she asks suddenly. 'He's got an elephant in his hall. A brass one, about two metres tall. He calls it Madagascar, after the old one at the zoo.'

It's coming back to me all right, the details. What Howard did to me when I finally arrived at his place after hitching a ride over the bridge. It was the day he'd been discharged from hospital and I was desperate to see him. He was all I had thought about for weeks.

The woman is writing something in her notebook. 'Who were the women who attacked him?' she's asking. 'A vigilante group?'

'My mother was one of them. I was only a kid. I had nothing to do with it.'

'Your mother?'

'And her girlfriend and some others. Chookie, who was off her head. An Australian called Kerry. What shits me is I can't remember the name of the girl he was supposed to have raped. They must have mentioned her name while they were planning it all but it's gone.'

'And you rang Howard? To warn him?'

'Yeah. And he laughed at me.'

'Can you remember the conversation?'

'It was quick. I was worried one of the women'd come out and catch me at it. I probably said something like "They're going to get you for hurting a lady in Sydney. They're going to beat you up."'

'What did Howard say?'

'He laughed. He said "How ridiculous", and he asked to speak to my mother.'

'Did you put her on?'

'What do you think? I didn't want her to know I'd rung him. Mum's all right, of course, and so is Scottie — they wouldn't have hurt me. But some of those others were heavy fuckers and would —'

'Sorry . . . Scottie. Did you say Scottie?'

I didn't mean to. This Marjorie or Melanie or whatever she's called is gaping at me. It's almost comical. She drops her gaze, sucks in her lower lip and flicks her ballpoint in and out. It's so quiet in here I can hear the spring inside creaking.

'What's your mother's name?' she asks quietly. 'Lena?'

'I can't tell you that.'

'Why not?'

I sigh. She must be a babe in the woods, this girl: she knows nothing about how the real world works. 'Because it's all been kept secret for years. Howard didn't want anyone to know, and the women didn't want any media attention either.'

'What about you? Didn't you tell anyone?'

I glance at the prison officer by the door and decide to chance it. I can talk about my relationship with Shag. It's all right. I was only a kid.

'Until the last time I saw him I loved Howard, like a father, or an uncle. I mean, I was very confused. I didn't want to believe what my mother told me later, afterwards, which was that he had raped someone. She said that the courts would never give him a sentence that fitted the crime, and that the girl would suffer all over again if she were put on the stand, so that was why they had to give him the payback. I tried to tell my mother she had made a mistake but she got angry with me and told me it was none of my business.'

The pen flies over the open notebook. This is my utu, Howard, I think. I'm certain now this biographer knew nothing about this before this afternoon . . . then it hits me. Of course. Cunning old fox. This is what he wanted: for me to spill the beans on all this so he doesn't have to talk about it.

'When did they carry out the attack?'

'That night. On the phone Howard had started to give me a lecture about the difference between fact and fiction. He thought I was having some kind of fantasy. He said something like, "When you're older you'll understand I could never have done this. It's more against my nature than it is most other men's."'

'What did he mean by that?' The pen has stopped and I can't help it — a kind of mucousy, incredulous laugh escapes from me.

'Some biographer you are! Was it Howard who jacked up Mr Lamb for me?'

She looks blank. 'Who's Mr Lamb?'

'My lawyer.'

'No . . . in fact, Howard has provided me with funds for a lawyer if you need one. He didn't know you had one already, otherwise he —'

'I'm very well looked after. Tell him not to worry. Even got my own private shrink. She's studying me, though she's pretending she isn't.'

The girl looks baffled. 'You should give her a ring. She's in the phone book. Franca Todisco. She could tell you all about me.'

'Have you talked to her about Howard?'

'Time's nearly up,' interrupts the bozo at the door. Shame, because I'm enjoying this. She's a pillock, this girl: a puritanical fuckwit. She looks at her watch again, eyes flashing, and tries another approach.

'When did you last see him?'

'My lawyer?'

'No, no.' She's sounding panicky, talking faster. 'Howard.'

'I tried to see him in the hospital but he had me sent away. They had him in a private room with a false name on the door, then he was shifted to another hospital. Amazing how the ranks closed around him. So it wasn't until I arrived uninvited on his doorstep in Takapuna, like I said before.'

'And this was in 1985?'

'Yes.'

'And he let you in?'

'I took him a get well card. It was bright yellow with a picture of a puppy on it. A black labrador.'

'Like Web Ellis!' says the woman, nonsensically. 'He bought a black labrador pup in 1988.'

'Time,' says the officer, just as I stand up. I'm the model prisoner: I don't give them any grief. I don't bother saying goodbye to Melanie, but I can feel her eyes coasting over my back, appreciating my tight buns in their prison greens — and I can lay money on the likelihood of her paying me another visit.

It isn't until I'm back in my room that I remember the letter. I've left it behind — not that I care. I don't want it.

1985

As soon as he was able to arrange it, Howard had himself transferred to a small private hospital where he hoped he would be better able to preserve a degree of secrecy. He declined to speak to the police, who had been alerted to his predicament by the elephant keeper. A senior policeman was dispatched to his bedside to interview him.

'Can we have your name, sir?' he asked.

'Gideon Mortimer,' Howard told him. It was the name of a minor character in *Tombolo*.

'Could you describe your assailants, Mr Mortimer?'

'I don't know anything about them,' Howard lied. 'I have no idea who they were.'

'These men have committed a crime,' said the cop. 'It's in your interests to assist the enquiry.'

'That's where you're wrong,' said Howard, and would contribute no more.

For some weeks, no doubt because of the blows to his head, his vision was blurry. Unable to read, he lay flat on his back and went over and over that humid and humiliating night. He wondered if one of them was Jasper's mother, and why it was that he didn't tell the women that he could find out who they were. He had been frightened. That was the shameful truth: he, Howard Shag, veteran of the most rough-playing, violent decades of rugby, a period when all the action was in the forwards — huge men of the likes of Tiny White, Pine Tree Meads and Kevin Skinner, men who ran and crashed and rolled, who would be remembered by rugby historians as thugs — had been terrified out of his mind by a group of women. In the first test against the Springboks in '56 he'd been crash-tackled by the massive Butch Lochner and had had to come off in the first half; he'd been brought down by Calvo in the third test against France in '61, which resulted in a cracked patella and broken ankle. The men in his day fought for the 'pill': they played to win, they feigned immunity to pain. There was hardly a game when Howard didn't come off the field bleeding, or with rounds of flesh purpling already to deep bruises, or broken bones.

So why didn't he fight back, push the women away, fight for all he was worth? Had he softened, grown frightened of pain, or was it simply that the first tenet of his upbringing — You Will Not Hit Women — had been so firmly ingrained that he couldn't bring himself to ball a fist or curl his toes into a kick?

It was all these things, Howard considered, as swelling subsided and bones began to mend. It was also because of Jasper.

'Is that you, Mr Shag?' the boy had said when he'd answered the phone. He still had his boy's voice: there was no sign of a rasp, a deepening, a 'breaking'. 'There's some women here who are really mad at you. They're going to get you back.'

'What for?' Howard knew the feminist perspective on his books was not complimentary. *Broadsheet* magazine had once gone so far as to include him in a list of writers and politicians who were most likely to hinder the social progress of wimmin. Another voice had sounded in the background and the boy had hastily hung up. Later on, Raymond, his staff, went out clubbing while Howard stayed home alone, writing.

Brightside Hospital was an old wooden building with wide

verandas and a garden of roses and shady trees. Howard's private room had French doors, which opened onto the veranda and sometimes the nurses would wheel his bed out across the shiny, squeaky floor so that he could catch the breezes. The summer of '85 was unaccountably hot.

The veranda was a place where he found himself thinking about his father's convalescence after the war in a converted Greymouth villa very like this one. He too would lie on a bed under the iron eaves among other mending soldiers. Howard's compatriots weren't soldiers, of course. They had variously had operations to combat melanoma, prostate cancer, varicose veins. There were no tales of glory to be told here, only accounts of the success — or otherwise — of surgical procedure and the degradation of middle-aged and elderly male bodies. His case being more ignominious than any of theirs, Howard never contributed to these discussions.

One day, as he lay propped on pillows and watching leafy shadows on the lawn tremble and muddle together like water molecules, a voice sounded behind him.

'I'm here to see my husband,' the woman said, her vowels rounded, anglicised. 'Hamish Mackinnon. He's recuperating from a hernia operation.'

Poor man, thought Howard, having his name and condition trumpeted around the hospital by his fool of a wife. He resisted turning his head to either side to see if he could identify him among his fellow patients by his expression of discomfort or embarrassment.

'He's on the veranda, around the other side,' the nurse's voice answered. 'Just go straight through and follow the veranda along, Mrs Mackinnon.'

Footsteps approached, the precise clip-clip of high heels, and began the circumnavigation of his bed, his being the first of the row beyond the French doors. As she passed him by he was aware of the gleam of red of the woman's skirt, a cream jacket, a multi-coloured scarf at her throat. The footsteps stopped. There was the clink of a wedding ring on the metal foot of his bed as she took hold of it.

'Is that . . . it can't be . . . Howard?' Whoever she was, she was coming closer. 'It is. My God. Howard Shag. You won't remember me. I'm Johnny's sister, Michaela.'

For the first time since the assault he thought he might weep, but he fought to keep his mind clear. He hadn't seen her since Johnny's funeral. She was ten years younger than her brother and had turned her eleven-year-old back on him to close ranks with her parents.

It was a blessing perhaps, that he couldn't properly perceive her. The dark, sleek hair framed the beige oval of her face, her brown eyes were darker patches on either side of the blur of her nose, a strong French perfume coursed through his nostrils. How old would she be now — he wondered, in her early thirties? She pulled up a chair to sit beside him and briefly — though not briefly enough — laid an elegantly cool hand over his sweaty one, its fingers bandaged. He yanked it away, his body stiffening against the resulting shaft of pain, a negative charge.

'Don't. I'm sorry. I can't — you see — I don't seem to be able to bear being touched.' His lungs heaved, his cracked rib resisted his breath. For a moment everything whirled; he closed his eyes against the suddenly too-bright light, the rising nausea. When he opened his eyes again he saw that she was sitting quietly, the obsidian shine of her lowered head burning at the corner of his vision.

'What happened to you?'

'I had an accident.'

'A car accident?'

'Yes. My own fault. Driving too fast.'

'There's been nothing about it in the papers. You'd think they would report a man as famous as yourself losing control.' She sounded suspicious. Was he that bad a liar? The chair scraped back again and he thought she was taking her leave, moving along to her hernia husband, but no, she was standing at the foot of his bed again, unhooking the clipboard that held his notes and leafing through them.

'Gideon Mortimer!' she said, with a short laugh. 'Didn't he die about halfway through the book?'

'You have no right to read those —'

'Assault. I thought so.' There was a pause while she studied the notes. 'You don't realise, obviously, how closely I studied Johnny when we had him home with us, all those months before he died. His superficial injuries were similar to yours. I used to sit beside him and read to him in the hope he'd suddenly come round. The doctors thought if we talked to him and stroked his hair he might wake up.' Her voice broke then, and he was aware of creamy wings flying out on either side of her body as she turned away — the empty sleeves of her jacket. It must just be resting over her shoulders, he thought. Concentrate on the minutiae. Do not remember how they wouldn't let you have Johnny back.

'Did you get the boxes of Johnny's things?' he asked instead. 'His paintings and books and clothes?'

'Of course,' Michaela answered, regaining her chair. 'My parents chose a reputable courier company to come and fetch them from you.'

'I would have appreciated a letter of thanks,' Howard said testily.

'Why should they have thanked you for returning their own son's belongings?' There was a metallic snap, a flare of orange, the scent of tobacco smoke.

'Can I have a cigarette?' Howard asked suddenly. He'd never smoked in his life. Johnny had smoked. One of the things he'd packed up for the Boswell family was a gold-plated cigarette lighter, which had been a gift on their third anniversary. It had been in his pocket when he was attacked and the police had returned it to Howard. 'J.A.B. from H.C.S.' read the engraving.

Michaela handed him the cigarette she held and selected another for herself. He could taste her lipstick on the filter.

'Who did this to you?' she asked. 'Was it the same people?' For a moment he had no idea what she was talking about. Then he almost laughed.

'No. They couldn't have been more different.'

'Who were they? Have the police arrested them? There could easily be a connection.'

'There isn't. It's a mystery, as they say.' It was that little throwaway comment, that innocuous and over-used word, that gave him away, Howard realised later. That and the idea that Michaela was a stupid woman and would not persist in questioning him, that she would believe he knew nothing.

'So it was you,' she said, amazed. 'It was you. You're the "mystery man" the papers are talking about. The one they found at Western

Springs.' Howard felt his belly go cold; an icy finger traced the length of his spine.

'It's in the papers?' he said, and wanted to swallow it back straight away. There would be no denying it now.

'They're calling it — catchily, I thought — "The Madagascar Incident". They've interviewed that Englishman who found you, the elephant keeper.'

'What does he say?'

'He's more interested in relating the story from the elephant's point of view. Attendance at the zoo has increased markedly in the last few weeks and it's that particular elephant they're all thronging to see. It is fascinating, I suppose, an instinct of altruism in an elephant.'

So like Johnny, Howard thought, to half answer the question and end on a whimsical, almost philosophical note. He felt as though his bones were dissolving, as though his skin were a sack containing toxic, liquid grief. He could hear it sloshing in his head, feel its violent tides shifting in his chest. He dragged deeply on the cigarette the way Johnny would. It comforted, he discovered.

'He does say,' Michaela went on, 'that the man was badly injured, especially around his private parts. Which is why I think it's the same people. The same men who did that to poor John. And the cigarette burns. Miss Kitsi or whatever your wife's name was didn't put them off your scent.'

How banal, how disrespectful, to discuss Johnny's last hideous moments of consciousness like this, thought Howard. How dare she?

'I'll tell you something, Michaela. The men who killed Johnny were gay-bashers, homophobic fag-killing Neanderthal sub-humans. And it was twenty years ago. I saw only a glimpse of my attackers — they were not the same. They could not possibly have been.'

'How do you know?' Michaela persisted. 'Can you describe them? If you only knew the agony my parents and sisters and I go through every day of our lives, knowing those pigs were never caught, never punished. It was the loss of my brother that destroyed my first marriage, a kind of delayed reaction —'

Howard stopped listening. He closed his eyes again and imagined himself sailing with his lover, like they used to when *Snow Blind* and

Flashpoint bought them the Takapuna house, launching the little yacht off the beach and sailing out towards Rangitoto. Puffy white clouds floated behind the volcano like smoke and sent amoebae-shaped shadows scudding over the grey-green scrub on the island's flanks. A gannet dived, a seagull screamed . . . Michaela had fallen quiet.

He opened his eyes to find her leaning over him. 'Don't do that to me!' she said. 'I thought you . . . you weren't answering, you were hardly breathing. I thought you had died!'

'How preposterous,' he said dryly. 'Before you run along to see your husband, Michaela, I wonder if I could ask you a favour. All I have left of Johnny is a sketch he drew of me in 1961, three years before he died. That was all I kept in a sort of, if you like, numbed, mindless reaction to his loss. There are one or two things I would like to have — things I put in the box that perhaps I shouldn't have.'

'Like what?'

'An engraved lighter, a silver hip-flask, a soft yellow shirt we bought for him in Bologna, his Mahler records — and any of his paintings you could give back. I packed those separately, in a crate.'

'I'll see what's been kept.' Michaela stood, brushing down her lap as if they'd been having tea and cake crumbs had caught there.

'What's been kept,' Howard echoed. 'You mean you threw some of it out?'

'As you did yourself, in a way,' said Michaela, 'though I suppose it was convenient, in the end, that you'd send his things to us. You would have had to dispose of any residue before you got married.' She sounded jealous, thought Howard, jealous on Johnny's behalf. 'What would she have thought, eh? The Greek heiress? She gave an interview about you in the *Woman's Weekly*, for God's sake. I remember reading it, I was about fifteen —'

'Being Greek she would have thought nothing at all, had I told her,' Howard interrupted. 'They have a cultural tolerance of love between men.'

'You're disgusting. You haven't changed.'

'And you seem to have clung to all the public details of my farcical, dreary marriage.' He turned his head to look at her and could perceive, just, that she was looking directly into his eyes. 'It was all such a long time ago, Michaela.'

'Goodbye, Howard,' said Michaela, 'and think about what I said. There could be a connection.'

On the day Howard returned, a month later, to his own home, he began making arrangements for Raymond to return to Taiwan. He rang a company about installing a remote-controlled gate and security bars on all his windows. He changed his telephone number and ensured it would remain unlisted. He packed his typewriter away and had it delivered anonymously to the local writers' organisation. He forced Raymond to take his current unfinished manuscript into the garden and set fire to it. He locked the door to his study and put the key down the toilet.

At three in the afternoon a tearful Raymond left the house, telling his employer he was going shopping for a farewell gift.

'Don't bother,' said Howard, but Raymond went anyway, leaving him alone. This is how it's going to be for ever, vowed Howard. I will be solitary for the rest of my life. I will be blameless; no one will hold me accountable for any real or imagined sin. When Raymond had asked him, 'But why I go home, Mr Shag?' he'd had no answer for him.

He took himself into the small sitting room on the northern side of the house and poured himself a scotch to accompany his next cigarette. An hour went by, another crawled past, and another, and Howard drank steadily, feeling himself recede into the smoke-filled corners of the room. He would obliterate the sad lizard-faced man who sat reflected in the black screen of the television, a man who would always deny the memory of his one true love, a man who had borne not only that lover's violent death but also the punishment for another man's crime.

There was a knock at the door — one of the workmen, he supposed, who were already busy building the three-metre-high fence and setting in the massive gateposts. He ignored it, but the knocking went on and a pleading voice began to ring out over the percussive, arrhythmic tapping.

In the twilight stood Jasper, his face pale and strained, although a delighted smile spread across it at the sight of the man opening the

243

door. He had hitched across the bridge, it transpired, which had taken him hours. Then he'd walked from the bottom of Esmonde Road and was hungry and thirsty. A drunken, uncontrolled rage blew up in Howard's head, blinding him, lifting his fists.

'How dare you?' he snarled. 'How dare you come here?' The first punch knocked the boy backwards off the step. 'What lies did you tell your mother?' He came after him, kicking him into the driveway, the toe of his shoe spraying up gravel. 'You lying shit. You fucking lying little cunt.' Curled into a ball, the boy began to sob. He was pleading, muffled inchoate words into the stones which Howard couldn't begin to decipher. He didn't want to hear him.

His rage evaporated. He saw how the back of the boy's T-shirt was torn, how the seat of his shorts was dirty, how the corner of a bright yellow envelope was sticking out of his pocket. Jasper rolled over, away from him.

'Stand up,' Howard said, weakly. 'Get up. I won't hit you again.'

The child stood, woozily, holding one side of his head. The envelope fell onto the gravel.

'Go.' Howard pointed towards the gate. 'Get out. Don't come back.'

And he took off, young Jasper Brunel, his arms crossed over his stomach, running doubled over like the back end of a pantomime donkey, past the curious stares of the workmen, past Raymond, who at that moment was struggling to lift a large brass elephant out of the boot of a taxi.

Howard stooped to pick up the envelope and crushed it in his hand before he turned to go back inside the house.

RICHARD

The Fourth Man

Since my luxury stay at Darling Harbour came to its natural end three
weeks ago I've been holed up in a one-star bug-house in Newtown.
There's no TV or video-player in my room, just a narrow bed with a dun-
coloured candlewick bedspread, a floral armchair with the springs gone
on it, a scummy handbasin and a window, which gives out onto King
Street. Night and day traffic roars along the skinny Victorian road, and I
woke this morning from a peculiar dream spawned by it: I had been lying
back to back to a great, grey-skinned animal, an elephant perhaps, which
was deep in snoring sleep. As I woke, it did too, with a great roar of pain.
When articulator trucks go by the building shudders, the delta of cracks
in the handbasin grows ever more complex and the shop-fronts opposite
my window are cloaked in a kind of Mediterranean haze.

Sydney is a city that bleeds you dry. My plan to break the story
about the prison computer failure was, of course, stymied — it was
front-page news four days before I arrived. Apparently it was a disgrun-

245

tled ex-prisoner with hacker skills. He's become a kind of anti-celebrity, enjoying his fifteen minutes of fame. There's a profile on him in *Time* magazine and he was on the cover of the *Bulletin*. At least I've got a gig this afternoon — an interview with the manager of a new league team that roared out of nowhere and beat the Bulldogs. It'll pay bugger-all but it's better than nothing and it'll give me something to do.

Until then I do what I've done most days since Michaela walked out of my life, which is have coffee in the bar downstairs and then return to my room where I lie flat on my back, smoking, playing Jasper's videotape over and over in my mind, since that's the only place I can play it, casting its three writhing protagonists over the cracked plaster sheet of the ceiling. One is much smaller than the other two and I can't decide if it's because he's younger or because he's Asian. His voice — he giggles now and then — is stoned, high-pitched and slow. The second boy is a silent Pacific Islander and he is perhaps sixteen or seventeen, with a man's broad chest. Pubic hair curls at the base of his erect cock, a livid red nylon petticoat froths around his sturdy thighs. I remember all this not out of salaciousness or, God help me, for some kind of cheap thrill, but out of a desperate, crazed, obsessive hope that some detail may lead to the redemption of my son. The third actor is definitely Jasper: there's no denying it. In one shot he lifts his mouth from the Asian boy and looks at the camera, or just beyond it, with an expression that is almost pleading. It's Jasper's drugged-out spinner's eyes, Jasper's olive-skinned brow, Jasper's long fingers splayed on the ivory-coloured abdomen. 'How am I doing?' he seems to be asking his audience, or his future viewing self. It's a moment of vulnerability and, paradoxically, innocence. He's a child showing his mother a kindergarten daub, or a C-grade student presenting to his old man a school report. Despite the blissful lipstick smirk of the pubescent receiving his attentions my son appears to seek further applause, a deeper assurance that his cock-sucking is vigorous enough, that his mouth reveals enough of that gleaming, spit-slicked shaft to the lens. The camera, after settling on Jasper's face for no more than a few seconds, pans up the boy's body to his beatific, satisfied smile.

Pans. Of course. Why didn't I think of it before? There was a cameraman, a fourth man, in the room. I had assumed — actually I hadn't given it much thought — that Jasper had set the camera on a tripod. But then the angle would have been fixed, there would be no panning, no pulling of focus, no shifts in perspective.

There is hope. I feel it pump through my sluggish veins, it lifts me from the bed, has me take up my jacket and head down the narrow corridor and beer-stinking stairwell to the street, at first with the intention of going to the prison. 'You must tell them you were coerced,' I will tell my son. 'Tell them you were forced by whoever that fourth man is. Tell them he fed you drugs, that he held a gun to your head. Tell them anything that will have them believe you acted against your will.' Comforted and strengthened by this realisation as I am, it occurs to me, just as I am climbing into a taxi, that the tape and Jasper's altered statement, presuming he's capable of following my instructions, will not be enough. I need further evidence. I need to know who that man was.

'Redfern,' I tell the cabby. 'Burnett Street.'

The flat Jasper moved to after Bonny kicked him out is on the bottom floor of a crumbling semi. A leafless frangipani stands in a ring of concrete in the tiny front yard, a pile of weatherbeaten circulars bleed their colours into the broken cement step. Someone, perhaps the police, has forced the front door and slammed it on leaving. The wood around the lock is split, enough to reveal a glimmer of the brass barrel inside. One by one, I start going through all the keys on my ring.

Maybe it's my bad luck with women that makes me hold on to every key I've ever had for decades. They weigh my pocket half way down my thigh: there's a key to the last place I ever lived with Lena; a key to the first place I ever lived with Lena; a key to the flat we had while she was pregnant with Jasper; a key to my old office at the *Herald*; to my offices at *Truth* and the *Evening Post*; a key to Michaela's tasteful Parnell townhouse; a key to my late mother's retirement unit; to the house in Sydney I lived in all those years ago; and several keys belonging to the dwellings of termagants I don't see any more. Some of them are motel keys I forgot to return or keys to cars I sold long ago, and it's one of these, a heavy, plastic-capped nickel job with Corolla written on it, that I use in the end. I prise the splintered edge of the door away from the jamb and lever the snib back into the barrel. A hefty lunge with my left shoulder later and I'm inside.

On the hall floor are some envelopes, mostly windows. Jasper's unpaid creditors, I suspect, bending to pick them up. 'Damian Frost' reads the uppermost one. I don't recognise the name — but then why would I? I don't know any of my son's friends. A tiny living room opens up immediately on my left, with a bricked-in fireplace, a brown corduroy sofa and a poster of a swaggering, pistol-pointing Arnold Schwarzenegger. In one corner stands a cheap veneer unit designed to hold a TV and a video-player: it's empty, as are the grey metal book-shelves beside it. An aerial lies discarded on the brown sofa, an empty cardboard carton lies on its side on a shelf. The police have taken them all, the equipment and the tapes.

The kitchen at the back of the flat yields nothing of interest. All the cupboards are empty but for a couple of mugs and a jar of instant coffee. He obviously didn't go in for cooking, my boy. A flick of the light switch tells me the power hasn't been cut so I fill the plastic kettle. While it creeps slowly to the boil I open the first of the bills I picked up in the hall. It's from a camera repair shop, for the replacement of a lens. I forget the coffee and go in search of the bedrooms. Did he live here, this Damian, this cameraman? There are no letters for my son — they were all for him. Perhaps Jasper moved out of here some time ago.

In the one and only bedroom there is a sagging double bed. A pair of thongs with the tooth-marks of a dog lie near the wardrobe door, which stands open to reveal one battered denim jacket. The sticker-covered chest of drawers is empty, except for the top one which rattles with a stump of lipstick and a blunted eye-liner pencil. The bottom drawer sticks — won't slide back in — so I pull it out all together and toss it to one side. It gives a satisfying hollow, splintering bang as it hits the wall and I'm just about to stand up, get out of this place, when a flash of fluorescent red catches my eye. Twisted among the dust balls inside the shell of the chest is a red nylon petticoat very like the one worn by the Pacific Islander in the video. Beside it, lying splayed open, is a leather wallet. There's no cash in it, only credit cards, which bear different names. Jasper is common to all of them, along with, variously, Brunel, Gilmore and Shag. There is also a piece of paper folded up small and stuffed into the coin purse: a bank statement, fairly recent, from March of this year. Automatic withdrawals to Social Security for Bonny and the boys feature regularly, and also eftpos transactions at supermarkets, petrol stations and liquor shops. Everything is what you would expect from a normal suburban separated husband and father, except for one item that recurs at weekly intervals. It's a deposit made in New Zealand dollars — two hundred clams each time. Somebody paying off a bad debt?

I take the statement to the window, which is masked with a square of white, translucent plastic, and trace along the line with my finger. H. SHAG. The letters are tiny, dot-matrix, pale — but there nevertheless. Fucking Howard Shag, although he has been a complete recluse for years, has continued to send my son money and fuck up his life.

Why? Why out of all the kids he could have chosen — blossoming young sportspeople, or kids who showed academic prowess, or girls who wanted to dance or sing or play the violin — why did he choose to patronise my Jasper, who never showed any talent for anything at all? As a teenager he'd run for an athletics club, but not brilliantly. He began his degree in chemistry but dropped out during his first year due to excessive cannabis consumption. Cannabis, I realise now, he must have bought with Shag's money.

The only possible reason I can come up with, sitting here on the edge of this foetid, sweat-stained mattress, is guilt. It's blood money, or hush money — money that cleared Shag's conscience. It can't have been pity money: Jasper's lot in life back then was no worse than the majority of boys who grew up with absent fathers. And Lena, for all that she failed me, was a good mother. What did Shag do to my son during all that time Jasper visited him, those three years between our visit and the summer Shag lost the plot and locked himself away?

It's time to go back home and ask a few questions. Pocketing Jasper's wallet I leave the flat and whatever dingy secrets it holds in its grubby walls, and make my way along Elizabeth Street into town. I have time, before I go to meet the manager of the Wellington Wolves, to duck into a travel agent and arrange a flight for the next day.

The bar of the Inter-Continental is crowded with enormous men with thick New Zealand accents celebrating their win. Most of them are well away: the tables bristle with empty green Steinlager bottles and shot glasses and the white-jacketed waiters stand around looking helpless.

This is not the sort of clientele the hotel encourages. One of them points out the team manager for me and I introduce myself to him. Just as we shake hands a young woman joins us. Pale and thin, she has a fresh slash of red lipstick across her mouth and the marks of a comb still standing in her lank reddish hair.

'This is Mel,' says Godfrey, hooking one mammoth arm around her skinny hips. At one time he could've been a sportsman himself — now he's running to fat. 'Mel, this is Richard Brunel, who's doing a feature on us for the *Herald*.' Mel, who is fairly sloshed — there are four cocktail glasses with soggy paper umbrellas lined up in front of her chair — looks at me with startled eyes.

'Brunel, did you say?' she whispers slurringly to Godfrey.

He nods. 'Siddown,' he says to me. 'What'll it be?'

While he orders me a beer from a passing waiter his girlfriend doesn't take her eyes off me. Perhaps she's read my articles. She looks like a reader — one of that dying breed. She has a bookish look to her. Suddenly she breaks her gaze, taps Godfrey on his shoulder and whispers in his ear.

'Excuse me,' she says, standing. 'I'm going upstairs.'

Godfrey catches at her hand. 'You got any more cash?' he asks. She obliges him instantly, just as Michaela would have done me, and hands him a hundred dollar bill. 'Good girl,' he says and pats her gently on her skinny rump as she turns away, stumbling a little before she makes off towards the lifts. 'It's a case of opposites attracting,' says Godfrey, watching me watching her. 'She's a clever clogs. Writing a book about a very famous man. Top secret.' He taps the side of his nose.

'You all staying here?' I ask, getting my notepad out. 'Must have some pretty solid sponsorship.'

'No!' The big man laughs. 'Melody and I are. The boys are some-where else, a bit cheaper.'

'What are your chances, do you reckon, for your next game? Eels, is it?' I'm glad I'm returning tomorrow, I think, as the braggart tells me how they're going to clean up. I'll dash this story off on my laptop on the plane and have it out of the way before I pay the visit.

Over the years Shag must have paid out thousands.

'Will you be coming to the game on Saturday, mate?' the manager is asking me, one fat fist around a dewy bottle. The waiters have provided him with a glass, which he ignores.

'Could be,' I lie.

'You follow the League, then? For yourself, not just work?'

I shake my head. 'Not really. Did you play yourself, once upon a time?'

'Was a Warrior. You don't remember me from that?'

There're still so many loose ends, I'm thinking, while Godfrey regales me with some of his more glorious moments on the field. There's the puzzle of why Michaela would fork out for my son; why Shag would; and even more mystifying than that — who this Damian is. As I've got older I've come to accept that loose ends are a part of life. I've got hundreds of them: wrongs I've never righted, small instances of dishonest, beneficial synchronicities. In this case I want to know everything, all the details.

I want to apportion blame.

Terrier doesn't seem to notice how my mind has wandered. There are enough shorthand squiggles on the notepad to satisfy him. At the end of the interview he stands to shake my hand and I make my way out into the evening.

The following morning I leave the hotel and take a cab to the prison, where an officer shows me the way to the hospital and I wait in the drab dayroom for my son. The walls are scratched and battered from hip height down, as if animals have been kept in here — big dogs who have pissed and scraped and hunted for an exit. There's that indefinable smell that makes my stomach roll: a smell of despair, of men herded together, of remorse and anger and disinfectant. When Jasper is finally brought through I hardly recognise him. Pale, thin, effete, he leans heavily on a bald and heavily muscled nurse who perversely looks more like a crim than my son does, his encircling arm thick with blurred tattoos. He helps Jasper into one of the yellow vinyl chairs and it seems to me, suddenly, unpleasantly, that my son is bunging on an act. Who for? The nurse? Me? Curt, impassive, the nurse nods in greeting to me and leaves the room.

'Gidday, son.' I get up, as if to embrace him or shake his hand, but instead I lay my hand briefly on his head. How can he be in his thirties already? He's just a boy, a defenceless child. He never grew up. Under his mat of hair his skull feels hot and fragile.

'Dad,' he whispers.

'It's going to be all right,' I say softly. 'I just need you to answer some questions.' He shrinks back into his chair, fumblingly crossing his arms, and looks up at me with frightened childlike eyes. It's no act. He's zonked on tranks. 'I've been to your flat,' I tell him, sitting down and leaning towards him, 'Who's Damian Frost?'

'Friend,' mumbles Jasper. 'He's dead.'

'Dead? How?'

He looks at me wearily. 'Drowned.' His voice is flat, almost nasal. 'Pigs killed him. He couldn't swim.'

'When did this happen? When you were arrested?' He nods and the movement seems to give him pain, or make him dizzy. He puts a hand up to his eyes, presses his thumb and forefinger into the sockets. 'Was he your . . . Were you and he . . .' There's an uncomfortable pause while I struggle to find the right words. 'Were you with him? In a um . . . in a relationship?'

'Not really,' says Jasper eventually.

'But he was the cameraman?' My son's nodding head flips suddenly to one side as violently as if I had struck him. 'Was he? Jasper, this is important. You have to tell me.'

'I don't have to tell you anything,' It's that flat, mechanical voice again. It sounds almost as if he's speaking to me through an ancient telephone, over a long distance. I leave the Damian issue alone for while: if it's true that he's drowned and not here to defend himself, then all the better.

'I found this.' I show him the bank statement and minutely he raises his eyebrows and lowers them again. 'How long has Shag been depositing money in your account?' He shrugs. 'Try to remember.'

'Years. Since I was a kid.'

'Why?'

'Because he wanted to help me.'

'Help you what?' His eyes flicker towards my face and away again.

'He was a kind of uncle.'

'So you've kept in contact with him? Even since he locked himself away?'

'Only a few letters.'

'What about?' Jasper is yawning, rubbing his red-rimmed eyes. 'What were the letters about?'

'Stuff.'

'Like?'

Jasper sighs hugely. 'Why do people keep wanting to talk to me about him? He's just an old man.'

'What people? What do you mean? Who's been asking you about him?' Jasper's eyes are fluttering and closing. 'Come on. Wake up, son. I've got a plane to catch.'

He stares at me then, his pupils dilating with fear. 'Can't you stay until my case, until I go to —'

'You'll be all right,' I continue. 'Your mother's still here, isn't she? And you've got your hotshot lawyer.'

'Yeah. Thanks, Dad.' He thinks I organised the lawyer. Why didn't I? Another failure. I fight a rising sense of remorse, swallow the lump that forms in my throat. Let him think it. I did, in a way. Michaela would never have sorted it for him if it hadn't been for our relationship. She would never have met Jasper, their paths would never have crossed, unless . . .

'Do you know Michaela's brother?'

'Didn't know she had a brother. Whatsis name?'

'Haven't got a clue.' I rack my brains for Michaela's maiden name. She must've told me at some stage. It was the same name as a famous dead English writer — Milton? Pope? 'Boswell! Somebody Boswell?' My son does his best to examine his memory, then he shakes his wobbly head.

'Who else has asked you about Shag?' Perhaps it was the prison authorities, wanting to know why he was using such a famous name. Maybe they presumed he was Shag's son.

'A girl. A woman. She was here yesterday. Mel someone. She's writing his autobiography.'

'*Bio*graphy,' I snap. 'You can't write another person's autobiography, only your own.' Shut up, arsehole. I hate myself more than ever; I hate myself as much as I love my poor bastard son.

Jasper's face closes off. 'I knew that,' he says softly. 'I did know that.' His eyes are shut, the lids flickering. His head nods over his hands, which are clasped on his chest.

'Jasper?' Infinitesimally his head turns at the sound of my voice. 'What did this woman look like? Was she thin? Dyed red hair and glasses?'

He nods. 'That's her,' he mumbles stickily, his tongue peeling away from the roof of his mouth with a click.

'Did she tell you she's here with the Wellington Wolves, that new league team?'

Jasper shrugs his shoulders, struggles to his feet. 'Have to go and lie down. Sorry, Dad. I'm pretty fucked these days. McCutcheon —' His voice lifts to a dry, high-pitched rasp and through the open door comes the same nurse as before. With great tenderness he takes hold of my son and leads him away. I can hear the two sets of footsteps heading down the corridor — the squeak of the nurse's white-soled shoes and the soft shuffle and pad of Jasper's bare feet. I listen until I can't hear them any more, until the sound of their progress is muted by distance and masked by the progression of other staff and patients. A man in a white coat with shoulder-length grey hair passes at a rapid clip but doesn't look in — which is just as well, because I'm weeping like a baby, searching for something to wipe myself up with. My own father always had a ready supply of big monogrammed handkerchiefs in his pocket for tears and snot, for bleeding knees and cut fingers, for the Sunday ice-cream my sister and I would spread across our faces as far as our ears. But then, he had a wife to wash and iron them for him.

I go to the barred window of the dayroom, pull my shirt tail from my pants and use that. I won't give Shag any warning. I'll arrive unannounced.

From the departure lounge I make one phone call to the Inter-Continental. It takes a while for the telephonist to find the room because it's not booked under Terrier's name, but hers: Melody Argyle.

'You're the one writing Shag's book?' I ask her.

'Yes. Who is this?'

'Leave Jasper Brunel alone. You fucking stay away from him.' And I hang up in her ear like some cheap mobster, like some mafioso boss protecting his gangster loser son, and go to board my plane.

FRANCA

The Biographer

Jasper sits beside her in her red Ferrari and he is greatly improved. His face is vibrant, his eyes alert and shining, his hand on Franca's thigh dry and warm. They are driving into the Centre, into the red heart of Australia, and as the car spins along the empty strip of road, great clouds of ochre dust kick up from the spinning back wheels and a flock of cockatoos, glaring white and multitudinous as static flecks on a television screen, lift from the sage-coloured gums. Shadows flicker over their heads: the cockatoos; the sparse, dry leaves; the fine speckle of golden dust. Jasper is laughing, his head thrown back, and Franca congratulates herself on her bravery and daring — not that she remembers in any detail what she did.

Only the bare facts remain — that she went to the prison hospital armed with a needle and syringe loaded with sodium amytal, that she drugged Nurse McCutcheon, that he fell resoundingly to the polished floor, and that somehow she and Jasper made their escape through a long, dark and terrifying tunnel and that now, in the car, she knows she and Jasper are from different countries. She says to him, 'Do you remember Carson McCullers, how she says in *The Ballad of the Sad Cafe* that the beloved is only a stimulus for all the stored-up love in the lover? I am the lover, Jasper, and you are the beloved.' Jasper's answering smile is one of complete non-comprehension but it doesn't matter to her. She throws her head back and yells to the sky: 'I am the lover and you are the beloved!' and the sky wheels around them, the car speeds away.

It wasn't one of those cognisant, lucid dreams where the dreamer is able to think while it is unfolding: This is an invention. It is not real. And how peculiar it was that her subconscious mind had remembered that bit of McCullers, a quote from a book she hadn't read since she was in her twenties. In the morning she found her old copy and checked it. 'And somehow every lover knows this,' it goes on. 'He feels in his soul that this love is a solitary thing. He comes to know a new, strange lone-liness and it is this knowledge which makes him suffer.' Jasper's laughing face beside her in the car was detailed, subtle, acute, an image stored more vividly than any that remained of her mother and it ambushed her, still, days later, whenever the world around her fell silent.

Arm in arm with Nònna as they bent to the roses growing outside the main entrance of Monigatti House it was very quiet — too quiet — and she felt the dream rise in her again: Jasper's face, the way the wind had moved in his hair, the weight of his palm on her leg . . . She quelled it, forced herself to focus on her surroundings.

Set back from the road behind a high fence, the modern brick complex oozed faux peace and tranquillity. Family groups wandered around, in and out of the display unit and the main office. MONIGATTI OPEN DAY read the sign on Ramsay Street, with red and yellow balloons bumping at its corners. BRAND NEW HIGH-SECURITY RETIREMENT VILLAGE. It had been raining and the grass was damp and glazed beneath their feet, the petals of the transplanted roses sparkled.

'This place will be too expensive,' Nònna said, straightening from sniffing a rose. A droplet of rainwater clung to her nose like a tiny diamond, as if Nònna had been hip enough, when it was in fashion, to have a piercing. Tenderly, Franca wiped it away while Nònna kept talking. 'Look at this. Not a weed. They must have a gardener. How will they pay him? Out of our money, that's how.'

'You mustn't worry about that, Nònna. The money doesn't matter.'

'In my case it's different,' Nònna went on, pulling her arm away from Franca's and setting off deliberately across the grass, her head down, wrapping her nylon raincoat more firmly around her. As she followed her, Franca sighed, knowing what was coming. 'Some of these people, they could take care of their own. Look —' she pointed vigorously to a middle-aged couple standing near a newly planted sapling. Between them stood an elderly man, and nearby two teenage boys pushed each other around on the lawn. They were hooting at each other, like seals, or dogs. Under his battered fedora the old man's face was bewildered, his gaze shifting from the boys to the tiled roof of the complex and back again. 'Those people,' said Nònna, in tones of disgust. 'She only have those two big boys, eh? Then she can look after her old father herself. My case is different, eh, Franca?'

It's as if she's trying to convince herself, thought Franca then, as if by repeating it over and over she would come to accept, finally, that Franca couldn't have her to live with her. 'You don't have to come here,' she said quickly, catching hold of Nònna's arm again. 'We only came to have a look.'

Nònna sniffed. 'Anyway, the kitchen is too small.'

'It's only for making yourself coffee and snacks. You have your meals in the dining room with the other residents.'

'I might not like their cooking.' Nònna was turning away up the white concrete drive to the carpark.

'You don't want to go to the presentation? Hear all about the things you can do here? What they have on offer?'

Her grandmother did not respond. Doggedly, she continued on, one swollen ankle in front of the other, putting Monigatti's luxury units, spa baths, rose gardens, craft rooms, chapel and private hospital behind her. She didn't want a bar of it.

The family Nònna had pointed out earlier were going slowly up the gleaming limestone steps towards the glass doors of the main entrance, the old man still between them. Franca watched them for a moment, saw how the man and woman talked gently and incessantly into the old man's leathery red ears. He offered no resistance. How many of them go willingly? she wondered. Most of them must require a degree of coercion, a spate of straight-talking. 'You're not coping any more, Nònna,' daughters and grand-daughters must tell old ladies all over Sydney. 'You'll be happier in a home. Safer. Fed and warm. We won't have to worry about you.'

Parents and Nònno vanished inside, the teenage boys took out packets of Marlboro and lit up. A light wind caught the banner stretched between two gums on either side of the driveway, making it crack and flap, momentarily effacing the bright red BUON GIORNO and the English 'Welcome', written in smaller lettering below.

On the short drive back to South Avenue Nònna wasn't talking. She was punishing her with silence, Franca realised. At the door she kissed the tiny, lined cheek that Nònna proffered and got back into the car. The afternoon stretched ahead of her with the same familiar, arid and empty feeling of so many of her weekends. She would not go to the prison, she resolved. She didn't trust herself — not until the dream had been returned to her subconscious, bundled away, forgotten, filed under 'Foolish Longings' . . .

Her cellphone was ringing. Nònna, probably, she thought, wanting to know why she was still sitting outside in her car and did she want to come in after all.

'Franca Todisco?' said a woman's voice, which sounded South African, with clipped consonants and dull vowels.

'Yes?'

'My name is Melody Argyle.' No, it was a New Zealand accent. 'I got your name from Jasper Brunel.' There was a pause then, as though the woman were carefully choosing her words.

'Yes?' said Franca again, more sharply than she'd intended to.

'Could we meet?'

'Of course. Are you a friend of Jasper's?'

'No. Not exactly.'

A thought occurred to Franca. 'You're not a lawyer?'

'No, I'm . . . Look, I'll explain it all to you when we meet.'

'When would you like to do that? This afternoon sometime?'

'Well — yes, that would be great.' The woman sounded surprised. 'If you can make it at such short notice.'

'Where?' That terseness again, thought Franca, entirely unintentional. Her throat felt dry. What would she learn from this Melody? Perhaps she was an old lover of his.

'My hotel if you like. We can meet in the bar at three o'clock.'

They sat against the wall of the atrium in the Inter-Continental on rigid, rather uncomfortable armchairs, avoiding the shafts of hot light that fell from the distant glass ceiling and fired off the reflective tables and floor. The bar was empty but for a group of three other women, the youngest of whom had a shiny new brass neck-ring, freshly soldered at the back, contrasting with the three duller ones below it. As she was short-necked it was pressing hard up against her jaw. It was only a matter of time before a girl died, thought Franca, her spinal cord severed. It was a decorative way to commit slow suicide if you shared the aesthetic — far more glamorous than smoking cigarettes.

Melody Argyle ordered coffee and they balanced the bone china cups on their knees, talking in hushed voices as though they were anxious not to be overheard. When the woman told her she was writing a biography and who her subject was, Franca felt her fingertips chill against the hot shiny sides of her cup. She was aware her mouth had pulled down — probably very unattractively — and that her feet were seeking shelter under her chair. Pull yourself together, she told herself harshly. Get a grip.

'It seems your patient —'

'He's not —' began Franca.

'I'm sorry. Client —'

'No, he's not that either,' said Franca, looking carefully at the biographer, whose eyes were hidden from her behind stylish chrome-armed spectacles, their lenses catching the light and flashing white and opaque. 'I just visit him now and again.'

What has Jasper told her? she wondered. It was impossible to guess the woman's age. Something about her said early thirties — the slight slackening of skin at the jaw, an infinitesimal stoop to her undernourished shoulders — but she had the demeanour and body of a girl: pubescent breasts and narrow hips.

'He says you're studying him,' Melody said lightly. 'For research purposes.'

'I was. I decided he didn't really fit the bill. Anyway, I interrupted you. Please go on.' She was a nervous character perhaps, this Melody. Her fingernails were so badly bitten the pads had splayed. She was pretty in that fragile, handle-with-care way that big men — paradoxically — found attractive. She was taking her glasses off now, folding them away and slipping them into the breast pocket of her shirt. Her hazel eyes were huge in her thin face. She looked hungry, her mouth thickly coated in a blood-red lipstick.

'What I'm interested in,' said Melody, 'is the relationship that developed between Howard Shag and Jasper between 1981 and early 1985. They met soon after the Springbok Tour of our country — which you may have heard of about?' Franca was shaking her head. 'Shag took an interest in the boy. He helped him out financially and acted as a father substitute while Jasper's real father was in Australia. Then, very suddenly, three and a half years later, their friendship came to an abrupt end.'

'Jasper's told me nothing about it,' said Franca. 'He's never mentioned it.'

'He would have been nine years old when they met, and twelve when it finished. Shag didn't abandon him, though — at least, not as far as the money was concerned. He kept his payments up, paying them into Brunel's account. It was set up as a kind of allowance for him.'

'Very honourable,' said Franca, dryly. Shag's biographer looked bemused.

'Yes, it was. Very. Howard's a very honourable sort of man. All those old-fashioned virtues like decency and discretion run thickly in his veins. At home he's famous for his philanthropic organisations, which he —' She broke off. 'I'm sorry. Am I boring you?' Franca had covered her mouth and was looking away, as if she were yawning. Or was she stifling a laugh?

'I do apologise,' said Franca smoothly. 'It's just that, you see, in my experience —' She took a deep breath: the wave of nausea receded. 'Yes.

My experience of Mr Shag is quite different.'

'Have you met Howard?' With quick jerking movements Melody put her coffee on the floor by her feet and dipped into the bulging cloth bag that was hooked over her seat back. Then she seemed to change her mind; she was looking at Franca with an indefinable expression and drawing her hand out again. 'Go on,' she said, and Franca, leaning back in the chair with her arms folded across her stomach, thought she would. She would go on: she would tell the biographer exactly what had happened. It would be the finish of it for her, it would — in the tired lexicon of pop-psychologists and badly trained two-bit therapists — give 'closure'.

'If I tell you what happened, and you decide to include it in your book, then it will be conditional on your changing my name. I don't want any exposure from it.'

Melody nodded. 'We can come to an arrangement.'

'The arrangement will be complete anonymity: my profession, my physical description. Nothing must remain that could lead to my being identified.' The woman nodded again. 'All right.'

'All right,' echoed Franca. 'In 1985, when I was seventeen, I went out one night with my friend Karleen,' she began, and described how she had met Shag in the club, and how he had taken her back to his hotel. She described how he had held the pillow over her face, how he had hurt her and how ill she had been afterwards. She told the story almost as if it had happened to someone else, as though she were giving notes on a clinical case. Without interrupting, Melody listened carefully, her head inclined, not meeting the psychiatrist's eyes. When she had finished, she waited a moment or two before she asked, 'What happened next?'

'I rang a cousin of mine in Auckland, who arranged to have him beaten senseless.' The biographer was certainly looking at her now, Franca observed. Her eyes, rounder than ever — startled even — were travelling from Franca's manicured hands with their ash-coloured nailpolish, to the black pearls circling her throat, to the sapphires in her earlobes. She was thinking, no doubt, that Franca was an appalling and violent human being.

'I think you are a little younger than me,' Franca said, inclining slightly in her chair. 'You won't remember how rape cases were tried back then. I would not have had a leg to stand on. After all, I had got in to bed with him, hadn't I? I had allowed him to penetrate me.'

Suddenly, vividly, the biographer blushed, which gave Franca a small pulse of amusement.

'Then you changed your mind?'

'Yes. Which I had every right to do. The possibility of successful legal action was further reduced by the fact he was a visitor. He was only in Sydney to promote one of his crap books, and would have returned home soon after. I was a student then. I had no money or resources to pursue him.' The girl had her hand in her bag again and this time drew out a packet of roll-your-owns. That must have been what she was going to do before, thought Franca. Smoke. Now I've made her really want one.

'Do you like Shag?' she asked her. 'Do you get along with him?'

'Mostly,' Melody answered, 'although he can be very taciturn and irascible.' The lighter flared, she exhaled. 'You do know, don't you, that Howard was broken by that experience? He has scarcely stepped outside his front door since his punishment. He hasn't written another book. You fucked his life.'

'I'm not sorry for what my cousin did. Nobody could predict that he would become a recluse.' Franca looked at her watch, then towards the doors, suddenly filled with misgivings.

'May I ask you a question?' asked Melody.

'Of course.'

'How did you know this man was Howard Shag?'

'Because he told me he was. There was no reason not to believe him.'

'What did he look like?'

'I'm sorry.' Franca stood, straightening her skirt and bending to pick up her bag. 'I've told you what he did. I don't want to be put on the stand twenty years after the event. You're completely out of line.' Was she shouting? The neck-ringed girl looked over, turning her whole body stiffly in her chair.

'Please —' Melody had caught hold of her hand. 'It's just that the photographs of Howard are few and far between. He's had none taken since he was an All Black. I just want you to . . . describe him for me.

262

Please?' The upturned face was contorting and for a moment Franca thought the girl might cry. The huge eyes were definitely a few degrees more moist, the vermilion lower lip trembled. She hesitated for a moment, then sat down again.

'Well, he was a big man, as you would expect in an ex-rugby player. Curly dark hair greying at the temples. Olive skin, blue eyes. In fact, strangely, he looked very like Jasper. Perhaps that's why he took such an interest in him. He must have recognised, even subconsciously, that similarity. It was a case of like attracting like.'

'Does Jasper know about this? Your previous association with Shag?'

'No. Very few people know.'

'Why did you tell me?'

'Because . . .' Franca almost shuddered at the woman's naïveté. It was almost repulsive. 'Because I think it's important that you portray your national hero in a realistic light. He hasn't always been the altruistic do-gooder he is now.'

'Neither is he a rapist. I know Howard well. I can't believe that he . . . I know he wouldn't . . .'

Franca almost laughed, but it died in her throat. There was a heavy, damp sensation in the centre of her chest as though something were weighing her down, pressing her into her chair. The little biographer seemed strangely enlivened by this unpleasant exchange. She had leapt to her feet and was gathering up her things.

'The coffees are on my tab,' she said. 'Goodbye, Franca. Nice to have met you.' Before Franca could reply she was vanishing in her quick, jerky, strobe-like way across the atrium and into the lift lobby. The girl with the neck-ring caught her eye. In the nineteenth century a phrenologist called Spurzheim believed suicide was a form of insanity produced by abnormal thickening of the skull, remembered Franca distractedly. What would he think now, of all these stretched necks, thickened by the rings?

Concentrate. Focus, she told herself. You've make a mistake, telling that girl the story. What on earth possessed you? You will be exposed, even if the biographer changes your name. It would be written down in black and white, in somebody else's words, in a biography that will no doubt sell by the truckload. You've given Shag a chance to answer you, to defend himself, to make public the reasons for his long seclusion. Perhaps he will even want to track you down and confront you.

The girl must have gone to her room. Franca stood, resolved to follow her there.

'I was just having coffee with my friend Melody Argyle,' she told the girl at the desk. 'She went back up to her room and left her handbag.' Franca lifted her own bag to show her, thinking as she did so that black Italian leather was probably not Melody's style — she seemed to favour ethno-hippie velvet — but the clerk was not to know that.

'I'll get a porter to take it up,' she said.

'Don't worry about that. I'll do it.'

'Suit yourself,' said the girl.

'She told me her room number but it went straight out of my head. Do you have it — is it four three something?'

'Just a moment . . .' How obliging she was, this girl. She was scrawling a number on a piece of paper and handing it over.

'Thank you,' said Franca, turning quickly on her heel and following in Melody's footsteps towards the lifts.

As she lifted her hand to knock she heard voices inside the room and nearly lost her nerve. It was another woman's voice, slightly muffled and oddly familiar. At the sound of the knock the voice cut off. It was only the television, thought Franca, as the door opened.

'I, um . . . I just wanted to make doubly sure you understand that if you include my story in your biography you must protect my identity. I will be talking to my lawyer about this this afternoon and —'

'Come in,' Melody interrupted, widening the gap in the door. There was a jumble of things on the unmade bed — a cassette recorder, clothes, folders of papers. The muffled voice she'd heard, Franca realised, was her own.

'Were you recording me downstairs?'

Melody looked towards the bed and back towards her. 'Yes. That's how I work. I never learned shorthand. All my interviews with Howard are —'

'Why didn't you tell me? Ask my permission?'

Melody sighed. 'Look. We've got something bigger to worry about.' She sat down on the edge of the bed next to her closely, too closely. Franca moved away, towards the window where there was a view of Circular Quay, the Opera House and the harbour. A ferry was streaming in; there were hundreds of Saturday yachts and pulling hard around the point from Farm Cove a Chinese dragonboat loaded with men dressed all in red.

'I'm not saying I don't believe you were raped all those years ago. I accept that. But it wasn't Howard. You got the wrong man.' Melody's voice was soft behind her.

'He told me his name was Howard Shag,' Franca said, not turning around.

'He lied. It wasn't.'

'How can you be so sure? How dare you?' She spun now and glared at her. The biographer looked nervous, those little bitten hands clasped in her bony lap.

'I just know. Howard would never do anything like that. He's too decent and kind.'

'You've only known him as an old man. Christ. I can't believe we're having this conversation.'

'Would you like to see a photograph of him?' Melody picked up a folder from the chaos on the bed and leafed through it. 'It's an old one. He hasn't been photographed for years. Not since the assault. Here —' For a moment she thought Franca wasn't going to take the picture from her. She came to stand beside her, twisting her gaze to rest on the little snap. 'Here,' said Melody again, pushing it at her.

'Who's that?'

'The woman? Howard's Greek wife, Ellie Kitsi. The marriage lasted a year.'

'He was much older than this when I —' Franca stopped suddenly, bit her lip. The young man in the photograph looked Greek himself: suntanned, nuggety, broad-shouldered. One of his hands, square-palmed with long, slim fingers, curled around a halyard above his head. The other rested lightly on his wife's shoulder.

Hands on flesh. Not that flesh — that firm, round, shoulder — but her own

265

*pale, drunken body. Not those hands, but smaller ones, with short, spatulate-
tipped fingers.*

She brought the photograph closer, examined the man's hair, which was
ruffled by the wind, cut short at the sides and longer on top — and, it
appeared, dead straight. There were no curls. Perhaps the man she
remembered had had his hair permed. There was a fashion for that in
the '80s, when the unisex hairdresser began to replace the corner barber.
Hair changes — hair can achieve all kinds of metamorphoses. But
hands don't. Hands stay the same. Franca sat down on the bed beside
Melody, noting the man's eyes, his nose, his high cheekbones. They at
least seemed familiar, though the nose, in profile, had been broken. A
rugby injury perhaps, corrected later — but still . . .

'Well?' asked the biographer.

'I, um . . .' She couldn't bring herself to reply. What could she say?
That she had been wrong all these years? It was impossible.

'If there are any doubts in your mind — any doubts at all — then
you should come back to New Zealand with me. You owe it to yourself.
And to him.'

'That's where you're wrong. I don't have a vendetta against him.
He's had his punishment.'

'You see, from what I can make out, Howard had no idea why the
women abducted him in the middle of the night and took him to a city
park, where they tortured him and left him to be discovered by a
stranger in the morning. He thought it was because of his relationship
with Jasper Brunel.'

'Relationship?'

'Friendship. I assume that he thought the women, among whom
was Jasper's mother, were under the impression that he had had . . .
improper relations with the boy.'

'Had he?' Franca felt as though she were standing in a very hot,
pure white light. It was as if some cosmic force were pushing its way
towards her. *You were wrong, all those years ago,* it was saying. *Your
assailant may not have been Shag — but Jasper's was. It's because of
him that Jasper is in the mess he's in. It was a kind of karmic exchange,
laid by fate years ago. You were destined for this, to help Jasper*

through. It's all right. You have not built your whole lonely life on a lie.'

'No, of course not.'

There was a chair in the corner, under a lamp. Franca groped her way towards it. 'But what does Jasper say?' she asked. 'Have you asked him?'

'His memories of Shag are fond ones, although there is some remorse and blame there for the way the friendship ended. He hasn't seen Howard since the attack.'

'So that was why their friendship ended? Because Shag thought the women were punishing him for the boy?'

Melody nodded. 'Yes, I think so.'

Moral conscience was not part of Franca's psychological landscape. She had banished it, she thought, along with fear. She avoided intimate associations with other human beings, which constantly presented participants with dilemmas of what was right, either for the lover or the beloved. Rarely could a solution be found that did for both. The idea of selfless, generous love was anathema to the real bones of human nature, she believed. It belonged to the old Christian world and was buried and gone for ever. The truth of modern love was something entirely different: human beings always take the most powerful course of action at any given moment, they do whatever will further their own interests.

'Perhaps,' she began, 'the reason Shag went to ground after the incident is that he felt he had been rightly punished. Not for what happened to me, necessarily, but for what he did to Jasper.'

'He didn't do anything to Jasper.'

'We don't know that. How could we? When are you going to Auckland?'

'Tonight,' said Melody. 'I could go back out to the prison to see Jasper, but there's no point really. I'm more use back home, putting in some solid work on the book. The boyfriend's pissed off, though.' She pulled a wry face and Franca wondered which Melody was, the lover or the beloved. She was opening her mouth to speak again and Franca had the feeling she was going to attempt friendship with her, to impart some intimate details about her boyfriend. Franca was not interested.

'I'll come to Auckland,' she said quickly, 'but not on the sa' flight. I'll try for tomorrow.'

'Really? You really are coming?'

'Why not?'

'You would like me to take you see Howard?'

'Absolutely.' Was it just bravado that had made the girl suggest the trip? Franca wondered. Now her skin had grown impossibly paler, her red mouth was slack with surprise. She extended a hand and the girl shook it. 'Have you got a card?'

'Oh. No. Hang on.' She tore a corner off a sheet of paper and scrawled an address and telephone number.

'See you, then,' said Franca at the door.

On her way out of the hotel she felt pleased with herself. When she had gone up to the biographer's room she had certainly been on the back foot. When she left she had the distinct impression she had the upper hand. It was the dream, perhaps, that had sustained and inspired her through the whole exchange. She knew what it meant now, its oblique symbols made clear: the love she had for Jasper would never be reciprocated, but it would run its course. She had to let that happen. It was a journey to nowhere. Eventually her love would die from lack of nourishment; it would just wither painlessly away. She knew that. In the meantime it was real to her, it was fierce and real and intensely private. Travelling to New Zealand to meet the man who with curious synchronicity had ruined both their lives was an entirely sensible thing to do. She would do it for Jasper.

JASPER

Letter to Damian

Is that you? That touch on my hair just then, the lightest pressure on the crown of my head, enough to make my scalp creep — that's how you used to wake me up when we were at sea, or if I'd fallen asleep after filming you'd brush your palm over the points of my hair and . . . I'm awake, Damian. I'm sitting up in my bed and looking for you, looking into the dark corners of my hut. You're here, for the first time. You've come to see me, you've swum in.

Damian?

You used to tell me I talked too much. You'd tell me to shut the fuck up. You were always a silent one. Shall I talk to you now, then? I'll tell you what it's been like for me.

Have you been outside, mate? Did you have a look around? My hut at Berrima is not so bad, eh? At least it's near the gates so I can watch the comings and goings. On the walls I've put up a photo of Mum and Scottie and one of you, which I cut out of the newspaper. There's no

269

Nurse McCutcheon here, but I've kept the dosette in memory of him. He said he'd come out to the highlands to visit me but so far he hasn't. It's not that I think he'd bring me anything to put in the dosette. He was kind to me in the hospital at Long Bay, but he reminded me too much of you and it didn't help my grieving. He wanted something from me and it doesn't take a rocket scientist to work out what.

When I went to trial, a year ago now, McCutcheon made sure I would be all right. Stambach decided quite suddenly I was in my right mind and next thing I knew my drug trial date was set for the following week at the Supreme Court. McCutcheon brought me my civilian clothes, which had been washed and ironed somewhere else in the prison, and he left a couple of Serepax in the shirt pocket. I took one just before I left, which was just as well. The judge was an old bastard — he blamed you for everything. He commented on my 'naïve and dependent personality', my 'eagerness to please the late Damian Frost', and my 'history of drug abuse, one of the most tragic he had known, which began in the prisoner's childhood'. He gave me eighteen years. After that I didn't care what they gave me for the boys. Mum came to the trial. I kept my eyes on her the whole time but she sat beside Scottie with her head bowed, not looking at me until the summing up.

'I sentence you, Jasper Richard Brunel, to imprisonment for eighteen years to date from the twenty-third of June, 2005. I fix a non-parole period of ten years to run from the same date.'

Despite all my boyhood reading it's numbers I remember. I remember every day the number of years I'll serve for the coke and the six I'm serving concurrently for the boys.

That red and orange lei hanging from the ceiling of my hut is from Lenny Fakafanua, who used to star in our films. He brought it with him when he came to see me — came all the way on the train with it round his neck matching his lipstick. It was the first time he'd been out of Sydney since his parents brought him to Australia from Auckland when he was a baby. He loved it here — the wide highlands, the clear skies, the farm and the bush. He looked at me with his big shining brown eyes and I reckon if he could have moved into my hut with me he would have.

'It's not a holiday camp, Lenny,' I told him. He just smiled.

The brochures on the table are from the university. There's a woman education officer here who thinks I should continue with my chemistry degree.

'You've got what it takes,' she tells me, as if she knows me. Which she doesn't. She has no idea how busy I am. After my day's work in the kitchens I like to come straight back to my hut and read my mail. I get at least one letter a day and I always write back. Since I came here I've had seven correspondents and all except one write once a week.

That drawer, the one in the table with the splintered leg, is full of letters. See, here's one from Vincent, my oldest son.

> Dear Dad,
> I hope your ok in the jail and not feeling too lonly. I
> got your adress from Granpa's old girlfreind who likes
> to visit Mum now and again. She sits on the edge of
> our couch and drinks tea and smils alot. She told Mum
> she was sorry the lawyer she got for you was so
> munted, but your case was hopeless anyway. Mum says
> she doesn't know why Mikaela comes here, but it could
> have something to do with her going round with a
> famous Maori activist who has full moko, Mickaela I
> mean, not Mum, and hanging round us gives her cred.
> That's what Mum says.
>   It's allright living here. We see heaps of our
> aunties and cousins. Blair at school, his Dads in prison
> too so were mates.
> Mum says hello.
> love,
> Vinnie.

His letters are short, but not as short as Jack's, which are usually two-liners. I write back to them, though: they each get a letter each week, and I just let my imagination fly. It was Lenny Fakafanua who gave me the idea, to make it seem like it's more fun than it really is. I make up all sorts of things — aeroplane rides, bungy jumping, hang-gliding, mountain climbing. A note came from Bonny the other day: 'Stop filling the boys up with shit.' Here it is. Look at that. One line, not even signed. She knows I'll recognise her handwriting.

This envelope, this long, narrow ivory-coloured one, is scented with something lemon. It's from Franca, who still hasn't forgiven herself for not attending my trial. She was in New Zealand at the time.

Letters to Vinnie and Jack zoom out of my pen but I struggle with my replies to Franca. I haven't answered this latest one yet because of this paragraph here — it freaks me right out.

'I have just come in from Nònna's funeral — my grandmother's, that is. She died very suddenly last Sunday morning, of a stroke. I don't think you realise that for a long time, apart from you, Nònna was all I had in the world . . .'

Apart from me? She hasn't even come out here to see me, not once in a whole year. There's a reason for that, though; it's in an earlier letter, if I can find it . . .

Here. She was using a packet of blue envelopes then. 'I am still unable to understand why they've sent you out to Berrima. You're not a homosexual. I wish you had told me more about your relationship with Damian. From what I do know, it seems to me it was more about power than sex . . .'

Pretty fucking desperate, in my opinion. She returns to that theme often; it seems to really rankle with her. It's even more complicated than that, for her, the homo thing. This torn, ancient-looking envelope is one that was forwarded from Long Bay and got lost for weeks somewhere in the prison mail system. She wrote it in New Zealand. There's a bit half way down the second page . . .

'I allowed my dreaming self to overwhelm the self that went about her daily life. My regard for you was completely out of proportion with what circumstances could ever allow us. That is why I've gone away for a while, to try to sort things out in my own head.'

The last sentence is fairly mendacious. It isn't why she went away. That Mel woman, the one who was writing the book about Howard, she got her to go to New Zealand to cure the old bloke of all his various phobias. I imagine that when she doesn't fall in love with her clients, she's a good psychiatrist.

There's one envelope in that drawer that could easily be confused with Franca's, but it's not from her, it's from Michaela. The first letter came a few months after I arrived at Berrima, hand-written on thick, rose pink stationery with a fountain pen. In places the ink has fuzzed into the paper as if the paper were a living thing, with capillaries. She writes in a large round script, similar to Franca's, but bigger, more assured, more aggressive in the amount of room each letter takes up. She leaves no margins.

> You might like to know who it was who footed the bill
> for Mr Lamb. I did, but you mustn't think it was out
> of any affection for you. You may remember the one
> and only we time we met was shortly before you
> separated from Bonny and your drunken, abusive
> behaviour on that occasion left much to be desired.
>
> My reasons for providing you with a top-ranking
> lawyer were personal ones, to do with the early and
> tragic death of my much-loved brother Johnny, who
> was my only sibling. Like you, he had come into
> contact with the devious and perverted Mr Shag, a
> man who spoiled him with drink and drugs and
> indirectly caused his death. You are the lucky one.
>
> It was in Johnny's memory that I helped you.
> Please do not reply to this letter. I do not require any
> thanks or acknowledgement.
> Yours sincerely
> Michaela Thompson-Boyd (née) Boswell

I like that one. It excites me. Reading it is like coming across a perfectly formed, symmetrical pond in a forest, ringed with trailing grasses, stinking of sulphur and so murky you can't see the bottom; you can only suspect that something primeval and viscous lives inches below the surface.

Of course I did write back. Why wouldn't I? Besides, I think if she were serious about me not writing back she wouldn't have used that pink stationery with her address stamped into the top. I can't remember much about what I wrote, except that it was cheeky. I thanked her for the Lamb and said how marvellous he was, how he got me off and how I was now living in Taiwan, like Harness out of *Fire Dragon*, with house-boys blowing me off every time I felt like it. Not that Howard's hero did the latter. That would have had an adverse affect on sales and Howard has never been one for niche markets.

The second letter tucked into the same pink envelope is from Lamb himself. One line.

'My client wishes to advise you that this correspondence is at a close.'

Just as well Dad never made her my stepmother, otherwise I'd feel really abandoned. My own mother is, of course, a brick. I've had to start throwing some of her letters out — there's so many I can't keep them all. She writes in a tiny, crabbed hand on those thin-leafed, black-lined pads you can buy at supermarkets, filling them with endless detail: what she and Scottie ate, movies they saw, books they're reading, walks they went on, how Vinnie and Jack came up to stay the weekend. Often she repeats her invitation for me to go and live with her and Scottie when I've done my time, and she always finishes with 'Lots and lots of love' and a line of x's. She hasn't been to see my father once, or at least, if she has she doesn't mention it. I think this is unfair, considering the amount of time she must spend writing to me. If she lived in this country she'd be out here to see me every weekend, I reckon. From Dad's letters — there's only four of them — he sounds really low. Mum must realise he has absolutely no friends who could visit him. It's his own fault, of course — he concentrated for too many years on getting his leg over, and not enough on making friends. He hasn't got any mates and he's been through hell since I last saw him.

Howard's letters I keep away from the others because they're special and I can't help thinking, worth a bit. Not that I'll sell them before he falls off his perch — I do have some principles. Until I decide to send them somewhere, which, given Howard's health, may not be very long, these letters are for my eyes alone. I keep them wrapped in a pillowcase under my bed, in chronological order. The first one arrived in early July, soon after my arrival here:

> It falls to me to alert you to some grave unpleasantness
> to do with your father. It seems he made up his mind

to do me damage, a course of action he perceived as retribution for imagined wrongs I had done to you. There was a time, as we both know, when I did take to you with my fists — and for that, Jasper, I am truly sorry. For many years my conscience has been plagued by the events of the day I was released from hospital, many years ago. There is no excuse for a grown man to hurt a child, as you were then, and this is something I can only hope you have come to understand yourself.

It was out of loyalty and commitment to you — and yes, guilt — that I continued to make regular payments into your bank account.

When your father came to visit me three weeks ago he made it abundantly clear he believed that I had, during our association, relieved you of your innocence, and that the money I sent you was to keep you quiet. At the time of his arrival I was, as usual, alone in the house. I tried to explain the truth, even going so far as to describe how the only shameful injury I had ever inflicted on you was an undeserved beating — which is bad enough — but he was blind with rage and bent on retribution. I am an old man now and a nervous one at that. For some years now I have had panic buttons installed in the house in various rooms and these set off alarms at a private security firm. As soon as I realised what was in store for me I was able to depress one of these buttons. Very soon after that I sustained a heavy blow to the head and fell to the floor unconscious.

Your father is now on remand at Mt Eden Prison and will stand trial for aggravated assault. I fully intended to drop the charges as I could very easily see — given the nature of your own crime — how his fevered mind had come to the conclusion that it was my influence during your childhood that had predisposed you to it. However, even after he was arrested, he continued to make threats against my life and police advice is to uphold the charges.

Jasper, I do not wish ever to discuss with you the crimes you and your accomplice committed against adolescents. It is something I would prefer to put aside, to — as they say — draw a veil over. It is abhorrent to me in the extreme and I can only presume that you had so weakened your mind with narcotics that you had no idea what you were doing. Should you decide to reply to this letter, please don't attempt any excuses or explanations.

I did write back, and I did as he asked: no details. I wouldn't want to go over all that anyway — I just rattle on about life inside. Maybe Howard will start writing books again and set one of them in a prison — I can help him with the research . . . but it'd be nice to tell him about Damian one day. Howard would understand. In one of his letters he tells me about Johnny, a letter which strangely enough arrived the same day as Michaela's:

He was the love of my life. Our relationship was utterly clandestine and I have wondered, since his tragic death, how it would have played itself out had he not been so brutally taken from me. Perhaps if it had been allowed to reach its natural end I would have loved again, properly. I have had other lovers, of course, in other countries — interesting and exotic men of beauty and grace, or of great physical strength, or in possession of incisive and fascinating minds — but none touched me as deeply as Johnny did. None came close.

After long and intense conversations with Franca about him I have come to the conclusion to allow Melody to include that part of my life in her biography. It is difficult for younger men to under-stand what it was like for us then, for men who led prominent public lives, as I did as an All Black. An

All Black! The last bastion of heterosexuals! I couldn't have made it more difficult for Johnny and myself if I'd tried.

For many years I was ashamed of my sexuality, bewildered and even frightened by it, and in this country, aside from Johnny and one or two friends of his who were of the same persuasion, it was a closely guarded secret. Imagine my horror, then, on the night I was attacked and left for dead in the park. I believed at first I had been found out. Later, during my convalescence, it seemed to me that it was worse than that: that you had told your mother a tall tale of pederasty and that was what they punished me for.

It was my turn to apologise then, in my next letter. Not for myself, but for my mother and her friends, who were only going by what the young woman in Sydney had told them. I suppose it's a common enough age-old ploy to use the name of a famous man as a leg-opener, though I've never done so myself. Never had to.

It's light now. The day is coming. See the soft grey chink in the curtains. If only you could write back, Dam, and tell me what it's like where you are. The chaplain here asked me if I worried about you in the afterlife — you know, he thought maybe I pictured you burning in the eternal hellfire of damnation. It's the opposite, I could have told him: I see you swimming in a vast tumbling ocean, your strong, wiry arms curling around, pulling you through, taking you down, down, down in your fluid, watery world where nothing is as it seems, which is just the way you like it. I didn't tell the chaplain this; I just fell silent and he made a little note in neat printing that I could read upside down: 'Prisoner anxious about lost partner'.

I'm not, though. You can be my eighth correspondent. You can swim up from the depths just as you did earlier and spend a couple of hours with me each day before sunrise. I won't write the letters down, there's no need. You can come to me, just as you did this morning, with a feather touch to my hair, and wait quietly on the chair while I lie here and write you a letter in my head.

LENA

Last Word

It was Helen, Melody's mother, who told me what was going on. It was just idle chat, the first time I'd seen her since her Womb Burial on that brilliantly sunny winter solstice a year and a half ago. I haven't felt like seeing people since Scottie and I came back from Sydney. I told myself to take my own advice, that if I were my own client I would recommend virtual seclusion, some solitary time, during which period I would fully experience all my rage and grief, until a day would come when I could let that rage and grief go . . .

What specious shit all that 'letting go' is. Anger, guilt, regret, despair, misery, desire for revenge — whatever species of black cloud hangs over my head at any given moment may pass on to another part of my firmament, but it will never dissipate completely. And why should it?

Shortly before Jasper was arrested I had a client come to see me, an Englishman. It is unusual for men to seek me out, unless they are friends or friends of friends, and I ended by sending him to a psychiatrist. It was either that or, if he had been a religious man, a priest. I couldn't help him, not with the wisdom gleaned from my twenty-year-old six-week course, my half-dozen weekend retreats, my library of Jung, Gestalt therapy, transactional analysis, psycho-drama, books on Buddha, the Bhagavad Gita and New Age takes on incest, ageing, mid-life transformation, psychosynthesis and countertransference. As a younger man he had been a mercenary in Angola. For entertainment he had shot and killed children; pushed terrified adolescents against trees with the bull bars of jeeps and crushed every bone in their under-nourished bodies. Now, in his new life in New Zealand, he discovered he couldn't sleep and he came to me for help. It was absolution he required, or sedation thick enough to stifle all consciousness. He gave his account of these unforgivable crimes dry-eyed, his voice flat, devoid of expression.

When he stood up to leave, rummaging in his pocket for cash to pay me, I stopped him. I didn't want his money. I wanted him away from my bright, welcoming Work Room, off the squashy lilac sofa and back out into the world without leaving a trace of himself behind. As I watched him go back down the curly path to our gate, a big, lumbering sandy-haired man running to fat, I found myself almost murmuring a malediction — Go home and suffer, I was thinking, full of the terrible realisation that I and my kind have led the world by the collective nose into a miasma of false hope. More than any priest who in the end must defer to the higher power or the punishing fires of hell; more than any shrink who will reach, eventually, for the prescription pad, we therapists promise a self-generated road to happiness and clean conscience — no matter the cruelty, no matter the crime.

I see that morning now as the beginning of the journey that has led me this point, here, walking along the sunny beach with Hausfrau home from Helen's. I remember that moment vividly: watching the man go down to meet the waiting taxi, which would take him back to the ferry. In our first five minutes together he told me he'd caught the boat out to the island just to see me, and that he'd selected me out of the plethora of counsellors on offer because I had the same name as his mother. Before he folded himself into the cab he'd crossed the road to stand above the beach and look out over the bay and our wide, clean sky, his pudgy hands on his hips. Even a man like him still has a human eye for beauty, I'd thought, watching him: he is still capable of awe and delight. Then I had turned away, allowing him his private moment, and gone to be with Scottie, who was working in the courtyard outside her shed on the other side of the house. A slab of swamp kauri lay across two trestles and she was planing the surface into wide stripes, feeling with her sensitive fingertips, then sanding, planing again and feeling for rough spots. Her big head bent in the sunlight, her face was intent, concentrated, and for a moment I envied her as much as I loved her. I wished I too had a trade that was all solid, warm wood and not human misery, bewilderment and neurosis.

Many of my colleagues like to believe they have dismissed any experience of guilt from their lives and encourage their clients to believe the same, but I have come full circle. I now accept its place in my life as a normal and necessary human foible. It was guilt, a tinge of it, that had me this morning put on my sunhat and go along the beach to Helen's.

'I'm going into town tonight,' she told me over our cups of hot water, 'for the launch of Melody's book.'

'I didn't know she was writing a book,' I said. In the light filtering through the moss and bird shit-covered glass roof, Helen looked thin and pale and I suspected she was on yet another of her crash diets — water and vitamin pills.

'Didn't you?' asked Helen. 'That's because the last time I saw you it was still top secret.'

'Really?' I can't imagine either of Helen's daughters keeping a secret, belonging as they do to the tell-all, reveal-all generation.

'It's a biography,' she went on proudly, 'on Howard Shag. She even got a trip to Australia out of it.'

In a country as small as New Zealand it is impossible to avoid certain names, certain people. Howard Shag certainly qualifies as one of these. No sooner do I think he is no longer part of my orbit than he pops up again. After Richard's assault of him, a misguided and violent demonstration of paternal love, I had hoped Shag would finally fade quietly from view.

'Does he live in Australia now?' I asked Helen, and as I spoke that crazy February night came back to me yet again, undimmed by the twenty-something years that have passed or by the substances I'd imbibed before going with the others to abduct him. I remembered pulling his dressing-gown down to cover him before Scottie and I sat on him for the drive from Takapuna to Western Springs. I remembered Chookie hitting him and burning him with cigarettes, I remembered tying my scarf around his face to gag him.

'No, he's in Takapuna. Lovely old place, Melody says.'

'He's been there a while,' I added inadvertently.

'Do you know where he lives?' Helen asked. 'Melody's always very cloak and dagger about which house it is exactly. Poor Curtis did a good job of finding her after Zin's baby was born.'

'It would be a good idea for everyone to stop calling him Poor Curtis,' I said.

Now, as I come up from the beach, across the road and in our gate, I'm worrying about Melody, whom I've known since her early teenage years, keeping company with an elderly rapist. Not that he'd be capable of anything now, I reassure myself. Scottie, who prior to having her consciousness raised was a fan of his books, had a story she'd gleaned years before from the *Woman's Weekly*. She told it to us as we prepared that night to go out and get him.

We'd met that Thursday night in the big old Herne Bay house, all of us excited and apprehensive. Being there all together like that brought back memories of the recent Springbok Tour — of the risks we took then. This action was different of course. For a start off we had to wait for it to get dark, and as it was summer we had to wait for hours. Jasper had come with Scottie and me as far as the house and he hung around watching TV while we waited. Kerry rolled up a powerful joint to help pass the time. Beck and Chookie practised the hold, using Scottie as a stand-in for Shag. Arms pinioned, she was marched up and down the long wooden hall, their voices echoey and intense. It wasn't as scary as the Tour either — although this venture didn't have the Tour's predictability. Back then we knew that if we stood in the front row we'd more than likely be pummelled by the long batons, have the hair that protruded from our crash helmets yanked from our scalps, have fingers or toes broken as we were shoved violently into waiting paddy-wagons. There was a cold, brutal inevitability about the Tour.

On that February night nothing could be predicted. From Jasper we'd learned that Shag lived alone except for an Asian valet and that the valet had Thursday nights off. My son, as it turned out, had been a reliable source of information. We even knew Shag had gone to Australia for a book tour before Kerry got the phone call from her cousin, because he'd promised Jasper an expensive toy on his return. A remote-controlled car, I think it was, or perhaps one of those little yachts that children sail around ponds. I'd asked Jasper, without letting him know what was going on, for the return date. Even though we were anti-hierarchy, Chookie and Kerry were the unacknowledged leaders of the action and they decided that payback time for Mr Shag would be a week after he touched down on New Zealand soil.

Having demonstrated that she could easily free herself from the hold, Scottie flopped into a couch and cut electrical wire into lengths suitable for binding Shag's hands. Beck poured tequila shots all round.

'D'ya know he was married once, this guy?' announced Scottie.

'Marriage is legalised prostitution,' said Kerry, rolling up again.

'Don't get too out of it,' said Chookie.

'He had this drop-dead gorgeous wife. I read a thing about her in the *Woman's Weekly*.'

'You buy the *Woman's Weekly*?' asked Chookie sternly. 'You read that shit?'

'Only in the doctor's waiting room. Or the dentist. You've got to do something. It was years ago. There was a photograph of her. She was a marine biologist. Greek. Bloody beautiful.'

'You've already said that once. Don't be lookist,' squeaked Beck through her toke.

'She's dead now, anyway,' said Scottie, putting down the pliers, the job done. 'She drowned.'

'Shag's wife drowned? Maybe he had something to do with that too,' said Kerry. 'Maybe he drowned her.'

'Shag?' Jasper turned his gaze away from the telly. 'Do you mean Howard Shag?'

'Yeah,' said Beck.

'Maybe,' said Kerry. I tried to hush them, then hoped that even though his name had entered the conversation Jasper may not put two and two together. He was staring at me, his eyes huge in his little pale face. Maybe he wasn't getting enough to eat, I worried — maybe he was sickening for something. He had panda rings under his eyes and his lips looked dry. He seemed suddenly thin and vulnerable, like a seedling raised on a windowsill.

'This prick,' resumed Scottie, who was fairly stoned, 'who may or may not be Howard Shag, was once married to one of the world's greatest beauties, who was obviously brainy as well, and the marriage only lasted a year. Not because she drowned just then — that happened later — but because they got divorced.'

'Why?' asked Jasper.

'Why does anyone get divorced?' asked Kerry. 'Because men are shits.'

Jasper regarded her, steadily, and I got up to put my arm around him. 'Not all men,' I said quietly into his pink ear, feeling woozy from the booze and dope. 'Not you, darling.' His shoulders were stiff and bony under my arm. After a moment he pulled himself away from me and went out into the hall.

'Where's he going?' asked Chookie.

'Fresh air, prob'ly,' said Scottie. 'It's pretty smoky in here.'

Out of the corner of my eye I saw Chookie and Beck exchange a glance — a why-don't-they-just-get-rid-of-him look — and I could have responded to it. I could have repeated my performance on the front steps of that very house when Scottie first took us to Auckland, and I could have thrown in a few punches as well — but I didn't.

'Why won't you tell us your cousin's name, Kerry?' Chookie asked for the hundredth time.

'Because you don't need to know it. I don't want gossip about her. All you need to know is the truth of what happened and I've told you that.'

'We're never going to meet her. She lives in Sydney,' I said. We thought it was unfair of Kerry not to tell us. She'd prepared a little speech to read to Shag once we'd got him, but Chookie wanted to stand around him in a circle and chant the cousin's name at him, which I thought could be very effective in terms of making him understand what he'd done. In the end Kerry never did tell us.

Perhaps it wasn't just guilt that urged me off to Helen's this morning but loneliness as well. Scottie is away in her truck on a wood-finding mission around Northland. Carefully I hang my hat on one of the crumbling driftwood hooks in the porch — a long-ago housewarming present from Helen — and make my way down the hall to the living room. The polished floors ring with my footsteps and when I clear my throat it sounds so inordinately loud it almost startles me.

Retracing my steps, I turn left at the front door. My Work Room, unused now for fifteen months, still retains its sense of healing calm. The green and red Guatemalan baby shawl drapes one wall, the Emily Karaka painting reflects the hot blues and greens of the sea beyond the window. There's a musty smell and on closer inspection the polished surfaces — the low table beside the sofa and my desk top — are mossed over with a fine patina of dust. I open the window and take in a lungful of the steamy outside air. There's the smell of dandelion and baked earth, the sticky scent of paspallum heads, a blue tang of monoxide from the outboard motors churning up the bay. A girl with a white mane of peroxide hair water-skis on a single ski towards the wider gulf, wearing nothing but a thong. Her slim brown body shoots on its one stalk back and forth over the tumultuous wake and once, just before the boat takes her out of sight beyond the point, she turns and waves. Ski skimming, one hand on the tow-rope, she maintains a point of perfect balance in a gesture of farewell to her friends on the beach.

As I turn away the girl's image burns into my retina and an idea strikes with such power that the room seems, for a moment, to darken. In my early years as a therapist I used to draw pictures for my patients, to give them a symbol for their problem, and I draw one for myself now, in felt-tip on the wall below the window: the point of the bay, the boat, the wake, the vanishing, waving, one-legged girl. The bay, I write beside my crude drawing, equals Scottie. She is the warm, sheltering harbour I have anchored in for the past twenty-six years.

The boat is my past. It's my mad bastard alcoholic immigrant father, my sad broken-down mother, both dead. It's my marriage to Richard Brunel, my neglectful mothering of his son, my almost mindless embrace of feminist theory because it soothed, it vindicated, it promised earthly righteousness. The boat is the emotional power-house of my life.

The wake is the turmoil caused by all those people and ideas, and that's me, the one-ski girl skimming over and around them. The wake is thrilling: it's dangerous, it's my own sacred stream of white water. I have been as cocky as that girl. I've risked losing my skin on sudden rocks and fatal blistering from the unremitting sun. This minute, I will take my hand off the tow-rope altogether and swim for the shore.

Already I'm heading down to our garage to drive the car to the ferry, on my way to visit Howard Shag. I will find out what lies he's told Melody.

In two decades the road to Howard's house has changed. Elaborately ornamented old wooden villas have been demolished to make way for townhouses and units; the expansive gardens of some of the older places are cross-leased. In the punishing sun the sea seems to simmer inside its skin, with burnt, darker streaks pointing up the currents, the bed of the channel. It's a weekday, a Thursday, I realise with a thrill of synchronicity — though I'm not sure if that qualifies as true Jungian synchronicity or if it's just coincidence — and the traffic is light. I park the car where we left Beck's car that night, complete with the jettisoned kiddie carseat. I don't think she ever went back to get it.

Yes, this was the way, I think: up the gentle slope and first left into Curnow Ave. Apprehension tingles in my fingertips: will I recognise the house after all this time? Memory flashes past me like a bright-winged bird, giving me Chookie sweaty in her balaclava, Beck pulling down the rim of her beanie and Scottie puffing beside me as we ran. Even then, when we were in our early thirties, Scottie puffed. I miss her terribly, suddenly: I want her here with me.

Last time I passed this way there were no gates. Now there most definitely are — two giant oblongs of massed cast iron curlicues, bolted at either side to steel posts. A honeysuckle, thick with bees and flowers, curls over the posts and flashing through the leaves is a red eye, a sensor. A driveway of finely raked orange gravel begins on the other side. Twenty years ago the approach to the house was luminous crushed white shells, which led uninterrupted up to the house. We'd skirted it, keeping into the shrubbery at the side before scooting along under what appeared to be kitchen windows. At the back of the house was a glassed-in porch and inside, lit up as if he were on a stage, was the man of Kerry's cousin's description: big, beefy, meat-fed, ex-All Black. He was sitting in some kind of exercise machine, which cupped him round like a throne while he pulled hard on two heavily springed handles. He was about forty years old and his strong arms and chest swelled and softened with each creaking of the equipment. A towel hung over the railing of a treadmill and on its black rubber mat stood one sweaty footprint. He had obviously just left it. A little further off, near the open French doors, was a set of dumb-bells and a bench press. The heaviest weight sat bridge-like on the floor.

Why didn't we go in straight away while he was contained in the machine? I wonder now. Why did Chookie wait until he got up, wiped himself down with the towel and left the room? She was counting on his leaving the French doors ajar, which he did, but it wasn't until we got into the narrow corridor beyond the gym that we had any idea how labrynthal the house was. We hissed at one another, arguing about what to do next.

'Shut up!' said Scottie, suddenly, holding up one hand. We all heard it then: the running shower in an upstairs bathroom. Chookie turned towards the direction of the sound, her face uplifted as if she were a fox scenting the air, her mohawk hairdo making a strange lump in the balaclava. She headed for the stairs . . .

Without warning the gates begin to swing open. I have been observed. The red eye flickers and a disembodied voice, a woman's, issues from a grey box higher up the post.

'Lena? Is that you?' There's an electronic crackle, a pause, and then it resumes. 'Don't look so startled! It's me, Melody. Come in.'

Just as the gates reach their terminus, bumping gently against the hedges, the front door bursts open and Melody comes hurrying down the steps to greet me. Two things almost stop me in my crunching tracks. The first is that she is, at a guess, about six months pregnant. Why didn't Helen tell me? The second arresting spectacle is the other woman who has come to stand in the doorway. Has Shag remarried? I wonder. She looks the type to hunt down an ageing wealthy writer: all flashy gold jewellery, heavy makeup and expensive tailored clothes. She reminds me of some of my Italian cousins.

'I thought you'd show up sooner or later,' Melody is saying, mysteriously, hooking one arm through mine. 'But more likely after the biography came out than before!'

'Why did you think that? I came today to see if you were all right.' My voice is trembling. What the hell am I doing here? If Scottie had been home this never would have happened — she would not have let me come.

'Because of your association with Howard. As well as all he's done for Jasper. This is Franca.' The tall blonde and I shake hands. 'This is Lena. Franca has come over from Sydney for the launch.'

'The launch?' I feel vague, almost faint. I stand in the centre of spinning, concentric circles.

'Of my book. Franca has worked miracles on Howard. She's got him going for walks along the beach with Web Ellis.' We pass through the door. Just inside there's a fat brass elephant with a pink bow around its neck, and a suitcase with the airline tickets still attached. 'Now he's almost back to normal. He's even going to speak tonight.'

'Web Ellis? Who?' From the back of the house comes the sound of heavy mallet blows and the grate of a saw on wood.

'Howard. At the book launch.' Melody stops suddenly, halfway down the hall, and takes me by both elbows. 'Are you all right?'

'I think so. You know, Melody, that I was one of the women who took action against Howard because he —'

'Yes. Jasper told me.'

'Jasper? But you've never met him. How could you —'

'I saw him in prison. Ages ago now. Don't worry. Howard's through there.' We have walked the full length of the house and paused at the end of the corridor.

'I don't want to see him, Melody. That's not why I came here —'

A frown creases Melody's forehead. 'Why did you, then?'

'Because I want to warn you, I want you to be careful.'

'Of Howard?' She finds the idea ridiculous.

'There are things I can tell you about him. Facts that will save your book from hagiography — the truth —'

'You don't need to worry, Lena. True.'

'But it's important that men as famous as he is are portrayed honestly. You don't know what he did.' Suddenly, the blonde woman has taken my other arm and they are half pulling me through the door.

'Here he is,' says Melody. Shag has his back to us, talking to a builder. A dining table stands between us, covered with a white sheet. The builder has removed a long narrow window and is now engaged in bashing away the seaward wall. 'He's replacing the French doors in this room,' Melody goes on. 'He had them taken out for security reasons years ago. Now he's better, he's putting them back.'

At the sound of her voice, Howard turns to face us. Franca has slipped noiselessly around the table to take his arm. She whispers something to him, watching him intently, and Howard lifts his gaze. One eye meets mine. It's sharp, scrutinising, intense. The other eye is skew-wiff, unfocused. Did we do that to him? I submit to a memory of fists, Chookie's and Beck's, striking his strangely impassive flesh.

'I wouldn't have recognised you,' he says finally. Nor I you, I think, but don't say. He's very thin, his face partially shadowed by the broad brim of a white panama hat. 'Not that I actually saw any of you, that night.'

'We didn't intend you to.'

'It wasn't him,' Franca says quietly, holding tightly to Howard's arm. 'We got the wrong man.'

'We? Who are you?' I ask her, though I'm beginning to suspect.

'We have a lot to talk about after all these years,' says Shag. 'We'll go to the other room, Melody.'

We go to another closed-in porch, where there is a cabinet stuffed with rugby memorabilia, a vast TV and a bookshelf crammed with his bestsellers. There is also an ancient, smelly black labrador and, displayed on a low coffee table, an advance copy of Melody's book, *An Interrupted Life*. I wonder, as I sit nervously on the orange sofa, if it was this woman Franca — and Scottie, Beck, Chookie, Kerry and me — who inspired the title. The old man is settling himself in an armchair and Melody, as unasked as a well-trained wife, is pouring him a scotch. She waves the bottle in my direction.

'No, thank you.'

'I'll make some coffee.' Franca leaves the sofa in a wave of perfume and pauses at the door. I'm aware of her at the corner of my eye beckoning to Melody, whose departure is reflected in the big screen: her big tummy bobbing along above her twig legs.

'Jasper has more of his father in him than he does of you,' announces Howard as he lights a cigarette. I can think of no reply to this. To search for one would be to return to the territory of countless tortured, sleepless nights. I never think now, ever, of who Jasper resembles more, Richard or me. 'Physically, I mean,' Shag goes on. 'He was a good boy, your son. I loved him.'

I am nodding like a fool, swallowing sudden, bewildering tears.

'And he loved me. Still does. He writes to me from Berrima.'

'Yes, I thought he might.' And I hated the idea, I could tell him, but I don't because, oddly, now I don't mind. What a trajectory my feelings for this man are on. 'Why has Franca changed her mind?'

'I recognise your voice, you know,' he says, ignoring my question. 'You were the one who smelt of frangipani. You put your scarf in my mouth.'

'Yes. I did.'

'You must have worried about repercussions afterwards?'

'When there was no investigation we took it as further proof of your guilt. Besides, you didn't know who we were.'

'Oh yes, I did. Jasper told me.' There is the clink of china and the clip of high heels and Franca is back in the room. She gestures for me to pick up the book so that she can set down the tray. Before I know what I'm doing I catch at her hand and the tray dips and coffee slops.

'Careful!' she says.

'Are you sure,' I ask, 'that it was someone else?'

'Oh yes. I wouldn't be here otherwise, would I?'

'Is it in here — in the book?' I wave it, *An Interrupted Life*. The cover is a montage of items from the display cabinet.

'I didn't mention names,' says Melody, sitting beside me with a mug of herbal tea. 'Howard didn't want me to and I agreed. There was no point.'

'That was . . . kind of you,' I say, lamely.

Howard smiles, showing stained teeth. 'Do you think so?'

'Look,' I'm standing, shoving my hands into my pockets, 'we were given the wrong information. As far as we knew it was you. So we took the only action we could.' I turn to face Franca. 'It was what you told us. You gave Kerry his name.'

'I gave her the name the man gave me. It's all right, Lena. Howard and I have talked and talked about it.' Franca's tone is slightly patronising, almost excluding of me. I tell myself she only means to placate, but it's no good — my hackles rise.

'Then who was it? Do you know?' I'm almost shouting.

'There's no need to be aggressive about this, Lena.' Franca leans back and crosses her legs. Her expression remains sympathetic. 'We don't know. And after all this time it doesn't matter.'

Howard clears phlegm from his throat. 'Obviously he was someone who bore enough of a resemblance to me to get away with it,' he says.

'Shall I give her Jasper's wallet?' Melody gets up and crosses to the cabinet where there is a squat, square black billfold beside the dusty football.

'It dropped from Richard's pocket,' Howard tells me, and I can feel him watching closely as I take it from Mel. 'The day he dropped in. It must have fallen when he took the swing at me in the kitchen.'

The moment the wallet is in my hand I know who it was who raped Franca. And I know that Howard probably suspects, that he's probably worked it out. And I know also that he hasn't told Franca or Melody, or Jasper. I try to catch his eye but the old man only allows me a flash of his before he turns away. I turn the little wallet over in my hand — it's soft and worn, the raised lettering of the credit cards inside pressed into the thin leather. I open it up, the tattered wings of an old moth. I wonder if he did it more than once — use Howard's fame as an aid to seduction. He may not even remember Franca: she would have been one girl among many. That's what he was like then. A lothario, living out his seventies dreams of free love. It took me years to recover from my relationship with him. Even now, rarely, I dream about him, always as a distant figure, giving off waves of cool indifference. It's as if we share a tiny subconscious piece of each other that, despite everything, never lets go. I feel as if I'm dreaming now, closing the billfold, turning it over and over.

'He kept yelling at me that it contained proof,' Howard is saying, 'but he wouldn't pause long enough to show me.'

'Proof of what?' I ask.

'Who knows? He was too excitable to tell me. Clobbered me fair and square.' Howard gestures to his forehead and then remembers he's wearing his hat. He takes it off and rubs one hand over his sallow balding head. The band has left a pink mark.

'You know he sat here and waited for the cops' — Melody is leaning forward, her cup on her knee — 'in this room. Drinking Howard's scotch. The security men found him. They rang the cops —'

'Yes, yes, of course, I followed it in the media. I was sick with it.'

Franca holds her hand out to draw me down to sit between herself and Mel again, but I'm paralysed before them, my sagging shins digging into the coffee table, my head whirling with what could easily be the worst and most labrynthal Kiwi joke ever told: a joke that spins on a tiny population of divided people, a litany of coincidence and old sins casting long shadows.

'Come on,' says Franca, patting the cushion beside her. I flop down gracelessly. 'What you did that night, it was a sign of the times, of the eighties,' she says. 'It would never happen now.'

The times have a lot to answer for, I think, these times and those times. I tuck Jasper's wallet into my breast pocket.

'Young women now are arch-consumers, completely apolitical. Witness the fashion for neck-rings,' says Franca, taking one of my hands in hers. 'What could that possibly mean but self-destruction and madness?'

'Come off it.' Melody's face pinkens. 'We're not that fucked in the head. My generation will have its own leaders, it's own revolutionaries.'

'I certainly hope so,' says Howard, surprisingly. 'The world is a far more complicated place now. I hope they rise up in bloodless rebellion and make it better for all of us. Just as long as nothing that I am gets in the way.'

'Nothing that you are . . .' I look at him, sitting relaxed in his sagging green armchair. A blade of sunlight has cut its way through the salt-frosted pane of the French doors to light up one side of his gnarled old face. 'What exactly are you, Howard?'

'Ah,' he says, grinning again. 'You'll have to read the book to find out.'

We fall silent, the four of us, and in that moment I feel the bonds that tie us together, willingly or not, reverberate down the years. The hot afternoon settles around us; our lives feel timeless. Eyes closed, Howard lets his head tip back against his chair and restlessly, in his lap, he fidgets with his packet of cigarettes. I can't take my eyes off him. Suddenly I find that I'm weeping for him, for me, for my poor damaged son, for stupid, blundering Richard, for all the wrong turnings. On one side Franca clasps my hand and I suspect, though I don't look, that she is crying too. Only Melody is dry-eyed. She takes my left hand and lifts it high to lie on the fulcrum of her belly and I feel, almost at once, the baby shift and kick.

'If it's a boy we're calling him Howard,' she says. 'You don't hear that name so much any more.'

The window behind Howard's chair shows the hip of Rangitoto and the smooth skin of the channel. Above the flank of the old volcano is a sky so blazingly blue that any idea of clouds — be they remorse, or guilt, or any of the cumulus that have tortured me since Jasper was arrested — is banished for a moment. The pure, high colour sings with the promise of a kind of peace of mind and I think, suddenly, for the first time, that there could be a way through all this.

MELODY

The Launch

The biography took me nearly two years to write. I jettisoned the idea of literary criticism, not because I didn't think Howard's books would stand up to it, but because nobody would ever read it: people who love Howard's books are not interested in criticism or literary theory. His themes and some of the non-stop action come into the main body of the text anyway, especially the ones he went away to write, like *Black Orbit*, *Fire Dragon* and *Tombolo*. I don't know if the book's any good or not — it's impossible to tell. Howard is pleased with it, and so are the publishers, but one disadvantage of having such a famous subject is that it'll sell no matter what. I'll sit tight and wait for the critics, of whom there are a few tonight in this crowded room.

I arrived here feeling very flustered, having rushed out to the airport to pick up Franca and drop her off at Howard's. Then of course Lena arrived and I was late getting home for my rest, which my darling Godfrey insists on. That made me a quarter of an hour late getting here.

I sip at a tiny half-glass of well-earned champagne and watch as Howard, in his favourite old yellow Italian shirt and highly polished shoes, moves towards the rostrum and lectern set up in the corner, half leaning on Franca's arm. Sometimes I feel jealous, left out, as if she and I are his daughters and she's the most favoured one, even though I wrote the book — but Howard is searching the crowd for me. He catches my eye and sends me a beaming smile and a wicked wink.

A hand grips my shoulder and I think at first it must be Godfrey, who last time I saw him was talking to Chris Laidlaw, but it's Dad, who has the writhing and exuberant Zanipula on his hip.

'Well done, girl,' he says. 'We're all very proud of you.' Mum stands behind him with her arm around Lena, who looks pale but resolute.

'As many of you know —' Howard has begun his speech. The room falls quiet, even Zanipula. 'For many years I rejected all offers from biographers. I did not consider that my life required any account. However, as time went by, it seemed more and more that my story must be told before I died, and as truthfully as possible. With this in mind I chose a young woman, relatively inexperienced, but who I believed had the necessary qualities. She is quiet, thoughtful, open minded and best of all has a great love of rugby union.' He gets a laugh on that, mostly male. 'Her only previous biography was of a masochistic Wellington poet, Lavinia Mann —' Laughter again, also male, 'and it seemed to me she could easily make the transition from that life to mine, a gay All Black.' Well, that's one way to come out, Howard, I think. The room falls eerily still. Even the small group of gay men over by the bar stand motionless, glasses in hand.

'If Melody were not a biographer, she would be a good private eye,' Howard goes on flatteringly. 'Eighteen months ago I reached the end of two decades of virtual seclusion. On my behalf Melody went to Australia to sort a few things out and returned, not only with the necessary information, but also a gifted and delightful psychiatrist — Franca Todisco — who has become one of my closest friends.

'I'm not going to tell you what those mysteries were, because Melody and I would rather you read the book. But before I step down I would like you all to charge your glasses and drink not one, but two, toasts. The first, of course, is to my dear Melody —' Howard turns towards me, his glass upraised. I'm blushing, smiling, my eyes are watering.

'To Melody,' says Howard.

'To Melody,' come a hundred or so voices and it's overwhelming. Godfrey materialises beside me and draws me close. I lean my new bulk into him.

'Secondly, just as importantly,' Howard goes on, 'I would like us all, just for a moment, to remember our friends, past and present. I would like to remember friends who were once very important to us and who were lost to us — not because of any design of our own or of theirs, but because forces of revenge, or ignorance, fear or pure evil put us apart from one another.'

Our guests listen carefully to what Howard says and one or two faces show utter bewilderment. For a moment he looks incalculably sad, his battered old face inclined towards the reading-light of the lectern, as if the colossal effort of appearing before so many people after so long a period of isolation has roused too many of his ghosts. Then suddenly he looks up at the assembled mass and raises his glass. His eyes flash with all the force of his considerable humanity and grace, and he says, in a strong, warm voice:

'To absent friends.'